The P.S. Wars

A novel

The P.S. Wars

Geoffrey Carter

Three Towers Press
Milwaukee, Wisconsin

Published by
Three Towers Press
An imprint of HenschelHAUS Publishing, Inc.
www.HenschelHAUSbooks.com

HenschelHAUS titles may be purchased in bulk for educational, business, fundraising, or promotional use. For information, please email info@henschelhausbooks.com

PB ISBN: 978159598-574-3
E-book ISBN: 978159598-575-0
LCCN: 2017955931

Cover design by Michael DiMilo
Photography by Robert W. Carter

Printed in the United States of America.

For my mother, Maryann Carter, my first and best teacher

And for all the public school teachers striving to give their students
the knowledge, the confidence, and the love that they need to flourish

Chapter 1

He woke with a start and lay huddled on the bed in a twilight state, not asleep but not himself. He had time before he had to get up; the shadowy light hadn't crawled very far up the wall, so he knew it was just before dawn. It would still be a few minutes before the alarm went off. He closed his eyes, trying to hang onto the last few precious minutes of sleep, but he found himself shivering. It was cold—and he realized there were no blankets on the bed. He raised his head and tried to focus. The quilt was half-off the mattress. He gathered it up and tried to cover himself and saw he was still dressed in yesterday's clothes. He didn't remember going to bed. And his stomach was churning. He sighed, unable to help it. The new day was already worming its way into his consciousness.

A dream had awakened him, he knew that, but he couldn't recall why it had brought him up so sharply. A feeling of anxiety was what he remembered from this one—that and pieces of conversations, arguments, and maybe a fight. Maybe more. Maybe violence. He'd been high up on the railing of a bridge near the end of it, he recalled suddenly, the stark black and white image of him hanging onto a suspension cable with one hand returning to him, hanging on until he couldn't anymore, hanging on with everything he had until his fingers had finally given out and he was falling, floating, air billowing up behind him, cushioning him. It had felt nice, comfortable, like sinking into a warm bath. Then he had rotated in the air, still falling, and saw the blacktop of the bridge rising up quickly, sickeningly, until he hit—and that was it.

Dave stretched and then curled back up under his lone quilt. He was still cold. He raised his head and looked around and saw his coat lying at the foot of the bed; he sat up, grabbed it, and covered himself. It helped, but not much. He closed his eyes and drifted. For a moment, he felt himself sinking, relaxing, returning to the brown layers of sleep.

The first bars of *Across the Universe* resonated shrilly through the room. He was wide-awake at the first note, reaching over to turn off the alarm, and automatically put his feet on the floor.

He had a monster headache and his mouth felt like steel wool. The night before started unfolding itself: the Cote du Nuits Burgundy, and then the Zin, playing old records on the stereo, and the airing of *The Man Who Shot Liberty Valance* at midnight. That damned Zinfandel. Why had he opened that second bottle?

Dave stood up and shuffled slowly to the bathroom. His knees creaked and popped and were their achy selves the first thing in the morning, but his foot hurt for some reason today, and his left hand felt numb on the side. And it was shaking a little bit. He looked at it, clenched his fist, and willed it to go away. When it didn't, he went into the bathroom, turned on the shower, and stripped off yesterday's clothes, taking a minute to assess any more damage in the bathroom mirror.

He could see a face that had a grayish tinge under the ruddy flush of the heavy drinker—broken capillaries were starting to crosshatch his nose; he really needed to start cutting back. He was starting to look like a drunk. His cheeks hung loose, flaccid flaps, and his hair, once blonde, was now turning a non-descript combination of gray and tan and stuck out from his head in every direction. Gray stubble lined his pointed chin. His eyes were still green, but barely. His lids hung heavily, like half-drawn blinds, over the bloodshot mess that used to be the whites of his eyes. Hard to believe he was only sixty-three years old.

You look like hell, he thought. Worse than hell. He didn't weigh himself—no need to pour it on—and stepped into the shower. He put his head directly under the nozzle, and the hot water streamed over his head and face, steaming out the cobwebs. After a moment of letting the hot sting seep into his scalp, he washed himself, shampooed, and shaved under the steaming water, watching himself in the foggy wall-mounted mirror.

Ever since he'd retired, things had been going to hell on a downhill slope. He'd had his pension, which was pretty substantial, and promised Valerie he'd work another job until the girls were out of school, but since he'd retired, she'd walled him out. Out of conversation, out of her life, out of their bed. Then, seven months ago, she had filed for divorce, totally blindsiding him. The kids were all out of the house, so they didn't have to be part of it—to see his humiliation—but that was small consolation.

Val saw his retirement as a defeat. She was a woman fascinated by wealth, and, more particularly, the show of wealth. Only God knew why she had married a teacher. But then she hadn't always been that way—at least not as extreme. Getting the newest trendy gadget was almost orgasmic for her. She had always wanted nice things: a new car every two years, landscaping, new furniture, and the remodels. Constant remodels. He hated the process, the dust, the mess, and especially the contractors who took three months to do a two-week job. He'd hated it all, but put up with it for Valerie. He'd also put her through real estate school and watched, proud, as her career blossomed. But she was gone now and had taken her money with her. He had even ended up paying her alimony.

He stepped out and dried himself, glancing up at the subway tile with the jade green and black accent. Another one of Valerie's projects: the bathroom remodel—her idea—that had cost him a fortune. And the real irony was that he was the one still paying for it while she was off cavorting in St. Thomas or whatever other fucking paradise she was in this week. He tossed his towel on the floor, brushed his teeth, combed his hair, and put on his deodorant. Then came the Visine. He still felt a little foggy, but a cup of coffee would fix that. He was even starting to look human.

Dave glanced at his watch. He was running late. He ran into the bedroom, dodging the heaps of dirty clothes and books, and dressed, putting on a fairly clean pair of khakis and a pullover crew neck. It would look okay with his blazer. He ran downstairs, found the shoes under the couch, put them on and ran to the coffee maker. He looked at it, cold and empty, and realized he had forgotten to set the timer the night before. Dammit. It just figured. He glanced at his watch. There was still time to stop at the drive-up coffee place on Brady. He just had to hurry. Trotting through the kitchen, glancing at the sink full of dirty dishes and the newspapers strewn on the floor, he grimaced as he grabbed his briefcase and ran out.

The cold walloped him as soon as he stepped out the door, the wind knifing through his cotton blazer. His eyes teared up as he leaned into the wind and walked to the car, clutching his briefcase to his chest. Good, he thought, the cold will clear out the cobwebs. He took out his keys, clicked open the car, got in, and started it. Seven twenty-five. He wasn't as late as he thought. He took a deep breath and rubbed his eyes with the heels of his palms. Coffee. He needed big coffee.

He backed the car out of the driveway, turned on the headlights, and headed toward school. Okay. Today was Thursday. Faculty meeting would be at eight. His first, second, and sixth hour would be taking unit tests. Third and fifth hour would be working on the Mayans and eighth hour, the freshmen, would be working on search and seizure in the Bill of Rights. Not a terrible day ahead. Pretty quiet, actually. The freshmen would be challenging, but they always were. He leaned over and flipped open the glove compartment. He kept his eyes on the road as he fumbled around for the bottle of Tylenol he always kept there.

"Shit."

He took his eyes off the road a moment and scanned the jumble of papers, pencils, old lottery tickets, and other junk in the glove box, trying to locate the bottle. It was in there somewhere, but he'd have to wait for a red light or the coffee shop to find it. His head wasn't that bad anymore anyway, just a dull steady ache. He remembered suddenly that Valerie had texted him yesterday, demanding to know why the alimony was late. He was only a couple of days behind with the check and she was already threatening to call the lawyer. True to form. She never wasted time busting his ass. He'd have to give her a call and tell her she was going to have to wait until Friday. That was if he could figure out where the hell she was now. She kept insisting that he text her, that she couldn't be reached by phone. He'd learned how to do it but still didn't like it. Compared to a phone call, it seemed like an incredibly convoluted and inefficient process. He'd get in touch with her his own way.

Well, he thought, turning onto Locust, thank god he only had the baby to support now. The other two were out of college and already working. Annie, their youngest, had just started at the state university. She was eighteen, but he intended—as he had with the other two—to help pay her way through college.

It was the principle of the thing. Val definitely didn't need his money. She had remarried a stock analyst ten years her junior, and was now—finally fulfilling her life's ambition—as rich as a Rockefeller. And here he was, living on a small pension and a substitute teacher's salary, stuck with a mortgage on a house he couldn't sell. And Valerie, because she was principled, too, was still insisting he pay alimony and help with Annie's college. Well, he didn't begrudge helping Annie. Alimony was a different story, but her lawyer had talked circles around his guy and he'd gotten nailed. But he didn't even put up a fight about paying tuition. Annie was his youngest, and his favorite, though he never admitted it. Val could tell, though, and blamed his favoritism for the other girls' problems. But Annie was special. Sweet, mature, and smart as a whip. He was proud of all his kids, but she was something special. It was his pleasure to help her out. It wouldn't have been right not to, no matter what he felt about his ex-wife and her fucked-up values.

He turned into the drive-thru coffee shop and nosed up to the car ahead of him. Only one in line. It shouldn't be that long. He leaned over, rummaged in the glove compartment, dumping old napkins and pens and pencils on the floor before finally finding his Tylenol bottle. He opened it. One left. A car honked, startling him. He turned and saw the mini-van ahead of him had gone through and that it was now his turn. He pulled up.

"One large house coffee. Black," he said, without looking up.

"Well," said the clerk, "we have two house coffees today. Panama Mountain Rico and Red Trotter."

He looked at the guy. He wanted to say that he didn't give a shit about the coffee brands; he just needed a cup. And now. But the clerk was just a kid, not much older than Annie, cultivating the groovy hipster look: goatee, black watch cap, and big plastic glasses. Just a kid.

"I'll take the Panama," he said.

"Good choice, Mr. Bell," said the kid, smiling.

"How do you know my name?" asked Dave, peering closely at him.

He smiled. "You don't remember me, do you? I was in your Creative Writing Class in summer school before my senior year. I'm Simon Baranski."

Dave remembered him now, vaguely, two or three years ago, before he retired, a quiet kid in the back of the class. Quiet, but a good writer. A very good writer.

"Yeah, sure," he said. "You were a good student, a good writer. Very good. You wrote that story about Tarzan in the nursing home—the fantasy—that was good."

"Thanks," said Simon, handing over the coffee and taking the money. "You remembered."

"Thank you," he said, taking the cup carefully. He wanted to say more, to ask Simon what he was up to, but the driver behind him honked again. He waved good-bye.

"Hey," said Simon, "I heard you retired, but that you're back."

Bell nodded as he put the car in drive.

"You were a great teacher," Simon said again. "It's too bad you're just a sub now."

He saw Simon smiling and waving in his rear-view mirror as he pulled away, not a trace of irony in his expression.

* * * * *

He walked into the library just as the faculty meeting was getting started. Mr. Ricks was standing in front of the room next to the Smart Board; he frowned at Dave as he sat down at one of the rear tables. Ethel turned around in her seat and gave him a look, too. His headache had subsided into a steady relentless throb—that was what only one Tylenol—an old one—did. He wished he'd had time to stop in his room. He always kept a jar in his desk.

"This being late is getting to be a habit, David," Ethel whispered loudly.

He pursed his lips as if blowing her a kiss; she raised her eyebrows and turned around in her seat.

Well, he thought, as he snapped off the lid his coffee, you can't please all the people all the time. I can only please none of the people most of the time.

"All right," said Ricks, "let's settle down. Now that we're all here, we can get started."

Mr. Ricks walked over to the laptop in front of the room and pushed a button. An image leapt onto the Smart Board, a logo. Dave squinted at it and adjusted his glasses. EduNet. The letters were filled in with bold primary colors and a huge green and black paint swish flowed behind it. A murmur ran through the audience. Ethel leaned over and whispered something to the teacher sitting next to her, a youngster, only teaching her second year.

Dave had known Ethel Benjamin for almost forty years. She had already been teaching English at George Custer High School for ten years when he started thirty-four years ago. Last year, when the state legislature had taken away public employees' collective bargaining rights, Dave had tried to persuade her to retire with him, and hundreds of other teachers, to preserve their pensions and other benefits before renegotiations started. Ethel simply looked him straight in the eye in the disquieting way she had that had silenced hundreds of students over the years—the laser gaze— one student had said, shaken her head, and smiled.

"No, David," she said. "I've been at Custer for over forty years now. I'll leave when I decide to leave, not when some screwy-assed politicians tell me to. Besides, someone has to work with all these youngsters and teach them how to stand up for themselves."

Ethel was a legend around the building, winner of state teacher of the year four times, the building representative to the union for three decades, and one of the main instigators of the big strike in 1978. She had a PhD in American Literature and taught part-time at the state college. She also swore like a sailor, but only when she was not around students. Though she barely topped five feet, Dave had seen Ethel face down some of the toughest gang-bangers the school had to offer. She was born to teach.

"All right," said Mr. Ricks, taking out his laser pointer. "Your attention, please. Thank you. Today we're not going to be talking about attendance or percentiles or achievement. Today is something new. This is about a new company, EduNet, that the school board is considering having come in and head the effort to replace some of our failing schools."

An angry murmur coursed through the crowd of teachers, growing louder and sharper as Mr. Ricks' words finally sunk in.

"Yeah, I got your attention now, don't I?" he said, smiling.

Dave smiled. Despite himself and their long-standing spats, he liked Ricks. He always had. A couple teachers were already pelting him with questions. Mr. Ricks held up his hands.

"Hold on," he said. "Hold on. Wait until you have it all."

The group quieted down.

"You know what's been happening. There's been talk of privatizing public schools for years. You know what they always say: failing schools are the fault of a broken public school system and a bloated union. Teachers and schools are the problem, not the solution."

Ethel started to say something, out of reflex, but then thought better of it.

"Now they're getting serious," Mr. Ricks continued. "The school board voted last week to allow this company, this EduNet, to file a proposal for opening a private charter to take over one failing school in our system. This takeover will act as a model for its program. And guess what school that's going to be?"

"That's not right," said John Reynolds, one of Custer's veteran science teachers. "We've shown improvement over last year in every area of need: graduation rate, test scores, ACT scores. We've done everything they wanted."

"And that's what I told them last week at the school board meeting," said Mr. Ricks, "and it didn't make a bit of difference. They've wanted to get their hands on this school for a long time. I'm not sure why, but we've always been right bam in the middle of their crosshairs."

Mr. Ricks took a deep breath.

"Now," he continued, "this EduNet is going to be sending in representatives starting this week to observe classes and—"

Another murmur went through the room. This was what the faculty been anticipating. And dreading. Mr. Ricks waited for the noise to subside.

"—and to make their analyses about the feasibility of installing their private charter in this building. Now I know this won't be easy, but I'd like for you to give them everything they need. Giving these people a hard time, even not cooperating, will not do anyone any good. If they do take over, those of you who want to continue working here will be working for them. If they see bad morale and antagonistic behavior, they'll use that as another reason to close the school."

Mr. Ricks paused a moment, surveying the sixty or so teachers in front of him.

"I don't like this any better than you. I went to public school my whole life. I taught in these public schools for ten years, and I've been here at Custer for six. I'm going to fight to keep this school and all of our schools public. I know you will, too, I expect you to, but fighting these people here in our building under these circumstances will not be the way to do it. We need to go about our jobs—as we always do—like professionals. If we do the best we can, good things will happen. I'll try to give you a heads-up when they get here, but I'm not sure when that'll be myself."

"All right," he said, glancing at his watch, "go get ready. Have a good day. Make education work."

Everyone started making their way out of the library, some of them hurrying, others moving more slowly, and a few still standing around and talking. There were only about fifteen minutes before homeroom and there were worksheets to copy, Smart Boards to turn on, and lessons to prepare. Dave got up and sidestepped his way through the moving throng toward Ethel, who was listening to Felicity, one of the young teachers sitting at her table.

"Don't worry about it, Felicity," Ethel was saying as Dave came within earshot. "Worrying about the things you can't control won't do you any good. Just do your job."

"I know, Mrs. Benjamin," said Felicity, a note of petulance in her voice, "but I can't afford to lose this job. What's going to happen to me if these new people take over?"

Dave smiled to himself. Some things never changed. When Felicity had first arrived, she'd been incredibly anxious about lessons, grades, parent conferences, everything, and she spilled her enormous anxieties, like vomit, onto anyone who would listen to her. She seemed so helpless everyone felt sorry for her and reached out to help. Now, with three years under her belt, she had become an adequate teacher, just competent, whose juvenile anxieties had now evolved into middle-aged angst. Already, thought Dave, after only three years. He reflected on it a moment: he supposed things did change. Felicity's whining had morphed into complaining: non-stop, virulent complaining.

Ethel shrugged. "I don't know, Felicity. I really don't know. You just have to do your best."

Felicity sighed and glanced around quickly, like a bird, seeking an-other sympathetic ear as if it were a worm to be pulled. Her glance landed on Dave.

"Dave, what the hell is this?" she asked, hands on her hips. "Can you tell me what's happening here? Who let this happen?"

He shrugged. It wasn't the first time he noticed the way she addressed him. It bothered him. Just a little, but it bothered him. Why did she call him Dave and Ethel Mrs. Benjamin? He had propped her up just as much as Ethel in the beginning.

"All I know, Felicity," he said, "is that these guys might be the face of our new administration. And even if they are private charter people, I think Mr. Ricks is right; for now, the best strategy is to show them our best side. Go about our business. Be civil."

She nodded and made a face as if to say I suppose, then glanced at her watch.

"Omigod," she said. "I have class in ten minutes. I have to get things set. Bye," she said, trotting off. Bell and Ethel followed her out at a much more relaxed pace.

"Well," said Ethel, "she sure as hell trusts your judgment. Even though you didn't even say one goddamned thing."

"Well, I am a man. Who can blame her?"

"Go to hell, Bell," she said.

"After you," he said, holding the library door.

"Thanks," she said. They walked along together, not saying anything, each lost in the implications of what might be beginning this morning. Dave had taught at Custer for thirty-four years before he'd retired last spring. Here he was back as a substitute for his thirty-fifth year at two-thirds the pay. Plus his pension. Ricks had called him back in August; he'd been short-staffed in the Social Studies department again and was wondering if Dave would like to come back for another year. His first im-pulse was to say screw it. He—like so many others—was still bitter about the way first the politicians and then public opinion had handed it to the teachers. Years, decades, of experience thrown out like yesterday's trash. It still knotted him up inside.

And Ethel. He stole a sidelong glance at her, his own mentor, with forty-four years of experience, who should have, if she'd been smart and not so goddamned dedicated to this place, left with him. She scanned the hall ahead of her, holding all of her five-foot something ramrod straight. Forty-four years—it was hard to believe. She'd been here since nineteen seventy-two, when Nixon was president and the war in Vietnam was still being fought, almost twenty years before computers entered the classroom. God knew how many kids she'd taught and guided over the years: thousands? Maybe ten thousand?

Her husband was a patent attorney; she'd been married a little longer than she'd been teaching. She could've quit years ago. With her husband's income, they certainly didn't need the money, but she'd taught all the way through raising three kids. They were grown now and out of college. Two of them were teachers.

"A penny for your thoughts, David."

He glanced up. Ethel was staring up at him, her eyes narrowed. He knew that look. She'd been concerned about him ever since the divorce and the aftermath. And vocal about it.

He shrugged.

"Nothing, really," he said, "just thinking about all the history here."

They stopped at Room 264, her classroom. Ethel unlocked the door and turned to look back down the hall.

"We've certainly seen a lot of young people come through here, haven't we?"

There was an underlying resignation in her voice, a sadness, something he very rarely heard. He remembered hearing it a few years ago, when one of her favorite students had been shot and killed during a robbery, and again, further back, when her youngest child had been diagnosed with cancer. And now, here it was again, when she knew her school was probably dying.

"Yes, we have, Ethel." Dave said, looking at her. She was still gazing down the hallway, a million miles away. She looked tiny today, a little tired, old finally. "We've seen more than a few. I'll see you later. You have a good day."

"Thank you, David. You, too."

She went into her room and shut the door behind her. He left and continued to his own room. A few other teachers were bustling down the hallway, getting worksheets or supplies or running last-minute errands. He hurried along, glancing at his watch; the homeroom bell was only a few minutes off now. He was running late again, something that never used to happen to him, not before his divorce. Now he couldn't seem to be anywhere on time.

His head had begun throbbing again, and the overhead lights seemed to shimmer as he walked along. He blinked rapidly, trying to clear his sight. The hallway ahead of him, empty now, suddenly stretched out crazily in front of him, like a rubber band, farther and farther, almost lost in infinity. The fluorescent bulbs buzzed overhead, and the light, suddenly painful, stabbed at his eyes. Man, he needed those Tylenols. Bad. The throbbing in his head became louder, more strident. The light receded, grew murky and thick, as if it were raining down on him, and images seemed to swim before him. Faces. Hundreds of faces. He reached his classroom and opened the door, stumbling toward his desk. He scrabbled through his desk drawer, found his Tylenol, and took three, swallowing them dry. He sat at his desk, rubbing his forehead with the palms of his hands. The pain in his head started to ebb just as the homeroom bell rang, just as the day was starting. Luckily, he didn't have any kids until first hour. He sat back, took a deep breath, and focused on the Gettysburg Address poster on the back wall. It was in perfect focus now; the lights, everything looked normal. His eyes were fine again.

He got up and turned on his laptop and accessed the day's warm-up activity. The Smart Board glowed and began to warm up. The day's journal activity slowly came into focus: "What's the worst thing that ever happened to you?" Dave smiled to himself. That was an easy one.

Chapter 2

I t was chilly but sunny, a perfect morning for a run. He glanced at the app on his smartphone: two and one-half miles done, one and one-half to go. So far, so good: not his best time, but that was all right. The object of the weekday runs was simply to stay in shape. Saturdays were for training. Saturdays were when he pushed himself to the extreme.

He turned the corner onto Bradford Boulevard and was greeted by a stiff north breeze that hit him like a brick wall. He grit his teeth and picked up the pace a little bit. Just ten more minutes, maybe only nine and one-half if he pushed it. A gust blew straight into him, almost altering his pace. He could feel his cheeks going numb. It was worse than he thought, and there wouldn't be anything between him and home blocking this wind, either. Bradford Boulevard ran straight as an arrow through the rebuilt SoLo, South of Locust District. There were towering new residential apartment buildings and condos on both sides of the street that seemed to channel and stream the wind straight down the boulevard. Ground floor coffee shops and boutiques dotted the buildings on every block. He ducked his head as a particularly nasty gust streamed past him, squeezing him with its icy fingers.

He glanced into a Starbucks as he ran past; he'd think about stopping if he'd brought his wallet, but the only thing in the interior pocket of his running tights was his apartment key. He glanced into the full-length window of the hairstyling boutique on his left; a tall figure clad in a red windbreaker over a yellow stretch crew running jersey, compression thermal tights, neon green cross-trainer running shoes, and polarized sunglasses was sweeping past. His head was bare and his closely cropped scalp gleamed with sweat, despite the cold. Two bright red spots, like clown make-up, highlighted his cheeks. That always happened to him when he exercised, and he hated his body for doing it. It looked stupid, weak, girly almost, although in this day and age nobody cared too much about that.

Masculinity was getting to be a lost art. He glanced again into the next storefront, a wine shop. All in all, he looked pretty good.

He took pride in his body, his appearance, and cultivated it for maximum effect. He wasn't a big man and didn't have an intimidating presence—not in the classic sense—but he tried to squeeze every drop of testosterone out of what he had. He lifted weights every other day, adhered to a strict daily calorie count, and ran at least four miles a day. The exercise wasn't only for health; he believed that it amplified his presence, his confidence, and that his feelings of inner health and self-satisfaction were transformed externally into a presence of dominance and superiority. He believed it made him a better person and a better corporate executive.

He was only four blocks away from his building now; this last stretch was on a slight upward grade that made the last leg of his run deceptively hard. The closer to home he got, the harder the road became, and it shouldn't be that way, not for him. He was a closer—the final push had always been his strength, never his challenge. He had thought more than once about changing his route specifically because of these last four blocks, but to do so would be to admit defeat, something he never did if he could avoid it. The wind leaned into him and he leaned back, gritting his teeth and pushing himself up to sprint—finishing—speed. Now was the time. Now. His chest burned and his breath came in gasps as he pushed himself up the grade, into the wind, and to the end.

The entrance to his building flashed past and he slowed to a walk, and, with hands on hips, walked around the block for his usual cool-down. As soon as he turned the corner off Bradford onto Locust, the breeze died. It figured. He would really have to think about changing the route. He didn't mind the extra effort, the extra pain; he knew that it was ultimately good for him. He just liked the easy ending.

He walked into the entrance of his building and unzipped his windbreaker.

"Hello, Mr. Paige," said the uniformed doorman. "I hope you had a good run, sir."

He nodded at him. Although he'd heard the doorman's name a hundred times, he could never remember it. The guy looked as if he had fought in the Civil War. They really needed to get somebody younger.

"Here's your morning paper, sir."

He took it and nodded to the old man, then walked to the elevator and punched the up button.

"Have a good day, sir."

Paige turned his back to the doorman, opened the paper and glanced at the headers of the front page. There was nothing about the education bill in the State Assembly there. He scanned the locals and the business pages. Nothing. The elevator opened; he stepped inside and pressed twenty-three. They were going to have to do more to stir up public sentiment on this issue. He made a mental note to call Sandra. She needed to get on the PR department to call two or three of the state representatives on board with this thing and have them issue some statements. A couple of radio interviews with the local conservative talk shows would be good, too. This stuff should be happening now. Sandra was slipping. She should've been all over this shit without being told. It should have been done yesterday.

The door opened and he stepped out of the elevator. John Kinney, his neighbor and one of the senior vice-presidents for RealCo, the city's leading commercial realty company, was just getting on the car.

"Hey, John," he said, smiling and holding the elevator door.

"Hey, Mitchell," he said, looking him up and down. "A little brisk for a run this morning, isn't it?"

"Not really. There's nothing like running in the cold. It really gets the blood flowing and the mind working."

"If you say so," said John. "I'm old school. I'll take my bacon and eggs."

They both laughed politely, and then stood looking at each other as the joke faded. Paige stood there smiling, still holding the elevator door. John stood in back of the car, smiling back.

"Okay, John, we'll see you," said Mitchell, releasing the door. "Have a good day."

The elevator door closed and Mitchell walked down the hall past the windows that showed a view of the lakefront and the river. Nice view, but it definitely wasn't Manhattan or The Loop. If he could ever get an in with John Kinney, maybe he'd have a better shot at a view like that. And the way things were going, that might not actually take that long. He might not even need a John Kinney.

Mitchell came to his door, opened it, and threw his key in the dish on the kitchen counter. The place was clean, spotless. Mitchell had a woman come in every day, but there wasn't much for her to do. He only came here to shower and sleep. He shed his running clothes, letting them lie on the floor where they landed, and climbed into the shower.

He started going over the day's schedule in his mind as he soaped himself up. Today was the day EduNet would begin the final process of privatizing George Armstrong Custer High School. The ball was really rolling now: today there were going to be three big meetings beginning the finalization process. First there was going to be the strategy session with himself and upper management to confirm the long-range planning, then the logistics meeting with the supervisors to make sure everyone knew their place in the day-to-day execution, and, finally, the last preparatory tactical session with the observation team, who would be gathering evidence for the concluding evidential reports.

That was going to be the key meeting; he was personally going to make certain that everyone was on the same page with this project; he didn't want any fuck-ups. There would be absolutely no room for bleeding hearts or liberal misgivings on this mission. Human Resources had a pretty good process for weeding that shit out, but nothing was infallible, and this was too important for any glitches to squeak through. The people on the ground were going to have to be hard-core, without an iota of pity. Whether or not EduNet would take over Custer was going to be a strictly business decision, not a sentimental one. He didn't want any people on his team who were going to be influenced by teary-eyed students or angry parents at school board meetings who wanted their precious children's public school experience to stay the exact dismal stinking same as it had been for years. He didn't any misguided white guilt clouding anyone's sound business judgment. He was sick of that shit. Public schools were dying. That was a fact, and it was time for them to finally get out of the way of progress. They were money holes that sucked up billions in tax dollars and had been doing an abysmal job for years—decades. Closing them would be doing society a public fucking service.

He got out of the shower and began toweling himself off. Three big meetings. Considering everything, the scope of the operation and its importance to him, he actually felt pretty relaxed. It was going to be a long day, but not a particularly tough one. At least not for him. His work was already done. There wouldn't be any big money or personnel decisions to make; those had been decided months ago. The observation teams on the ground were pretty well set, too; there were a couple tweaks he might want his team to make, but nothing major. That ex-teacher from Ohio made him a little bit nervous, but even that would be an easy fix. The toughest task of the day might be tearing someone a new one for fucking up. But even that, he thought, wouldn't be that hard. Management was easy. Being a leader was hard. Having a vision was hard.

This project was his baby. This project was going to make him. He had boldly promised the Executive Board and the CEO that he'd have the project done by the end of the year. Well, they were down to the last two months. It was going to be close, but everything was falling into place. This was going to be his tour de force.

And, besides, he really believed in what they were doing. He'd been working fourteen-hour days getting it ready and he had left nothing—nothing—to chance; there were not going to be any surprises. By this time next year, no one would be able remember the old Custer High School. It would be another in a long line of bad memories that started in the liberal holocaust called the sixties.

Mitchell wrapped his towel around himself and started his shaving ritual. This was one thing he loved to do old style. A roommate of his in college had done it this way, and Mitchell had co-opted the process for himself. He loved the deliberateness, the completeness of it. He took his shaving brush out of its cup and swirled it on the bar of soap he kept on the sink especially for that purpose. After he had it foamed up, he started brushing the suds onto his cheeks.

Once this Custer thing was settled and put away and his senior-vice-presidency was—hopefully—in the bag, he was going to have to figure out what to do with Sandra. The kid was out of her depth—not nearly tough enough for his world. She wasn't tough enough, she wasn't smart enough, and she wasn't nearly ruthless enough. The absence of the EduNet presence in the paper this morning was evidence of that, as if he needed any more proof. Any executive worth his salt would have taken care of something as simple as a press release. And the personal thing they had was going nowhere fast.

She tried too hard. He swabbed his upper lip and then put the brush back in its cup. Too eager. Trying to anticipate his every need was flattering at first, but it got tiresome after a while. When she could tell he was getting bored in bed, and she did have a good sense of that—good antennae—she immediately changed up what she was doing. Trying a new position, more oral sex, even massagers. He liked her eagerness to please, but he didn't like the fact that she needed to please him so badly. It was as if she, and her desires—whatever they were—didn't even exist in their bed. And she wasn't inexperienced; she did enjoy it, but she subsumed herself entirely to him and expressed no kind of sexual identity herself. It smacked of desperation. And, besides, bottom line, he didn't really even find her that attractive. The relationship was going nowhere. He was going have to end it.

And, he thought, picking up his razor, she did not have the looks to be the wife of a top executive. She was sort of attractive in a boyish kind of way, but only pretty, not beautiful, not a woman to stop conversation in a room, and that was what he would need. And Sandra—for all her subservience in bed—could be confrontational. She could definitely hold her own in an argument. There was that time at the last company Christmas party when she took on equal rights in the workplace, arguing her case—and doing it well—in front of three senior vice-presidents. But she obviously didn't realize that was the sort of shit that kept the glass ceiling in place. He'd tried to tell her that, but she wouldn't listen. Funny. Sandra could be that assertive about an issue in public, but have absolutely no confidence about herself in bed.

He scraped at his chin. The Custer Project, if everything went well, would be done in about two months, by the end of the year. Sandra, like all the junior execs, would be under continual evaluation until they were finished, and he would be part of her review team. It could very well be that her managerial strengths might lie in another area. He and the other guys on the review team would have to determine that. Sandra might find a better fit in their Omaha or their Portland office. A move, even a lateral move, for her would probably be the best for all concerned.

Mitchell rinsed off his face and stared at himself in the mirror. Not bad. He was no Chris Pine, but his looks were passable. Strong chin, small full mouth—he didn't like his mouth, it was too feminine—a straight-edged aquiline nose, and light brown, almost tan-colored, eyes. He had reddish-blond, almost strawberry blond hair that he kept short, almost short enough to deny the color.

He leaned closer to the mirror and tilted his head, attempting to focus exclusively on his right eye. The right eye, the stronger eye, his stronger side. He peered deeply into the iris and pupil, trying to plumb the black depths behind the gleaming cornea and desert-colored iris. He leaned even closer, almost touching the mirror, and could detect dominance in that darkness: the power, strength, and ruthlessness; he could feel it. Mitchell just had to mine those depths, harvest those iron qualities and hone them into weapons of power and conquest, tools that would propel him to the great heights, pinnacles of power and wealth and influence. Success was his best friend and ambition was his teacher. He would have it all. For him, and men like him, it was inevitable. That was only his due.

Chapter 3

The bell to end second hour rang. The thirty-four students in the classroom seemed to exhale simultaneously, a sound between relief and exasperation. Almost no one finished early, except Eloise, who always finished early, but that fact didn't surprise Dave. This was one of his tougher tests.

"Time's up," he said, "please put your unit test in the basket up front on your way out."

Dave's AP U.S. History class stood up and filed out slowly, putting their tests in the basket as they made their way out. None of them looked too happy. Antoine was grumbling under his breath as he put his test on the pile.

"Problems, Antoine?"

"Mr. Bell, I need to you to tell me something. When did we talk about this Saratoga thing?" he demanded, standing akimbo with one foot forward, reminding Dave of his Aunt Gloria. "I did not remember that at all, and I remember everything you teach. Everything. You know I do, Mr. Bell."

If you remembered everything, thought Dave, you wouldn't be cutting a 'C' average.

"We covered Saratoga last week, Antoine. You should remember it was one of the last decisive battles of the Revolutionary War."

"I was sick last week."

"You know the rules, Antoine. If you can't make it—"

"You got to make it up," said another student behind Antoine.

"Who asked you, Shaquanta?" said Antoine, turning to face her. "This ain't none of your damned business, now is it?"

"Shut up," she retorted.

"Enough," said Dave, in the voice that showed he meant it. This was an AP course, Advanced Placement, supposedly the cream of the academic crop at Custer, and he still had to put up with this middle-school crap.

"Get to your next class, Shaquanta," he said. She left, smirking at Antoine.

"You swore again, Antoine," said Dave. "I thought you were going to work on that. You know that's another phone call home."

"Mr. Bell, I don't care if you call my house—" began Antoine.

"Watch your tone, young man," said Dave. He knew he couldn't afford to let Antoine get started. There had been at least one Antoine every year of his career: part lawyer, part preacher, part bullshitter; if you let them drag you into negotiating, you were sunk. You had to nip it in the bud with them. Antoine looked at Dave, decided he meant it, took a breath, and clamped his mouth shut.

"If you'd rather not get the phone call, Antoine, we'll go right ahead and refer this matter to Mr. Ricks."

Antoine squared his shoulders, turned and left, maintaining as much dignity as he could.

Dave sat down, made a note to call Antoine's house that night, and then leaned on the desk, rubbing the bridge of his nose. It was only third hour coming up, his junior World History class, and it already felt like it should be the end of the day. Dave closed his eyes. He never used to feel this way in the middle of the day. He must be getting old. Burnt-out.

Dave felt a presence nearby and looked up. Darrel Ridgeman, all five foot two of him, stood there at the edge of the desk, staring at him. Darrel was an odd kid, smart, very well-educated, but socially awkward, quiet most of the time, but still prone to odd little outbursts—nothing serious or disruptive, just weird, like the time they were studying the Ancient Greeks about a month ago.

Dave had been leading a class discussion about ancient governments and asked the students to give examples of the two most dominant city-states in ancient Greece. No one had volunteered anything, and Dave was about to call on someone when Darrel stood up and said, "The only true wisdom is knowing you know nothing," and sat back down.

A few members of the class snickered; a couple laughed outright. Dave looked at Darrel a moment, nodding and smiling to himself.

"Little nigger be crazy," said Daquone under his breath, quietly, but not quietly enough. Dave could hear him fine, even from the back row.

Darrel heard him, too, and hung his head. He might be socially awkward, but he knew when he was being made fun of. A few of Daquone's cronies laughed out loud; he was the starting guard of the basketball team, tall, good-looking, and lazy as the day was long.

"Making comments like that, Daquone," said Dave, "means I'll be coming down and seeing Coach Martinson tonight."

"Mr. Bell, don't do that, I didn't mean nothing. You—"

"I don't negotiate, Daquone. You know that."

Daquone knew that was it; any further argument would get him sent to the office and mean even more extra laps at practice. He put his head down on his desk.

"Darrel," said Dave. "What did you mean by that, by what you said before?"

Darrel stood up, something he always did when he spoke in class.

"Sir?"

The class tittered again. Dave gave the usual suspects a look and they quieted down.

"You don't have to stand, Darrel."

He sat back down.

"The quote, Darrel. Could you repeat it, please?"

"The only true wisdom is knowing you know nothing."

"Good," said Dave. "Thank you. Now please tell us what that has to do with the ancient Greeks?"

"Socrates said that," said Darrel, staring straight ahead.

"Continue, please. Who was Socrates?"

Darrel took a breath. "He was a philosopher, a student of Aristotle's, who was a resident of ancient Athens, a city-state skilled in the arts, culture, and which is widely regarded as the birthplace of democracy."

The rest of the students were staring at him as if he were a three-headed jellyfish. Tiana Parker was actually glaring at him as if to say who the hell do you think you are? Daquone was sneering.

So this is the way our society treats intellectual prowess today, thought Dave. What a shame. Things had never been easy for the smart kids, the nerds, the outliers, but it seemed to Dave as if the climate had become worse for them these days, that things were tougher for the achievers. He knew Darrel had been having problems with the other kids after school.

He'd gotten a call from his mother a few days ago asking if there was anything he could do to help the kid. Apparently some of the other boys were jumping him after school, beating him up and taking his stuff. He'd lost an iPad and some money already but wouldn't say who did it. He knew to keep his mouth shut at least. Probably saved him a couple of more beatings.

"What is it, Darrel?" he asked. Darrel looked over his shoulder at the other students starting to filter in for class.

"I was wondering if I could talk to you after class about a personal matter," he said very softly, almost whispering.

Dave nodded and said sure. Darrel thanked him, more audibly this time, and went back to his seat.

Daquone walked in, talking to Olive Williams, which was unusual. Olive usually kept to herself. She didn't have much to do with the more popular kids, especially the athletes. Dave was pretty sure that was her choice. He could see that Daquone was trying to put the moves on her, and that Olive was having none of it. She looked uncomfortable. Dave needed to talk to Daquone anyway; now was as good a time as any.

"Daquone," said Dave. He stopped and Olive continued straight to her seat, holding her books to her chest.

"What is it, man?" asked Daquone, smiling and sitting on the edge of Dave's desk. He smacked his gum.

"Well, Daquone, I got caught up with grades last night and it seems as if you're just holding at sixty percent. You're getting a 'D'. Barely. "

Daquone shrugged and smiled. "Yeah, so?"

"So you need a 2.0 grade point average to play sports."

"Yeah?" He laughed and looked back at his buddy Travion, who was already in his seat.

"Sixty percent is a 'D'. A 'D' is 1.0. So unless you bring your grades up in this class, you won't be able to stay on the basketball team."

Daquone wasn't laughing now. He actually looked a little worried.

"Hey, Mr. Bell," he said. "You gotta give me a better grade."

"The grade you get is up to you. It's what you earn. I give you nothing." He glanced up at the clock.

"Take your seat now, Daquone. We'll talk after class." The bell rang. Dave went to close the door. Daquone still stood at his desk.

"Mr. Bell—"

"We're not going to talk about this now. I have to teach my class."

Daquone glared at him and stalked back to his seat.

Dave went over to the Smart Board, ready to start the daily warm-up activity when it came to him—a thunderbolt. A solution so neat and so simple it was almost too good to be true.

"Okay," he said. "Today's warm-up is a short journal question. It's right up here on the Smart Board. Who would like to read it for me?"

Tiana raised her hand.

"Tiana."

She cleared her throat theatrically and said, "What are some parts of our culture today that originally came from the cultures of the Aztecs and the Mayans?"

A few students applauded. Tiana got up, bowed, and sat down.

"Thank you, Tiana. If you'll remember, we spoke about this yesterday and have been studying it all week. Write down—"

A knock sounded at the door. Dave frowned. If there was one thing he hated, it was being interrupted in the middle of class.

"Someone's at the door, Mr. Bell," said Damien.

"Thank you." He strode over and opened it. A man stood there, looking uncertainly about him. He was middle-aged, graying around the temples, and wore tortoise-shell frame glasses. Bifocals. His face was tanned and looked a bit weathered, and his apparel was nondescript. In fact, that was the word to describe his visitor: nondescript. Or maybe two words: completely nondescript.

"Can I help you?" asked Dave.

"Mr. Bell?" The man's voice was lower than Dave expected. It was resonant and contradicted his seemingly meek appearance.

"Yeah, that's me."

"I'm Scott Brown. I'm here from EduNet. I don't know if you've gotten word yet, but we're going to be coming in to observe your school in action."

EduNet. The company that wanted to take over Custer.

"Yes, our principal mentioned you might be coming."

"Well, if you don't mind, I was hoping to come in and take a look-see at your class."

Dave took a step back and motioned him inside. "Sure, come on in and have a seat. Sit anywhere." Brown came in and sat at the teacher's desk. "Make yourself at home. This is my World History class. Students, this is Mr. Brown, here to observe us today. I would like you to show him every courtesy."

He glanced at his watch.

"Write down the answer to the warm-up activity. I'll give you two more minutes to finish up."

They were being pretty good today. Tiana, who was a mediocre student at best, was hard at work. A couple kids in back were talking quietly, but when they saw Bell looking at them, one of them raised up his paper, indicating they were done. Dave nodded to him. Daquone had his head down on his desk, either pouting or sleeping. Dave would ordinarily roust him, but he wasn't going to rattle his cage anymore today; he was going to talk to him after class, anyway.

He glanced back at Brown, who had parked in Dave's chair and was surveying the class and writing busily on his little laptop. Wonderful. He was sure Ricks had picked him on purpose. Use a veteran teacher to show off the school. The little worm was probably already writing about Daquone being off-task and how he was not redirecting his behavior. Well, he couldn't worry about a worm and teach at the same time.

"All right," he said. "Time. Who's got an answer?"

Tiana raised her hand.

"Yes, Tiana."

"One thing we got from the Aztec and Mayan culture was squash."

"Excellent. Anyone else?"

"We got calendars," called out a voice from back.

"Close, but not quite," said Dave, "but you are on the right track. Did the Europeans not have calendars before the Mayans?"

Darrel raised his hand.

"Yes, Darrel."

Darrel started to stand up like he usually did, but stopped himself.

"Another thing we got from Mayan culture," he said, "was a better understanding of astronomy, which helped us make better calendars."

"Very good," said Dave, smiling and nodding at him approvingly. Not only had Darrel given a concise answer that was on point, he'd kept himself within the social norms while doing it. He was learning. Dave glanced back at Brown to see his reaction and noticed he was tilting the back of his laptop toward the back of the classroom, as if aiming it. Wait a minute, thought Dave. Is this son of a bitch videotaping the class? Not that he minded personally, but there was a strict district policy against taping students in class. At least not without parental permission. He'd definitely have to tell Ricks about it.

"Can we think of anything else we have today that came from the Central American civilizations? Dave asked.

The kids sat in their desks, avoiding eye contact with him.

"What about architecture?" Dave continued. "Were these people pretty good builders?" He looked around the classroom. Daquone still had his head down. Tiana was whispering something to Laqueesha.

"Laqueesha?"

She turned her head around slowly to gaze at him. Depending on the day of the week, or the phase of the moon, Laqueesha could be compliant, engaged, and industrious, or disrespectful, confrontational, and disinterested. Her special ed instructor had told Dave Laqueesha was bipolar and was supposed to be on meds. Dave believed it. Today did not look like a good day for her.

"What?" she said.

"The question was whether or not the Mayans or Aztecs had an influence on architecture in our culture."

Laqueesha looked at Tiana and shrugged.

"Yeah, I guess so, Mr. Bell," she said, slowly and sarcastically, curling her lip.

Dave looked at her a moment; she had definitely skipped the meds that morning. He could let it go, and probably should; otherwise redirecting her would turn into a huge production that would suck up a lot of instruction time and probably end up getting her suspended anyway. Usually he would never let something like that go, but today they had the visitor. And, honestly, he was tired. He didn't really feel up to another battle royale with Laqueesha. He decided to simply call her up and speak to her after class.

"Any other opinions?" he asked the class at large.

No one answered. More kids staring up at the ceiling or down at their books.

"All right. Well, I guess we'll just have to do a pop quiz then. That might show me what you really know."

A chorus of groans and objections rained down from the students.

"No?" asked Dave. "What's wrong?"

"Man, we don't need no quiz."

"C'mon, Mr. Bell, we got a quiz yesterday."

He scanned the room, smiling a little, when his eye caught Laqueesha, glaring at Daquone. He and Travion were looking and her and laughing. He had obviously just said something to her, something she didn't care for. She looked ready to blow. He needed to get him out of her way.

"Okay, then," he said. "Daquone, could you come up here, please?"

"What for?" he asked.

"Excuse me?" said Dave. Daquone looked at him and shook his head.

"Sorry," said Daquone, and started walking to the front of the room. Laqueesha watched him like a hawk as he went by her desk, but, as Dave had suspected, she didn't go off on him after he'd been called up to the front.

Daquone stood in front of the class with his hands folded in front of him.

"So, Daquone," said Dave, "I bet you're wondering why I called you up here."

"Not really."

He had been intending to use him with this lesson anyway; the situation with Laqueesha had just precipitated it.

"Well, we need your expertise."

Daquone shrugged.

"How long have you been playing basketball?"

He shrugged again. "I don't know. Since I was about five, I guess."

"Are you any good?" asked Dave.

Travion laughed out loud in back and a few of the other kids chuckled.

"Yeah, you know," said Daquone, nodding, "I guess you could say I'm pretty damned good."

"Language, please."

"I just said damned, that's not swearing."

"Careful, Daquone. That's your one warning."

The boy scowled and stared at the floor.

"Now," said Dave, moving behind his desk and side-stepping Mr. Brown, who was still sitting there with his laptop, "the Mayans played a game the Spaniards called 'Juego de Pelota'. Does anyone know what that means?"

"Ball game," said Carlos, a smaller kid who was usually very quiet.

"Ball game. Correct," said Dave. "Now," he continued, opening a cabinet behind his desk and getting out a small rubber ball, "does anyone know how this game worked?"

"Yeah," said Carlos. "We learned about it in our middle school. They're not sure about the way it happened, but it was kind of like soccer. The players couldn't use their hands. They had to get the ball through a really tiny hoop. And they were like twenty feet away from the court. It was up high."

"Very good, Carlos," said Dave. "Thank you."

"Sure, Mr. Bell," said Carlos. "Glad to help."

"So is that where basketball comes from?" asked Travion.

"Not exactly," said Dave, "but that's a good question, Tra."

"So why do you have the little ball?" asked Daquone.

"To demonstrate how tough this game was," said Dave. "Although court sizes varied tremendously, the hoops were at least six meters, or about twenty feet away from the playing field. How far up is a regulation basketball hoop, Daquone?"

"Ten feet."

"So this was twice as high up."

"If you say so."

"The numbers say so, Daquone. History says so."

He rolled his eyes and grunted.

"Okay, take a look on the back wall," said Dave, pointing. There, attached to the top of the metal cabinet, was a hoop he had made out of the top of used yogurt container. It was barely wider than the ball. In the twenty years he'd been demonstrating this lesson, not one student had ever sunk the basket.

"I'd like everyone in the range of fire to move your desks out of the way."

The students scooted their desks back toward the wall, leaving a four or five foot lane down the center of the classroom.

"Carlos, I'd like you to go stand underneath the hoop back there."

After Carlos had placed himself under the yogurt cup, Dave waited for the class to quiet down. All it took was his sternest look and a momentary pause. The kids knew what—and what not—to do.

"Are we ready? Good. Here, Carlos. Catch."

He tossed the ball across the room. Carlos caught it.

"I'd like you to put the ball into the cup and tell us how tight the fit is."

Carlos stood on his tiptoes and placed the ball in the cup. It went through.

"It's really tight, Mr. Bell. It barely fits."

"Thank you, Carlos. You can sit down. Now," he said, "the reason I'm showing you this is not because it's fun or goofy; it's to teach you something about Mayan culture. Now the teams that played this game were warriors, sometimes captured prisoners, sometimes people from that community. It was played to please the gods, and the winners got a special prize. Anyone know what it is?"

"Money."

"Women."

"They got to do whatever they wanted."

"They got NBA contracts."

That one got a laugh from the class. Even Dave caught himself smiling.

"Nope, nope, and nope," he said. "Any other guesses?" He glanced at Carlos and then at Darrel. He was pretty sure they both knew the answer but neither one was volunteering. That was fine. Darrel was learning not to shine too much in the classroom, which was a good thing for him.

"The winning team," said Dave, "was granted the privilege of giving their lives for their gods. They were sacrificed."

"What?" asked Tiana. "What do you mean?"

"I mean that after the team won, and all you had to do to win was score one basket, the winners were sacrificed to the gods."

"That would suck, man," said Daquone.

"I don't believe it."

"It's true," said Dave, "and quiet down now."

He waited until the murmuring died down. "Why the winning team? Wouldn't it be more appropriate for the losers to die?"

"No man," said Travion, "the gods would want the best we had to offer and the priests from Maya knew that. So that's how they picked them."

"Good, Travion. Very good. So what does that say about their culture? What motivated them? What made them do what they did?"

They sat quietly, wondering about it. A number of the students, the ones who despised thinking, looked bored and exasperated, but they knew enough to keep quiet until the discussion was over. That was the way things worked in Mr. Bell's class. The others were really wondering about it; Dave could almost hear them thinking.

"Any ideas?" he asked, after a moment. "No? We'll come back to this. Now, I'm going to ask Daquone to see how he would have done at this game. Stand on the tape right there. You see it. I marked off seven paces, about twenty feet, earlier today. We'll see if Daquone, one of the best basketball players in the school, can hit that bucket from here."

He gave Daquone the ball. He glanced at it, then looked at the yogurt cup taped to the cabinet.

"There's no way, Mr. Bell. Nobody could hit that."

"It's tough, I know, but why don't you try it anyway? Maybe the gods want you to make it."

Daquone looked at him moment, shook his head, and looked at the basket again. Some of the students started whispering and giggling. A couple shouted encouragement to Daquone. He squared up and shot the ball. Time seemed to take a breath as the ball arced through the air closer and closer to the cup and then—without any interference from the rim— went straight through. A tremendous cheer went up from the students. Dave shook his head. The first time it had ever gone through and it had to be a kid like Daquone.

"Good job," he said. "Everyone put your desks back into the rows." He waited until the students complied and settled down. "That, ladies and gentlemen, is a first," he said. "Let's hear it for Daquone." He stood up as the rest of the class applauded him.

"All right," continued Dave. "What would have happened to Daquone had he lived in the ancient Mayan culture?"

"He would have been sacrificed," said Carlos.

"That's right. The cultural standard would have said he belongs to the gods now, and we would have to sacrifice him to gain their favor. What does that tell you about how they felt about their gods? And, by extension, about their world?"

Darrel raised his hand. Dave nodded to him.

"I think," said Darrel, "it showed they were scared of the gods. It's like when people are scared of bullies. They give them stuff so bullies leave them alone. It usually doesn't work, but sometimes it helps."

Carlos was looking at Darrel and nodding. Daquone leaned back in his desk and was staring hard at Darrel.

"So, Darrel," asked Dave, "why do think these people were scared of these gods? How were they being bullied?"

He shrugged. "I don't know. Maybe disease, rain, the crops were dying, other stuff they didn't understand. They thought the gods controlled everything and they must have thought they were really mean."

Dave nodded. "Very good, Darrel. I think you're on to something there. I'd like you to complete your exit assignment. You have three minutes. Answer this question: How much did the Mayans trust their gods?"

He went back to his desk and started putting together the warm-up activities. Mr. Brown, the EduNet rep, was busily writing on his laptop. Dave had almost forgotten he was there.

"I hope you enjoyed the class," said Dave.

"I certainly did, Mr. Bell. You have some very effective, though unorthodox methods."

"I try to use as much differentiated instruction as I can." It couldn't hurt to throw some eduspeak at this guy; sometimes a little jargon could go a long way.

"Indeed," said Mr. Brown, still busily writing on his desktop.

Dave could see the conversation was over. Well. So much for that. Dave turned and appraised the class; most of them were still writing. It would be interesting to see what they took out of this lesson. Darrel had really hit the mark with his bully analogy: Dave hoped the kids felt the same way.

The bell rang. The students got up, gathered their things, and started to leave. Mr. Brown also rose from his desk, folded his laptop, nodded to Dave, and left.

"Leave your papers in the basket," said Dave to his students. "You know the drill."

Darrel stopped at his desk, waiting to speak to him.

"Just a second, Darrel," said Dave. "Daquone."

As he expected, Daquone was almost out the door, trying to leave without speaking to him first.

"Yeah, Mr. Bell."

"I think that until your grades come up, you'll need to come in during your lunch hour for extra tutoring."

"Forget that, man. I need to eat."

"You can eat here," Dave said as he sat on the edge of a desk, "but I'll let you know right now. You don't come in, you don't play ball. It's that simple."

Daquone shook his head but sighed and said, "All right."

"Come in tomorrow," said Dave. "We'll get started then."

Daquone left. Dave turned his attention to Darrel.

"What is it, Darrel?"

"I was wondering, Mr. Bell, sir, if I could come here during my lunch hour. It's really noisy in the cafeteria and I don't really like it there. My mom said I could probably ask you. I bring my own lunch and I would clean up afterward if that would be okay."

The poor kid was probably getting harassed or beat up or worse during lunch. Dave smiled to himself; it was funny the way things worked out sometimes.

"It's funny you should ask that, Darrel. I was about to ask you a big favor. One of my students needs to be tutored during the lunch hour, and I thought you might be the person to do it."

"Daquone?"

Dave nodded. Darrel thought a minute. Dave could tell the idea kind of scared him, but that it was kind of appealing, too.

"Would he mind being tutored by me?"

"I'm sure he'll be fine with it. You are one of my best students."

"Okay," he said. "Yeah, I could do that."

"I'll see you at lunch today," said Dave, writing him a pass. "Now hurry to class."

Darrel nodded and walked out.

Chapter 4

Sandra was late, which was not like her at all. The strategy session with all upper management had been set to begin at nine-thirty. Mitchell glanced at his watch. It was now nine thirty-five. He looked over the table at the array of executive talent the company had deployed to implement the EduNet Project. Bill Jackson, graying, near retirement age, and overweight; he looked ready for a nap even at nine-thirty in the morning. They should have put him out to pasture five years ago. Mark Phillips, the ultimate yes-man, scared of his own shadow, but an excellent detail man. Jimmy Gaston, assigned here because he was the CEO's nephew and useless as tits on a boar hog. Simon Vasquez, an able executive, but one who was distracted by office politics. A game-player. Angela DiCaprio, a yeller. The female Vince Lombardi. She felt the only way to motivate her people was to terrorize them through fear and volume. And, finally, the empty seat next to him: Sandra, who was able—relatively—reasonable, and conscientious. But not ruthless. And late.

The door opened and Sandra came in, holding her laptop tight against her chest.

"Ah," said Mitchell, "glad you could make it, Sandra."

"Sorry, Mr. Paige. Sorry, everyone," she said, nodding to the table. "I had a flat tire on the way here and Triple A took forever."

Nods and commiserative noises floated around the table as Sandra set her laptop down. Mitchell watched her as she got up to get some coffee. She seemed flustered this morning; her face was flushed and that flattered her complexion, especially with the forest green dress she was wearing. The stress and excitement sharpened her eyes—dark brown and in turns, indecipherable, depthless, or as trusting as a child—as the nearness of a predator might sharpen the reflexes of a rabbit. He eyed her as she bent over the table. She was a thin woman, not model-thin, but she took good care of herself. Her legs displayed great muscle definition. It was one of the first things he had noticed about her. She was physically strong, as strong as some men. She turned and caught his eye; she shrugged slightly and raised an eyebrow, not exactly in apology, more of an 'I don't know what the fuck happened' look. She had good bone structure, a strong chin and well-defined cheekbones, but it was not delicate structure; in fact, in the right light, she had a relatively masculine look. Her mouth was not ultra-feminine either; it was wide and her lips thin. Sandra sat and brushed back her hair with her hand. Auburn. Dyed.

"Okay," said Mitchell, "today we're going to review the key strategic objectives for the EduNet Project. We can start with Bill, who will be handling the public relations side of the project. Anytime, Bill."

As Bill lumbered to his feet and slogged his way to the board at the front of the conference room, Mitchell glanced furtively at Sandra, who was leaning forward over her laptop, ready to take notes, her breasts straining against the green fabric of her dress. He turned his attention back to Bill.

"Gentlemen. And ladies," said Bill, nodding to Sandra and Angie, who both smiled at him, "things are looking pretty darned good."

In spite of his porcine appearance, Bill had a magnetic personal presence. He was personable, funny, and, once you got past the fat, charming. But old school. Mitchell—anyone—could see he was part of a dying breed, an anachronism. Charming executives were useless, vestigial, like appendixes. Today's business climate demanded the ruthless, the cunning, even the killer.

He half-listened as Bill went over the campaign to blanket the media, especially local talk radio, with ads selling a better education, a better future for your kids through EduNet; Bill was excited to tell them about the latest public relations coup—they'd managed—somehow—to hire William Shatner as spokesperson. Imagine that. A TV star irrelevant to anyone born after 1975 was going to be their spokesperson. Bill was marching on: the website was up and running, billboards were going up all over town, and on and on. It had all been said one hundred times before, but they weren't here today simply to get another rehash. Mitchell had other things in mind; he was being patient, waiting for the correct moment to pounce.

"And that," said Bill, "is where we are right now. Everything is in place; all we are waiting for is the go-ahead."

They all applauded and a few of the vice-presidents voiced their approval. Mitchell glanced over at Sandra, who was looking at him appraisingly, maybe apprehensively.

"Well done, Bill," he said. "Very comprehensive, very detailed. I just have one question."

The table quieted. All eyes turned toward him. Bill's smile faded and he looked at Mitchell, still standing with his hands folded in front of him. He knew he had done nothing wrong, and he was right. The presentation had been impeccable. Every base had been covered.

"Who is our clientele?"

Six sets of eyes turned to Bill, who frowned.

"Well, it's the parents of our prospective students, of course. The media campaign is meant to convince them that EduNet is the best educational choice for their children."

Mitchell held up his hand.

"Don't quote the brochure to me, Bill; tell me. Who are these people? Where do they live? What do they want?"

"They're just like you and me, Mitchell. They want a better future for their kids."

Mitchell slapped his hand on the table. Several people jumped. Not Sandra, Mitchell noticed. She was expecting this.

"No, they're not like you and me. Most of the students in the district live in abject poverty. Most are African-American. Most of them are involved in crime or drugs. Most of the boys will end up in prison. Many of the girls are or will be pregnant before they're eighteen."

He paused, daring someone to challenge him, to show political correctness. No one said a thing. Not even Sandra. Six months ago, she would've been all up in arms. Now she knew better.

"Do you think, Bill, that they know or care who William Shatner is?"

Bill shrugged. "Probably not."

"Probably not."

"But, Mitchell," he protested, "we followed the guidelines set down by the research department. They picked the target audience, we didn't. They suggested we hit the political right with the ad campaign and that we hit it hard."

"That makes sense to plow the road for the legislation, but we're into the selling phase now, Bill. What do we do at this point?"

Bill glanced around the table and sighed.

"I guess we go back to the drawing board. I'll suggest we find a more suitable spokesperson for the target clientele and parcel out a portion of the ads to the urban radio stations."

Mitchell looked at him long and hard, a gaze he imagined a serpent would employ to hypnotize its prey. Bill started to fidget. A small bead of sweat was running down his temple.

"You'll have to reapportion the budget, Bill," he said, fixing him with his cold passionless eyes.

"That's going to be tough, Mitchell. We've already spent the lion's share of it on the present ads. Where's the rest supposed to come from?"

"You're a resourceful executive. I'm sure you'll figure out something, Bill. Let's move on."

Angela was next, outlining the technical side of the school curriculum. She stood up, swallowing nervously. Mitchell frowned slightly; she didn't seem to be herself today. The woman usually had confidence pouring off her like heat off a radiator. She seemed fidgety, and maybe a little disoriented. She began by reiterating the fact that most of the curricula would be presented online and proctored by teacher's assistants. They would utilize the present hardware of the school, after updating it, and the projected ETA of the software would be two weeks after that.

"So, if all goes well," she concluded, "Custer High School should be completely free of licensed teachers by the beginning of the next school year."

Everyone around the table nodded. A couple of them applauded softly as she took her seat. Mitchell looked across at her, studying her hands, which lay clasped on the table in front of her. A grim silence fell around the round table. He waited. When Angela wasn't in action, she was a twitcher; she couldn't sit still. He knew she was sweating underneath that suit and that her heart was going a mile a minute. She was in misery, and he knew it. She knew he knew it. She would crack any minute.

She cleared her throat.

"Moving from licensed teachers to teacher's aides should save the company almost two million dollars."

36

Heads nodded. Angela smiled and hesitantly took her hands off the table.

"Very good, Angela. Very good," said Mitchell. "I'd like a complete hourly projected schedule of the hardware installation and the software implementation. By Monday."

Angela nodded and smiled over a pained expression. Coming up with a detailed schedule such as the one he requested would take at least a day; her weekend had just been erased.

The meeting went on. The other vice-presidents reviewed their basic overall strategies for implementing their program. Everything was running smoothly; overall, Mitchell was satisfied. Very satisfied. They had done a good job, which didn't keep him from assigning them status updates and other tasks, but that was mostly to affirm to them that he was on top of everything—to keep them under his thumb. Which was the point of the whole meeting. The last thing he needed at this point was a mutiny. The more fear he held over them the better.

After Jimmy, whose presentation was entirely inept and useless, but whose uncle was CEO, caught high praise from everyone at the table, and no retribution from Mitchell, he turned to Sandra.

"Sandra," he said, smiling, "as assistant executive vice-president overseeing this project, I'd like for you to take us through the steps we'll be taking to bring us to the next stage."

"Thank you," she said, standing up and looking around the table. "As you all know, the EduNet Project has always had Custer High School bookmarked as its model for takeover. This is because it has so many characteristics that are typical of an urban public school. Attendance hovers around seventy percent, the graduation rate is about sixty percent, and its composite ACT scores are about fifteen out of a possible score of thirty-six. There is, obviously, a lot of room for improvement."

She paused to take a drink of water. Mitchell watched her throat as she tipped the glass back. Her neck was neither long nor elegant; in fact, it was lot like the rest of her body: a little thick, showing well-defined muscularity, but average overall. Still, there was something about the way she possessed herself, the way she moved, even when she drank. She was confident, self-possessed, but strangely hesitant, almost jerky, at the same time.

"Custer," she continued, "also has a high population of students with special education needs. Nearly forty percent of them are classified as special education. The beauty of our situation is that we can pick and choose who we want in our school, and if we decide that having a special education program would be too expensive, we can simply refuse to enroll those students."

"Is that legal?" asked Angela.

"Perfectly. Under the present state charter law, we are not entitled to serve every student in the district like the public schools are, so all the specialized programs like gifted and talented and bilingual programs are not mandated for us. "

"What happens to these kids?" asked Angela.

Sandra paused, exhaled, and glanced at Mitchell, waiting for his cue. The question was from the no-go zone, part of the takeover that was never to be mentioned. As Mitchell had stated at the meeting introducing the no-go zone, "We cannot afford to be distracted by issues of sentimentality. This is a business proposition. Any issues like the history of the school, the fabric of the neighborhoods, or the fate of students ineligible for enrollment in EduNet schools, are irrelevant. Let the bleeding hearts deal with that crap. We're a business. I don't want any discussion of these other factors in my presence. As of today, we don't go there: it is now the no-go zone."

Mitchell inclined his head to Sandra slightly. Let her handle the intrusion into the no-go zone. She nodded back slightly and turned to Angela.

"Well, as we said when we went over this before, Angela, this situation is a win-win for us."

A look of pure fear crossed Angela's face; it had finally dawned on her that she'd gone into the zone.

"We don't," Sandra continued, glancing back at Mitchell, "have the added expenses of hiring special education teachers, aides, or any of the other accompanying personnel. Under a federal mandate, these children have to be taught. But not by us. Public schools will continue servicing them, and, as a result, because these students don't achieve as well, attend as much, and get into more trouble, it makes our statistics look that much better. That's the second part of our win-win."

Sandra looked down at her laptop as Angela nodded, trying to hide her sigh of relief. She knew she had gotten off lightly, that Mitchell would have absolutely blasted her for asking such a stupid question. Now, thought Mitchell, she knows Sandra is the one who will get screamed at for not being ruthless enough. As does Sandra, who had taken one for the team. Another bad habit she had.

"As we've seen today," she continued, "everything seems to be in place. The computers we will be using are the ones that are currently installed at Custer, the software is in our warehouse, currently awaiting distribution, our people are in the process of being trained and will be ready for the classroom as scheduled. As Bill told you, the PR machine is ready to roll. And, as of yesterday, the first shot, if you will, was fired over the bow. We had observers come in to some of the classrooms at Custer to gather data concerning the effectiveness of the current curriculum there."

She gave a nod to Mark Phillips, who acknowledged her with a slight smile.

"Thanks to Mark for getting all the logistics of hiring and data collection and collation down for us. He did an outstanding job. The data to be collected, which will consist of observable material, such as classroom movement, student behaviors, and on-task behavior, will be collated after the two-week collection period. This report, which we expect will reflect substandard teaching, an unsafe environment, and unacceptable student behaviors, should be the final piece that pushes our program through the last phases of legislation and public acceptance. Thank you."

There was a polite smattering of applause around the table. Mitchell did not look toward her as she sat. He leaned back in his chair and looked at each one of them in turn, appraising them silently.

"Good," he said, finally. "Everything seems to be on track. I don't need to tell you how important this current stage of the project is. The data we gather from these teachers will be instrumental in our mission to elevate these schools. Unfortunately, there is a human element here that could not be subtracted from the equation. As part of our permission to come in and do this, it was mandated that some of these observers be retired teachers and administrators. Even though we were extremely careful in the application process, some sympathetic souls may have slipped through the cracks."

He leaned forward in his chair, placing his elbows on the table.

"I want none of it," he said, his voice sharp. "I want you all to be my watchdogs. Each one of you will see the raw data at some point in this process. Keep an eye out for anyone who thinks this might not be the right thing to do. We're not going to jeopardize all of our hard work for some misplaced sentimentality."

He glanced at his watch.

"All right," he said. "That's it."

They stood; he took out his smartphone and started checking emails as they left.

"Sandra," he said without looking up, "stay a moment, will you?"

"Sure."

He waited until everyone had left. He put away his phone and glanced up at Sandra, who was standing next to her chair, clutching her laptop under her arm.

"You did a good job today."

She nodded slightly. "Thank you." She knew the other shoe was already falling.

"Why did you let Angela off the hook?"

She shrugged and he felt his frustration rising. He didn't like this passive aggressive sort of thing and she knew it. If she had a good reason for not tearing Angela a new one, or even a reason that wasn't that good, he had to hear it. He didn't want any of this 'it didn't feel right' or 'I couldn't' bullshit.

"I need a reason," he said, his voice clipped and closing in on harsh.

"I knew," said Sandra, "that she had just messed up a little bit. I knew she knows the zone. It was just a glitch, Mitchell."

"What the fuck?" shouted Mitchell, rising and smacking the table with his open hand. "What the fuck? Do we tolerate incompetence? Do we tolerate sloppiness? No. So what the fuck were you thinking?"

She didn't flinch; she knew him that well. And she didn't seem intimidated by him anymore, either.

"I had my reasons," she said, her face composed, consciously impassive.

"Like fucking what?" he said, his voice bouncing off the walls.

"I don't know if you knew," said Sandra, "but Angela had lung cancer. She was diagnosed last year. She went through chemotherapy for six months and is now cancer-free."

"So? She's all better now, right?"

Sandra looked at him a moment, her lips pressed firmly together.

"The cancer's gone, but I think she's suffering from what they call chemo brain. It's an after-effect of the medication; you have memory lapses, you freeze under pressure at times; there's a whole host of symptoms. You can find it all on the Internet."

"Why wasn't I told about this? Why is she still on the project?"

"Because she knows this area better than anyone. And she told HR she didn't want anyone to know. She has that right. She told me as a friend, and I thought that I should let you know so you understand her circumstances."

"I don't want any weaknesses, any infirmities on my team."

Sandra sat down on the edge of the table, facing Mitchell.

"You know Mitchell, when Angela was going through chemotherapy, she never missed a day of work. She would do treatments in the afternoon and come in the next day without a complaint, without whining, without telling anyone what she was going through. She's been with the company over thirty years. I think she deserves more than browbeating and intimidation."

He leaned back and stared at her a moment, openly amazed. This was mutiny. Open mutiny. He had underestimated Sandra's balls.

"So you don't like the way I manage the team?"

She looked at him, her face softening a little.

"I do. You know I think you're a great executive, Mitchell. I don't think there's anyone as efficient or as hard-nosed as you. That's why I really appreciate working and learning under you."

She stood up and folded her hands in front of her.

"I'm sorry if you think I showed you up in front of the team, Mitchell. I would like to make it up to you if I could."

He nodded.

"Ordinarily, I don't stand for this sort of thing, but you know my rationale. If you break one of my rules, have a good fucking reason for it."

"I know," she said. "I thought my reason was a good one."

"I'm glad you have loyalty for the team," he said, shifting in his seat and pulling down his zipper, "but your reason came very close to our own no-go zone. You can't get too close to your co-workers."

"I know," she said, kneeling down and putting her hands on his thighs. "Let me make it up to you."

Chapter 5

Dave threaded his way down the crowded hallway, past the throngs of students talking and laughing and congregating in front of their lockers, doing everything, as usual, but going to class. He nodded to the children he knew, or who greeted him, and acknowledged Beverly Finster as he passed her standing outside her classroom, badgering students to hurry to their next class. Privately, Dave thought Beverly was not looking that great these days. She'd put on a little weight and her face had a puffy, pasty quality that she had unsuccessfully tried to cover with make-up. It was understandable, though. She was under a lot of strain. But for all that, Dave reflected, she still looked pretty good. Beautiful shoulder-length auburn hair, natural, sharp blue eyes, and a well kept figure, a little too Valhalla-like for his taste, but still nice.

She smiled and waved at him enthusiastically, almost buoyantly, when she sighted him. He smiled back. Bev was newly divorced and—he suspected—looking for somebody to rebound with. Some of his friends on staff told him he was a marked man. It was an interesting thought, but he wasn't sure it was a good idea.

Not that he didn't like Beverly; she was funny, smart, and had been very supportive of him during his own divorce. And she was also a wine enthusiast. Since Ethel had accepted the Faculty Chair position, Bev was also now the chair of the English department. Fully a third of the English teachers had retired during the enactment of the anti-union legislation— the great migration as Dave had termed it. Beverly wasn't at the minimum age for early retirement, so she'd had to stay. But she was also the sole surviving English teacher with seniority enough to lead and was there-fore—by default—selected to become the chair.

She was also recovering from a very nasty and a very messy divorce, even a year after the legalities were done. It seemed her husband Roger, a sax player with a local band, had gotten busted with over a pound of pot in his car and had been charged with possession with the intent to distribute. He was looking at serious jail time. She'd been fighting with him over his drug habit for years, and this had been the final straw. Beverly filed divorce papers the next day.

They had three children; two were grown, but one, Celia, was twelve years old, and like Solomon's baby, was caught in the middle. Even though Roger was very likely headed to prison, he wouldn't let go of custody. His attorney was filing every sort of delaying action, motion, and tactic he could employ to stave off the inevitable. Roger kept trying to see Celia, coming to the house at all hours of the night, leaving phone messages, and harassing them to the point that Beverly had to take out a restraining order—which he was still routinely violating. His sentencing for the drug charge was coming up soon, so she was hoping he—and his attendant problems—would go away.

Since her divorce, Dave had been picking up signs that Bev might want to be more than friends—nothing too obvious: a little more touching than necessary, a little more dropping in to see him than usual, and a little more smiling and laughing at his jokes than was appropriate. His jokes just weren't that funny. They never had been.

He waved, smiled back at Bev, and continued on toward the teachers' lounge, already visualizing the cup of rank coffee he'd have there.

A sudden burst of motion in the distance caught Dave's eye. He turned and saw a quick turning of heads, then a few kids trotting, then suddenly running toward the commotion about halfway up the corridor. He heard shouting and a general rumbling of noise: talking, screaming, cursing, and a mass of humanity surging to the action. Fight. It looked like a big one. He started running, trying to keep up with the tidal movement flowing toward the disturbance.

He reached the fringe of the crowd, tried to shoulder past the ring of spectators shouting encouragement, cheering, pushing, and shoving. He saw a few smartphones raised up overhead, recording the altercation on video; he knew they'd be on Facebook within a few minutes. Out of the corner of his eye, he saw Mr. Allen, a security aide, also trying to break through, yelling at the kids to move out of the way. He was a big man and was making progress to the inner ring. Mr. Ellerby, one of the math teachers, another big guy, was right alongside him. Dave fell in behind them, and after a moment, they finally broke through.

Three boys were kicking another who was down on the ground, trying to cover up. Mr. Allen immediately went for the most aggressive one, who was leaning over and punching the kid on the floor. Allen pinned his arms and lifted him up in the air. Dave saw he had five rings on his right hand, all of them bloody. Mr. Ellerby walked toward one of the others, his arms raised, shouting for him to back off. Dave ran up to the other assailant still standing over the boy, yelling at him to leave, to get out of there.

"Fuck you, teacher," he said, giving the boy on the ground another kick in the back. "This ain't none of your motherfucking business."

"Get off him, now!" screamed Dave, and the kid actually took a step back. The third assailant had already melted back into the crowd and Ellerby was moving back toward them, also yelling at the kid.

Dave got between the second kid and the boy on the ground.

"Go on," he said. "Get out of here."

The kid glared at him and, for a moment, Dave thought he might go after him. He finally stalked off. Dave knelt down next to the boy lying on the ground. He had several gashes in his scalp and was bleeding hard from the mouth. He was conscious, however, leaning up on an elbow, his eyes darting over the crowd.

"All right," said Dave, "I think we need to get you cleaned up. Can you stand up?"

The kid looked at him a moment, blinking. Dave could see the swelling already coming up under his left eye. He was probably going to need some stitches. The kid nodded and started to rise. Mr. Ellerby squatted down beside him and peered closely at the wound.

"That's going to need some stitches," he said. Dave nodded.

"All right," he said. "Let's go."

He and Ellerby helped the kid up and started walking him toward the nurse's office. By this time, more security had arrived to disperse the crowd. Most kids had left peacefully, but a few stayed around to relive the excitement. Two kids watched the three of them move slowly down the hall.

"You see that motherfucker go down? Bang. That was the shit, man."

"Yeah, man."

Mr. Allen appeared behind them.

"What are you talking about? You need to get the class, the two of you. You go now. Y'all get to class."

"All right, Allen, just a minute, man."

"Now. You all go now."

The kids shrugged and, muttering, started walking off down the hall. Mr. Allen came over to Dave and the beat-up kid, taking Ellerby's place to support him on his other arm. Blood was dripping from his mouth onto the floor. Mr. Ellerby hung back, peering down the corridor over his shoulder.

"It's clear," he said. "All clear."

"Let's get him in the bathroom," said Mr. Allen. "Try to put a stop to that blood."

They got him to the bathroom and sat him down on one of the commodes. Mr. Allen tore a sheaf of paper towels off the roller. He went and started dabbing at the kid's lip. The boy tried to push Allen away, but the big man told him not to worry, it wouldn't hurt for long.

"Stop that now," he said gently, "you can't be bleeding all over Mr. Bell and everything."

The kid let him press the towel onto his face.

"Hold this on there," he said, pressing it to his bloody lip. The kid did. He looked up at Allen, and then at Dave. He no longer looked completely dazed but still seemed disoriented. Shock, thought Dave. He knew a fair amount of the kids at the school, through class or activities or reputation, but this one was new to him. He glanced around to see if Ellerby knew him, but he hadn't followed them into the bathroom.

"All right," said Mr. Allen, "we'll get you straightened up and send you in to Mr. Ricks' office. We'll find those other two boys who jumped you and make sure they get what's coming to them."

The kid said nothing, staring at the ground in front of him.

"What's your name, son?" asked Mr. Allen. "I don't believe I know you."

The kid fidgeted a little, dabbed at his lip, looked at the blood on the towel, and finally said, "Marcus. I'm Marcus DePierre."

"What happened, Marcus? Why were those boys on you?"

Marcus shook his head and dabbed at his lip again. He put his head in his hand and stared at the floor.

Mr. Allen motioned to Dave and they moved to the bathroom door.

"I'll talk to him, Mr. Bell, and get him down to the office. He needs a little time to gather himself, I think. You can go on now."

Dave nodded. The kid was still in a daze and would be humiliated when he started to realize what had happened. Probably the fewer people around, the better. Mr. Allen knew what he was doing; there wasn't anyone in the school better with the kids than him.

"All right," said Dave. "Did you know any of those other kids?"

"I knew one. The ringleader. Damarius Como. I handed him off to Mr. Z. who's taking him down to Ricks. He's some kind of knucklehead."

"Okay," said Dave, telling himself to remember the name. "We'll see you, Mr. Allen."

"Hey," said Mr. Allen. "Thank you, Mr. Bell. You and Ellerby probably saved this boy a few extra stitches by getting there when you did."

"Hey, I just followed you, Mr. Allen."

"Well, thank you just the same."

Dave went out in the hallway; there were still a few stragglers—hall walkers—wandering around, but by and large, things had calmed down. He continued to the lounge, got there, unlocked the door and entered.

There were four other people inside. Eric Knox, a first-year English teacher, was lying on the couch with a wet towel on his head. Triage. Zoe Ralph, a second-year math teacher, was absorbed with texting or e-mailing or doing some other damned thing with her smartphone. Mr. Ellerby was getting his morning soda out of the vending machine. Will Baker was sitting at the table correcting papers; he preferred working here rather than his classroom, where he said he was less likely to be interrupted.

Will and Dave went back a long time; they had begun their careers at Custer only a month apart. They'd lived through at least ten different principals, three or four district superintendents, and 9/11. Will had lost a nephew in the South Tower that day. After absorbing that tragedy and never getting satisfactory closure—they never did find any remains—Will had begun changing subtly. His politics started leaning right, which, Dave supposed, was not completely unreasonable. It had happened to a lot of people.

But every now and then Will would stop Dave in the hallway and tell him about a website that proved Bush was behind the towers falling or that Osama had spent a night in the White House. Dave was taken aback; he'd always known Will as a very steady guy. He knew it would pass. And, for the most part, it had; still, every now and then he would surprise Dave with some whacked-out conspiracy theory.

Will was married, but you wouldn't know it from his appearance. His gray hair was perpetually standing up at all sorts of odd angles; he often wore the same shirt two or three days in a row, and was the clumsiest person Dave had ever seen. He had never seen the man not spill food on himself.

"Hey, Will," said Dave, as he got his coffee. "What's the story?"

"Same old, same old. There was a big fight last hour right by Finster's room."

"Yeah, I was there. Mr. Allen and I broke it up. Mr. Ellerby was there, too."

"I was indeed," said Ellerby. He was a middle-aged balding black man who—in Dave's estimation—had probably been teaching three years too many. His heart didn't seem in it anymore. Every day he seemed to grow a little less committed and a little more cynical.

"Who was it?" asked Will.

Ellerby shrugged. "Don't know," he said.

"I didn't know any of them, either," said Dave. "Freshmen, proba-bly, by the looks of them, but the kid said he was jumped by a student named Como."

"That prick," proclaimed the couch. Or rather, Mr. Knox on the couch.

"Hey, Knox," said Dave. "Another hangover?"

"Huh," he said, sitting up. "Hangovers are easy. It's that fucking sec-ond hour. Those kids are insane."

"Freshmen?" asked Zoe, who had—only briefly, it was never for long—glanced away from her cell phone. She was small and thin, always very tidy-looking. Her blondish hair was usually tied back in a ponytail or braids or something else, never hanging loose. She dressed in slacks and blouses mostly, occasionally a dress, but not often. She was almost but not quite pretty, but not unattractive either, which probably had to do with the permanent smirk she had on her face; Dave had come to the conclusion that it probably wasn't intentional—that was just the way she looked. She had big brown eyes, even, almost delicate features, and a little pointy chin.

Dave liked her. She could be funny when she put down her phone long enough to hold a conversation and she was already, after only one year, a very good teacher. For a woman who stood five foot four in flats, she could handle a classroom of rowdy freshmen quite handily.

"Of course," said Knox, with a tone that sounded as if he was speaking to someone with a learning disability. "Who else?"

Mr. Ellerby padded out without saying good-bye to anyone. Will looked at Dave and raised his eyebrows.

"Hello, Ralph," said Dave, sitting down.

"What up, Bell?" she said, working her gum. That was the other thing; the woman chewed gum constantly, smacking it as if she were a cow chewing its cud; she was worse than any of his kids.

"Nothing much. Oh," he said, suddenly recalling it, "I had one of the EduNet observers come in my third hour."

He saw Knox sit up on the couch out of the corner of his eye. Even Will looked up.

"What did he do?" asked Will.

Bell shrugged. "Sat down, took notes, looked like he had a gigantic stick up his ass."

Will chuckled and Zoe smiled while poring over her smartphone. Knox sat up on the couch, staring at him.

"Oh," he continued, "I couldn't be sure, but I thought he was video-taping the class."

"Is that legal?" asked Knox, an edge creeping into his voice. He had come into teaching late, in his early thirties, out of some misplaced sense of civic duty. Dave had co-taught with him a few times and thought he was an all right teacher, but wanted to tell him that if he could get over his fear of the kids and anxiety about himself, he might be really good. When not lying on the couch, Knox was average height and a bit overweight. He had a pasty complexion and wore dark hipster glasses and almost always dressed in a sport coat, tie, and Dockers. The kids had taken to calling him Mr. Doughboy almost immediately, and unfortunately, the name had stuck. But he was earnest about the profession and worked diligently on his lesson plans, classroom management, and parental contacts. It was just going to take him a while. He reminded Dave a lot of Felicity during her first year.

"I think it's legal," said Dave. "Since the union downsized, we don't really have much say in it anymore. I think it's more or less up to the schools."

"I do think there is a liability issue," said Will. "Parents have to sign off or something."

"Well, it definitely used to be that way," said Dave, "but who knows nowadays?"

"Hey," said Zoe suddenly. "Should I join the union? What do you guys think? My mentor was mentioning it to me, but if it's as useless as you guys keep saying, then what's the point?"

"Well," said Will, pushing back from the table, "it's definitely not as strong as it used to be, but I still think it's a good idea to join."

"Why?" asked Zoe, poking at her iPhone. Dave resisted the impulse to tell her to put it away and pay attention.

"It's kind of an insurance policy," said Will. "Let's say you're alone with a kid after school, say giving him a test or something. What do you think would happen if that student decided to accuse you of sexual assault?"

"Well," said Zoe, finally looking at Will, "it would be my word against his, right?"

Will shrugged. "Probably," he said.

Zoe shrugged back. "Then I'd be okay. I mean who's the administration going to believe?"

Dave snorted. Zoe rounded on him.

"What?" she asked.

"Well," he said, "we're assuming there's nothing to the charge, but what would the administration—any administration—do in a case like that? A kid accuses a teacher of sexual assault, and let's also assume the parent comes in raising hell."

"I'm not sure," said Zoe, taken aback. She hadn't expected to be surrounded.

"Think a minute," said Dave. "What is their prime number one all-powerful concern?"

"Students?"

"Really, Zoe?" piped in Knox. He was sitting up with his feet on the floor, suffering from a sudden surge of energy.

She glanced around the table, looking like a cornered bird.

"What?" she said.

"Covering their own ass," said Dave. "Or is it asses? What would be the correct form in this case?"

"Asses," said Knox. "It's a collective thing, but they're covering the individual ass, too."

"Oh," said Zoe. "Yeah, I see your point. That's kind of what they do all the time. Yeah. Duh."

"So," said Will, "if they decide to hang you out to dry on something like this, you're pretty much powerless."

"And that," continued Dave, glancing over at Will, "is where the union can help. If you're a member. They can demand a hearing, give you counsel, they can do a lot of things. It is like an insurance policy."

"And not only in instances like that," continued Will. "They're still somewhat of a political force, our lobby if you will, in the state capitol."

Somewhat is right, thought Dave. He wondered, not for the first time, why he and Will still advocated so strongly for the union. Everything they'd been saying was true, of course, and he himself was still a member—actually a member twice: once in the active teachers union, and again in the retirees' union—but he wondered what a teacher Zoe's age must think. Since they'd been stripped of collective bargaining rights, the unions had no, or very little, input about hours, working conditions, or wages. The new kids had to be wondering why bother?

He turned as the door opened and a smaller middle-aged man entered. Dave recognized him immediately and smiled. It was Scott Brown, the EduNet observer. He glanced over at Will, raised his eyebrows, and made a slight motion with his head toward Brown. Will furrowed his brow, glanced at Brown, and then nodded. Dave glanced over at Knox, who was digging something out from under one of his nails. Zoe was engrossed in her cellphone, texting or something.

"Hello, Mr. Brown," said Dave, using his boomiest teacher voice. Knox and Zoe looked up almost simultaneously. "How are things going with the observations?"

He nodded and smiled slightly. "Very well, Mr. Bell. Thank you." He walked to the vending machine, bought a Diet Coke, and went over to the table. "Do you mind if I sit?"

"Not at all," said Dave, motioning to a chair. Mr. Brown sat. Will was watching him intently. Zoe had stared at him at first but was now only stealing glances between texts. Knox was staring at him with a look of utter distaste.

"I have to say, Mr. Bell," said Mr. Brown, oblivious to the tension, "that was a very interesting class you had this morning."

"Oh?"

"Yes, the students seemed quite engaged. I thought it was an outstanding lesson plan."

"Really?" said Dave. "Thank you. It's nice of you to say so."

He glanced at Will, whose expression had not changed. He was staring at Brown as if he were a cockroach in his kitchen sink.

"You know," continued Mr. Brown, " I was a high school teacher myself once upon a time. English Literature and Composition. My specialty was Shakespeare and Medieval Literature."

"Where did you teach?" asked Knox, a sneer in his voice.

Mr. Brown turned around in his chair. "Oh, hello, young man. I hadn't seen you sitting there."

"Mr. Brown," said Bell, "this is Knox."

"Just Knox?"

"Just Knox," said Dave.

Knox gave Dave a look, and then turned his attention back to Mr. Brown.

"Well, Knox," said Mr. Brown, glancing again at Dave and smiling tentatively, "I taught twenty-two years at Central High School here in the city before I was offered a job at Elysium Junior College, where I taught another ten years. I retired seven years ago."

"How did you connect with EduNet?" asked Will, never one to beat around the bush.

"This is Will Baker, Mr. Brown, and while I'm at it, this is Zoe Ralph, another one of our young teachers."

"A pleasure," said Mr. Brown, rising to shake Zoe's hand. "It's nice to see that someone has two first names. As opposed to Knox."

"Ah, Mr. Baker," said Mr. Brown, glancing at Dave, "I can see my reputation precedes me. Yes, I work for EduNet, and, yes, I did observe Mr. Bell's class this morning."

"And you liked it?" asked Knox. "You liked the class. Is that what you're telling EduNet?"

"Of course," said Mr. Brown, "what else would I say? I thought it was an exemplary classroom and an outstanding lesson plan." He coughed and glanced around the room. "Of course," he continued, "they'll have more objective evidence than my own opinion."

"The videotape," said Dave. Mr. Brown nodded.

"Yes," he said deliberately. "We were instructed to videotape every class we observed with our laptop computers."

"Were you supposed to conceal that fact?" asked Dave. "I mean it wasn't very obvious that's what you were doing."

Brown suddenly looked very nearly sheepish, his self-assurance evaporating.

"I'm afraid," he said, standing up, "that I can't really discuss this matter any further. I'm under certain obligations—because of my contract, you see."

"You taught in public school, Mr. Brown," said Will, "and you obviously know what EduNet is planning to do to the public school system here."

"I'm sorry," said Brown, moving toward the door. "I really have to go."

"How can you do something like this?" asked Will.

"You're helping to kill public schools," said Knox, suddenly standing and looking pastily vehement. "You're ruining the future. Our future."

Brown walked out quickly, not making eye contact with anyone.

"Bastard," said Knox, after the door shut behind him.

"He didn't seem like such a bad guy," said Zoe. "In fact," she said, smiling a little, "he reminded me a lot of Bell."

Dave nodded to himself. Zoe was right. Brown was a lot like him, retired, a teacher who probably took another job to make ends meet a little more neatly. In different circumstances, Dave knew that he very well could have ended up in the same place. Knox, still huffing and puffing and spewing invective all over the lounge, was too young to know what simple survival meant yet. Will knew. He'd been around long enough to see the cost of survival. He'd seen most of his friends retire and then return in some faint semblance of themselves: substitutes, mentors, consultants—a legion of ghost educators. Zombies. Dave glanced at Will, who was staring out the door after Mr. Brown, eyes furrowed in thought. Bell knew that look.

"Penny for your thoughts," he said.

Will blinked, looked over at him, and smiled.

"Nothing much there," he said. "Just wondering how a guy like that would end up with EduNet. You think he'd have more respect for the public education system."

"He probably just needed the money," said Zoe, gazing down at her smartphone screen.

Will nodded. "Yeah," he said. "That must be it. It's just that simple."

Zoe still poked at her smartphone. The sarcasm rolled off her like water off a duck.

"He's a fucking traitor," said Knox. "Just a fucking traitor. There's no goddamned excuse for his behavior."

Dave nodded. "You're right," he said. "No goddamned excuse."

They fell silent then, all of them—except Zoe—staring at the closed door.

Chapter 6

Sandra pulled up in front of the shabby one-story ranch house, the definition of ordinary; it was a house that could be anywhere, in any town in America. There were hundreds, thousands of houses like it, prefabbed white cracker boxes. Cheap early sixties starters, fine when they were built, but run-down and shabby now. Many of them were still occupied by their original owners, men and women in their eighties—and beyond—who didn't like anything new. She knew these people; when they looked down their street they only saw things the way they used to be.

She knew what these houses were like inside. Three tiny bedrooms huddled around one end of the house like sheep hiding from a dog, one tiny bathroom—unless the dad had been ambitious enough to add one downstairs, and a ten by twelve living room with shag carpeting presided over by a Magnavox Console 32" television set. She knew these houses because she and her brothers had grown up in one just like it.

She glanced at her watch: 9:45. Past visiting hours, she knew, but she hadn't been in to see Jimmy for over three weeks. And it wasn't as if she'd be waking him up; Sandra knew he'd be up watching his TV. *The Brady Bunch* came on at nine-thirty. He would definitely be watching; Jimmy was nothing if not consistent.

Sandra sighed and shut her eyes a moment, leaning back into the leather seat of her SUV. She could fall asleep right here without half trying. It had been a hellishly long week. Mitchell had not been very happy when some of the initial evaluations had started coming back from Custer. Most of them were fine, but despite all their efforts to stack the deck, a few of the evaluators had come back with satisfactory or superior reports of teaching.

She tried to tell him it was only one or two outliers. There had been a total of only four bad reports out of almost fifty, but Mitchell didn't care.

He was making life hell for everyone else around him. She leaned forward, opened her purse and dug into it. She found the unopened pack of Marlboros near the bottom, bent a little, but still looking okay. She picked up the pack and tamped it against her other hand, breathing in the tobacco aroma and remembering the satisfaction. No.

She got out of the car, put her purse and briefcase in the back and then locked the door. She glanced up and down the street before going up the sidewalk to the porch, which was lit up by a huge florescent light. It was as bright as an operating room. Moths and other bugs fluttered through the dripping light, their final summer fling before winter set in. She rang the bell and waited half a minute before ringing it again. Nothing. She was about to press it again when she finally heard footsteps approaching. Someone started fiddling with the lock. She stepped back into the bright part of the light.

The door jerked open and a thin pasty face thrust itself out at her.

"What?" it asked, squinting into the glaring light. "Who is it?"

"Hello, Larry," she said. "It's me. It's Sandra. Sorry I'm so late. I should've called."

"Oh," he said, pushing his glasses up, standing up straight, and then gesturing jerkily with his hand. "Hello, Sandra. I didn't recognize you there. It took my eyes a minute to adjust. It's sort of dark inside." He shrugged and then threw back his shoulders in an effort, she supposed, to look cool. He wasn't quite there yet. Larry had a crush on her; he had ever since they'd met. It was touching, she supposed, and she used it only when she needed to.

"Yeah," she said, giving Larry a sweet smile. "I came to see Jimmy. "

Larry let out a deep breath and looked off to one side of the porch, shaking his head disapprovingly.

"I know it's late, Larry," she said, "but I haven't had a chance to see him in over three weeks."

"Sandra," he said, blowing out his breath in an exasperated fashion, "you know the rules. Nobody, no family, no strangers, nobody comes in after nine. You know that. You know that."

"I do know it, Larry, and I'm sorry to impose on you, but it's been so long, and my work is so busy, I just don't know when I'll be able to get here again."

She stepped nearer the open screen door. Larry moved back like she was a hot coal and let the door slam shut.

"Has anyone else been here to see him?" she asked, putting her hand on the screen.

Larry stared at his shoes and shook his head.

"Same old story," he said. "You're the only who ever comes to see poor old Jimmy."

"He must be really sad," she said.

Larry shrugged. "He seems okay to me."

"C'mon, Larry," she said, putting her hand on the screen door and opening it. "I'll be in and out before you know it."

"I don't know," he said, glancing nervously behind him.

"How about," she said, cocking her head and crinkling up her face with a smile, which used to drive the boys nuts in high school, "how about if I sponsor the next movie outing?"

"What movie?" he asked, perking up.

"Isn't the new *Star Wars* coming out soon?"

He nodded. "That would be really cool."

"And," she said, "I'll bring a fifty-pack snack box with me next time."

"Frito-Lays?" he asked.

"Yes," she said, "of course. Nothing less. And I'll pay for all ten of you to go."

"There's eleven now," he said. "We got a new brain injury."

She smiled. "Eleven then."

"Okay," he said, opening the door and gesturing her in, "but you've got to be really, really, really quiet. The boss isn't here, but these guys will talk to anybody, including him. They'll say anything to anybody. Absolutely no discretion. No discretion at all."

"Okay," she whispered and made a show of taking off her heels, which were killing her anyway.

Larry glanced back and then looked at her more closely. He seemed to be paying special attention to her legs.

"You're really short without your shoes," he said.

She put a finger to her lips; he nodded and moved stealthily down the hall and into the main living area, which was illuminated only by a television. One man lay slumped sleeping in a wheelchair while another

57

middle-aged woman sat on the couch engrossed in *The Brady Bunch*, covering her mouth and giggling at the Brady antics.

Popular show, she thought, among the Down syndrome population, the emotionally impaired, or whatever other brain damage cases were being parked here nowadays: a representative slice of the American public taste. Sandra wasn't surprised. She couldn't speak for all the people here, but she knew Jimmy had always liked his life structured, set into solid routines. That kept Jimmy happy, which kept their mom happy. He loved aa the old reruns, and he lived his life just like the TV Bradys: there was never anything new in their experience — or his — and once he got into the reruns everything was gold, solid golden oldies, when it became physically impossible to experience the unexpected.

In a sudden flash, she realized her life had become eerily similar to Jan Brady's: like Jan she was never happy, never satisfied, ever envious, and always forced into the master Brady mold of conformity. Always trapped in a routine. That was her, all right — Sandra, Sandra, Sandra.

She caught herself smiling as Larry led her to Jimmy's door. He stopped and peered down the hall, watching for — for what? There was no supervisor here, no one here to reprimand him, so what was Larry so afraid of? He was slightly impaired, she knew, but he still didn't have to be such a baby. She knew the type, impaired or not. She worked with them every day in the corporate world: scared of their own shadows and overly concerned with covering their own asses. Larry turned back to Jimmy's door.

She saw that the tattered *Incredible Hulk* poster that had hung in his bedroom at home was still taped to the outside door. The Hulk, she thought. Another survivor. She had bought the poster for Jimmy as a Christmas present at least twenty years ago. Somehow it had survived three brothers, moving, and all the assorted group home residents.

Larry knocked quietly.

"Jimmy," he said, his voice barely above a whisper. "Jimmy."

Sandra heard movement in the room, slow, ponderous, and very deliberate. Very Jimmy.

"Who is it?" he asked. It was definitely Jimmy. Other people sometimes found it hard to understand him, but she knew every one of his misarticulations and slurs.

"It's me, Jimmy," she said, louder than she had intended.

"Jesus," squeaked Larry, "for God's sake, Sandra, keep your voice down. You want to get me fired?"

The door popped open and Jimmy stood there, beaming at her with his snaggle-toothed smile, all two hundred and forty pounds of him. His round face was getting lined now; he was nearly forty, old for someone with Down syndrome. She ran her hand through his sandy brown hair. It needed cutting.

"Hello, Sandy," he said, reaching up to hug her. He was a full six inches shorter than her. She hugged him back and glanced over at Larry, who was looking as if he were about to crap his pants.

"Let's go inside, Jimmy. We don't want to wake anybody up, do we?"

"No. Okay," he said, grabbing her hand and pulling her into the room.

"Thanks, Larry," she whispered, leaning back out of the doorway. "I won't forget this."

"Don't forget our bargain," he whispered and shrank back into the shadows.

She shut the door and turned back to the room. As usual, it was a shambles. Dirty clothes littered the bed and floor. Empty chip bags and candy wrappers were everywhere, on his desk, next to his bed, on the bed, and on the television. A couple of dirty plates were on his desk. She turned and glared at Jimmy, who was sitting on the edge of the bed and staring at the TV.

"Jimmy, this place is a pigsty. What did we talk about last time I was here?"

Jimmy looked up at her, his face blank. She knew that this was one of his oldest tricks, playing dumb when he got in trouble. He knew exactly what they had talked about, and he knew exactly what he was supposed to do.

"Jimmy," she said, her voice sharper this time. He looked up, blinking. "I'm talking to you."

"What?" he said. "Why are you yelling? You shouldn't yell at me all the time. You just got here."

"I'm yelling because this place is a pigsty. We talked about you cleaning it up, didn't we?"

Jimmy screwed up his face, started making oinking sounds, and giggled.

"That's not funny, Jimmy. Do you want them to move you out of here?" She sat down on the bed next to him.

Jimmy went back to staring at the TV. The ending credits for *The Brady Bunch* were rolling.

"Jimmy, look at me," she said, more gently. "Don't you want to stay here?"

"No," he said, suddenly. "I want to go home."

Sandra sat up straight on the edge of the bed.

"Jimmy, you know we had to sell the house after Mom died. You couldn't stay there by yourself."

"I could have. I could have. I'm a man. I work at a real job and I get a real check. I'm a man."

Sandra sighed. When their mother had died three years ago, none of the children could, or were willing, to take Jimmy into their homes. Two of her brothers, Dennis and Al, were married with families and said they didn't have the time or the extra room for Jimmy; Matt had the space but was more interested in his sailboat and making his yearly trip to the Caymans than boarding his brother.

When they had sat around the old kitchen table, all siblings with no spouses invited to the meeting—Al's idea: he said it was Feeley business, nobody else's, and a very sound one, Sandra had thought—trying to decide what to do with their brother, Matt had said wryly that Jimmy simply wouldn't fit on the boat, that he'd sink them both: the little prick. He'd wanted Sandra to take Jimmy; he said as much, that she was closest to him, and it was the best fit. Though Al and Dennis wouldn't say so, she knew they'd wanted it, too. She'd always been the most protective of Jimmy, the sister who'd beaten up anyone who dared call her brother a retard in the schoolyard. What they didn't say in their most sexist of hearts was that taking care of their little brother was woman's work, never mind that Sandra made twice as much as any of them.

She told them that she thought the best solution would be the group home, and, after hours of haggling, she had finally convinced her brothers of it. She was the one who had found a place and checked out all the references and the history; Al came with her once to check the place out, but Matt and Dennis had never even bothered.

"It's nice," Al had said, looking around. "He'll have company. People he can relate to."

"It'll be a lot better than being alone in my apartment all day."

"Yeah," said Al, running his hand over the woodwork. "It's just too bad he won't be with family."

He looked at her then, smiling a sad little smile.

Fuck you, she thought. You take him if you're so hot on family, you and your fat wife and moronic kids. I'd like to see that. Jimmy would be the smartest one in your fucking two hundred thousand dollar over-bought house.

So they had moved him in, and, true to form, Jimmy had not made a fuss. As long as he had his TV and his DVDs and his coloring books, he was fine. Sandra was pretty sure Jimmy still missed the house, his old room, and their mom, but it had been over three years now. She had thought they were over the hump.

"Hey, Sandy," said Jimmy.

"What?"

"Gas leak," he said, and started giggling just as the smell hit her.

"Jesus, Jimmy," she said, waving her hand, "what the hell do they feed you here? Dead dog?"

"Hey," he said, suddenly serious. *Bewitched* is coming on."

"Okay," she said, leaning back on the bed. "We can watch that."

She leaned back, feeling weariness pulling at her like a needy child. She lay back on her elbow and watched as the familiar title screens and theme music came on.

"You going to stay and watch?"

"For a little while," she said, clearing some of the empty chip bags and candy wrappers off the bed. "Maybe I'll just stay a little while."

"Good. You always liked this show, especially the one with Sam's twin sister."

Sandra looked at him, shaking her head. Some of the things he remembered were uncanny. Who knew what the hell went on inside that thick noggin of his? His teacher at the high school had always said he had one of the best memories—for a Down syndrome kid—she'd ever seen. What was her name again? Conner? Cooper?

"Hey, Jimmy?"

"What?" he said, not turning around. He didn't like to be distracted from his TV.

"Who was your teacher in high school?"

"Mrs. Conway," he replied without turning around. "Beatrice Conway. She was from Indianapolis and went to school at the University of Wisconsin at Whitewater. Can I watch my show now?"

"Okay," she said.

Mrs. Conway. She had been Jimmy's teacher all through high school and had taught him how to cook simple meals, how to take the bus, how to do and fold the laundry, and how to read, even though all he ever wanted to read was the TV Guide. She had been beautifully patient, yet tough, with Jimmy and all of her other kids. Their mother had loved her, called her a gift from heaven for little Jimmy. Sandra closed her eyes, thinking of their mother.

And there, amidst the paraphernalia from Jimmy's—and her own—childhood, the *Incredible Hulk* poster, the sixties television shows, the toys and books rescued from her mother's house before it was sold, gone from their lives and their pasts forever; there, in Jimmy's room, with the dialogue from *Bewitched* playing over her half-conscious mind, she closed her eyes and fell into a deep dreamless sleep, the best and most satisfying sleep she'd had in weeks.

Chapter 7

Mitchell stood at the window in his office, squeezing his stress ball and staring out at the river below shimmering in the brassy autumn sunlight. It was a beautiful day for late October: Indian Summer. The trees in the park were at the height of their fall color, the aspens glistening gold, their leaves almost glowing in contrast to the deep impenetrable scarlet of the sugar maples. It was beautiful: a fucking postcard.

He turned around and glanced at the scattered papers of today's observation reports on the floor and felt himself getting worked up all over again. Things were not going according to plan. Things were fucked up. Fucked up in a major-league way. When the first teams from Custer had filed their reports a week ago, Mitchell had devoured them immediately, eagerly anticipating the final nails in Custer's coffin, but, apparently, things couldn't be fucking rosier over there: he found himself reading about the excellent displays of exemplary teaching skills, creative and effective lesson planning, and significant student engagement.

These reports were the exceptions. His staff told him that. He knew that. Most of the observation ratings were exactly where they were supposed to be; they ranged from unsatisfactory to barely satisfactory with reports of fighting, widespread student misbehaviors like swearing, gambling, and suspicion of in-house drug use. Some of the teachers could not control their classrooms and many could barely keep their students on task. But being a mostly failing school was not good enough. For EduNet to get control of Custer without any backlash from the community, without any doubt whatsoever, this study had to be an absolute slam-dunk. Nothing good, nothing positive could ever come out of that building. Never, not until EduNet had control of it.

How many fucking times had he hammered that point home to his people? How many times had he said it had to be a slam-dunk? How many times had he said exactly that exactly like that?

His staff had paraded expert after expert in front of the observers—their observers, their—his—fucking employees—testifying to the fact that schools were sinking into a pit, that they were lucky the police weren't hauling body bags out of there day after day. So how, how the hell had this happened? How the fuck had they failed? How had he failed? It was all falling apart.

He turned back to his desk and looked down at the scattered pages of Sandra's last summary, then with one great sweeping motion, and an animal noise tearing from his throat, he swept everything from the desktop onto the floor. A great roaring filled his ears, a red mist swept over his vision, his thoughts, his whole consciousness, and he found himself grasping the desk, lifting it, and pushing it over with a great crash.

Mitchell dimly heard a faint noise from somewhere, a rapping, and slowly became aware that someone was knocking on the door. He was standing next to his overturned desk, sweating and panting like a dog.

"Sir? Are you all right, sir?" called a voice on the other side of the door.

He took a deep breath and glanced at the mess on the floor. The glass top of the desk had fallen off, but, miraculously, had not shattered. Everything else was smashed: his trophies, knick-knacks. Everything was broken.

"I'm fine, Monica," he called out. "I'm fine."

"Yes, sir."

He heard her walk away without any further ado. Well, it wasn't the first time unusual noises had come from this office. He sat down and surveyed the mess in front of him. His mess.

How the fuck had this happened? All the planning, all that work, all of it straight down the fucking toilet. All right, he thought. All right. Enough. It had been a week since this had first happened, and it was continuing to happen, and that wasn't good, but he had to get control of himself; he had to look at the situation coldly, objectively. He could not afford to be weak and emotional, to lose control of himself again. Women lost control, women let their emotions control them, and he was not a woman. He had to bring it back into line. He took a deep breath, let it out, took a deep breath and let it out. Control. Calm. Control. Calm. Breathe.

Mitchell sank back into his chair. He needed to get things moving in the right direction. He looked for his landline and spied it halfway across the room, lying in three pieces. He took out his cellphone and dialed Sandra's number. It rang once, twice, three, then four times; he took a deep breath, trying to bury his impatience.

"Hello?" she said.

"Sandra," he said, the tone of his voice flat, the diction deliberately clipped.

"What's up, Mitchell?" She sounded tired to him, and maybe a little irritated.

"The rest of the observations came in and there's more of the same. I need to fire these people. This is unacceptable." He struggled to keep his tone even. Breathe.

"How many bad reports are there now, Mitchell?" she asked. "Totally, I mean." She was writing everything down. He could visualize her doing it.

"Four."

"Four out of how many? Fifty-four? The positive ones are from how many evaluators?"

"Two."

"And you want to fire them all, right?"

"Yes."

"I know you don't want to hear this right now, Mitchell, but I think that would be a mistake." She paused. Mitchell took deep even breaths, bringing himself back to a state of equilibrium. After five breaths, she continued. It was uncanny, he thought, just like she was counting with him.

"I think we can talk to these people, Mitchell, and get them to massage these written reports. We're good with the video."

"Massage them?" said Mitchell, "I thought these were already submitted electronically to preserve their objectivity."

"Right," said Sandra, "but we can persuade these observers to add addenda to some of the written reports. And I think there are a few other alternatives we can look at." She paused again, and he heard her take a breath.

"Like what?" he asked, sitting back in his office chair, still concentrating on his breathing.

"Well, the objective data for one: the videotapes. Those are going to be fine. We can use those to ask the evaluators to re-examine their data. We'll sit down with them and watch the videos and steer them toward a more guided type of interpretation. I think we can make them see reason. Or we can possibly offer some other incentives for them to reconsider their judgments."

"Okay," he said. "That doesn't sound bad. Okay, let's work on that."

It was such a practical solution; he was amazed he hadn't thought of it himself. Massage the artifacts. Reinterpret the evidence. And if that didn't work—and he wasn't overly hopeful—pay them off. He kept breathing. No, he wasn't dead yet. Not by a long shot.

"What else did you have in mind?"

"Well," she said, "I think there might be another alternative to persuade some of these observers that they were mistaken about Custer."

"Like what?"

"Like a fixer."

He leaned back in his chair and stared up at the ceiling. He realized suddenly he wasn't breathing regularly anymore.

"It would be expensive," she added.

He knew that. It would put them way over budget. But if it meant keeping the project afloat, he would work it.

"Let me worry about that, Sandra."

"Okay, Mitchell," she said. "Don't worry," she added, "we'll get this figured out before you know it. You'll see."

"This is going to be handled," said Mitchell, his voice grating and harsh even to his own ear. "You needn't worry about that."

He paused, waiting for a response. Her could almost feel her exasperation over the line. Enough, he thought. He didn't have time for this. There was too much work to do.

"I'll be letting you know what we'll need when I see you," he said and hung up abruptly.

He got up and paced over to the mess in front of his desk. He glanced down, saw the humidor that his mother had given to him for Christmas last year, nudged it with his toe, and then leaned over and picked it up. Somehow, in the upheaval of the desk, it hadn't broken or even opened up. He turned it over in his hands. It wasn't an expensive piece; it looked like something you'd get from Amazon or L.L. Bean. But it was a tough little number, exactly like something his mother would get.

She always got the most for her money, finding the best buys, nothing flashy or anything, but merchandise that lasted.

His mom was still living in the house he had grown up in back on the cold hard plains of Illinois. He had tried to get her to move into a condominium the summer before, but she had refused. She was seventy-nine, and, as far as he knew, still mowed the lawn in the summer and shoveled the sidewalk during the winter.

She was alone out there on the big prairie, but she never minded the isolation. And she didn't just say she didn't mind and yearn for company; he knew her better than that, much better. He knew the solitude never bothered her. She actually preferred it. She didn't like people. She didn't even like him.

There had been times during his childhood when she had dismissed him summarily, like a servant, when all he wanted was to be near her. She hadn't wanted him. It had hurt when he was younger, and he had hated her because of it, but she didn't seem to care. As he grew older, he began to realize she had nothing against him personally. She excluded everyone. She simply didn't like people. That was a hard thing to for a child to understand about his own mother—that she couldn't love—but he had figured it out eventually. And he learned to live with it.

He accepted his mother; in fact, he admired her. After all, he owed her everything. She had taught him about being tough, about not depending on anyone, about holding onto his love. About only trusting himself. That was the hard lesson she had learned herself when his dad had left them. He'd been three, and she'd been left alone without a job, without prospects, and with no one to lean on. And she had not only gotten by, but she had started her own cleaning business, growing it into a concern profitable enough to support them and three other employees. She was tough and she hadn't been born that way. And she'd passed that on to him. She'd taught him to trust nothing or no one.

Mitchell snapped open the humidor, fished out a cigar, rolled it between his fingers and placed it in his mouth, chomping down on it. Los Puros. Only the best. He sat back in his chair and wheeled it around to take in the view of the park. Mitchell stared at a gull just outside his window, balancing on the wind, his wings outstretched. It didn't look easy adjusting to the variable air currents. The bird was constantly twitching, compensating for the changes in wind. Balancing. Keeping himself on top of things. Adapting. That was true. You needed to change in order to survive. He'd adapted. He was no longer the little boy yearning to be held by his mommy. He was a man of means. And he was on his way to becoming a mogul, a tycoon.

He had changed, adapting himself into a cold, calculating, and ruthless engine of capitalism. He would do whatever would be needed to ensure EduNet would eclipse the public school system and give the children of this city the education they truly deserved. And, he mused, smiling to himself, make him an extremely wealthy man in the bargain. But they weren't there yet. There would be some tough decisions to make in the future. He might have to use the company fixer: he might have to use Adrian Cole.

He leaned over the junk from his desktop, looking until he found the lighter stand. Mitchell picked it up, inspected it for damage, fired up his cigar, puffed it a few times, and returned to his chair. He leaned back.

Adrian Cole. This was a serious man, a man who wasn't afraid to do whatever was necessary by any means necessary. A man like himself. Cole cleaned up messy situations discreetly. He eliminated problems quietly. He persuaded people. Mitchell spun around the chair, looking out the window for his bird balancing in the wind. It was gone. The sun had gone behind the clouds. All that was left was the reflection of himself in the window shrouded in a cloud of smoke. He stared back at himself, presiding over the wreck of his office.

Chapter 8

Dave woke with a start, sat up on the couch, and looked out the window. The light outside was dim and the small slice of sky he could see out the window dark, bluish-gray. He glanced at his watch: 4:38. Dawn? Had he slept through the night? He swung his legs to the floor and sat a moment, gathering his thoughts. No, the light was wrong. He had come home from work and lay down for a minute and fallen asleep for about an hour. It was dusk, evening. The night is young, he thought, but he felt wrung out, drained.

He got up slowly, his knees popping and creaking, and went into the kitchen. The sink was still filled with dirty dishes from the night, no, two nights before. He sighed, stacked the dishes on the countertop, turned on the hot water tap, and started looking under the sink for the dishwashing detergent. He found it finally and, with an effort, stood up straight. The steaming water, covered with an oily film, rose slowly toward the top of the sink. Dave squirted it with the detergent, watched the edges of the grease slowly retreat, and then foam up under the roiling tap. He took the dishcloth and started into the hardened crust of the night before last's spaghetti sauce.

Dave sighed. It had been a long day, anyway, but then he had run into Mr. Ricks on his way out the door today. He had been standing in the main office, leaning on the counter and staring out at the main concourse of the school, and, to Dave's eye, looked more worn out and tired than usual. Some students were still milling around outside the office, talking and laughing.

"How's it going, Mr. Ricks?"

He looked up suddenly, as if awakened, and nodded at Dave.

"Hello, Mr. Bell. We're all right. My, it's been a long day, hasn't it?"

Sometimes Ricks had a habit of referring to himself in the plural: the royal we. Dave had noticed he tended to do it when he was tired or upset. He couldn't tell which it was tonight.

"Yes, it has," said Dave, thinking of the conversation with Knox, Ellerby, Zoe, Will, and the EduNet observer. What was his name? Scott Brown.

"You know," continued Dave, "I got observed during third hour by an EduNet rep."

"Really?" said Ricks, glancing over at him. "How did it go?"

"Okay. It was a good class. He came into the teacher's lounge and complimented me on the class. Will and Knox and Zoe were all there, too. And Ellerby."

"Hmm," said Ricks, looking at Dave and smiling. "That was probably an interesting conversation." He glanced over as Felicity Simmons clomped into the main office wearing her gigantic boots.

"Good evening, Miss Simmons," said Ricks, smiling.

"Hello, Mr. Ricks," she said brusquely, hanging her keys on the rack while balancing her bag on one knee. "Hello, Dave."

"Hey, Felicity. How was your day?"

"All right," she said, putting her valise on the floor with a thud. She fixed Ricks with a look. "I heard that EduNet was in the building today."

"That's right," said Ricks. "I understand that they began their observations with some of our teachers today."

"Oh, my God. I cannot believe they're doing this to us. Do we have to let them into our classrooms, Mr. Ricks? Isn't there anything we can do?"

"I'm afraid not," said Mr. Ricks. "It's part of the process that the school board agreed to. And like I said this morning, they would like nothing more than to report that the staff here is surly and uncooperative." He fixed her with a look. "So," he continued, "we need to extend these observers every professional courtesy and to make them feel welcome in our building."

She turned to Dave, ignoring Ricks.

"Can't the union do anything, Dave?"

"They're fighting it on the local and the state level, but EduNet has the okay from the school board to do the study. I know there's been a lot of work being done to rally families and the community. In fact," Dave continued, "we could use as many volunteers as we can get to man the phone banks and go door-to-door. Do you think you could you help us out Saturday or Sunday?"

"Oh, I'd love to," said Felicity, smiling, "but, you know, I've got this thing going on this weekend."

"A thing?" asked Dave, raising an eyebrow.

"Yeah," she said, walking backwards out of the office. "I'm getting together with our group of old college friends. We do it every year."

"Sounds great," said Dave. "We'll miss you during the canvassing."

She waved, said her goodbyes quickly, and left.

"Well, she couldn't say no to that volunteer shit fast enough, could she?" said Ricks, raising his eyebrows.

"Because of that thing. Her thing," said Dave.

Ricks chuckled. "That big thing," he said, under his breath. "That college thing."

"Yeah," said Dave, moving to the rack to hang up his keys. "I guess Knox and me are actually pretty lucky. Can you imagine working with that one all day?"

He glanced back at Ricks, who was leaning on the counter and staring out at the concourse again.

"Mr. Ricks?"

Ricks looked up. "Sorry," he said. "I guess I'm distracted today."

"Yeah, don't worry about it. Listen, I just wanted to let you know I'm pretty sure the EduNet guy videotaped me today during the observation. I wasn't sure if that was part of the agreement." He shrugged. "You know how they are about videotaping anything in the classroom."

The school board, because of legal liabilities—read fear of being sued—had strictly banned anyone from videotaping students or faculty in its district buildings. The only exception was if all the children in the classroom, whether they were to be on the videotape or not, had presented a waiver signed by their parents to the administration. The waiver had to be subsequently approved by the board, a process that could take up to three months. The whole production was so cumbersome and ponderous that almost no one bothered with it anymore, which was exactly what the board had wanted in the first place.

Ricks thought about it. "I don't think that's right," he said finally. "I don't recall anything about videotaping being allowed in the memo of understanding. You know what, let me check that out."

Dave picked up his case and walked out of the office, smiling. He was glad he had remembered to mention the videotaping to Ricks. Even if it didn't matter in the long run, and if probably wouldn't, it still was something for Ricks to use, to fight back with, even if it was precious little.

"Hello, stranger."

How could he not recognize that voice after thirty-four years? He turned and saw Ethel walking toward him with her briefcase and umbrella clutched in her left hand. He waited for her to catch up to him and then fell in step with her.

"Hello, Mrs. Benjamin. How are you?"

"Oh, I'm tired, David."

"You? I didn't think you got tired."

"We all get old."

Dave felt himself frowning. It wasn't like Ethel to complain, much less to feel sorry for herself.

"What's the matter, Ethel?" he asked. "Did you have a bad day today?"

She looked up at him and smiled, some of her old spark shining through. "What's the matter with you, David? You know I don't have bad days. What, do you think I'm finally starting to crack?" She laughed.

He laughed with her, but something seemed off. It was as if as if her antennae, usually preternaturally sensitive, weren't working very well. Over the years of working with her, Dave had discovered that Ethel had a special awareness of students, the faculty, the school itself: a radar; she sensed things in the building he—and everyone else—were oblivious to: tensions building, fights brewing, and students' stresses, the last especially. She knew—sensed—when one of her children was going through a tough time or about to get into trouble. It was extraordinary how she could do it. She seemed a little off tonight; the radar was jammed.

"I got observed today," he said, by way of making conversation. He'd also been telling people that to get a sense of where they stood with the takeover. Some teachers, like Will and Knox, would fight to keep the public schools public no matter what, whereas others, like Zoe and Felicity— probably—and Ellerby and some others, mostly newbies, would go with the flow and simply take whatever they could get. He'd been assuming that Ethel would be on his side; she always had been, back to the old original union battles, the great strike of 1978, when they were young and hard-headed, and he knew she loved Custer like a second home, no, like a child: an obstreperous, spoiled, difficult child.

"Don't you want to know how it went?" he asked, opening the vestibule door.

"Well, I shouldn't have to ask, should I?" asked Ethel, stopping to button up her old wool coat. "I know it went well." She smiled. "I trained you, didn't I?"

He nodded. "I think the observer actually enjoyed the class despite himself. He was very complimentary to me."

She nodded as she put on her scarf over the top of her head, old school, the way his mother used to wear it, and then began putting on her gloves. He thought she looked old, even fragile, quite the contrast to the sassy attitude she'd been carrying around all day.

"Ethel," he said. She stopped pulling on her glove and looked up.

"Where do think we'll end up with this mess? You've been around longer than anybody. Who's going to win?"

"Win?" she said, her voice rising. "Where's the win? The students won't be any better off. The teachers certainly won't be. The city won't be." She gazed down the main concourse. "No one wins. Not even the people who will make all the money."

Dave was a little stunned by this outburst—a relative outburst for Ethel—not because she hardly ever raised her voice, but then she never had to, not even when dealing with the most blustery student, but because through all the years they had worked together, he had never known her to be quite this cynical. Or, he recognized, quietly furious.

"You don't think we have a shot at keeping Custer the way it is, keeping it public?" he asked, feeling he sounded like a little boy even as he was asking it.

She looked at him levelly, her bright blue eyes boring into him. Her teacher look, he thought, that had intimidated thousands of students through the years.

"Come on, David. Think. You know history. What chance in hell do we have against a corporate conglomerate that has the entire legislature bought and sold and unlimited financial resources in its back pocket?" She shook her head and smiled at him. "What do we have to fight them with? We don't have the political clout anymore, and almost no support from the public. Most people still think teachers are lazy creatures who only work part-time and sponge off the state like welfare queens. Honestly, David, sometimes I can't believe I trained you to be a thinking man's teacher. Good night."

Dave opened the door for her as she strode out into the gray October afternoon and gazed after her. Ethel Benjamin never had been afraid of speaking her mind. Speaking the truth. And she had just chillingly, finally, and decisively done both. She's right, he thought. We're screwed.

Yes. Ethel and Ricks had both been right. It had been an extremely long and an extremely discouraging day. He finished the last dish, wiped down the counter, and took a quick look around. The kitchen was very nearly presentable. It would never have come up to Valerie's standards, but he didn't have to worry about Valerie's standards anymore. She could take her bleach sprays and scrubbing bubbles and shove them up her ass. This was clean enough for him, clean enough for anybody with no germ neuroses.

Dave went into the living room, sat down and took off his shoes, wiggling his toes on the cool hardwood. He leaned back and found his gaze drawn to the mini wine rack next to the television. It was nearly depleted, but he saw that the lone bottle of his Willamette Valley Pinot was still there. And, yes, it had been a long day.

He stood up, went over to the rack, took out the bottle, and started hunting for the corkscrew. Where had he opened that Zinfandel last night? He tried to recall: *Liberty Valance* had just begun and he thought he remembered opening it while watching the credits. Dave scanned the shelf next to the television and there it was, right next to the family pictures: a portrait of his Mom and Dad taken the Christmas before standing in front of the monstrous and perfect tree at his sister Sarah's house. They looked old, and they were old, doing all right but getting older. Dad couldn't remember things the way he used to, but fuck it, who could? I sure have my days, thought Dave. Except that his Dad's memory loss was looking more and more like Alzheimer's.

He was forgetting common words, familiar places, and how to do the simplest tasks. His mother had told them that he had been donating money to any Tom, Dick, or Harry who called with their bogus charity stories. She was as sharp as ever, and as feisty, but she was consumed with taking

74

care of Dad, and it was draining her. Dave knew he needed to call them this weekend—he'd been putting off doing it. Talking to them had become depressing. Dave filed off the foil around the cork and started turning the screw.

His dad had always been disappointed that he had chosen teaching as a career. He'd never realized that education had chosen him. Dave had started out as a pre-law student at the state university, but after Bob died, he had gotten absorbed in the anti-war and civil rights movements. Vietnam was a horrid joke, an ugly bait and switch for well-intentioned heroes, innocent kids raised on John Wayne and 12 *O'clock High*. He began to feel alienated from school, but, because of his father, he had kept it together and graduated with a decent grade-point average in political science.

The cork popped out. He sniffed the bottle. Nice. There was nothing like an Oregonian Pinot. He went into the kitchen to look for a clean glass. He found one with relatively few fingerprints and returned to the couch. Now where the hell had he put the remote? He got up again, looked around the television trying to retrace his steps and finally spotted it on the floor next to the wine rack. It figured. He must have knocked it over at some point during the movie last night. He leaned over to pick it up and found his gaze drawn to the picture of his brother Bob, dressed in his army fatigues. The picture was a good likeness, taken just eight days before Bob had stepped on a landmine in the Mekong Delta.

Dave had been a junior in high school when his brother died, and while he had to register for the draft, he never had to go. But Bob did. He was in the last wave of draftees. His birthday was the third lottery number picked. It was back in '71, the year he'd graduated high school. Bob had been planning to go to the University of Wisconsin after taking a year off to work and earn tuition money, but he figured he'd just have to put everything on hold for his two-year hitch. It won't be bad, he had told Dave. I'll probably just get stuck in some clerical job behind the lines, he said, and he smiled his toothy, crooked smile.

Bob was two years older than Dave and, in their small town at least, was the closest thing they had to a hippie. He was listening to Bob Dylan, Joan Baez, and Tom Rush before anyone else had ever heard of them. He introduced Dave—and most of the kids in their high school—to the Beat-les and the Rolling Stones.

That was one of the great things about Bob. That and those long dis-cussions they would have walking to school together, talking about girls and football and movies amidst the falling leaves and snow and budding leaves over the dozen years they'd shared the same elementary, middle, and high schools. It had only been seventeen years of growing up together but seemed so much longer: the Halloweens, the dances, the basketball games, and the games of Kick the Can, Freeze Tag, and Red Light, Green Light during those long summer afternoons and evenings: all now seen through the haze of years.

Dave took a sip of the Pinot. The Bob in the photograph was the same guy he'd grown up with, the brother who'd always looked out for him, but not quite the same guy after the army. When he'd come back on furlough from basic, Bob had displayed an aggressiveness, an intensity, a reckless-ness he'd never had before. Over the years since then, Dave had seen that same quality again and again in former students who'd enlisted coming back to visit him at school. Something about basic training made them that way. He took another sip of his wine. Bob was still the same guy when he'd come back—basically—except that he'd been trained to kill. He was home for two weeks, then they shipped him out to Vietnam, and then six months later he was dead. And everything had changed.

It was mostly Bob's death, along with the idiocy of the war in general, that had turned Dave toward the counter-culture. He rejected law as a profession, realizing it was only another way to pick the common man's pocket, and decided to major in political science, to change the system from the inside. He'd worked as an activist and community organizer for a few years after college, even running for alderman. Twice. Then, on his twenty-seventh birthday, he realized he could keep trying to change the world, living paycheck to paycheck, or latch onto something more stable. He decided it was finally time to grow up and join the mainstream. He went back to the university and got his certification to teach school. Two years later, he met Valerie, and they married and started a family and he became a teacher. That was how teaching had chosen him.

And here I am, he thought, draining his glass. Here I am, alone and drinking. Where do I go from here? His conversation with Ethel had shaken him up a little bit; what she had said not only felt right, he knew she was right. They were screwed. And if EduNet takes over Custer, he thought, I don't think I'll be able to stay. Even though he was a sub, and cheap to keep on the payroll, he doubted they would keep on a sixty-three year old ex-union rep and activist, although if he'd learned anything from thirty some years of public service, it was that anything was possible.

And they might want him, but would he want them? Could he jump ship with the other rats and betray public education? Or should he officially and completely retire? And do what? Work at Dunkin' Donuts next to some loser ex-student? Or find a job at a private school or maybe do something in the private sector? Consulting? Or retire and perhaps go off to teach English in some exotic country. Maybe, he thought, sipping his wine, maybe. I could hook up with one of the natives and become an embittered expatriate like Hemingway. He smiled as he sat back on the couch and pressed the power button on the remote. Spend the rest of his life drunk and oblivious on a tropical beach. Leave behind the ex-wife, the kids, the life he'd built here for anonymity, oblivion, and relaxation. The TV flickered on. *Lost* was coming on. How appropriate, he thought. How appropriate.

Chapter 9

Sandra watched from her car as the students spilled off the line of yellow buses onto the sidewalk. She'd parked across the street from the main entrance of the high school to get an idea of what she might be in for today. Some of the kids came out of the buses laughing and joking, a couple of them chasing each other around the trees in the front yard, full of hormones and youthful high spirits. Most of them simply went about their business, socializing as they made their way into the building. She knew from the extensive studies EduNet had done that the school population was eighty-seven percent African-American, six percent Hispanic, four percent Asian, and three percent Caucasian. Most of them were eligible for free lunch, a euphemism for living beneath the poverty line.

Some of them were dressed pretty well, but a lot weren't. Under Armour was big, she saw, but Nike was still hanging in there, too. Even Reebok. She noticed a lot of the local pro team t-shirts, usually given away at free camps or clinics to underprivileged kids. Her brothers had brought home a few back in the day. The baggy pants thing for the boys was still hanging on, so to speak, and some of the outfits the girls were wearing were amazingly skimpy. Some things never changed. Sandra thought she had pushed the envelope back in the nineties with high crop-tops and short skirts, but these went over the line. That skinny girl's skirt is almost up to her panty line, she thought.

It was a cold morning, overcast with a clammy feeling in the air. More than a few of the kids had no winter coats. Many of them were still wearing thin windbreakers or spring jackets. A few were wearing only t-shirts or thin blouses. Sandra wondered whether wearing a winter coat was a fashion choice or an economic privilege for this generation. Being the only girl in the family, she never had to wear hand-me-downs like her brothers. Al didn't mind so much, but Matt had hated them. Maybe that was why he'd turned out to be such a selfish prick, she thought, because he never had his own stuff. But at least they'd had hand-me-downs. She watched one boy wearing a coat at least two sizes too big trudging up into the school and another wearing gym shorts sprinting up the steps. Some of these kids don't even look like they have anything, she mused, just give-away t-shirts and gently handled — and not so gently handled — donations.

She glanced at her watch. Ten minutes to eight. She was supposed to meet the principal at eight. She took a final sip of coffee, grabbed her briefcase and purse, and got out of the car. The cold wind hit her as soon as she stood up, taking her breath momentarily. She walked briskly across the street through some milling groups of students. A few of them stared, but most of them ignored her.

She opened the front door. A large doorframe metal detector stood immediately in front of her. Two men in district uniforms stood there, channeling bodies through. Students and guests alike had to separate themselves from their metal, walk through, and then reclaim everything: just like the airport. Sandra had been mentally preparing herself for spending the day in an urban high school, but somehow this surprised her. She knew she should have been expecting it — common sense would say so — but it was still, well, shocking to her. She'd gone to a high school like this not very far from here. The doors had always been open there, and a metal detector at the front entrance would have been unimaginable. This wasn't even like school anymore.

"Hello, ma'am," said one of the security guards. "You'll need to place your bags on the table, put your metal belongings in the tray, and step through."

"Ma'am?" Sandra asked the guard, undoing her wristwatch. "Do I look that old?"

He chuckled. "No, you don't. But compared to the children, you look like you should be called that. Anywhere else, I would say no, you are not a ma'am, you are a miss."

Sandra stepped through without setting off anything.

"Okay," she said. "I guess I'll buy that. Thank you."

"Anytime," the guard said, "Miss."

She chuckled and nodded as she walked toward the office, weaving her way through kids going to homeroom, teachers getting to their rooms, and the knots of students just hanging around and talking.

As she passed one group of kids, a girl dressed in a yellow print crop-top called out to her in a voice that would have carried over a jackhammer.

"Hey, lady, you a sub?"

Sandra looked over at her and shook her head. "No," she yelled over the clamor, "just visiting."

The girl grinned at her and nodded. Friendly. Sandra smiled back as the girl turned and continued yakking it up with her friends. Sandra watched them a moment: teenaged girls talking about what? Boys, make-up, clothes? What she had talked about with her friends? Or had things changed and if so, how much had they changed? What would it be like to be a kid in this place?

Sandra entered the main office, stood at the counter, and took in the scene. A steady stream of traffic pulsed all around her. Students and a few parents stood at the counter waiting as the secretaries fielded phone calls and scribbled out passes to students. Teachers streamed in, emptied their mailboxes, and got their keys off the main rack. She started studying the instructors more closely. One African-American woman with salt and pepper hair walked to the rack, looking very stern, very business-like. Getting her game face on, thought Sandra. A younger woman came in clutching her valise to her chest as she searched frantically for her key ring. Not scared, thought Sandra, not exactly, but I'd say she was apprehensive, preparing herself for something not so good to happen.

An older woman, gray and tiny, but standing ramrod straight, exchanged greetings with the apprehensive girl, walked to the rack, and picked up her keys almost without looking to see where they were. She turned, eyes scanning the office, spotted Sandra, and nodded in acknowledgement while appraising her with a slow measured look. Sandra nodded back without changing expression. She'd seen looks like that before, usually on the other side of the corporate bargaining table. The woman strode through the office and was greeted by a rumpled middle-aged man as he entered the room.

"Hello, Ethel," he said. Sandra marked the name.

"David," she said, "how are you this morning?" They had moved behind her. Sandra turned to see them better.

"I'm good, Ethel," he said. "A little tired. I didn't sleep particularly well last night."

Sandra took a closer look. His shirt and tie were stained with what was probably coffee, his khakis had not been ironed, and his gold blazer didn't match anything else he was wearing. He looks single, she thought, and hung over. Probably divorced.

"You need to take better care of yourself," said the woman as Sandra watched them walk out together.

"Miss Feeley?" said a voice behind her.

She turned. A compact but sturdily built African-American man was leaning on the counter with his elbows and smiling at her. He was wearing a suit and tie complete with a tie clasp, cufflinks, and was half-smiling as he scanned her face. Joseph Abboud, she thought. This one knows how to dress.

"Yes," she said, extending her hand. "I'm glad to meet you."

"I'm Ryan Ricks, the principal here," he said. Even though he was soft-spoken, his voice carried over the chaos in the office.

"How did you know it was me?" she asked, raising her voice.

"Just a lucky guess," he said. "That and the fact we don't get too many guests here from the corporate world." She smiled, suddenly feeling self-conscious in her Calvin Klein faux-suede.

"Well, we all dress the part," she said. "And I have to say that's a very nice suit you're wearing. Joseph Abboud?"

"Calvin Klein." He stepped back and gestured for her to come around behind the counter. "Why don't we talk in my office?"

She made her way through the milling bodies and stepped around the counter and came up next to Mr. Ricks. He was taller than she first thought and had a very confident bearing. His coffee-colored complexion shined under the fluorescent lights. Not a bad-looking guy, she thought.

"Shall we?" he asked. She nodded and they went to his office. It was furnished in the usual institutional style, nondescript and ugly at the same time. She sat and Mr. Ricks brought her coffee.

"So," he said, "I was a little surprised to hear from you so soon. I know we had some observers in a while ago, but I didn't think the corporate office would be following up so quickly."

"Well, first of all, thank you for being so hospitable to our observation team," she said. "I know this is a difficult situation for your staff and that tensions can run high in circumstances like this."

Ricks sat back in his chair and nodded. Waiting.

"We wanted to do a comparative rating of the in-class observations," she continued.

Ricks nodded. Waiting.

"We have our observers impressions but we would like to cross-match those with the impressions of the classroom teacher, and to do that," she continued, hoping she wasn't sounding as if she were rushing it, which was how she felt, "I would like to conduct a short interview with a few of the observation subjects."

She couldn't tell Ricks that what she really wanted was to get a first-person view of the teachers on those observation videotapes. She wanted to know who EduNet was going up against and what angles they could use to help their observers reinvent their interpretations.

"So you want to interview some of the people you observed?" he asked. She noticed a slight change in his demeanor. He was still the model of courtesy, but there was a reserve, a calculation in his manner that hadn't been there before.

"Yes," she said.

"Today," he said. She nodded.

"Well, this is rather short notice. Let me see." He pulled out a building schedule. "Who exactly are we talking about?"

"Well," she said, pulling out her ledger. "I have a Miss Ralph."

Ricks shook his head. "I think she's out on a field trip today."

She nodded. "A Mr. Knox?"

"I think he might have called in sick. Who else do we have?"

"Mr. Reynolds?"

"He's here," nodded Ricks. "Let's see where he is right now. Oh, this is almost perfect. He's got first hour prep, so you can probably catch him in his room this hour."

"Good," said Sandra. "There's one more we wanted to talk to." She riffled through the pages. "A Mr. Bell."

"Okay," he said, looking at the schedule. "Mr. Bell has a fourth hour lunch and a seventh hour prep. He'd be available at eleven or at two."

"That's too bad," she said, smiling. "There's no other way I could have a meeting with him this morning? Could he have a substitute or something?"

He looked at her, calculating. Not waiting now. Thinking. Moving. Balancing the needs of his school with the instructions from the school board.

"Okay," he said. "I think we can do something with his second hour. Why don't we go down and talk to Mr. Reynolds and while you're doing that, I'll speak to Mr. Bell and arrange for someone to take his second hour class."

"Thanks," she said, standing up. "I really appreciate your flexibility, Mr. Ricks. All of us at EduNet do."

"We aim to please," he said. A bell rang. "That's the first hour warning bell. We'd better get going."

They walked through the main office, now virtually deserted, and into the school proper. Some students were still in the halls, but most of them were moving toward their first hour classes. A few clusters of students stood at their lockers, talking. They started moving as soon as they saw Mr. Ricks. Another group of four girls stood taking a selfie together at a locker.

"First hour begins in thirty seconds," said Mr. Ricks, his voice now heavy as iron and carrying through the corridor. "Get to class, now," he said. "Aryanna, if I see that cellphone again, it goes in my desk drawer until Christmas. You understand?" The cell phone disappeared into the girl's back pocket.

One of the girls, dressed in a black and silver crop-top emblazoned with a label reading "Bling" put her hands on her hips and glared at the two of them. The rest of the girls scattered.

"You having a problem hearing me today, Dominique?" asked Ricks, his voice low.

"I don't know why you always singling me out and picking on my ass," said the girl, her voice blaring like a foghorn. She took a step closer to them. "Everyday, it's Dominique this, Dominique that. I don't know what the fuck you're after with calling me out all the time. I be sick of it, Ricks. I don't want you calling out my name no more." By this time, the girl was only a few feet from them, gesticulating angrily. Sandra took a step back and sidled in behind Mr. Ricks, who hadn't moved a muscle.

A security guard had appeared at the other end of the corridor during the girl's tirade and moved toward her. Ricks, almost imperceptibly, nodded at him.

"Hey, Dominique," said the guard, "I think you need to relax a little bit."

She turned around and glared at him. "Relax?" she shouted. "I relax when this motherfucker leave me be." A few teachers—and some students—were now peering out of their classroom doors.

"Okay, Dominique, let's go and talk about it," said the guard. He came up next to the girl, holding up his arm behind her without touching her, trying, Sandra realized, to shepherd her. Another security person, a younger short heavyset woman, came out of one of the classrooms and walked up to the girl from behind the other security guard.

"Dominique," she said softly. "What in the world is going on with you, girl?"

Dominique looked at the woman, shrugged, and mumbled something, looking hangdog suddenly.

"Let's go and talk, baby," said the woman. Dominique left and the male security guard followed.

"Thank you, Ms. Michaels," said Mr. Ricks. "Will you take her to the security office?"

"Yeah, we'll let her calm down a little bit."

"Okay," he said. "Give me fifteen minutes and I'll be in there."

"All right", she said, and left with the other two.

"Wow," said Sandra. "Does that happen every day?"

"Sorry you to had to see that, Miss Feeley. Yes, we have outbursts like that about two or three times a week. Some of our students, like Dominique, have difficulties dealing with authority. Many of them are in our special education program. Dominique and Ms. Michaels have bonded, and that's how we've been helping her through some of these difficulties. Many of our students aren't so lucky."

"How many of your students qualify for special education?" she asked, even though she already knew.

He glanced at her a moment before answering. "About forty percent."

They continued on toward the science department without speaking. Forty percent: two hundred accidents like Dominique waiting to happen every day. If she had been that out of control with the principal, God only knew what that girl would be like with the staff or the faculty. And one hundred ninety-nine more like her. Sandra shook her head. She just hadn't realized. Jimmy had been in special education and she'd imagined, somehow, that most of these kids were as agreeable and compliant as her little brother had been. She just hadn't realized.

They were coming up on the science wing. There was a distinctive smell, a chemical odor Sandra remembered from own days in high school. Formaldehyde? She couldn't identify it. It did bring back memories, though. Frog dissections, the movie she'd seen of a woman giving childbirth, and Billy Wentworth, her sophomore lab partner in biology, on whom she'd had a crush all year.

Mr. Ricks stopped at an open door and knocked on the window.

"What?" a voice rapped out abruptly.

"Hello, Mr. Reynolds," said Mr. Ricks in a pleasant tone. "How are you doing this morning?"

Sandra walked up behind Ricks and peered around him into the room. A man with a mane of wild silver hair sat at a desk correcting papers. He was scowling at Ricks and then switched his blazing gaze to her. She saw he was wearing wire-rimmed glasses that were bent in about a dozen places and a white shirt with a paisley tie underneath his light blue lab coat that had been stained so many times it gave only faint hints of its original color.

"What is it, Mr. Ricks?" he asked, his voice like a shovel dragging on concrete. "I've got a lot of work to do."

"I've brought someone to see you, Mr. Reynolds." Sandra, right on cue, stepped around Ricks and nodded to the man in the semi-blue lab coat.

"Pleased to meet you, sir," she said, more meekly than she'd intended.

Something about this old curmudgeon was very intimidating. He sort of reminded her of her seventh-grade English teacher, Mr. Binkman, who on occasion would come up behind boys goofing around in class, grab them by their hair, and slam their heads on their desks.

"I'm Sandra Feeley," she continued, "from EduNet."

"EduNet," he muttered, glaring at her over the bent tops of his wire-rims. "What is it? Do you want your pound of flesh already?"

"No, sir," she said, "I was just here to do some follow-up on the observation we did in your class recently. I wanted to come in and get your perspective on how the lesson went and how you felt about the observation."

She sat on a lab stool opposite Mr. Reynolds. Mr. Ricks waved good-bye and left the room.

"It stunk," he replied. "These kids come in here without any of the tools they need to succeed. They can't do math, they have no idea of biological processes—half of them have never even heard of photosynthesis—and they don't know how to think. And they're too lazy to do it. They don't even want to try."

"Well," said Sandra, pulling a folder out of her valise and opening it, "Mr. Willard—respectfully—disagrees with you. He said the lesson concerning—" she scanned the page, looking for the lesson name.

"Evolution," said Mr. Reynolds, scratching at one of the papers in front of him with a red pen. "I assume you've heard of it."

"Yes, that's it. He mentioned in his report that you had an innovative lesson demonstrating cell mutation using a drawing?"

"Yes," he said, not even looking up from the paper in front of him.

"Would you like to tell me about it?" she asked after a moment.

"Why?" he asked, looking up for a brief moment. "It's all on the videotape."

That stopped her for a moment; how did he know about the video?

"Well," she said, smiling, "the reason I'm here is to get your input on the lesson. We already have Mr. Willard's feedback and now I'm here to get yours."

He snorted and turned to his next paper, scratched a few marks on it with his red pen, and then slapped it onto the completed pile. He leaned back in his chair, crossed his arms over his chest, and glared at her.

"You really want my input, Miss Feeley?"

She leaned forward on her lab stool and planted her elbows on the counter.

"Yes, Mr. Reynolds," she said, looking him straight in the eye. "I really do want your input."

"All right," he said, after a moment. "I'll play." He looked down at his pile of papers for a moment. "It's a fairly straightforward lesson, Miss Feeley. If you knew anything about education, you would be able to see that. The lesson goes like this. I place a line drawing of some sort of geometric shape and have a student copy it. Then the next student takes the first student's drawing and copies that. That student's copy moves on to the next until everyone has had a chance to copy a copy."

"What's the objective of the lesson?"

He almost smiled. "After they're done, I have the students compare the original drawing to the next, and then to their own copy, and they see subtle changes. As these changes mount, they eventually result in a striking change from the original to the final copy. Which," he continued, "is an illustration of the process of evolution, how minor changes will, and do, eventually make for wholesale changes in animal species."

"Here," he said, tossing two papers across the lab counter at her. "Guess which is the first and which is the last."

Sandra picked up the sheets. One was obviously professionally drawn and showed a rectangle inside a triangle inside a circle. She picked up the next, which showed a circle and triangle inside a square.

"You're kidding," she said.

"Nope," he said. "The results might seem surprising at first, but this data becomes more and more predictable over the years. The deviation from the first to the last drawing seems almost constant from year to year." He leaned back and actually smiled. "After a while, nothing they do surprises you anymore."

"Mr. Reynolds," said Sandra, "I just ran across a student in the hallway who was cursing at the principal. That doesn't surprise you?"

He shrugged and leaned back in his chair. "It's not unusual," he said. "Not here."

"Students cursing at their principal is not unusual?" she asked, hearing her voice becoming somewhat strident.

"Where did you go to high school, Miss Feeley?" he asked, folding his arms over his chest. "Are you from around here?"

"Yes," she said, "in fact, I grew up not far from here. I went to school at Central High."

He smiled. "Nice school. When did you graduate?"

"1999."

"And how was your school experience different from what you saw today?" he asked.

"Well, we never had anything quite like that," she said, gesturing toward the open door, "that explosion."

"Like the girl's outburst just now?" She nodded.

"Why not?" he asked.

"I don't know," she said. "We just didn't act like that in school. Nobody did."

"Well," he said. "I guess that begs the question—what happened in those eighteen years between your idyllic high school experience and this?"

He gazed at her, smiling slightly. Sandra shrugged, suddenly not willing to answer the question. Somehow, she smelled a trap.

"Come now, Miss Feeley," he said. "I know you're bright enough to come up with some sort of theory. I'm sure your expensive EduNet analysts and spreadsheets have given you some sort of insight into what's happening here."

He looked up at her, smiling a bit more broadly, his yellowing teeth almost shining underneath his mane of wild hair. An image came to her suddenly, an illustration from one of her favorite childhood books: Alice standing meek and submissive before a fading and insanely grinning cat. She looked at Mr. Reynolds, holding his gaze steady in her own: a smile full of riddles, questions, rebuses, and enigmas.

"I'm not sure why the school climate would've changed so much," she said finally. "I can't explain it."

"Well," said Mr. Reynolds, "I give you credit for being honest, but don't you think it would have been prudent for you and your company to understand how this institution works before trying to acquire it?"

"EduNet has done dozens of exhaustive studies on this school, sir," she replied testily. Who the hell did he think he was? "Including studies of demographic patterns and cultural shifts within the urban community." She stood up. "We've looked at achievement gaps and the effects of single-parent households on student achievement."

Mr. Reynolds sat back in his chair and looked up at her, still smiling slightly. He didn't look impressed.

"We also are going to implement a new literacy program which we expect will raise ACT scores significantly over the next few years."

Mr. Reynolds raised his eyebrows and whistled.

"That sounds quite significant, Miss Feeley. But you still haven't answered my question."

"What question?" she asked, standing up and grabbing her things.

"After all your studies and profiles and analyses, can you tell me what has happened between the school experience you knew eighteen years ago and what you just saw today?" He stood up and started stacking his own papers. "Can all of your data—any of it—start to approach answering that question?"

She stood with her briefcase in hand, thinking, trying to come up with an answer for this old son of a bitch.

"We have all the data we need," she said. "It's just a matter of analyzing it and formulating the right conclusions."

"Statistics, facts, spreadsheets," he said. "That's not the sort of answer you're looking for, young lady."

Young lady? What was she, fifteen years old? She opened her mouth to answer with some scathing retort but held her tongue. She'd said too much already.

"What happened to you in the hall just now," he continued, rising, "wasn't about science or statistics or ACT scores; it was about you and your past. Your sensibilities. Your memories of growing up in a school like this. You are from here after all, aren't you? You're a city girl. Dominique, that girl who blew up, could have been very like you eighteen years ago." He glanced at his watch. "And," he said, opening the door for her, "you could very well have been her today. I'm sorry, but you'll have to excuse me. I have to prepare for my next class now." He stood by the open door and gestured in an exaggerated manner toward the space beyond. "Goodbye, Miss Feeley."

She stood up straight, and mustering as much dignity as she could, left the room and walked out into the corridor. The door closed softly behind her. It was near the end of first hour, but the bell hadn't rung yet. There was a knot of boys down at the end of the hall hanging around a locker and talking in low voices. A couple of them were kneeling. They glanced up, looked her up and down, and then simply ignored her. She looked the other way. The hall was completely empty, although she heard voices echoing, an argument happening somewhere around the corner.

She felt a tingle, almost a shiver. Mr. Reynolds was right; this looked just like her old school, down to the puky green paint and the dented orange lockers, the color of spoiled tangerines. She was a part of this place—

not this place exactly—but a place very much like it. And now she and Mitchell were getting ready to take it apart. What it might look like after they put it back together was anyone's guess. As Mitchell had said—dozens of times—they would have to follow the money and go where it took them. These schools were failing, she knew, experiencing momentous and egregious problems, problems that they—she and Mitchell—had no idea how to solve. But she believed in EduNet and she believed in Mitchell; they would figure it out. She had faith.

Sandra heard footsteps behind her and turned to see the girl Dominique, flanked by Ms. Michaels and Mr. Ricks, listening and nodding as the woman spoke to her in a quiet voice. Mr. Ricks caught sight of her and waved. He said something more to Dominique, who smiled at him and nodded. Sandra looked more closely at her. The girl was tall and rangy, as she had been as a girl—a lot like me, she thought. Spirited, too. Just like me. The illustration from Alice came to her again, quite suddenly. Mr. Reynolds had been right; the situation did beg a question, but not the one he had posed. Not that one, but another. What side of the looking glass was she actually on?

Chapter 10

Mitchell glanced at his cellphone. 11:12 a.m. Just late enough to show his importance to these drones, these minions. He stood up from behind the desk, strode out of his office and down the hall to the corner conference room. He pulled up outside the closed door and then stood still a moment, gathering himself. Breathing deeply, evenly, five times, he stilled himself, swung the door open and stepped quickly inside.

Two people were sitting at the massive oval table: the one on the left, a balding middle-aged man with a salt and pepper mustache, half-rose out of his chair when Mitchell entered. The other, a lean, older man with hair graying around the temples, raised his head a bit and nodded slightly. A cool customer, thought Mitchell. We'll see how long that lasts. Without taking his eyes off the two men, he walked slowly to the head of the conference room table and sat down very slowly and very deliberately. Two folders had been placed carefully on the table in front of his chair. He glanced at them: the personnel folders containing all the information about these two observers, these two traitors. Mitchell raised his eyes to stare at the both of them.

Bald boy started fidgeting almost immediately. He turned this way and that in his chair, trying to get settled, but he couldn't seem to make himself comfortable. The other, the lean man with the graying hair, sat leaning forward on his elbows with hands clasped, returning Mitchell's stare ounce for ounce.

Mitchell opened the first folder in front of him. Joe Willard. He glanced at the picture clipped to the file. This was Bald Boy. Apparently, he'd taught high school in the district for over thirty years. Math. He'd been retired for five years. Willard had gone through the EduNet training program with no problem. His psychological profile demonstrated compliance, respect for authority, and a high degree of conformity in daily behaviors. Everything had checked out. So why had this guy gone against the grain, and, against any kind of common sense, given out a positive review?

"Mr. Willard," he said.

"Yes, sir."

"As I'm sure you know, my name is Mitchell Paige. I'm the vice-president in charge of operations for EduNet. I'm in charge of everything from acquisitions to personnel. Which is why we're here today. Personnel." He settled back in his chair. "Mr. Willard, you went through the EduNet Orientation Program." He paused a moment, leaned back in his chair, and gazed up at the ceiling. "What is our mission statement? Could you tell me that? Please. If you don't mind." He could hear Willard shifting in his chair, still trying to get comfortable. The man cleared his throat.

"Well," said Willard, "the purpose of EduNet is to reinvent and reinvigorate the educational process. According to the latest research, public education is dying. Teachers no longer teach and students no longer learn. The system has been broken for years. It leaches the money off of our state, municipal, and county taxes." He paused and Mitchell closed his eyes. They'd taught this one well.

"In short," Willard continued, "it's time for the private sector to take over our public schools. Government has ruined public education, like it ruins almost everything else it touches." His voice had taken on almost a singsong rhythm as he concluded, as if reciting from memory. Mitchell opened his eyes.

"Good," he said. "Now tell me about your task. The task," he said, bringing his eyes down from the ceiling to rest on Willard, "you were paid so handsomely to perform."

A sheen emerged on Willard's forehead. He grabbed a Kleenex from the box in front of him and wiped his nose.

"Well," said Willard, "I was paid to go into an at-risk high school and observe a teacher conducting a class. I was to observe student engagement and behavior, the professionalism of the teacher, and the atmosphere of the building. I was to gather artifacts, including lesson plans and student work, and to videotape the class from start to finish." He paused and took a breath. "The video was supposed to be taken surreptitiously through our laptops, which was how I accomplished it during my observation."

"And you are aware of the fact that public schools are failing, correct?" asked Mitchell, staring fixedly at Willard.

"I know they have problems, a lot more problems than they used to have," he replied, with sudden and unexpected authority.

Mitchell almost smiled. Our Mr. Willard might actually have some balls, he thought. But he wouldn't have them for long.

"And why do our public schools have the problems they do?"

"Well, according to EduNet," said Willard, glancing back at the other observer, who had not moved, "schools here are failing mainly because of the teachers' union and the school board. Local and municipal governments are also at fault. They've been sitting on their hands and not interceding on behalf of the children—our children. According to EduNet research, teaching has become an irrelevant and outdated profession. Teachers have lost touch with the students, the community, and society at large. They're liberals whose beliefs are outdated and out of touch. They're protected by the labor unions and their pensions and huge health benefits are bankrupting us all."

"According to EduNet," said Mitchell, reaching into his breast pocket and pulling out a cigar. "All of this is according to EduNet. What about you? What do you think?"

Bald boy shrugged. "Our schools are definitely in trouble, there's no disputing that. The kids are out of control. I mean the swearing, the disrespect, the way they are dressed, everything. They don't seem to care about anyone or anything."

"The kids, Mr. Willard," said Mitchell, leaning forward to light his cigar. "You're going to blame this on the kids?"

"I don't believe there's one simple answer, sir. I think that yes, part of the problem is the way these kids are brought up. They come from environments of poverty so profound that—"

Mitchell held up his hand. "I don't want to hear any of that bleeding-heart liberal shit," he said. "I know better. I grew up poor, rural poor, which is a lot worse than urban poor. These kids have all the opportunities they need. Poverty is no excuse. Neither is race."

He took a puff from his cigar and looked at Bald Boy again through the white-blue cloud of smoke. He smiled.

"So, Mr. Willard, tell me. Why are these schools failing?"

Willard looked down at the table, then back up at Mitchell.

"I know what you want me to say, Mr. Paige," he said, his voice quiet. "You want me to say that the teachers at Custer are the problem, that they can't manage their classrooms, that they can't teach, that they don't care. That was the implicit message behind every session in your indoctrination program, behind every speech that Ms. Feeley made. And it's true that some teachers have problems. But," he said, "I cannot in good conscience state that the teachers I observed were not trying to do good jobs. I've been there. I know. One was definitely struggling, and two were holding their own, but one was absolutely excellent." Mitchell ashed his cigar and leaned back in his chair.

Willard took a deep breath. "I know what you want, Mr. Paige, but I cannot in good conscience blame all of this on the teachers."

"Hmm," said Mitchell, without looking up. "I guess I should just go ahead and fire you."

Willard looked down at the table.

"I should fire you," he repeated. "But I won't. You have integrity and I respect that. That might surprise you, but I do. So I won't fire you. But we need to reassess your analysis and your tape, so until we've completed that process, we won't be able to use you."

"How long will that take?" asked Willard.

Mitchell shrugged. "Four to eight weeks. Give or take."

Bald Boy fidgeted and finally said, "That seems like a long time to evaluate a single review."

"Well, I'm sure you understand we need to be thorough," said Mitchell. "You'll just have to sit tight until we've completed the process. I'm sorry we won't be able to offer you any jobs until we're completed. We'll be in touch."

Willard mopped his brow, took a deep breath, and then nodded. "I understand," he said, "but I need to work. I still have two kids in college."

"I'm sorry you're caught out in the cold," said Mitchell, "but hey, you were trained. You knew what you needed to do. And did you do that? No. You suddenly developed a conscience. You fucked up." He took another puff from his cigar. "You fucked up, but you're lucky. You're able to keep your job. Thanks to me. Now get out."

Willard stood up, flushing, and walked slowly to the door. He turned. "I'll be ready when you call, sir." He started to leave.

"Unless," said Mitchell. Willard stopped in his tracks. "Unless you might want to reconsider your evaluation. Perhaps—after further re-view—you might decide you were far more lenient than you should have been."

Willard took a deep breath, looked at Mitchell, and then glanced at the other evaluator.

"Okay," he said, in a low voice. "I'll review it tonight. I probably could make a few revisions."

"Good," said Mitchell. "Excellent. Now get out of my sight. I'll want that new evaluation on my desk first thing in the morning." Willard nodded and left.

Mitchell glanced at the man at the other end of the table.

"Well," said Mitchell. "I thought he'd never leave."

The other man leaned back in his chair and smiled slightly.

"So," said Mitchell, reaching for the second file, "you must be Mr. Scott Brown. Is that correct?"

"That is correct," said Brown.

"Let's see," said Mitchell, opening his file, "it seems as if you also had a questionable review." He riffled through the file until he found the pa-per he wanted. "Yes, here it is. You reviewed a Mr. Bell during his World History class. Is that correct?"

Brown nodded. Mitchell glanced at him a moment, gauging his reac-tion. There wasn't much to see.

"You said," Mitchell continued, "that Mr. Bell utilized a creative and diversified lesson plan which did an excellent job of engaging his stu-dents. This lesson had to do with the ancient Mayans, correct?"

"Yes, it did," said Brown, looking up and smiling slightly.

"And he had a kid shooting a ball through a hoop?" Mitchell laughed. "You're kidding me, right? Is this the creative and diversified lesson plan you were writing about?"

"I believe I said differentiated," said Brown drily.

"However you put it, it sounds like a lot of touchy-feely horseshit. Are you really telling me that this," he waved the copy of the review, "was a good plan?"

"I am," said Brown, in a quiet yet firm voice. "I know a good lesson plan when I see one. I also know a good teacher when I see one."

Mitchell leaned back in his chair. "Refresh my memory," he said. "How much do we pay you per review?"

"Including the background research on the teacher, analyzing the lesson plan as it pertains to the Common Core Curriculum, and the review itself, including the video and our explanation of it, I was compensated about six hundred and fifty dollars."

"Not bad," said Mitchell, pulling his cigar out of the ashtray and examining the end.

"Well, I did a little analysis of my own," said Brown, pulling a folded sheet of paper out of his jacket pocket and opening it, "and considering that the background research—the way EduNet wanted it done—took over ten hours, the lesson plan analysis took five, and the expiation of the videotape took two, and the final report took eight, I averaged about twenty-six dollars an hour."

Mitchell nodded as he relit the cigar. "That doesn't sound too bad."

Brown shrugged. "There are worse ways to make a living, although the truth is I could make more money working as a substitute teacher."

"But this way you don't have to put up with the kids," said Mitchell, blowing smoke at the ceiling.

"True," said Brown, "but I do have to put up with politics—like this. And, besides, I don't look at working with students as putting up with them."

"Teachers," said Mitchell, leaning forward suddenly in his chair. "You know I don't get you guys. Either one of you. Do you still think that there's something worth saving in public schools?" He stood up and took a breath. Stay calm, he told himself, then glanced at the smug little prick sitting at the other end of the table. Well, fuck moderation. Fuck being cool.

"Do you really think these schools are going to survive? What you call politics, I call business and business is telling me that you need to shape your shit up or get out. Is that clear?"

Brown sat completely still during the tirade. Mitchell watched him, his chest heaving. The bastard was even smiling a little.

"Would you like me to answer your question?" asked Brown softly.

Mitchell looked at him, trying to remember which question he'd asked.

"Your question," said Brown. "You asked if I think that there's anything worth saving in public schools."

"Sure," said Mitchell suddenly. "Go ahead." He sat down abruptly. "Why the fuck not? Tell me what's worth saving in public schools."

Brown reached down and brought up his book bag. He took out his laptop, opened it, and clicked a few keys. He turned it around to face Mitchell. He recognized the program immediately—the EduNet video observation program. Brown pressed the play arrow and sat back. The video started. It was a classroom, a very full classroom. The children—hardly children, really—some of these kids looked like they were in their thirties, were raising their hands and answering questions. One fat girl was talking about squash for some reason and then another geeky looking kid got up and started talking about calendars and astronomy.

How in God's name, thought Mitchell, is this going to help any of these kids find jobs? Why were they studying history, anyway? An absolutely useless subject for the real world. He shook his head and glanced up at Brown, who was watching him with that same half-smile on his face. Little asshole, thought Mitchell. Thinks he's smarter than me. Brown glanced back down at the computer and Mitchell followed his gaze. The teacher had the class lined up on either side of the room. A boy was standing with a ball in his hand while the teacher was talking about some ancient Mayan game called frijole or Pelota or something.

Mitchell actually found himself drawn in as the voice began describing the traditions of the game, the hard-fought three-day battles, and the bloody sacrifice of the winners. He found himself caught up in the energy as the students started chiming in with opinions and answers and insights. He found himself becoming absorbed as the talk ranged over to the Mayan gods and their anger and how their own culture feared them and everything unknown and transformed their own loving gods into the faces of their own deaths. He found himself—for the first time in a long time—imagining, wondering. He found himself watching as the kid lofted the tiny ball and somehow—impossibly—sank it into that tiny yogurt cup basket. A bell rang and the videotape ended abruptly. Mitchell stared at the blank screen. That had been a good class. The little prick was right. Shit.

"That," said Mr. Brown, closing his laptop, "is good teaching." He folded his hands in front of him. "You can demonize public education however you want, Mr. Mitchell; you can frame it as nothing but government waste, union corruption, incompetent teachers, you can say test scores are down, or that it's the cause of our rotten culture. And, you know what, some of that, a tiny portion of that, might even be true. But it doesn't change the fact that this," he tapped the laptop, "is good teaching. Almost great teaching."

Mitchell turned his chair to stare out the window. It was overcast and hazy. He could see them both reflected in the floor-length windows.

"And," said Mr. Brown, packing away his laptop as he prepared to leave, "it's alive and well in one of the worst high schools in the city." He walked toward the door and then stopped when he came abreast of Mitchell, who kept his gaze locked on a distant point outside the window.

"You have," continued Mr. Brown, "done everything in your power to sabotage this school, these teachers, and this administration. I've seen exactly what you've done. Firsthand. I was there. And I think it's disgusting."

Mitchell swiveled his chair around to stare at him.

"Disgusting?" he asked.

Brown nodded.

"Well, I guess that means we've come to a parting of the ways," said Mitchell.

"Yeah, I'm done here," said Brown. "I collected my paycheck before I came here today, and since I trust you so much, I deposited it, too."

"You signed a non-disclosure statement—" Mitchell began.

"I'm fully aware of my obligations," said Brown. "You have nothing to worry about."

He left. Mitchell swiveled to the window and stared again. It was cloudy and looked like rain. Or snow. He wasn't worried about Bald Boy, Willard, but Brown could be trouble—they needed to keep an eye on him. At the very least. He leaned over and picked up the phone.

"Monica," he said. "Could you call Mr. Messerschmidt for me?" It was time to bring Mr. Adrian Cole into the picture.

* * * * *

His cell rang. Cole opened his eyes, reached over, and picked it up.

"Mr. Cole," rasped out the voice on the other end. "Are you there?"

"Yes, sir." It was Mr. Leach. This was only the second time he had ever spoken to the CEO directly; this had to be quite important for him to call in person.

"Cole. I need to see you in my office immediately. I have a job for you to do. It concerns one of my vice-presidents. Mr. Paige."

"Yes, Mr. Leach."

"It's a very delicate matter and will need to handled discreetly and neatly."

"All right. Mr. Leach?"

"Yes?"

"Just to let you know. Mr. Paige called just a few moments ago and wants me to meet him tonight. In his apartment."

"What about?" asked Mr. Leach.

"He didn't say. Only that it was quite urgent."

"Excellent. That is perfect. Come to my office. Come now. We'll see what the raven has brought and work our plans accordingly."

He hung up. Cole stared at the cellphone a moment, and then put it down. He stood up, stepped out of the bathtub, and reached for the towel.

Chapter 11

Sandra walked with Mr. Ricks and Dominique down the hall. The girl seemed quite calm now and even smiled when she caught Sandra casting her a sidelong glance. They stopped outside a classroom. Sandra looked over Mr. Ricks' shoulder as he peered into the classroom through the tiny pane in the door. It wasn't quiet; she could hear kids talking, some excitedly, and she glanced over at Ricks with her eyebrows raised. He motioned her in to take a closer look.

The class, a big one—maybe forty-some kids—had been divided into groups and looked as if they were presenting a speech or something— maybe a role-playing bit—to the other people in their group.

"That be Mr. Bell," said Dominique. Sarah glanced behind her. The girl was hanging over her shoulder and also peering into the classroom. "I had him last year. He be doing the group role-play."

"What's that, Dominique?" asked Mr. Ricks, straightening up.

"After he break us into groups, he give us a situation. One of mine was to illustrate search and seizure from the Fourth Amendment."

Sandra looked at her and nodded.

"From the Bill of Rights," added Dominique. "In the Constitution. You know."

"Yeah," said Sandra. "Okay."

"So we had to write up and act out a role play about how that works. I played a cop who busted into somebody's house without a warrant. I found cocaine and guns and shit—"

"Dominique," said Mr. Ricks quietly.

"My bad," said Dominique. "I swear too much."

Sandra nodded again and smiled—sympathetically, she hoped.

"Anyway, it was a bad arrest because we didn't have no warrant and the criminals went free. But it worked good, because I still remember it a year later, and I don't usually remember nothing."

"Do you like going to school here?" asked Sandra.

The girl scratched her neck, frowned, and said, "Yeah, I guess. Mr. Ricks be okay most of the time and we do have some other good teachers here."

Sandra opened her mouth to reply as the bell rang. Dominique waved and smiled and trotted off down the hall.

"What a nice girl," said Sandra, trying to keep the irony out of her voice, as she and Ricks watched her leave.

"Yes," said Mr. Ricks, "she can be." He looked at her and smiled. "She really can be." They stepped back as the kids started pouring out of the classroom.

A middle-aged man with blondish graying hair and wearing plastic-framed glasses was talking to a student as he walked him to the door. Sandra recognized him as the rumpled man she had seen in the main office earlier that morning. She and Ricks stepped inside the classroom.

"You will," he was saying to the student, "have to know facts and dates for the AP test, definitely, but you are also definitely going to have to know the causes of certain conflicts or historical movements and the effect they had on society."

The kid, looking a little overwhelmed, nodded and made his exit, threading his way between Mr. Ricks and Sandra. The rumpled man came to the door.

"Hello, Mr. Ricks," he said, glancing at Sandra and furrowing his brow. "Did you bring me a new student today?"

They laughed. "Very funny and very flattering, sir," said Sandra. "Thank you." She held out a hand and he shook it. "I'm Sandra Feeley, and I'm from EduNet."

"This," said Mr. Ricks, "is Mr. Bell."

Kids started threading around them into the classroom.

"I'd love to talk," said Mr. Bell, "but as you can see, I have my U.S. History class this hour."

"I'm going to sub for you, Mr. Bell," said Ricks, "while you have a meeting with Ms. Feeley. Apparently, she has some pressing business from EduNet to discuss with you."

"Really?" He glanced at her again with a look that was not nearly as pleasant at the first. His eyes were very green, she noticed, and also blood-shot. She nodded, smiling her nicest smile.

"All right," he said, giving Ricks a 'what the fuck, are you kidding me?' look. "You can go over the Revolutionary War stuff that's on the PowerPoint. Just have them take notes and tell them I'll check them off when I get back." He turned to Sandra.

"Will this take all hour?" he asked her.

She shrugged. "Probably not. It depends."

"Okay," said Mr. Ricks. He handed Dave a key. "Why don't you two meet in my office? It's quieter there."

Mr. Bell nodded and motioned her to follow him.

"Hey, Mr. Bell, where you going? That white lady your wife? She coming to get you?"

"No, she too young to be his wife. She his baby." Some of the kids giggled and tittered.

Mr. Bell turned as they got to the door and addressed the class. "Mr. Ricks will be watching you until I get back," he said. "He will also be presenting today's assignment." Sandra noticed the change in his voice immediately. It had become official and businesslike but had not lost its friendly tone: tough but not stern. "Do everything he says and have your notes done when I return." He left the room abruptly.

She followed him out into the hall and fell into step with him as he strode down the hall.

"Thanks for your time, Mr. Bell," she said. "I appreciate it."

"Well, that's fine," he said, "but I'd appreciate it from here on in if you would try to schedule these things during my prep time. These kids need every bit of instruction they can get."

"I understand that," she said, "and I apologize for scheduling this during class, but it couldn't be helped. I'll make this as brief as possible so you can get back to your students as soon as you can."

He nodded. "I appreciate that."

They walked down the hall. His pace was surprisingly quick and she had to rush to keep up. "So, Miss Feeley," he said, "what exactly do you do at EduNet?"

"I'm the assistant executive vice-president overseeing this project."

"The EduNet Project itself?" he asked. "Or do you mean the project of installing EduNet in Custer after you dismantle it?"

"The first," she said, looking him straight in the eye and smiling. He grunted in reply. She noticed, close up, that there was a very subtle grayish tinge to his complexion. Having grown up at least for a few years with an Irish drinker of a father before he passed out of their lives, she knew the look of an alcohol abuser. But there was something underneath that hazy veneer, something coiled up under that gravelly voice, something very alive in this man, something very—what? Powerful? Energized?

Mr. Bell opened the office door, then stepped past her and led the way into the main office. It was less crowded than it had been in the morning, but there were still quite a few students milling around. Mr. Bell led her around the counter, past the secretaries, who watched them quizzically, and opened the door to Mr. Ricks' office.

"So," he said, after seating himself in Ricks' chair. "What's up with EduNet, our favorite corporation?" He started playing with a pencil, dropped it, and then leaned over to pick it up.

"I'm here," she said, after waiting for him to get upright, "to get a comparative analysis of the evaluation that took place in your classroom. We have the observer's report and the lesson plan, but we would also like to get your input on the observation."

"My input?" said Bell, leaning back in the chair and frowning.

"Yes. We'd like to know if you thought it was an effective lesson, and, if so, where its strengths lay and where you think it could possibly be improved."

He leaned his elbow on the desk and ran his hand through his hair.

"All right," he said, sounding all the world like a tired and condescending parent. "Ask away."

"So," she asked, taking out her notebook, "what were your impressions of the class?"

"Let's see," he said, swiveling around in the chair and staring up at the ceiling. "Was that the World History lesson with the Pelota hoop?"

"Umm," she said, looking into her case and digging out the report, "I believe so."

"All right," he said. "I remember that class. The lesson went pretty well as I recall. My objective with that one is to get the kids to understand cultural differences between us and the Mayans, specifically how religion influenced their world view."

"Why did you choose Juego de Pelota?" asked Sandra.

He smiled. "Your Spanish is pretty good, Ms. Feeley. How do you know about Pelota?"

"Well, I read Mr. Brown's report," she said, holding it up, "and I also had to write a report about it in high school." She smiled back. "And you can call me Sandra."

"I guess you can call me Dave," he said. "If you want."

She smiled at him but said nothing.

He cleared his throat. "To answer your question," he said, "I felt Pelota was a sort of bridge between our cultures. All of these kids know sports to one degree or another, and Pelota, as you may have noticed, has more than a passing resemblance to basketball. Putting a kid in the place of a successful Mayan athlete and comparing the rewards the two cultures deem proper give the kids some insight into the values of that culture."

"That sounds good," she said. "Very engaging."

"The kids do seem to like it," he said, rocking in the swivel chair. "They have for years."

"We never did stuff like that in my high school," she said.

"Where did you go to school?"

"Central."

"Here? In the city?"

"You sound surprised," she said, folding her hands on the desk.

"I am," he said. "I had you pegged as a suburban girl, growing up out there in Franklin or Greenfield or some other piece of the promised land."

"Nope," she said. "I grew up over on Roosevelt."

"And you're a product of the public school system," he said slowly, rubbing his chin and staring at her—through her—with those green eyes. "Our public school system," he continued. "And apparently, it gave you a pretty decent start to your education. It got you a college degree and took you all the way to EduNet where you are now vice-president in charge of dismantling public schools." He smiled. "We did well with you."

"I have no complaints," she said, looking up. She caught his eye and held it. "I also have nothing to be ashamed of."

"So, Sandra," he said, picking up a pen, "if I may be so bold as to ask. What are you really doing here? You don't think I bought that stuff about you wanting feedback from me, did you? I know Ricks didn't."

She considered a moment; part of her wanted to level with this guy. It was weird, but she kind of trusted him. No. Better to play the comedy through.

"I'm sorry you feel that way, Mr. Bell," she said, "but, what, do you think I'm here on some sort of industrial espionage mission to steal your lesson plans or your curriculum?"

"Or our jobs?"

"I'm not here for that," she said. Not today. "We simply are trying to determine at what level of effectiveness Custer is currently functioning."

"Uh-hum," he said, twirling the pencil between his fingers.

"So do you have any other insights about this lesson that I could add to my report?" she asked. She felt lame asking it; she hoped it didn't sound that way.

"Just that these kids deserve the best," he said. "Dedicated and well-trained professionals."

"That's what they have now—" she began.

"No," he said, his voice getting an edge. "That's what we had before. Now these kids are getting everything from the best teachers still out there to emergency permits given to any and every damned fool that comes in through the front door."

"You're still here," she said, regretting it the moment it came out of her mouth.

He snorted. "I'm retired. I had to retire, after collective bargaining became illegal for public employees."

She felt herself frowning.

"I'm subbing," he said. "Ricks called and said he wanted me back. I figured what the hell, I could use the extra money. So I came."

"You're double dipping?" she said. His face clouded over.

"I don't acknowledge that term," he said, his voice even. Too even. She could tell he was angry. Really angry. "I'm earning money substituting while collecting my pension; money that I earned and money that I saved through my pension program. Okay, Sandra. Let's do a hypothetical. If you supplemented one of your paychecks with your savings account, would that be wrong? Would you call that double dipping?"

Sandra leaned back in the chair, folded her hands on her lap, and said nothing. Better to let him get it all out and say nothing. Mitchell—and her brothers—had given her an abundance of experience dealing with angry men. With Mitchell, she had learned, much as it was with her brother Matt, it was better to let the tantrums run their course. This, however, she thought, considering Mr. Bell's demeanor, was no simple tantrum. Mitchell's anger was never measured, never controlled like this. Mr. Bell's eyes were still fixed on her. He was thinking, deliberate, pondering the next move. She nodded to herself: an anger like this sharpened instinct, honed the senses and the mind, lent a clarity and fine pitch to the emotions. Anger like this was perfect for strategizing, planning, and, she thought, returning Mr. Bell's stare ounce for ounce, destroying. She knew because she had used it herself. And she would use it again. She stood up and extended her hand.

"I'm sorry if I offended you, Mr. Bell," she said, smiling.

He shrugged and smiled. "It's all right," he said. "No harm taken." They shook hands and she turned to leave.

"Sandra," he said. She turned back to him. He stood with his arms folded, gazing at her. She waited a moment.

"Yes?" she said finally.

He took a deep breath. "You seem like a decent person," he said. "I'd like to ask you not to do this."

"Do what?"

"To work with EduNet. To take over our public schools. Don't do it. You're from here. You're one of us."

She shook her head and smiled.

"Mr. Bell, even if I wanted to—"

"No," he said, his voice sharp. "Don't give me that I'm a small cog in a big machine. Don't give me that crap. It all comes down to our personal choices." He came around from behind the desk. "You're not one of them," he whispered, coming closer, his face filling her field of vision. "I can tell," he said. "I can tell."

Enough. She took a step back.

"I have to go, Mr. Bell," she said. "Thank you for your help."

Sandra hurried out of the office and into the hall before he could say anything more. She could hear the sounds of students laughing and shouting echoing far down one of the empty hallways, hollow disembodied voices seeming to call out to her. She scurried out the front door and got into her car. The wind howled past her car and seemed to echo the voices from the school, from her own past, and from her own conscience.

Chapter 12

The parking lot of the Riverwest Providence Baptist Church was about half-full. Not bad, she thought, not too bad for a Wednesday night. Well, she wasn't surprised; a lot of people had been stirred up by this school takeover thing. She opened the car door, braced her arms against the seat and pushed herself to her feet. She went around into the backseat of the car and hefted up the baking pan covered with aluminum foil. Her Apple Crumble: so good God himself would have loved it. Now she would never say that, but deep down in her heart of hearts, she knew it must be so. She closed the door and walked slowly with short steps, ever on the watch for those nasty invisible ice patches—black ice, they called it. Ever since her neighbor Zola had fallen last winter and broken her ankle, she had taken extra care not to make herself a casualty. She would not have been able to stay inside for eight weeks like Zola had to; she would have gone crazy and probably gained fifteen pounds to boot. Just like Zola did. That girl never could stay away from her macaroni and cheese.

She got to the door, opened it, and stepped gingerly down the wet stairs into the basement. They had set up some of the old wooden folding chairs in rows. She didn't trust those chairs anymore; they were old and moved sideways when she sat on them. More dangerous than that black ice, she thought.

"Millicent," she heard and turned around. It was Serena McDaniels, the salt of the earth. Not only had they gone to high school together, but the woman had been with Riverwest Providence forever and knew simply everybody: black, white, Puerto Rican, Somalian, it didn't matter; Serena would talk to a rock if she had to. But everyone loved her; she had the brain of a scientist and the silver tongue of a roadshow preacher. And she knew how to listen.

"Oh," said Serena, her eyes lighting on the pan. "Is that the Apple Crumble? The world-renowned dessert?"

Millicent smiled and cocked her head.

"Oh," said Serena, "I cannot wait. I might even cut short my comments to get at this a little sooner than I might have. How are you, honey? I don't believe I've seen you since, oh, last summer?"

"I believe so," said Millicent. "The picnic."

"That's right." Serena chuckled. "I remember it was hot. The Reverend Lee had a tremendous thirst that day."

"He did, didn't he?" giggled Millicent. "The way he kept going on about the sin of the flesh and looking at Miss Fletcher, I was almost expecting a visual demonstration."

Serena whooped with laughter and said, "I heard that, darling."

"I thought I heard a familiar voice."

Millicent turned and saw a youngish man in a suit. Well-kept. Clean. Had a good job somewhere. He looked like a teacher. She didn't know how she knew that, but he did; he looked like a teacher.

"My God," said Serena. "Ryan Ricks, I haven't seen you since I don't know when. How have you been?"

"I'm doing well," he said. "How are you since retiring?"

"What are you talking about, retiring?" she asked, putting her arms akimbo. "I'm working harder than ever now. I am working part-time. And part-time for me is better than full-time for most people."

He smiled. "I know it is," he said.

"Millicent," said Serena, "let me introduce you to Ryan Ricks, who worked as an assistant principal when I was the principal over at East. He was one of the best assistants I ever had. He had those kids wrapped up tight, I can tell you that. Ryan, this is Millicent Maxwell."

"Well, Ms. McDaniels was one of the best principals I ever worked for," said Ryan. "She knew how to take care of her people."

Serena raised up a finger and said in that proclamation voice of hers, "You have to let the leaders lead. And Ryan was a true leader. I even saw it in him when he was a student of mine."

Millicent looked at him. "You had her as a teacher and as a supervisor?"

"Yes, ma'am," he said, smiling again.

"Well, all I can say is you should thank God you made it through." Serena whooped again and all three of them joined in the laughter.

"So," asked Serena, "how is that school of yours doing?"

"Well, you know," said Ricks, "we're doing our level best to hold on but they're creeping in like cockroaches. EduNet has already sent in some of their representatives to—" he held up his fingers in a quotation mark gesture—"observe some of our teachers in action."

"What is EduNet?" asked Millicent.

"They are the company that wants to take over the education of our children," said Serena.

"They're the ones?" asked Millicent. "And they're in there already?"

"They are," said Mr. Ricks. "Just today a young woman from EduNet came in to talk to some of the teachers who'd already been observed. I think she wanted to get some adjustments to their data."

"What do you mean exactly by data?" asked Serena.

"Well, they came in to observe some classes but several of our teachers, including Mr. Reynolds and Mr. Bell, suspected they were videotaping."

"You put them in classes with veteran teachers," said Serena. "That's smart. And," she added, "they don't get much more veteran than Mr. Bell and Mr. Reynolds."

"I had Mr. Reynolds," said Millicent.

"What?" exclaimed Serena. "You did not."

"I did," said Millicent. "I had him for biology." She turned to Mr. Ricks. "You know we graduated together from Custer, Mr. Ricks, back in 1982. I was in the top eighty percent of our class," she said with a sly grin. Mr. Ricks smiled and chuckled a little bit.

"That's an old one," he said. Serena gave him a puzzled look and then turned back to Millicent, who waited, smiling. She knew she would get it. Eventually. It took Serena a minute, but then she chuckled and put her hand on Millicent's arm.

"Eighty percent. That's some joke, but I know you're smarter than that, girl. That is very easy to see." Serena looked around. "I think we better find us some seats. It's getting a little crowded in here."

She was right. More people had been coming in while they were talking; it was going to be pretty near a full house.

"Well, this is a pleasant surprise," Mr. Ricks was saying. Millicent turned. He was taking the hand of a tiny white woman, no more than five foot nothing. She had snow-white hair and stood as straight as a flagpole. She smiled graciously at Mr. Ricks and then started scanning the crowd.

Somehow she seemed familiar, but from where? Millicent was pretty sure it wasn't from the church. And then it hit her.

"Oh, my lord," she whispered to Serena, tugging at her sleeve. She turned from her conversation.

"What is it, Millicent?"

"Do you know who that is?" she whispered, gesturing toward the woman.

Serena glanced over and smiled. "Oh, she made it. This is powerful. Do I know who that is? Is that what you asked me? Well, of course I do. That is Ethel Benjamin. She's been teaching at Custer High School since dinosaurs roamed the Earth."

"I know," said Millicent. "I know that, Serena. I had her. She was my American Authors teacher sophomore year."

"She is also one of the strongest voices for our cause," said Serena. "She'll have every teacher in that school on our side in no time."

"She was scary," said Millicent. "She had this look. Oh, she'd stare you straight in the eyes and it felt like there was an icicle going through your brain. And she knew, I can tell you, she knew if there was something going on."

The woman, Mrs. Benjamin, had caught Serena's eye and was making her way through the crowd to her. It was slow going. It seemed as if every other person there knew the old lady. Millicent smoothed out her blouse and stood up straight. She wasn't quite sure why she was so nervous. After all, she was a fifty-two year old woman who had four grown children and two grandkids. She'd buried a husband and beaten off cancer, but as the tiny woman walked slowly toward them, she felt her heart pounding.

"Hello, Serena," said Mrs. Benjamin, embracing her. "It's so good to see you again."

"That is beyond true," said Serena. "I wish our meeting was under some more inviting circumstances. Ten years ago, I never would have thought we would be fighting for the lives of our public schools."

From what Millicent could see, Mrs. Benjamin hadn't changed much. Of course, she recognized the voice immediately. She might have closed her eyes and been back in the eighties, sitting in the back of the American Authors class and passing notes with Dorena Evans. And those eyes — that look—had not changed one bit. Dorena used to say that woman could make ice cubes with that look.

Mrs. Benjamin was talking now about some of the other teachers still at Custer, Mr. Reynolds, Mr. Bell and some few others, some of whom Millicent knew, some not. It was funny, she found herself thinking—remarkable—how well she still remembered that time. Not only her classmates and friends and the good times, but the other students, the coaches, the teachers, and even some of the lessons. She still remembered Mrs. Benjamin and the story about the boy wanting the blue suede shoes. "Thank You, Ma'am" she suddenly remembered, with the big old tough woman, Ms. Luella Bates Washington Jones. She shook her head. Where that name had suddenly come from, she couldn't say: but there it was.

"Hello, Millicent."

She looked up. Mrs. Benjamin was standing in front of her and smiling. She couldn't help smiling back.

"Hello, Mrs. Benjamin. How are you?"

"I'm good," she said. "It's very nice to see you again."

"I cannot believe, Mrs. Benjamin, that you actually remembered my name. How long has it been?"

"A long time," she said. "You were in my American Authors in eighty or eighty-one. I remember you used to sit in the back with Dorena Evans."

"That's right," said Millicent. "We were best friends."

"I gathered that," said Mrs. Benjamin, smiling slightly. "You two certainly had a lot to talk about."

Despite herself, Millicent giggled. "We did."

"Who," asked Mrs. Benjamin, "was that boy who played guard on the basketball team? He was skinny as a rail and had one of those flat-top haircuts that were so popular at the time."

"That was Levon Angelo."

"That's right. Levon."

"Oh," said Millicent. "I had a terrible crush on him. Dorena, too, but she never told me until after we graduated."

"Well, I guess that figures," said Mrs. Benjamin, glancing around the room. "Well, it's been a pleasure talking to you, Millicent, but I should go and find a place to sit." She turned to leave.

"You know who I was just thinking of just now?" asked Millicent suddenly.

Mrs. Benjamin stopped and raised an eyebrow.

"I was thinking of Mrs. Luella Bates Washington Jones."

The old lady smiled.

"I don't know why," said Millicent. "Her name just sort of popped into my head. After all these years, I hadn't given her a thought and then, boom, there she was. Her and the boy with the blue suede shoes."

"Roger," said Mrs. Benjamin softly. "I believe his name was Roger."

"That's right," said Millicent. "It's funny how some things stay with you. I hadn't thought of that story in nearly forty years, and when I saw you, it popped up as clear as if I had read it just yesterday."

"Memory is a funny thing," said Mrs. Benjamin. "I can remember almost every one of my students, and I've had a few of them, but I don't know if I can tell you what I had for dinner just two hours ago."

"It's odd what stays with you," Millicent agreed, "but it's almost always the important things that stay with you the longest. That was one of my favorite stories you taught. It meant a lot. Thank you for giving it to me."

"No," said Mrs. Benjamin, touching her arm and leaning close. "No, Millicent," she whispered. "Thank you."

She walked away, fading into the crowd. Millicent stared after her, high school memories crowding in around her: she and Levon kissing behind the pool, she and Dorena and Serena sharing a bottle of Ripple wine at her parents' house, the prom. So much of it was a part of her, not forgotten but dormant, part of her substance that she didn't have to think much about, like breathing or dreaming. This was part of her and most of the people she knew, people in her neighborhood, in this church, and in this community.

She looked up, startled out of her reverie, as Serena took her arm and guided her to a seat, a rickety old wooden chair she had promised herself to avoid. Well, she thought, settling herself gingerly. I will take this risk. Body and soul.

Chapter 13

The church basement was full, standing room only. Millicent guessed there were over one hundred people there, maybe more. Serena walked across the floor to the podium and stood there a moment, surveying the crowd, her angular face lifted high and proud. Like a queen. She stood straight, radiating nothing but dignity, her mouth set in a strong firm line. She knew she could wait. Some people could just do that, walk in front of an audience and own them. Public speaking had always terrified Millicent; she never could stand facing that many people at once. But Serena, that was a different story: that woman could face down an army of KKK members and have them eating out of the palm of her hand within five minutes. She'd always been that way, as long as Millicent had known her.

That's because she has the word inside, Millicent thought. God put it there. She carries the word with her—she radiates a light that shines throughout this tiny and dingy basement.

"We are here," said Serena, her voice ringing throughout the low-ceilinged basement, "to talk about what is happening to our public schools in this city."

A murmur ran through the room. A lot of yeahs and uh-huhs.

"You've been hearing a lot about companies coming into our city and our neighborhoods, saying they're going to improve our schools. They say they're going to get rid of the inefficiency and waste that happens with a government-run program. They say they're going to get rid of teachers who do not care about our children and our communities. They say they're going fix it. They're going to fix our schools, fix our communities, and fix our lives."

Millicent glanced around her. Some people were nodding. The woman next to her was leaning forward and clutching her purse, one hundred percent certified attention.

"Well," said Serena, and then paused, looking out over the crowd. "I don't know about you, but I don't need any fixing."

Applause rose up from the room like a flock of startled crows.

"I don't need somebody from out of town coming in and telling me how to live my life. I don't want someone who doesn't know my community, who doesn't understand my community, and who doesn't even like my community coming in here and telling me how to fix my community."

Millicent applauded and cheered, feeling herself carried along on the wave of enthusiasm.

"These people," she continued, "are not coming here to educate our children, to improve the community, or to invest in the future. They are coming here to make money by privatizing our schools."

Murmurs, affirmations, and a few amens swept over the crowd.

"Privatization," she continued, "does not work any better than public education, and in fact, it ignores some of the students already in our system, some of our very own children. Private charter schools pick and choose who they want to come into their schools, and then they kick out whoever they don't want for whatever reason suits them: discipline problems, low achievement, or special needs. Anyone that holds down their numbers, anyone that affects their profit margin they can suspend, dismiss, or expel. Just like that. They don't need a reason. If our children don't fit into their mold, they throw them away like so much garbage."

Another angry murmur swept through the basement. Serena waited for the crowd response to die down.

"These privateers—which, for your information, is also a term used to describe pirates hired by European governments in Napoleonic times to destroy the enemy—that's right, I said pirates. These pirates take our taxpayer money to run their schools, hire their teachers, and buy their supplies, but, unlike our public schools, they are not accountable to any government oversight. Now I want you to think about that a minute."

"Imagine you are building a road," she continued. "You get a government contract and start building it but halfway through, you realize you're over budget, so oh-oh, what do you do? You look for ways to cut costs. Maybe you look to buy cheaper materials, concrete that isn't quite as strong as the best you can get. Maybe you try to find workers who are less experienced, less qualified but who are willing to work for less. Maybe you get rid of your chief engineer and find somebody who has an idea for a less expensive design. So you cut costs, you make sure your profit line is stable and that all your investors get their return. But to do that, you have to buy cheaper materials, unskilled laborers, and inexperienced designers. And you ask, wait a minute, is this road going to be safe? For me, the privatized road-builder, that is not my problem. Safety is not my concern—profit is. I mean we've cut every corner we can—who's going to tell the people whether it's safe to drive our school buses on this road? Who?"

Some people were standing and applauding. Others voiced their anger.

"Well, I'll tell you who. Nobody. Remember, in this state, these private charter schools, these voucher schools, these pirates, are not accountable to the Department of Public Instruction or any other government entity. Public schools have to submit test scores, attendance figures, suspension rates, all of that and more. I know that because I've been there. I've been in the classroom and I've been in the principal's office."

She stopped a moment and cocked her head. "What I mean is, I worked in the principal's office." She waited for the laughter to die down before continuing. "Yeah, most of the time. I worked all over the public school system. For thirty-five years."

"But these private charter schools," she continued, "protected by special interests in state and local governments, do not have to submit a single page of reports, figures, or statistics. Nothing. Not one thing. They can do whatever they want to do and do not have to answer to the same authorities that people in our public schools do."

"Stop them," shouted the woman next to Millicent.

"That is not right!" shouted someone else.

"Uh-huh. It is not right. Federal law states that in the Individuals with Disability Education Act that all students must get an education. These are fair laws, they are just laws. They ensure that students with all sorts of disabilities, physical, emotional, or otherwise, should be able to have their special needs addressed in school. And let me tell you, our public schools do an exceptional job at this. Our district has some of the finest special education departments, facilities, and personnel in the country. And I'm not going to lie to you; this costs money. A lot of money. Each one of these students has to have their own individualized education plan and many others need specialized curriculum and modified equipment. Our public schools take care of these students. We give them what they need to learn. We do it because it's the law, but we also do it because it's the right thing to do. We cannot afford to leave any child without an education."

The room exploded into applause.

"These private schools, and specifically, the entity we are now dealing with, this EduNet, is not required to deal with students with special needs. They are driving themselves and their program through a loophole as big as the moon in order to avoid serving the students in this community, our community, with the educational services they need to succeed. And they are doing it to make money. They have no other reason. Money is their driving force."

Serena took a deep breath and grasped both sides of the podium. She put her head down. Millicent grasped her hands, waiting. After a moment, Serena's head finally came up and she gazed out at the room, smiling.

"I know we have our problems. We always have. Life has never been easy for us. Never. From the first days of slavery, to freedom, to the sixties, to today, it seems as if we never get ahead. We take one step forward, and then we get pushed back three. There's poverty, there's the racism, the discrimination, the hatred: you all know what I'm talking about. It seems like we fight and fight and fight, but never ever seem to get ahead, and it also seems that even though we try as hard as we possibly can, we work and strive and pray and parent, our children never seem to get ahead, either. Oh, and there are so many more dangers and hardships out there now facing our babies than we ever had to deal with when we were young. Drugs, gangs, guns, and all the rest of it: the streets have always been hard, but it seems like they're getting harder. Well, some of you might be thinking maybe these charter schools, this EduNet, might be the answer. Maybe this might be the key to help us rise up and claim our due."

A man two rows ahead of Millicent stood up slowly, like his knees hurt. He was a middle-aged man, portly, and simply dressed in a pullover sweater. He hesitantly raised his hand.

"Yes, sir?" asked Serena.

"Well, Ms. McDaniels, I have a question. You've been saying that these private charter schools are bad and will not do our community any good. Well, my question is what good have public schools done for us? Unemployment is bad as it's ever been, dropout rates are high as they ever been, and we're as poor as we ever been."

Serena nodded as he spoke.

"What I'm wondering," he said, "is can they do any worse? Maybe we deserve to give them a chance."

"Thank you," said Serena, "for bringing that up. You're right. Things are not much better here than they were twenty years ago. The job is not getting done. But do you think blaming all of our troubles on public schools is fair? Problems facing our community have been here for years. We have poverty, we have crime, we have violence, and some of us live in distrust of the world. And what I mean by distrust is distrust of the system, of the government, of the establishment. Some of us don't trust the police. I can't blame you. Some of don't trust the mayor or the city council. I can't blame you, either. Some of us—myself included—no longer trust the politicians in the state capitol. Some of us," and here she paused, "do not trust the people trying to teach our children."

A murmur, not so friendly this time, rippled over the audience.

"I know," said Serena, raising her arms, "that not all of us have had positive interactions with the teachers and administrators in the public schools. I know that. I was in some of those interactions. I've been there. I know that some of you feel your children have been unfairly singled out and picked on."

Millicent saw a few heads nodding out of the corner of her eye.

"And I know some of you are scared. You don't want to lose your children to a different life."

Serena paused and reached to take a drink of water. Millicent saw something in her movement uncharacteristic of Serena McDaniels: a hesitation, an uncertainty.

"Now I know this might sound like an odd thing to say, but I also know it is there in each one of us. I've felt it myself when I sent my daughter away to college. I watched her drive off, thinking it's all going to be different now; my baby is going into the wide, wide world. She'll come home and she'll look around and she'll say this ain't me. This ain't who I am anymore. This place is sketchy, raggedy, and not the place I want to live in and not the place I want to raise my children. I'm moving on."

She glanced out over the crowd again, and Millicent saw the steel returning to her eyes.

"My baby lives in Chicago now, and she is doing just fine. She got her college degree and has a good job. And she has public schools, Central High School, in fact, to thank for that. The education is there if you want it. The truth is that all of us in public schools are not only fighting ignorance; we are also battling poverty, discrimination, mistrust, and apathy. We are working hard. Are we as successful as we should be? No. Could our public schools do better? Yes. But ask yourself this. Look in the mirror and ask yourselves this. Couldn't all of us be doing better for our children?"

She grasped both sides of the podium and stared out at the crowded church.

"And, finally, one more question. Will these strangers coming into our neighborhoods, our communities, and our cities care more about our children than we do, than our teachers do?"

Serena slapped her open palm on the podium. "No. I say no. No. I say EduNet is not the answer. It is the wolf in sheep's clothing. It is lies. They will tell you that they'll raise test scores and achievement and that they will be the ones who will get our kids into college. The truth is that they have nothing behind them to back this up. And statistics will bear me out on this; the truth is that voucher programs, and some private charters, do no better, and, in fact, many times do a worse job than public schools. They want government money and to get that money, they need to take down our public school system."

Applause tore through the room. A few people shouted approval.

"Where will they start?" asked Serena. "Well, let me tell you that they already have started. You know they haven't been sitting around. The devil doesn't sleep. They've already been at it. Oh, and they've been at it for years. They've been making friends with some of our politicians in the capitol and working with them to get into our schools. When our legislature took away collective bargaining rights from our teachers, many of our best instructors left. That was because companies like EduNet are putting those politicians in their pockets. With their union decimated, teachers knew they would lose health benefits, raises, and maybe their pensions that they had worked so hard for over the years. Many of them retired. I don't blame them. A few stayed on, but they knew they were taking a risk with their own welfare."

"Now EduNet wants to get rid of our remaining veteran teachers and hire unqualified and underqualified candidates, people who never took a college course about education in their lives, people who've never set foot in a classroom, and people, in some cases, who have never even been to college."

Angry murmurs started up again.

"And why?" asked Serena, raising her arms, "Why do they want to do this? Because it's cheaper to hire unqualified teachers. It's cheaper to give our children second-best."

"Now lately EduNet has been getting all tight and cozy with the city government and our school board. Oh, they're friends with everybody: the county executive, the mayor, even some members of our school board. You may have noticed that a majority of our own board, that we elected, agreed to go along with EduNet's original business plan to take over one school, which is what they are trying to do right now. And we know why EduNet makes so many friends, don't we? We surely do. Campaign contributions, lobbying for pet projects; it's the same here as it is in the state capitol. We're being invaded by pirates."

She paused, took a deep breath, and smiled out at the crowd.

"Now I've been up here talking a long time."

"I heard that," said someone from the back of the room. A chuckle rose from the back and Serena joined in, smiling.

"I know," she said. "I get carried away talking about this, but it is the most important thing out there right now facing our community, facing our city, and facing our children."

She stared out over the crowd a moment before continuing.

"I've been telling you about the problem, about this cancer coming in to take over our schools. What I'm sure you're wondering is what can we do about it? How can we fight a company as big and as powerful as this EduNet? And, you know, this is a very consequential problem, but it is not insurmountable. We do have a plan. We sat down, myself, some members of the church, some members of the community, some school officials, and some parents, and we talked it out, and we now believe we have a strategy that we think will work. If our community and the schools work together, we can beat this thing, but we have to work together."

More sounds of assent.

"Now this will not be easy. It took a coalition of community leaders, many of whom are here tonight, to put this together. You know most of them. It also took some members of our education community. Many of the people working with us are fighting in the trenches alongside our children. These are the principals and other administrators, the paraprofessionals, and, most importantly, the teachers."

She raised her arms high above her head and the crowd stood, applauding.

"I would like to introduce you to Mr. Ryan Ricks, the principal at Custer High School, and Ms. Ethel Benjamin—" Here the noise level rose even higher. "—who has taught English at Custer High School for over forty years."

Millicent wondered how many people in this room had been taught by Mrs. Benjamin. It made you wonder, she thought, how many lives that woman has touched over the years. Hundreds, definitely, maybe thousands.

"We have these representatives from the schools here tonight, and I'd like to give them a chance to speak. But first, I'd like to also present you with our state assembly representative, Mr. Alvin Fox."

He is a wily old fox, thought Millicent, as the representative stood up and waved. He was wearing his signature three-piece suit and bowtie. He'd been in the assembly for at least twenty years and stayed just popular enough to get re-elected every cycle. The heartening thing about seeing him here, she thought, is that he always seems to end up on the right side of an issue.

"Mr. Fox," continued Serena, "will be spearheading our efforts in the state capitol to keep our schools funded and to make these companies like EduNet accountable. He has just sponsored a bill that would make companies that set up voucher programs accountable to all state and federal standards, but in order to pass this bill, we're going to need a lot of community activism. Remember," she said as she gazed out over the crowd, her mouth set in its firm line. "By any means necessary."

Millicent stood with the rest of them, cheering and clapping and carrying on. She was caught up in the excitement in a way she hadn't been for years. This is what the sixties must have been like, she thought. The excitement. The purpose. The hope.

"Now," said Serena, "now I would like to present Mr. Ricks to you."

Mr. Ricks came up and, mercifully for Millicent's back, his comments were short and to the point. He said he was working with the teachers' union, represented by Mrs. Benjamin, to help mobilize the teachers and students in Custer to save their school. He said he was depending on everyone here to help man the phones and to spread the word.

"I know some of you might find it surprising that administrators will be working with the teachers' union. It's not often that we see eye-to-eye on any issue, but these are different times. We, and by we I mean everyone involved in education, recognize that this proposed takeover of a public school is a threat to everyone and everything we hold dear. I've always loved school from way back when I was a little kid. It's been a very special place for me, and I still love going to work there every day. And now I see these people coming in to take all that away, and I tell you I will do anything and everything I can to save our schools."

"There will be," he said, "a meeting of the school board next Friday evening to determine whether or EduNet will get the go-ahead to take over Custer. It will be conducted in a town-hall format, so many of us will get a chance to speak. We hope to see a good number of you there. We also expect to have the local media there, so if you've ever wanted to see yourselves on the television, now might be the time."

Scattered laughter and a light sprinkling of applause. The man is no Serena McDaniels, thought Millicent, and that is for sure.

"You will find a sign-up sheet in back where Mrs. Benjamin is standing." Millicent craned her head and looked. Mrs. Benjamin stood there, hands folded. "Please fill it out if you're interested in volunteering on our phone banks or going door to door to spread the word," continued Mr. Ricks. "And remember, we need you. Our children need you. Thank you." He left the podium to a round of applause led by Serena, who came to the microphone and said, "And we do have some refreshments in back near the sign-up sheet. Help yourselves."

People stood up and started milling around. There were a lot more than Millicent had thought. Maybe more had come in during the speech. It was tight down there in the church basement. And warm. She made her way over to the snack table and snuck a peek. Sure enough. The Apple Crumble was just about gone while most of the other treats had not even been touched yet. God himself would love it, she thought, and smiled.

"Well, sister, what did you think?"

Millicent turned and there was Serena standing at her elbow.

"Think of what, Serena?"

"You know of what."

"Oh, your little foray into public speaking? I guess it was all right, although I think you could use some work on your delivery." She leaned in close and whispered, "I do think it was a little flat."

"Oh, shut your mouth," said Serena. "You know who the best speaker is in this building. I can put the Reverend Lee to shame and I'm not afraid to say it."

"I only wish I had your gift for speaking," said Millicent. "It is a gift."

"Thank you, darling," she said, grasping her hand, "but remember, God gave us all gifts. Some of them are just louder than others. There is no one that can bake like you, Millicent. No one. You have that gift."

"Well, maybe so," said Millicent, pleased, "but I don't think my Apple Crumble, as good as it is, would ever do the kind of good that you do."

"Well, I don't know about that," said Serena. "I just hope my little piece got some bodies moving. Do you see a lot of people signing up?"

"I can't really see," said Millicent, trying to get up on her tiptoes. "It's crowded, but I don't know if they're signing up or if they're just eating."

"I might go back there and do a little nudging," said Serena. She leaned in and gave Millicent a big hug. "We'll see you, honey, and I expect you'll be signing up to do something."

"Oh, yes," said Millicent.

"Good," said Serena, her eyes roving over the crowd, "we'll need you."

"All right, then."

"Millicent," said Serena. There was a question in her voice. Millicent turned.

Serena was gazing toward a corner of the basement, near the back row of seats, where a man was putting on his winter coat. It was one of those black wool Navy pea coats like she used to wear when she was younger. He was white, average height, with thinning brown hair that he wore combed straight back. Average size: not skinny, but not fat. If Millicent had to guess, she would say he was about fortyish or so, but he was one of those people who didn't wear their age on the outside. She thought he realistically could be anywhere from mid-thirties to fifty. The man reached into his coat pocket and pulled out a pair of black leather gloves. It was when he was pulling on the glove that Millicent noticed the ring finger on his right hand was missing. He finished putting on the glove and took a look around the room, not a glance, but a full measured look, like he was searching for a specific person.

"Do you know him?" asked Serena, gazing right back at him.

"Can't say as I do," said Millicent. "I don't think I've ever seen him before just now."

"He's up to something," said Serena, half to herself. "He doesn't belong here."

Millicent glanced back at him and saw only the back of the pea jacket as he was making his way up the stairs to leave. She looked back to Serena who was standing with her arms folded.

"What is it?" asked Millicent. "What's the matter?"

"If I didn't know better," said Serena, "I would swear that man is the police or something very much like it."

"Like what?" asked Millicent. "FBI?"

"No," said Serena. "I don't think he's on that side of the law." She shivered and then smiled, looking back at Millicent.

"Honey," she said, linking arms with her, "why don't we go tackle some of that Crumble before it's all gone?"

"I think you might be too late," said Millicent.

"Well, I hope we're not too late," said Serena, glancing at the exit. "I do hope that."

Chapter 14

Mitchell abruptly stopped pacing the floor of his living room, strode across the area rug, took a tumbler from the glass-topped bar, and leaned over to grab the bottle of Scotch, his good stuff, the Lagavulin 16 year old single malt. He poured himself a solid slug, replaced the bottle, and sat on the leather couch. Typically, he would have hidden his good stuff behind his other, more pedestrian brands, but he wasn't going to mind sharing his best tonight. Not with this guest.

Mitchell was excited, and despite himself, nervous. He was finally going to meet Adrian Cole, the company fixer, the enforcer. He'd heard him mentioned fleetingly at executive lunches and golf outings, but always furtively, quietly. He'd heard him described as a cunning man, a ruthless, dangerous man. Mitchell was eager to see how he'd measure up.

Boldness, he thought, raising his glass and gazing at the amber liquid. Balls. That was the name of the game. He took another sip of the Scotch and rolled it around slowly in his mouth, savoring the caramel overtones. What he was planning would move the takeover agenda along a little more precipitously, which was exactly what he needed—to strike now; he'd promised the CEO that he'd have the takeover accomplished by the end of the year. If he was to prove his worth to Mr. Leach, he was going to have to follow the original schedule and get the takeover finalized before January.

He knew, from some of his sources, that the opposition was mobilizing, preparing to skew the media—public opinion—against EduNet. He also knew the Mr. Leach would freeze the deal—albeit temporarily—if any controversy arose against the takeover. He could not prevent the demonstrations, the public outcry, and all the bleeding heart bullshit; no, Mitchell would have to steer the public opinion into a different direction and vilify those who would stand in the way of a better education. To do that, he needed an expert, a professional, a master of manipulation. And that man would be here within the hour.

The buzzer for the door sounded. He sprang up and strode to the intercom.

"Yes," he said.

"Hello. It's Joe Sykes."

Cole's assistant. Mitchell pressed the button to open the door without answering. He strode to the bar, finished his Lagavulin, put his empty glass on the counter, and then placed the bottle in full sight on the bar.

Joe Sykes came in the room quietly, scanning it from side to side as he did so. Mitchell appraised him as he closed the door and took his jacket, a Navy pea coat. Not especially fashionable, although it did make its way back into the retro fashion cycle every five years or so, but very warm. It stopped the winter wind dead in its tracks. He knew from having worn them growing up out on the prairie. His mom had loved them because they were warm but inexpensive. Mitchell had grown to hate them for the same reason; he had worn them all through high school and those jackets had become a badge of his poverty. But those Navy peas had kept him warm.

Perhaps, he thought, hanging it up, our Mr. Sykes spends a lot of time outside doing surveillance. Or maybe he's just cheap.

He turned. Mr. Sykes was handing him his gloves. Mitchell took them smiling and couldn't help noticing that one of his visitor's fingers was missing. He took the gloves and placed them on the foyer table.

"Welcome, Mr. Sykes," he said. "Would you like something to drink?"

"Bourbon," he said, taking a few steps into the living room. He spoke quietly; Mitchell had to strain to hear him. He nodded, went back to the bar, and took out one of the nice tumblers.

"Would you like a traditional bourbon? I think I have some rye in here, too."

"Whatever's handy," said Sykes, examining a print on the wall. "I'm not especially particular."

Mitchell poured out half a tumbler, refreshed his own Scotch, and came out from behind the bar. Sykes was leaning forward at the waist slightly, still examining the print. Mitchell saw he wore a dark sport coat over a button-down shirt open at the collar. He certainly didn't look like an operative—if that's what he was. He wasn't very tall or very big, although he moved well. His brown hair was thinning a little on top. Sykes combed

126

it straight back, exposing a high forehand. His hands were clasped behind his back; Mitchell noticed he had exceptionally long fingers, and the hands themselves were very massive, like paving stones. Sykes heard him and turned while simultaneously straightening up in one single graceful movement. Mitchell smiled and handed him the glass. Sykes took it, never taking his eyes from Mitchell's face. His eyes were easily his most striking feature, as cold and pale blue as lake ice.

"Thank you," he said, reaching for the glass and taking a good belt without even stopping to savor it.

Mitchell smiled politely and sipped his own drink. Sykes turned and took a few steps into his living room.

"Very nice," he said, walking over to the floor length window. The city lights—such as they were—stretched out beneath him. "I bet you have a hell of a view in the daytime." He gestured toward the vast stretch of darkness beyond where the lights ended. "I'm assuming that's the lake."

Mitchell nodded. "Yep," he said, walking up to stand next to Sykes. "That's Lake Michigan."

"You know," Sykes continued, still gazing out the window, "there are at least fifty shipwrecks in that lake. Cargo ships, passenger ships, fishing boats, ferries, pleasure craft, you name it. All the way back to the eighteenth, maybe the seventeenth century. And those are just the big ones, the ones that make the history books. Who knows how many small craft, how many little boats went under? Or even canoes. How many of the Indians did the lake get before we got civilized?"

He looked over at Mitchell. "That's a lot of bodies," he said, his voice supple, still quiet. "The lake doesn't give everyone up, you know. It keeps its secrets." He paused, letting his arm drop to his side as he gazed out the window past the glowing lights of the shoreline, and then, without moving his eyes, he raised his arm toward Mitchell and shook the empty glass. Mitchell paused, waiting a beat, then finally took the glass and went back to the bar and refilled it. He walked in front of Sykes and held it up.

"Thank you," he said, nodding and taking it. "Do you dive, Mitchell?"

Mitchell realized it was the first time Sykes had addressed him by name.

"Dive?" he asked.

"Yeah," said Sykes. "Scuba diving."

"No, I don't."

"I've dived into some of those wrecks down there. I don't anymore. There are a lot of old ships down there. Some fine old ships. The Prins Willem V. That's one for you. The Willy."

Mitchell nodded politely and surreptitiously glanced at his watch.

"You know you can die down there."

Mitchell glanced up at Sykes. Those icy blue eyes were on him now, unwavering and intense.

"What?"

"It's easy to die down there. It can kill you. The lake. The ships. You might think they're defunct, gone, part of history, but they still claim their lives, they still claim their tithes."

"What are you talking about?"

"Divers go in and start exploring in those dark places, Mitchell. And these are big ships, seventy-five or one hundred foot or longer. These divers get excited wandering around down there and sometimes they get lost and can't find their way out. And then they run out of air. Then they panic." He took another sip of bourbon. "And then they drown."

Mitchell took a deep drink.

"A friend of mine died doing just that. He didn't take precautions. He didn't prepare. He was overconfident. And now," Sykes gestured with his glass, "he's out there."

"I see," said Mitchell, smiling and starting back toward the bar. He never saw Sykes' hand; he only felt it grasp onto his arm like a claw.

"You know," said Sykes, his voice suddenly in Mitchell's ear. "I don't think you do understand. When you're in that deep, you need to be twice as careful, twice as prepared. You don't get more than one chance inside old Willy."

Mitchell pulled back, but Sykes held on tight to his arm and pulled Mitchell closer, so close their faces were almost touching. His eyes bored into Mitchell's.

"And remember," he continued, "it's not just you that's inside that wreck. It's me and Mr. Cole, too. And I'll let you know this now, Mitchell," he said, pulling him even closer. "If you get stuck down there and run out of air, well, that's that. That's your skin. But you need to understand that me and Mr. Cole won't get stuck down there with you. We escape. We get out. Whatever it takes, we always get out."

"Get the fuck off me." Mitchell pulled away and stared at Sykes, who stood there smiling.

The buzzer sounded.

"We always escape, Mitchell," he said. "Remember that."

Mitchell swallowed and rubbed his arm. Sykes smiled. "You'd better get the door. That'll be Mr. Cole."

Mitchell buzzed him in and stood to one side of the door, keeping an eye on Sykes, who had gone back to examining the print on the wall. Sykes looked up suddenly and smiled. He opened his mouth to say something just as a knock came at the door. Moving more quickly than Mitchell expected, Sykes brushed by him and opened the door, stepping aside as it opened, creating, Mitchell realized, an entrance for his boss. He wondered if the effect was circumstantial or deliberately contrived.

Adrian Cole stepped into the room, nodded to Mitchell, and looked over to Sykes, who cocked his head slightly and lowered his gaze. Cole inclined his head slightly toward him. He was a big man, tall and broadly built, but well proportioned. He didn't seem to carry any unnecessary weight.

"Mr. Paige," said Cole, shrugging out of his jacket. Sykes moved to take it and then handed it to Mitchell. "It is a pleasure to meet you." His voice was deep but not particularly sonorous. It sounded flat, deadened, like the sound of bread dough dropped to the floor. But his eyes resonated; they were a deep and dark green, the color of a swamp on a cloudy day. He had a wide mouth with thin ruddy lips. His dark hair was slicked back and wavy on top, and was combed behind the ears. In spite of his physical bulk, the face was gaunt but without austerity: it seemed a generous face.

Mr. Cole was wearing a black suit and tie, and, while presentable, his appearance was not very worldly. The cut didn't look exactly right for him. In fact, Mitchell wouldn't have been surprised to learn the suit had come straight off the rack. From everything he'd heard about Mr. Adrian Cole, Mitchell had expected someone a little more sophisticated, a little more continental. He hung up his jacket and went over to the bar.

"Would you like something to drink, Mr. Cole?"

"Yes, that would be very nice. Do you have any Scotch?"

"Yes, sir," said Mitchell, sidling his way behind the bar. He took out a glass, poured out some of the Lagavulin for Cole, and then refreshed his own glass.

"Here you are," he said, handing it over the bar and raising his own glass.

"Here's to success," he said. Cole smiled, raised his glass in return, and took a drink. He raised his eyebrows and sipped the Scotch again.

"Very nice," he said. "What are we drinking?"

"Lagavulin 16."

"Never had it before," said Cole. "It's very interesting."

"Shall we sit down?" said Mitchell, walking out from behind the bar and motioning toward the living room. Cole followed him with Sykes close behind. He hangs close to him, thought Mitchell. Just like a dog. They made their way around the coffee table and sat down on the sofa. Mitchell sat opposite them on the armchair. He looked out the window, out at Sykes' lake for a moment, and then back at his guests. Cole was looking at him, smiling slightly, while Sykes sat further down the couch, staring at him with those icy blue eyes. They were waiting.

"I wanted to thank you again for making the time to see me, Mr. Cole. I know how busy you are."

"As I said on the phone, Mitchell, it is no trouble at all. So," he said, leaning back on the sofa and draping his arm over the top, "what can we do for you?"

Apparently, Mr. Cole was not one for small talk.

"Well, I don't know if you're familiar with the EduNet reorganization plan."

"Somewhat," said Cole, "but why don't you refresh my memory?"

"Well, EduNet, and a number of our investors, have been working on a plan to reorganize some of the city's underperforming public schools. About three years ago, our company wrote the business plan, lined up a curriculum, vendors, the whole nine yards, and then we started working the system." He glanced over at Sykes, who was still fixing him with the same look.

"Our investors," continued Mitchell, glancing away, "made it known to some of their friends in politics what was at stake, and then our representatives set out to persuade them that the age of the public school was over. Once we had worked our magic and finally had some sympathetic ears in the statehouse, especially the State Senate, we were able to help them pass a bill allowing the school board to privatize public schools in an emergency, which they will do when the time is right. Once we fulfill certain legal and contractual obligations, we can step in and start the take-over process. So that, in a nutshell, is how we did it."

"I see," said Cole, looking at his drink. "It sounds all very neat and clean. It sounds as if you—like you said—have all your ducks in a row."

"Pretty much," said Mitchell, who took a sip of his own drink.

"Which begs the question," said Cole, his low voice creeping through the room like a cat, "why are we here?"

Mitchell shifted in his chair. "Well, to tell you the truth," he said. "There have been a few complications." He smiled.

"I'm listening," said Cole, not returning the smile.

"Well, when I took over leadership of the project almost nine months ago," Mitchell said, "I was promised a certain incentive if the takeover would be completed by the end of the calendar year—this December. We were right on schedule until we ran into a bit of a speed bump a while ago."

Mitchell stopped. Cole was staring at him with hooded eyes, still half-smiling. Sykes had finally looked away and was staring down into his empty glass.

"Part of the contract proposal we drew up stated that we had to compile hard data proving that Custer is completely dysfunctional. Typically, the data we use is test scores, grade point averages, graduation rates, and attendance rates, you know, that sort of thing."

Mitchell paused to take a drink and realized his glass was empty. He arose to refresh it.

"Would you like another drink?" he asked.

Cole shook his head; Sykes handed him his glass. Mitchell walked behind the bar and filled both his and Sykes' glasses half-full. He rounded the bar and handed Sykes his glass. The man accepted it without comment.

"So," Mitchell said, " to continue. One of the school board members, Lilly Robinson, is a real die-hard advocate for public schools. During negotiations, she forced a provision into the contract proposal that the data compiled by our company had to consist of observations and evaluations of teachers and classrooms performed by objective parties—non-employees of EduNet. We fought it, but she had enough clout to push it through. So we oversaw the hiring of a group of ex-teachers and administrators, trained them how to compile data, and set them loose at Custer. In effect, they were our people and it should have been a slam-dunk, and most of the reports turned out fine; the data conformed exactly to what we expected. But a few of the reports, about ten percent, came in with satisfactory or above satisfactory results."

Cole nodded.

"We've been able to accomplish a fair amount of damage control with these reports," Mitchell continued. "One of my associates had the foresight to insist that the observers videotape the classes. This has given us an objective record that we can refute some of the subjective data with."

"But I take it your attempts at damage control were not enough," said Cole, his voice as still and flat as the sound of a skull striking the pavement.

"No," replied Mitchell. He glanced over at Sykes, who had already finished his bourbon. The man was staring at the bottom of his glass and frowning. "No," he continued. "Even with us massaging the observation results, the percentages still aren't there. We need at least two of the reports to rate the teaching at Custer as less than satisfactory."

"And," said Cole, rising and going to the bar himself. "I'm assuming you need these results to be revised by the original observers."

"Yeah," said Mitchell, watching as Cole stepped behind the bar and poured himself some more of the Lagavulin 16. "That's about it."

"And I'm once again assuming that's the reason you asked us over tonight." Mitchell nodded, glancing over at Sykes.

"That's part of the reason," said Mitchell. "I'm also worried about the public backlash. We heard rumors that elements of the community will be trying to disrupt the process. I have a few ideas how to stop them, but I wanted to talk with you about it."

"I'm sure we can handle that. We've worked on issues of public opinion before, haven't we, Joe?"

"We have indeed, sir."

"Would you like to tell Mr. Paige how we did it?"

"I'd love to," said Sykes, "but first I have to take a piss."

He strode to the bathroom, walked in, and then stood at the commode without closing the door. "The first time it happened was when we did that job in Chicago. When those groups came in to protest, we just caught them before they got too close and beat the shit out of them."

He lifted the toilet ring and unzipped his pants. Mitchell looked away as he hauled out his business and started to urinate.

"The second time we got smart," he called out. "The second time, in New Orleans, we went to the meeting and waited for an opportune moment." Sykes chuckled. "Then two or three of our guys got pushy. They said things and did some things to get the crowd going."

He finished and hauled everything back inside. Mitchell felt a little short of breath. "The trick of it is," Sykes continued, zipping up, "to make it look like the other guy started it.

"Could you guys do that at our school board meeting?" asked Mitchell. Sykes shrugged and looked at Cole.

"Yes," said Cole, "we could do that." He sat back down.

"Okay," said Mitchell. "Good." That had been easy.

"So," said Cole, leaning back. "You said you wanted to meet me. Well, here I am," he said, sitting up suddenly. "What would you like to know?"

"Yes, I heard from some of my associates that you can be very persuasive, that you're the man to call when there's—" Mitchell paused a moment, searching for the right word—"tricky work to be done." He took a sip from his drink. "I guess what I'd kind of like to know," he said, leaning forward in his chair, "is how exactly do you persuade people? I mean, what do you have to do to get them to come around?"

Sykes snickered. Mitchell glanced at him as he got up to refresh his bourbon.

"Well," said Cole, brushing some lint off his trousers, "that depends on the subject. Some respond to reason, others to fear, others to different types of psychological pressure. For our more difficult subjects, we sometimes have to resort to other means."

"Like what?" asked Mitchell, never taking his eyes off Cole, who lifted his own eyes to Mitchell's and held them a moment. Mitchell looked into that face, stern now, not generous, but harsh and closed off.

"We never like to resort to anything beyond simple persuasion, but, unfortunately, sometimes we are forced to. I'm sorry. It's also a matter of professional integrity that my associates and I never discuss these matters. They can be very sensitive. I'm sure you understand."

"That's disappointing," said Mitchell, thinking of a new tack to take. He knew it was morbid, perverse even, but he wanted—needed—to know. He wanted to know exactly what tools they used, how often, when, why, and to whom. How much pain to administer? How little? He'd read a lot about the waterboarding during the Iraq War and the psychological warfare at Abu Ghraib. It fascinated him.

"Fucking dilettante," muttered Sykes from his corner on the couch.

"What?" asked Mitchell, standing up. "What did you call me?"

"You heard me. You're a dilettante. You want to hear all the gory details and be in on all the war stories, but you'd never get in there and get your own hands dirty."

"That's enough, Joe," said Cole, in a tone that made both the men look at him. "Mr. Paige is our employer. You need to show him his due respect."

"That's right," said Mitchell. "That's right. You both work for me and don't forget it." Sykes laughed. "And I'll tell you one thing, Mr. Cole, when I ask an employee a question, I expect it to be answered."

Cole said nothing. He sat quietly, staring up at Mitchell, a smile playing around his mouth. Mitchell stood, fists clenched, breathing hard, and watched him. Sykes was smiling.

"I said I wanted answers," said Mitchell, glaring at them.

Nothing. Cole smiled slightly. Sykes glared. Mitchell realized he was getting nowhere, and that he probably was looking like an idiot. He took a series of breaths and then sat, looking from one man to another.

Sykes looked up suddenly and said in a voice full of disdain. "How come it was you that called us, Paige?" He stood. "You're not our contact."

"I got your number from Mr. Messerschmidt. He offered to contact you, but I told him that I wanted to meet you in person. I was intrigued by your reputation." He could hear the sarcasm in his voice.

"Mr. Messerschmidt did vouch for you," said Cole, "and that's why we are here. So now you have what you wanted. You have resolved your situation and you have met me. Is your curiosity satisfied?"

"Somewhat," said Mitchell, sipping his own drink and leaning back in his chair. The anger still simmered, flaring sporadically. "I do have to say you weren't quite what I expected."

"Really," said Cole, crossing his legs. "What was it that were you expecting?"

Mitchell knew—he'd been expecting a man with a more intense physical presence: dominant, menacing, but urbane: a godfather, but also a cultured man: a James Bond—but he'd gotten this lawyer instead: this smooth talker.

"I didn't think," said Mitchell, deliberately putting sarcasm in his voice, "that you would be quite as cautious as you seem to be."

Cole smiled and chuckled.

"You were expecting someone a little more rough around the edges? Someone who reeked of the criminal element, an outlaw, perhaps, or a gangster? A Marquise de Sade?"

Mitchell shook his head.

"Is that the source of your fascination with me?" asked Cole softly.

Mitchell frowned. That was an odd way to phrase it.

"I wouldn't say fascination," he said, speaking quickly. "More of an interest, I guess."

"That's just splitting hairs," said Sykes suddenly. Mitchell turned to look at him.

"What are you saying?" he asked, his voice rising. Careful, he warned himself. Stay cool.

"Attraction, fascination," said Sykes. "There's no difference. That's just splitting hairs. They both get you hot." He laughed. "Maybe passion would be the better word. Or obsession." He laughed again.

Mitchell felt himself flushing. Cole actually chuckled and nodded to Sykes. They rose to go.

"All right, Mr. Paige," he said. "Get the names of the people we need to speak with to Mr. Sykes here. We'll start work tomorrow. We'll also need details about the meeting."

"Everything you need is in the black folder on the bar."

Sykes grabbed the folder. Mitchell rose to let them out. He started to say something, but Cole raised his finger to his lips.

"I think you need to learn, Mr. Paige, that there are times when it is better not to speak. We understand each other. Nothing more needs to be said."

"But—" Mitchell began.

"Hush," whispered Cole. He stepped close to Mitchell, cupped his face in his hands, leaned in, and before Mitchell could react, he kissed him full on the lips. Mitchell stood still, frozen with surprise. Cole lingered with the kiss for a moment, leaned back, patted him on the cheek, turned and left the apartment, Sykes trailing close behind. He stepped through the door, turned back, leering, blew Mitchell a kiss and giggled before turning to leave.

Chapter 15

The conference room off the main office was nearly full. Dave stepped inside the doorway and counted heads. Forty or so. Not too bad. Not great, but not bad—a little more than half the staff and faculty. He glanced at his watch. A little after eight. Ricks had said he'd probably be a little late; he had been attending the public rally over at Riverwest Church earlier, and those things had a tendency to run over.

He walked over to the podium and tapped the microphone.

"Is this thing on?" he said, tapping it again. A keening noise rose from the speakers. Feedback.

"Okay," he said. "All right. Mr. Ricks said he might be running a little late tonight, and he asked me to get things rolling if that was the case. It's good to see such a nice turnout here." He looked around the room and saw Knox and Zoe Ralph sitting in the back row. Zoe, predictably, was bent over her smartphone while Knox, catching his glance, gave him the thumbs up. Will Baker leaned against one of the chalkboards, bending over as Beverly Finster whispered something in his ear. Ethel wasn't there yet, either, but she'd said she was going to the church, too. Hopefully, she'd show up with Ricks.

It was a good mix, all in all. The old guard was well represented but there were a fair amount of the newbies, too. And not just the licensed teachers, either. Some of the newest teachers, the ones earning their degrees while working, the emergency permits, were also there. Dave didn't know many of them—as most of them were in special education—but he had been hearing from some of the other teachers that the emergency permits were only taking advantage of the short-term situation, and that they didn't really care about the big picture or a long-term teaching career. Well, if the turnout meant anything, it would seem as if the doubters were wrong. Good, he thought. Good. This would be a great first step to getting things back to where they should be.

"So," said Dave, "we all know why we're here. We've been hearing about EduNet for months now, and from all the latest indications, it now looks like they're finally moving to take over this school. Our school. We've all seen the EduNet observers and a few of us, myself included, have had them in our classrooms."

A few of the teachers nodded their heads and a small murmur swelled across the room. "We know," Dave continued, "that we're going to be the first, the bellwether. If we fall, the takeover of all our public schools won't be far behind. Nobody's quite sure exactly what that's going to look like, but if recent history is any indication, it won't be pretty."

He paused and glanced around the room. Most of them were with him. Knox was nodding in agreement. Will stood with arms crossed watching with—as usual—no expression on his face: inscrutable. Beverly made eye contact and gave him a slight smile. Zoe was watching; she had actually put away her smartphone. Bell smiled to himself; sometimes the small victories were the best.

"Not only will our school system be affected," he continued, "and our community torn apart, but this will affect everyone in this room and in this building on a profoundly personal level. If EduNet takes over our school system, we will probably lose a large chunk of our health and pension benefits. We will also be looking at profound salary cuts. If they decide to keep any of us at all."

A murmur swept across the room.

"The union has already been eviscerated by our governor's recent legislation, and membership has dropped almost forty percent. But that's still enough to keep our heads above water and to make sure our voices will still be heard in the state capitol."

The door opened. Mr. Ricks came in, closely followed by Ethel. Ricks seemed buoyant. Must have been a good meeting.

"As you can see," said Dave, gesturing toward the back of the room. "Mr. Ricks has arrived and he looks as if he's got some good news. God knows we can use it."

A younger teacher got up and offered Ethel his seat; surprisingly, she took it.

Ricks walked quickly up to the microphone, nodded to Dave, who moved aside, and looked out over the crowd.

"This," he said, "is a great turnout. I have to say I'm proud of my school and proud of my staff. You are standing up for yourselves, but even more, you are standing up for something greater than yourselves. You are standing up for your students, your school, and your community."

Dave smiled to himself. Ricks was definitely feeling it.

"I," Ricks continued, "have just come from a community rally over at Riverwest Providence, from a meeting full of concerned and committed community members dedicated to preserving this school and this school system. I can assure you that they are behind us one hundred percent."

A smattering of applause rippled across the room.

"I also met with some community officials and with our state representative, Mr. Alvin Fox. We have decided that there will be a combined protest against this public school takeover at the school board meeting here next Friday evening. As you may know, this will be the meeting where they will vote on final approval of the EduNet contract. If they approve it, our days as a public school will be numbered. We need to be there. We will also be encouraging our students and their families to show up, too. Until then, we need to be spreading the word. Mr. Fox will be working all the media outlets: radio, print, and television. Our friends in the clergy will be carrying the message to their congregations. The union will be sponsoring phone banks and going door to door raising awareness as to what is happening. They may not realize it, but the people of this city are living in a bubble. We know how important this issue is, how dangerous this takeover might be, and how vulnerable we all are. We know it, but our community does not. Not yet. We need to mobilize ourselves to spread the word. We need you to volunteer."

He paused and scanned the crowd. "Are you with me?"

Dave started clapping and others chimed in immediately, followed by cheering and shouting; Knox started whooping. He looked around the room, alive with energy, and caught Ethel's eye. She was looking straight at him, unaffected by the tumult around her, a crooked half-smile on her face. If he didn't know better, or know her better, he'd say that she looked cynical. Ethel could be pointed, painfully honest, and aggravatingly exacting, but for as long as Dave had known her, she had never doubted herself or her mission as a teacher. That was her touchstone, her rock: education and her place in it. The Ethel he knew would've been on her feet, circulating, encouraging the other teachers to champion the cause. But not today. He watched as Ethel rose, excused herself, and walked out the door without looking back, brushing past a man that looked vaguely familiar.

Dave started after her, pushing through the crowd, but as he reached the doorway, someone caught his elbow. He turned. It was the man he had recognized: slender, tortoise-shell glasses, graying temples, nondescript. He glanced out the door; Ethel was already gone.

"I don't know if you remember me," the man said. Dave recognized the voice immediately.

"You're the observer," he said. "Scott—" He snapped his fingers, trying to remember.

"Scott Brown."

"That's right," Dave said, crossing his arms. "You came into my room and observed me."

"Yes, and I have to say again that you did an outstanding job. In fact, that was one of the best examples of classroom instruction I've seen in a long time."

"Thanks," he said.

"I know it must seem odd to you that an EduNet employee would be so positive about a public school."

"I would say so," said Dave. He noticed a couple other teachers had recognized Brown and were glaring at him. Dave had to admire the guy a little; it took some guts to come into this den of lions.

"So," said Dave, "why are you here exactly? Did EduNet send you?"

"As a spy? No. Heavens, no. I no longer work for EduNet. I quit. I had quite enough of the corporate culture and their high-handed tactics."

"Really?" asked Dave, trying to suppress the irony that was trying to creep into his tone.

"Yes. One of their higher-ups called me and another teacher in and tried to get us to change our evaluation scores."

"Change them? How?"

"I did three observations for this school: one unsatisfactory, one basic bordering on unsatisfactory, and one proficient. That was you. The executive in charge of the takeover called me and another evaluator in for a conference. He also had completed a proficient evaluation. This executive,

Mr. Paige, made it clear that we had disappointed him, that they had not expected any sort of positive results."

Dave nodded.

"He also said that the observation training we had gone through should have precluded these sorts of results. He asked if we were truly satisfied with our observations. I told him that yes, I was." Brown paused and then said, "He was a pushy little son of a bitch "

Despite himself, Dave smiled. He hadn't expected language like this from Scott Brown, the little professor. Dave looked down at the little man, staring at him unabashedly, hands behind his back. He certainly told an interesting story. Dave wondered; could they use this in their campaign against EduNet? Had they been breaking the law by coercing their observers? Even if it had been done legally, it might be a good tool for raising awareness in the community. It would be a good story: EduNet was cheating, trying to fudge their own results.

"Mr. Brown," said Dave, regarding him closely, "would you be willing to tell this story about your boss, the EduNet guy — "

"Mitchell Paige."

Dave nodded. "Would you be willing to make a written statement as to what happened, that EduNet tried to get you to change your scores?"

"Well, I did sign a non-disclosure agreement when I was hired. Swearing out a statement would mean I would be in violation. I think that would mean giving up any compensation I received and also paying a fine."

He adjusted his glasses and smiled at Dave. "That would be something I could not afford."

Dave nodded, his mind racing. How could they make this work? If Brown's statement could be disclosed anonymously, they could hand it to the press on a silver platter and let them run with it, and that way at least get it out in the open.

"I'll tell you what, Mr. Brown. Let me talk to the union lawyers. I think there might be a way you could make a statement as an anonymous source."

"What would be the purpose of my testimony?" asked Brown.

"I'm not sure at this point," said Dave. "I'm thinking that maybe EduNet broke the law by messing with your evaluations and coercing you into changing your reports. Perhaps the statement itself will serve to sway public opinion against EduNet."

"But," he said, putting his hand on Brown's shoulder, "I guarantee that we will protect you however we can. If they come after you, we'll provide you with counsel."

"Well," said Brown, "if everything you say is correct, I certainly would be more than willing to help."

Dave put out his hand and they shook. Brown turned to leave.

"Mr. Brown," said Dave. "I'm curious. Why would a man like you with your experience and knowledge take a job with EduNet to begin with?"

"Well, first of all, I didn't really realize what I was getting into until we were pretty far along in the training program. The rhetoric in the course absolutely appalled me. Every negative thing you've heard about public schools was presented, represented, and drilled into us until they figured we were brainwashed. It was terrible."

Dave nodded.

"So I went ahead and passed the course and began observing. I figured I should do a few and see how it went but the whole process turned my stomach. They hadn't told us we would be surreptitiously videotaping classes until the day before we left."

Dave nodded. It figured.

"And when they called me in to tell me my report was not what they wanted, I knew I could not deal with these people anymore. I quit."

"And you came here to help our school? That's quite a turnaround."

"I know," said Brown, nodding quickly, "and I would understand it if you wouldn't trust me, but I want to help undo any damage I've done, and I want you and everyone else to know I had no idea that this EduNet operation would be so malevolent, so malicious. They have no idea the damage they're doing to education; all they can see is the profit line. That's truly the only thing they care about."

"Okay," said Dave. "Could I have your number or your e-mail address? We'll need to be in touch."

They exchanged numbers and Brown shook his hand again and left. They surprise me every time, thought Dave, watching the slender man walk through the darkened hallway. Just when you think that there's enough greed and avarice in the world to take it all down, you run across a little patch of decency. He glanced around the room; it had thinned out considerably during his talk with Brown.

Dave felt a nudge at his elbow and turned. It was Beverly, fellow wine-lover and teacher extraordinaire. Well, maybe not extraordinaire, but satisfactory; she tried.

"Hey, Dave," she said, smiling, "who was that you were talking to?"

"A surprise," he said, "a real surprise and a fine man to boot. What are you up to tonight, my fellow wine-lover?"

Beverly giggled and shrugged.

"I don't know. What do you have in mind, Mr. Bell?"

"I'm not sure, but I know we have to go somewhere else to find whatever it is we're looking for."

"Lead on, MacDuff," she said, holding out her arm.

He bowed ceremoniously, took her arm, and they left.

Chapter 16

Mitchell sat on the couch, his bottle of prized Scotch within reach. The inside lights were turned off, but the glow of the city below illuminated the room well enough. He could see what he needed to see, even his faint reflection in the window, the pale glow of his face. Mitchell still could not believe what had happened; that Adrian Cole had kissed him, hard, like a man kissing a woman, right on the lips. He reflexively took another sip of Scotch as if trying to cleanse the taste of another man's lips from his own: a mineral taste—iron—with an odd blend of spice mixed in. He felt repulsed, yet also oddly energized, animated, and—almost an afterthought—angry.

He stood up and strode to the window, his glass dangling from his hand. What right did the son of a bitch have to do that? It was disgusting: an intrusion, a violation, an assault. And that little fucker Sykes, standing there laughing like a goddamned hyena. A movement caught the corner of his eye; he turned and saw his reflection clearly: his small full mouth, high red flush in his cheeks. The anger erupted, and he threw his glass against the window. The windowpane vibrated and shook in its frame but remained unmarked. Mitchell stood a moment, staring at it, then collapsed on the couch. God, he was drunk. He sat up, staring at his upturned glass and then at the window.

Cole's face rose to him beyond his own reflection. Those lips rose in his mind like the petals of a flower and the green of his eyes swelled and deepened like an ocean that he found himself falling and sinking into. The green surrounded him, cushioning him, insulating him. Mitchell felt safe, as safe as he had ever been. The feeling enveloped him, erasing everything else. The kiss returned to him, the taste, the brush of those lips, and the sudden fleeting feeling of utter abandonment and submission.

Mitchell felt his own hand moving down, finding his zipper, undoing it, and then reaching, rising at his own familiar touch, swelling with agonized pleasure. Adrian. The face floated before him, lips slightly open. Waiting. Adrian, my Adrian. Mitchell flailed furiously. Everything came crashing together. He: the farm boy watching cows fucking in the field, in the boys' locker room, on the team, winning, everything was winning, getting ahead, being the best, being seen, known, loved. Cole: the man, the authority, the power, the man. The man. The man.

And he came and came and came.

* * * * *

Dave poured another glass of the Folk Machine Pinot and listened as Beverly continued on about the production she'd seen of *Hamlet* streamed live into a local theatre as it was being performed in London. It sounded great; he wished he would have known about it. He hadn't wanted to, but now as he looked at Beverly and smiled as she prattled on, he couldn't help noticing a button on her shirt—the third one—had come undone, giving him flashes of curved flesh, the ivory orbs. He caught himself glancing down there again and consciously, probably guiltily, looked up at her.

"And," she was saying, "the scene when he was pretending to go insane—you remember that one?"

He nodded. Sure. He didn't know shit about *Hamlet.*

"They dressed him, Benedict Cumberbatch, who was playing Hamlet, in a uniform so that he looked exactly like a toy soldier. And he was pretending to be insane; it was a perfect comment on the text. It was so subtle." She smiled. "I am going on. Am I boring you?"

"You?" He shook his head vigorously. She giggled.

"What?" he asked.

"You look like a big bear when you shake your head like that, like a grizzly shaking after he gets out of the water."

"A bear, huh?"

" Yes," she said, still giggling.

"I'm not a bear," he said, taking another drink of wine. "I'm not grumpy enough."

"You're drunk."

"Bears don't drink either."

"Actually," she said, "I read about a bear, he was a circus bear, a performing bear, and how they used to feed him beer and get him drunk for laughs, you know the other performers, the circus folk."

"The clowns," he said, and she giggled again. "They were all clowns."

"But this bear," she continued, grabbing his arm for emphasis, "became an alcoholic. He would steal beer and drink all day if he could, and he got so bad, he couldn't perform anymore."

"That's sad," he said.

"Yes," she said, "and it's a true story."

"You're drunk," he said.

"Yes," she said. "A little." She brushed her hair back and smiled again.

"So," he said, "I'd invite you over to try some of my Pinot collection, but I know you've got Celia at home."

"Yeah," she said, glancing at her watch. "I just texted her and she's still over at a friend's house doing homework."

"What time is it?" asked Dave. He was hungry; other than some bar food, chips and beer nuts, he hadn't eaten since lunch.

"A little after nine," said Beverly, looking at him soulfully with her deep and beautiful blue eyes. "I have to go home and do the mom thing."

Dave nodded. Doesn't look like any action tonight, he thought. God. He smiled to himself. He sounded just like a teenager, at least like a teenager back in his day.

"How are things going with the divorce?" he asked. "Is Roger still being a pain?"

She shook her head. "No," she said, "my lazy-ass attorney finally refiled the restraining order and it seems to have stuck. We haven't seen him in two weeks." She sighed deeply and drained her glass. "I'll be so glad when all this shit is over with." She glanced over at the bar. "Is that bottle gone?"

"Dead as the proverbial doornail," said Dave.

"Well," she said, "I guess it's time to go home."

"I guess," he said. "Here, let me walk you to your car." He stood up, pretty steadily, he thought, and slid into his sport coat. Beverly stood by her barstool, her hand still on the bar, and shrugged her purse strap onto her shoulder.

"Thanks," she said, "not that I have to worry about getting assaulted or anything. Who would want a middle-aged divorcee?"

"Oh, stop it," said Dave. "You are a beautiful intelligent woman who is very, very, very sexy."

"Well," she said, starting toward the door, "they certainly aren't beating down the doors."

"They will be," said Dave, following behind her, his eyes on the rear of Beverly's skirt, the tight black fabric surging with her every step. She did look good. He wasn't sure if it was his own judgment or the Pinot, but she was looking mighty good. They'd had a good time tonight. They reached her car, some kind of a Saturn, and she opened her purse to fumble for her keys.

"You know," he said, "we'll have to get together and do dinner and a movie. Or a play. Sometime."

"I would like that," she said. "I really would. It's just trying to work around Celia. You know, volleyball, the play, sleep-overs, all that."

"You just have to reserve a night for yourself, my dear. You are worth it."

"Thank you, David. You are so kind."

She put her hand on his arm, and he leaned into her and kissed her; he hadn't meant for it to be anything more than a friendly smooch, but as their lips touched, he felt a thrill run through him, almost like an electric shock, and felt himself leaning further into her, his arms encircling her, red mist rising behind his shut eyelids. He felt Beverly sigh and tense next to him, the warmth of her body searing through his clothes. Her arms clamped tight around his waist, reaching down. They broke it off and stared at each other.

"Oh my," she said.

"Oh, yeah," he said.

"Yeah," she said, reaching behind her and opening the backseat door. "Come here." She—somehow—backed into the car, pulling him along with her until they plopped onto the backseat. They kissed again and again, one long one really, hands all over each other. He tried to reach around her and found his right arm caught in the seatbelt. He pulled back and felt himself falling backwards, tumbling down in the tight space between the seats. Beverly leaned over, looking at him, smiling. He squirmed, trying to free himself, but couldn't pull himself up. She started giggling.

"You're a big help," he said. "How am I supposed to make out with you from down here?"

"I'd come down there, but I'm afraid I'd get stuck, too."

"Give me a second," said Dave, attempting to turn sideways, but he only succeeded in wedging himself in tighter. Beverly lay down on the seat, her head propped up by her arm, and gazed down at him, smiling.

With a mighty heave, he managed to turn himself onto his hands and knees and rise up; he turned sideways and brought himself into the seat next to Beverly's outstretched legs. He was breathing hard and sweating. God, he was he out of shape. He couldn't even crawl up between two car seats. Not that that was a common activity.

"Hey, stranger," she said, still smiling. "You come here often?" He could see she was trying not to giggle.

"Hello," he said and tried to smile back. Even with all the wine they'd had, this was embarrassing. "Well," he continued, "I guess that's what you call a mood-killer."

"I don't know," she said. She reached up and grasped him by the shoulders, pulling him down to her. They kissed and his hand found its way to the open front of her blouse. He felt her hand making its way down the front of his shirt, slowly unbuttoning it. Their kisses no longer had their previous urgency from outside the car; they were long and lazy, as if they had all the time in the world, as if two middle-aged teachers making out in the back of a used Saturn was the most natural thing in the world. Their hands explored each other slowly and deliberately: two experienced lovers checking and gauging their reactions to each type of touch. They were, Dave thought drunkenly, feeling each other out—out and up.

Beverly pushed him away suddenly and gazed up at him a second, no longer smiling.

"This is really nice," she said, "but we can't do this," she said. "Not here."

"Why not?" he said, shifting a little on his side to ease the ache in his pants.

"Sitting here like two teenagers in the back of a car? What if somebody saw us? What if a cop came by?"

Dave sighed. She was right, of course, but that didn't make it any less frustrating. He hadn't touched a woman for over seven months.

"Why don't we plan for a date in the next week or so?" she said. "We could go to dinner and a movie, or," she smiled, "we can just say that's the plan."

"And go to my place," he said. "Have takeout."

"Chinese is good."

"What if your daughter asks about the movie? What if she wants a review?"

"I'll have to wing it," she said, "or we could go to a movie or a play she would never see in a million years."

Hamlet, he said.

"No," said Beverly, with a sudden gravity, "Shakespeare is going to be something she really appreciates. And loves. And she does know *Hamlet*."

"How will you manage that?" he said, hearing the irony in his own voice.

"I'm her mother," said Beverly, starting to button up her shirt. "She listens to me."

Dave nodded. Sure. Pre-teens. Shakespeare. Whatever you say, Bev.

"She already knows quite a bit of it. We've read quite a few of his plays together: *A Comedy of Errors, A Merchant of Venice, Othello*—"

"You let your twelve-year-old read *Othello*?"

"Yeah," she said, a note of defiance in her voice. "Why not?"

"I don't know," said Dave, shrugging. "Isn't it a little risqué?"

"Not really," she said after thinking about it a moment. "It's no worse than any other Shakespeare work. There's blood and sex and crime and passion in every one of them."

"All right," he said. "We'll figure it out."

He worked his way out of the backseat door and watched as Bev got out and came over to his side.

"I'm glad we got together tonight," she said, grasping the sleeve of his sport coat and hanging onto it.

"Me, too," he said. And he was. Except for the rather quirky Shakespearian fan club thing there at the end, they'd had a great evening. He liked her; he wasn't sure he knew what had taken him so long to figure that out. She stood on tiptoe and pecked his cheek, then climbed into her car and drove out of the lot. He waved as he watched the taillights disappear and then started looking around for his old beige Escort—his flesh-tone Escort—with over one hundred twenty thousand miles on it. Still running like a top. Knock on wood.

There it is, he thought. He walked up to the car and looked down at it; the nicked-up rear fender, the rust spots around the wheel wells, the pits and scratches in the car door, the cracked windshield; it looked pathetic. It was dependable, got great mileage, and had given him more than his money's worth, but still. It looked pathetic. Old. What little appeal it ever once had was completely gone. He smiled and put his hands in his pockets. He could relate.

He wondered what to do now. He leaned up against the Escort and surveyed the parking lot. He needed to eat, but he was sick of take-out and didn't really want to go to a sit-down restaurant. Maybe he could get a burger down at Otto's. The thought depressed him, but then all his choices depressed him. His little bump with Beverly in the backseat had jazzed him at first, but now the idea of facing another evening alone at home seemed almost unbearable. He realized he'd been by himself in that house for seven months, alone in that king bed, the bed that seemed to get bigger every night, for almost a year, and had to get sloppy drunk every night just to get any sleep. He only ate take-out or frozen shit and probably wouldn't know a fresh vegetable if one came up and bit him in the ass. Pathetic. He was absolutely pathetic. Well, he thought, shrugging his shoulders. Enough self-pity.

Dave unlocked the car, got in, and turned it on. He always waited three minutes for it to warm up, something his dad had taught him to do. Knox had been telling him didn't need to do that with modern cars, that their electronics didn't need it or something, but old habits died hard. He would go to Otto's, eat his burger, go home and drink to get drunk, and get up tomorrow to do the same thing. But, he thought, smiling, tomorrow, or something close to it, was going to include Beverly. And whatever it turned out to be, one casual encounter, a strictly physical relationship, or something more, although he was not going to be ready for something more, it had to be better than burgers at Otto's. Yep, he thought. Things are looking up.

Chapter 17

Sandra liked to walk at night. It was cold tonight, but she welcomed the sting in her cheeks. She liked the cold. It kept her alert, fresh. And it burned calories. She stopped under a streetlight and fumbled in her coat pocket for her pack of cigarettes and lighter. She found them, tamped one out, and lit up. She felt tired and wound up at the same time, a feeling she hated. It had been one hell of a day, she thought, a day to forget.

After her depressing morning at the high school, she'd driven down to the lakefront and parked in a lot facing the lake. It was windy, and ice was starting to form along the edges of the shore. She had wanted to visit Jimmy, but he worked at Goodwill until three, so she'd sat in her car watching the waves crash into the breakwater, and thought about things as they came to her: Mitchell, EduNet, the teacher Dave Bell, Jimmy, her other brothers, and a lot of different stuff. She stayed in her car, watching the waves, and didn't end up returning to the office until after one. There were a few messages on her desk but nothing from Mitchell, which was surprising.

She leaned back in her chair, pondered a moment, and then pulled up some of the background material the team had compiled about Custer over the past year or so. She began scanning present achievement test stanines, the EduNet predictions for improvement, and the school district demographics. What was it Mr. Reynolds had said? "Statistics, facts, and spreadsheets. That's not the sort of answer you're looking for, young lady." She half-smiled to herself again: young lady. But, she thought, scanning through the data, he's right: what is the answer here, and, in fact, what is the question?

The demographics reflected the poverty, the splintered families, and the low achievement; the testing scores affirmed the deficiencies in curriculum, and the evaluation scores reflected the quality of instruction, but those weren't answers to the question nibbling around the edges of her consciousness. She kept scanning, hoping something would push it into the open: income projections, the business plan, the school mission statement—nope. She opened the next folder labeled support staff. The first file was special education, then social work, guidance, and then it hit her. None of the data explained what she had seen happen to Dominique and how that girl, that textbook picture of an emotional train wreck morphing into a meltdown, had been transformed, even temporarily, into a functional human being. It wasn't the curriculum or the money or the shine and gloss of a new program; it was, she realized, simply the human touch, people, professionals that helped these damaged kids adjust to school, to life, to social norms.

Somehow, Sandra realized, as she strode along with her hands in her pockets and her cigarette hanging out of the corner of her mouth, she had never really thought through—not completely—the implications of the takeover project: she knew what it would mean from EduNet's end, sure, of course. Once the contract went through the school board, when Custer had been acquired by EduNet, the entire takeover team was set to get huge bonuses. She and Mitchell would be getting the lion's share of the credit and the money and her reputation would be made; she'd be able to go to just about any company she wanted. It was everything she'd been working for the past fifteen years.

But she hadn't thought too much about what it might mean for everybody else. She'd bought into Mitchell's "no-go zone" as a way to dismiss any—as he put it—bleeding-heart liberal ideals or bullshit sentimentality, but now, now that she had been there on-site and seen it all up close and personal, it was different. How would a girl like Dominique do in an EduNet program? What, she thought, taking another puff, would've happened to Jimmy without his special education program at Central, without Mrs. Conway? Would he be in an institution now? And what would happen to the good teachers like Mrs. Conway or Mr. Reynolds or Mr. Bell, the ones who provided that human touch? How long would they have or would they eventually be forced out of their jobs by EduNet?

Sandra kept walking in the same direction, not ready to go home yet. She turned left on Bradford, heading for the lake again. It was close, only about seven or eight blocks. It's too far gone, she thought. The machinery is moving. Even if she wanted to, there would be no way to stop the take-over from happening. There were a lot of people who wanted to see this thing done—powerful people. People who would be making money, a lot of money, herself included.

She stopped to light another cigarette. It was funny. She'd been look-ing forward to closing this deal for over a year. All the years she'd spent growing up in the tiny little cracker-box ranch house, she'd dreamed of having a home with an upstairs, imagining what it must be like to run downstairs on Christmas morning instead of barreling down a narrow hall being body-checked by four brothers, imagining being able to get a brand-new car instead of a new used car, imagining eating something else besides tuna casseroles and day-old bread and having stinky egg salad sandwiches for lunch. Imagining herself as sophisticated, elegant, and ed-ucated, like Mrs. Peel on *The Avengers*.

Sandra stopped. The lake, a vast plain of darkness, an oblivion that encompassed sea and sky, stretched out before her. She threw away her cigarette. I've already done most of those things, she thought. I'm smart, educated, sophisticated, sort of elegant, and even a little dangerous. I earn good money. I don't have to do this—I don't have to go along with the takeover. She stared out at the solid wall of blackness, a darkness bor-dered only by the feeble harbor lights. But she did; she knew she did. If she bailed on Mitchell now, at this point in the process, she'd be finished. No more six figure income, no more company perks, and she'd probably have to move into a tiny studio somewhere in the suburbs, and probably with Jimmy. Or, she thought, smiling to herself, he might actually have to move in with Matt on his precious sailboat. That would be rich.

She crossed her arms and gazed at the lake. All her life she had been the middle child, the girl, the one who had to stay home and watch Jim-my or help Mom and be the responsible one. Before he left them, she had to help her mother clean up her father when he'd been out drinking and came home sick. Even when she was in her teens and being asked out for dates, she'd get stuck with the extra chores or sitting with Mom at home.

She had her sights set on moving to Madison long before her gradu-ation date. She knew she would never ever let herself be caught at home holding the bag like her mom; no, she was going to make good and god-damned sure that she wouldn't have to depend on anyone for anything.

Or that anyone would be depending on her. And she'd done it, graduating with honors, getting good jobs, working her way up until she was at the pinnacle, so close she could touch it.

Her cellphone rang suddenly, almost startling her. She glanced at its face. 11:36.

"Hello?" she said.

Nothing, although she thought she could sense someone there.

"Hello?" she said again.

Someone cleared his throat.

"Miss Feeley?" a man's voice said. It was a deep but flat voice.

"Yes," she said. "Who's this?"

"You don't know me. I work for a company you're very familiar with and I am also quite intimate with a good friend of yours. Mitchell Paige."

"Okay," she said, noting the strange way he phrased the statement and his diction. "What is it you want? It's late."

"I would like to meet with you tomorrow concerning the Custer Project. Mitchell got in touch with us and it seems as if we've run into some small problems."

"What sort of problems?" she asked, racking her brain as to who this could be. Not anyone on the board; she would have recognized their voices. "Who are you?"

"That's something we should get into tomorrow, I think," he said. "Would you be able to meet me at seven-thirty at Eddy's Café on Water Street?"

"How will I know you?" she said.

"I'll call you when you arrive there and describe myself," he said, and before she could reply, he had hung up.

She put her phone away and turned toward home. That was odd, an odd call and an odd conversation. A little bit too cloak and dagger for her. Even, she thought, smiling to herself, for Mrs. Peel. Well, maybe she should call Mitchell.

Sandra dialed his number and started walking home. It rang and rang until his voice-mail came on. She frowned and tried his other number, his private cell. Still nothing. Odd, she thought, walking more quickly. Very odd.

Chapter 18

Joe Sykes considered himself a patient man. He knew how to wait, how to pass the monotonous hours of a stakeout. He'd been here since four; they had no idea where Scott Brown was now working, so Joe had ended up sitting in his car since before dawn, waiting. No need to take chances. The sky was gray now and the birds that were left, the ones that hadn't migrated, had started to sing. Sparrows, perhaps, or some of the hardier robins, the ones that stuck around. Cardinals. Sunrise wouldn't be far off. He glanced at his watch: five-thirty four. He glanced at Brown's house: yes, there was a light on. Their man was an early riser. And his dossier said that Brown lived alone, so—unless the old man got lucky last night, that had to be him.

Joe fidgeted in his seat and rubbed his hands together. It was cold in the car; he didn't like to run it during a stakeout; it looked suspicious and it made you lazy. He thought about the mark: Scott Brown, an early riser and a stubborn man, and, apparently, a man of principles. A bad combination when it came to persuasion. Usually in these situations a simple talk would do the trick, but sometimes more extreme measures might be necessary. Well, if that did turn out to be the case, Sykes, as always, was prepared. For instance, Mr. Brown's daughter Lilly was going to college at St. Louis University. She lived in Marguerite Hall, Room 325, and was majoring in English Literature. Her best friend was named Rachel and she was going out with a boy named Peter Haskell—and he bet even Dad didn't know that.

Brown also had a sister living in Aurora, Illinois and another one in Rochester, Minnesota. Sykes had memorized their addresses and even their pets' names. Such details could be very useful, very persuasive. He also had Lilly's picture. She had a nice look: pretty but not overly aware of it. He liked that lack of self-consciousness. It was very sweet. Sykes hoped it would not be necessary to steal her innocence, to make her world a darker and more fearful place.

Darker, he thought to himself, as it was beneath the waters of the lake. Silent and black. It was cold down there, too, frigid, much colder than a November morning. Many things were hidden under the surface; some were things he had concealed himself, concealed most carefully. He sometimes liked to imagine he was there again, floating between the decks of a ghost ship, an underwater tomb, oblivious to the outside world, living but not, dreamlike but not. No, he thought, closing his eyes. That wasn't right. Not like a dream. No.

He saw another light go on upstairs. Out of the bathroom and into the bedroom to get dressed. Probably another half-hour or so. Sykes leaned back in the seat and glanced up at the photo he had attached to his dashboard. Adrian Cole. The picture had been taken the year before. Adrian hadn't known Sykes had taken the picture. Joe knew he wouldn't have liked it. It was a candid moment; Cole had been leaning back in his chair and listening to a client when Sykes had snapped the photo; he had caught him in the perfect moment, the perfect Adrian Cole moment: he looked engaged and detached at the same time, yet there was that coiled presence there, that ever-present sense of menace, power.

Sykes reached out and touched the photo lightly. The man radiated power; through all his years as a detective, on the force and off, Sykes had seen many facets, many reflections of power. The punks who threw out their cheap bluster, the professional gangsters who used it through their lawyers, and the real thing: the criminals—and a few cops—who could stop a room when they walked into it. But none of them compared to Adrian Cole. Old King Cole.

And together they could get anyone to say anything. Anyone, Joe thought, who wanted testimony, a confession, or, as in this case, a specialized type of agreement or cooperation, would use Cole. And Cole, thought Sykes, smiling to himself, uses me. Not just because I'm good or quiet or efficient or that I know exactly when to stop. No. It's mostly because we're perfectly matched—we have perfectly complementary abilities and demeanors. Adrian is cool, sophisticated, urbane. Very, Sykes thought, looking for the right word: European. Very civilized. Whereas, he, Joe, was completely American in his approach. Violent—when necessary. Intimidating—when necessary, and extreme—only when extremely necessary. They had it down to an art. Cole was the front man, the boss.

He, Sykes, was the helper, the lieutenant, the man behind the man. It was the perfect blend of European sophistication and American practicality.

The front door opened suddenly and Scott Brown walked out with a valise in hand. Sykes started the car. Brown was wearing a suit with an overcoat but no hat. He locked the front door and began walking to his car. As he got in, his back to the road, Sykes edged his car forward so that it blocked Brown's driveway. He started backing out, looking both ways, but then saw Sykes' car blocking his and stomped on the brakes. Sykes looked at him closely as Brown turned around to stare at him. At this point, some marks would beep the horn, others would start swearing and flip him off and others would do what everyone ended up doing: getting out of the car to speak to him and to tell him to get the hell out of the way.

Brown, he thought, might be stubborn, but he looked like a talker. He'll be out in a second. Sure enough, Brown opened the door, looked at him a moment, and then came around to the driver's side of Sykes' car.

"Excuse me," he said. "You seem to be blocking my way."

"Is that so?" asked Sykes, smiling. He knew it was a nasty one because he'd been working on it since his years in the force: just the right combination of contempt and malice, just enough to get their blood running cold.

"Yes, I'm afraid it is," said Brown, his voice stern. The smile hadn't worked. Sykes nodded to himself. This was going to be a tough one. He started to get out of the car. Brown took a step back. Sykes stood, stretching himself, and looked at the other man.

"Well, Mr. Brown, you see the truth of the matter is that we need to have a talk."

"How do you know my name?" the man asked, his voice sharp, his eyes aware.

"Let's say," said Sykes, "that we have a mutual friend."

"Where are you from? What do you want from me?"

"Well, I was sent to," said Sykes, leaning on his car, "let's say, try to persuade you to come around to our mutual friend's way of thinking."

Brown frowned, the lines between his eyebrows furrowing. Don't hurt yourself, thought Sykes.

"Were you sent by EduNet? By that Paige brat?"

Sykes nodded to himself. He was almost starting to like this guy. He cleared his throat. "Well, technically, no, but we do have common concerns. All three of us, I mean."

"So what do you want exactly?" asked Brown. "I don't have time for any of this nonsense. I have to get to work now."

"I'm afraid you're going to have to call in sick today, Mr. Brown," said Sykes, his own voice sharpened now. "Our business cannot wait."

"That's impossible," said Brown, turning away. "I need to get to work. I'm substitute teaching today."

"Mr. Brown," said Sykes in a tone that made the other man stop. "Scott," he said more gently, more quietly. "I think you need to take a look at this."

Sykes took out the picture of Lilly Brown and handed it to him. Brown looked at the picture and then back up to Sykes.

"This is my daughter Lilly," he said.

Sykes nodded.

"I don't understand."

"She lives in Marguerite Hall at the University of St Louis. She's taking a course on Chaucer this semester as well as a Shakespeare forum, a creative non-fiction course, and, let me think, oh yes, another course on the Modernists."

"How do you know all that?" Brown asked, his voice light, almost feathery. This was Sykes' favorite part. It was beginning to dawn on Brown, and then Sykes saw it—he saw the understanding cross the man's face. He was a smart guy. Sykes waited in anticipation for the flash of terror that inevitably followed the understanding. It always did when he had to use the kids. He saw the expression changing, and oh. There it was. Suddenly comprehended but very quickly hidden. He was a smart one.

"You bastards," he said, his voice still low but no longer feathery. "You leave her alone."

Sykes shrugged. "It shouldn't be necessary to bother her, Mr. Brown. Once we reach an understanding."

"All right," said Brown, his eyes wide, the pupils dilated. "All right." Sykes motioned for him to get into the car on the driver's side.

"You drive," he said. "I'll tell you where to go and how to get there." He got in and Sykes got in on the passenger side. Sykes motioned him to go. Brown pulled out into traffic driving south.

"All right," said Sykes, "take this to Water Street and go straight downtown all the way to Jackson. You got that?"

Brown nodded without looking toward him. Sykes leaned back in the passenger seat and closed his eyes. It must be difficult having children, he thought, having to worry and protect them from the minute they were born to—he glanced over at Brown hunched over the wheel, his face frozen into an angry mask—to always, he guessed. This guy's kid was an adult he had already sent out into the world and here he was, ready to throw away all his principles in one red hot second in order to save her from he didn't know what. Yes, he thought, opening his eyes to the gray morning, watching as the first snowflakes of winter started to come down, people are inherently weak, susceptible to fear. Most of the time their fears were exaggerated, blown up beyond all recognition. Sykes knew that; this was one of his best tools. Show a guy a picture of his kid, especially a daughter, under circumstances like these, and he imagines the absolute worst.

"So," he said, looking straight at Brown and in the most conversational tone he could muster, "what is your daughter majoring in?"

Chapter 19

Mitchell raised his head and tried to focus, but there was nothing to focus on. All he could see was gray, as if he were inside a cloud. He blinked, every movement of his eyes accenting the throbbing in his head. Gray, yes, but gray with a little variance, a few lighter patches. He hadn't gone blind. He turned his head slowly, his brain clinking and poking at him like a piece of broken glass. He saw the top of a piece of furniture, light brown, leather, nice workmanship. His. That was his couch. He was home. He was lying on his back in the living room. The gray was the sky outside his window; somehow, he'd landed with his head tilted toward the outside view. He looked, moving his head slowly and deliberately, toward the other side of the room. A shattered tumbler. The broken glass was everywhere. He slowly rolled to his stomach and pushed up to hands and knees. The glass was broken, and there was a scuffmark on one of his windows. Other than that, there didn't seem to be much damage. He sat up and took a deep breath and noticed he was naked. His clothes lay in a heap nearby.

What the fuck had happened? He glanced around. His eyes landed on the empty bottle of Lagavulin, lying on its side, a puddle on the carpet at its mouth. And it all came back to him. Cole. Sykes. The kiss.

And then? He remembered them leaving and then, then what? He remembered his anger, his blind, blind raging. He remembered Cole, his face, the dank green of his eyes, his presence, his glow, how it had surrounded, flooded, drowned him. He remembered how he had fallen into the flower of his mouth, how the taste of his lips stayed on his, how he couldn't stop, how it all combined to sweep him up and away to—God, what had he done? Cole. His face, his taste, and then, then the touching, the flailing, the clothes coming off, and then; Mitchell closed his eyes, remembering: the most intense sexual experience he'd ever had. Ever.

Mitchell pushed down on that realization as soon as it surfaced, trying to drown it like a sack of unwanted kittens. But it kept coming back up, clawing and mewling at him. He pushed down harder, more furiously until it stopped. It was quiet for now, but he knew it would be back. He'd seen it first in middle school, during gym class in the boys' locker room, and then, subsequently, in nearly every locker room he'd ever been in. So he had avoided gyms and worked out on his own. He'd told himself it was in order to concentrate on his workouts, to save time.

Then, later, in college, a friend of his roommate, Larry Little, had gone midnight skinny-dipping with them in Lake Williams after an all-night drinking session. The way Larry had looked at Mitchell confused him; he liked the boy's smile, his mouth, but these feelings were immediately tamped down by a surge of anger so intense he nearly went after the boy. Instead, he stood up, glaring at Larry, and then flung himself off the pier, narrowly missing the breakwater.

He heard his friends laughing and cheering as he surfaced, the rage still hot inside him. The boy was looking at him sadly. Mitchell flung himself away and started swimming like a maniac.

"Hey, Mitchell, take it easy."

"Hey, dude, come back, don't go too far out."

He swam and swam, numbing the rage and pushing down the desire until he felt in control again. He came back as his friends were preparing to go out in a boat to look for him. They looked down at him, concerned, maybe a little scared. Mitchell scanned the faces. Larry Little had gone. And the worst of it was that something in him was disappointed. Mitchell had gone home that morning and vomited and vomited and vomited until there was nothing left. He'd gone beyond the dry heaves, beyond alcohol—it was disgusting, execrable, and he was still making himself ill with it; every time he looked in the mirror that morning and saw those high cheekbones and that small pretty mouth, he saw what he never allowed himself to see—or to comprehend—that he was pretty. That he was a girl—should have been a girl. Should be a girl. Whenever that glimmer of knowledge rose in him, he would eject it, puke it out, get it out of his system—as literally as he could. But it was there. With every physical spasm, his conscious being would bury it again and then wait to hit it over the head if it ever tried to rise up from the dead. And it had worked. Until now.

Mitchell rose to his feet, shakily, and looked around the room. His head was still pounding, but not nearly as badly as before. He gathered up his clothes, wiped up the mess, rushed into his bedroom and flung them into the hamper. The maid was coming today, and she'd send them out and the cleaners would take care of all the rest. Evidence erased. He walked into the kitchen, searched under the sink until he found the whiskbroom and dustpan; he cleaned up the glass and looked around again. The scuff on the window where he'd thrown the glass. That needed to be fixed, too. He went into the kitchen again, found the Windex and paper towels and started working on the scuff. Three, four times he rubbed at it, but nothing. He would tell the landlord that the cleaning lady was responsible.

Was it Wednesday or Thursday? What time was it? He glanced at his watch. Eight-thirty. Shit. He was late. He'd shower and call Sandra and tell her some cock and bull story about car trouble. He felt a sudden yearning for her—well, not her—but her support, her companionship. No, her, he told himself. Her body. He wanted her tits, her ass, and her sweet snatch.

He hurried across the living room toward the shower when he felt a sharp pain in his foot. He hopped over to the couch and pulled up his leg to look at it. There was a jagged piece of glass sticking out of the sole, near the arch. It was already bleeding like crazy. He looked around, but there was nothing to wrap it in. Holding his foot up and covering it with both hands, he rose and started hopping to the bathroom, hoping the blood would stay on him and off the carpet. He reached the bathroom, put his foot down and looked back. Droplets of blood, tiny rubies glistening on his beautiful carpet, looked up at him, reminding him about what lived, about what could not be extinguished, about what would be lying inside him, curled up like a kitten, forever.

Chapter 20

The basement of the Riverwest Providence Baptist Church was starting to fill up. Millicent glanced up at the wall clock: ten minutes to nine. She made her way over to the refreshment table and poured herself a cup of coffee, picked up a vanilla glazed doughnut, and found a seat close to the stage. It wasn't that she wanted to be noticed or even to be heard; at her age, she just didn't hear as well as she used to, and she didn't want to miss anything. She settled herself in the rickety folding chair and glanced around the room. There were a few regulars here she recognized from Sundays, but for the most part the people here were strangers to her.

Serena was the one who called her about this meeting to coordinate their "resistance efforts". That was how Serena put it. She also told Millicent she'd be there, but that she'd be a little late. Millicent smiled to herself: as if that was anything new. Serena would probably be late for her own funeral.

Millicent saw Representative Fox standing up near the podium, chatting with a young man she thought she recognized. She saw a Catholic priest who didn't look quite comfortable; he was awkward. She thought he might be one of those African imports the Catholics so often brought into their parishes these days. And there was Brother Malcolm from the AME Church on Center Street: now he was a fine man; he'd marched with Father Groppi during the civil rights protests of the sixties and gone to Selma. He'd even shaken hands with Dr. King.

A young black girl dressed in a business suit stood up near the front podium, on the other side of Representative Fox—who kept glancing at her—clutching a leather binder tight. She glanced nervously around her. That is one uncomfortable young woman, thought Millicent. She looks like she's never been in a church basement a day in her life. I doubt if she's ever been west of Holton Street. Young, educated, and probably thinks she knows everything.

The girl happened to look over at that moment and made eye contact with her. She smiled, nodded, waved a little bit, and then starting walking over. Millicent settled herself in the rickety church chair and put on a big charitable smile.

"Hello," said the young woman. "I'm pleased to meet you." Millicent noticed she spoke very well; she was right, this girl obviously had an education.

"Hello," she said. "My name is Millicent Maxwell."

"I'm Celeste Hightower. I work in the mayor's office as a community liaison; he wanted me to come here today to find what the feeling about this situation is in the urban community."

Urban community, thought Millicent. You mean the inner city, the black community, the ghetto, and the hood. She had never liked that last term: too many negative implications. Hoods. In her time, that used to mean thugs, criminals.

"So the mayor is worried about this, too?" asked Millicent.

"It is worrisome," repeated Celeste—evading the question about where the mayor stood—and shrugged, "but it's also a very complicated issue."

"How do you mean?" asked Millicent, taking a sip from her coffee.

Celeste sat down on the chair next to her and folded her hands over her leather portfolio. If this girl tried to, thought Millicent, she couldn't look any more like a snotty little know-it-all getting ready to explain the world to a feeble-minded old lady.

"I think the first thing to understand," said Celeste, "is that over a period of years our city schools have not been doing the best of jobs." She leaned back in her chair and looked sideways, as if she were trying to think of the best way to say something difficult. "Graduation rates are low, poverty levels in the urban community have not improved, and crime is on the rise."

Millicent looked at her closely and said, "And all this is the fault of our city schools?"

Celeste smiled condescendingly and said, "No, of course not. In fact—"

"I went to public school my entire life," said Millicent quickly. She usually didn't interrupt people, but this girl was rubbing her the wrong way in three different directions. "I was taught by some of the same teachers still working at Custer today. They taught me my math, history, and English. I can read and write, and, best of all, I can think."

This girl—this Hightower—looked a little surprised that an old lady could speak to all of her double talk and ten dollar words. Well, thought Millicent, as bad as I am, when Serena gets here, this little girl will be more than a little surprised.

"I should make it clear to you that at this point Mayor Ledanski has not taken any kind of position on this situation. I'm here," she said, with her little Barbie doll smile, "to simply take the pulse of our community."

Our community indeed, thought Millicent. You've never been part of this community. In fact, this girl had probably been born with a silver spoon in each hand.

"Well, Ms. Hightower," said Millicent, "I think you can see where I, as one simple old publicly educated woman, stand. I do not want privateers coming in and taking over our schools. I pay my taxes for city teachers and principals to run the public schools, not to pay some corporation to try their hands at teaching. Teachers are professionals. And EduNet wants to replace them with who?"

Millicent glanced around her and noticed a few heads had turned their way; she hadn't meant to raise her voice, but she had gotten carried away with this little snippet.

"I'll be sure to relay your point-of-view to the mayor," said the girl, standing up. "Your opinion is very important to him. But please remember, that above all, Mayor Ledanski wants to make sure that every child in this city gets the best education possible."

"The mayor. He's never been for the public schools. I heard tell that EduNet has been lobbying him big time and helping him out with campaign contributions. Is that so?"

The girl swallowed and then began speaking quickly. "Every one of the mayor's campaign contributions has been documented and verified. He is not beholden to EduNet or anyone else in this situation."

Millicent nodded and turned away. That girl was lying. She'd raised enough of her own children to know when someone was not telling the truth. She saw the little know-it-all leaving out of the corner of her eye.

Millicent took a deep breath and looked down at her hands; they were trembling. Well, she thought, that certainly hadn't been a very Christian way to act. That poor girl was just trying to do her job; it was just that uppity attitude of hers. Millicent caught herself. Why, she thought, why in the name of the Lord would I use that term to describe this girl? Why would I use a term like that, a term I heard about myself back in the day? I shouldn't judge her for just being educated and articulate. She glanced up; the girl—Celeste, her name is Celeste—was standing and talking to Alvin Fox. She is only what she is: a politician.

She glanced up at the clock. Three minutes to nine. It looked as if they might actually start on time; people were finding seats and Alvin Fox kept drifting closer and closer to the podium. Millicent put her hat and gloves down on the seat next to her. Serena was running late: true to form. She noticed that Celeste Hightower had taken a seat directly across from the podium.

Mr. Fox finally reached the podium and tapped the microphone. It screeched a little bit and he leaned into it.

"Sorry," he said. "I think we're about ready to get started. Could we all please find our seats?"

People started sitting down. Millicent craned her head behind her and counted about twenty-some people. It seemed low, but these were the community leaders and men of the cloth who were going to spread the word about EduNet to their own flocks. The door opened suddenly and Serena bustled in. Millicent waved and pointed to the empty seat next to her. Serena nodded and started slowly making her way down the aisle. That woman does have to say hello to everyone she meets, doesn't she? thought Millicent.

"I'm sorry I'm late," she said, huffing and puffing as she settled herself into the chair.

"You're always late," whispered Millicent.

"That is not so. You need to stop spreading these lies about me, young lady."

"Speaking of lies," said Millicent. She pointed with her chin toward the Hightower girl.

"What do you mean?" asked Serena. "Who is that person? She's not much more than a child."

"Her name is Celeste Hightower and she says that she is from the mayor's office. She was just telling me that the mayor has not decided where he stands on this issue."

Serena leaned back in exaggerated surprise.

"No. Just what did she say?"

"Just that. And that the mayor finds this whole process worrisome. I swear, Serena, she must have used that word five times."

"I wonder why she is here," mused Serena.

"I think she's a spy," said Millicent, "and that she is going to go right back and tell our good mister mayor exactly what we have in mind."

"Millicent, I don't believe I've seen you this worked up in a long time. You clearly do not like this person."

"I try to be a good Christian, Serena, but that girl just rubbed me the wrong way."

Mr. Fox was tapping the microphone again. Predictably, it screeched.

"Good morning, everyone. Let's get started, shall we?"

The room slowly grew quieter.

"Thank you. First of all, I would like to take a moment to introduce all of our esteemed colleagues. I am Assemblyman Fox of our very own sixth district. We also have Father Bartholomew from the St. Matthias Church. Please stand up, Father, and let everyone have a good look at you."

The father stood up. He was young, slender, and very dark-complected. I bet he is African, thought Millicent.

"Brother Malcolm Beamon from the AME Church." Brother Malcolm stood to another smattering of applause. His hair had turned almost completely white; Millicent hadn't realized how old he'd become. He'd been famous in his day, and people still talked about everything he'd done during the struggle.

"And next," continued Fox, "our host, Reverend Lee, from Riverwest Providential." The reverend stood up and waved. He was a big man with a radiant smile who usually carried his weight well, but now, mused Millicent, just lately, it appeared as if his weight had begun carrying him.

"I think," continued Fox, "that between these esteemed gentlemen, we have most of the district's main denominations represented. And," he added, "with this much spiritual clout in the room, how can we fail?"

A general laugh, then a small round of applause followed.

"Moving on," continued Fox, "we have our Alderman, Patricia Samson."

She stood, a middle-aged black lady, hair done up nicely and smartly dressed in a sky blue business suit, and said, "Alderperson."

"You're right," said Fox, smiling. "Alderperson Samson."

"We also have Celeste Hightower who is appearing here as a representative of Mayor Ledanski's office."

The princess stood and waved. Just like the Thanksgiving Day Parade, thought Millicent. There was a little muttering in the back of the room. They're thinking what I was thinking, thought Millicent. They're wondering why she's here.

"We also have the director of our local Boys and Girls Club Program, Mr. Ulysses Ewell." He stood up and nodded to the crowd. He was tall, definitely over six feet, and thin, athletic thin—trim was the word—and also had a very nice smile, though it didn't glow quite as much as Reverend Lee's. Nothing did. That is a nice-looking man, thought Millicent. I'm glad I came today.

"Jerome Johnson from the local chapter of the Guardians."

He stood and surveyed the crowd without smiling, hands clasped in front of him. He was a young man, no more than thirty, short, dressed in an army jacket over a t-shirt, and wearing a light blue beret over those snaky braids the kids liked so much these days. He had a light complexion and looked like he had an attitude.

"And, finally, we have Serena McDaniels, whom most of you know as a former educator and administrator in our school district." Serena stood and waved to the now predictable smattering of applause.

"We are all here because we have shown a commitment to fighting for our community and our schools against this unprecedented threat," said Fox. "And the reason we're here is to mobilize our communities from the pulpit, from our schools, and from our boardrooms. First of all, I'd like to present a man we all know and respect, Brother Malcolm Beamon, to explain how the churches will be mobilizing their congregations to help us fight this threat."

Brother Malcolm rose and walked stiffly to the podium. He looked skinnier than when Millicent had last seen him. Almost frail, she thought.

How old is he? She did a little quick math in her head. If he'd been thirty during the movement, he'd be in his seventies now.

"Hello, everyone," he said, his voice still rich, full, and vibrant. That part of him had not aged. "It's good to see everyone here, prepared to fight the good fight to keep our community free from this invasion of corporate greed."

He coughed softly, a rasp that sounded like the tearing of butcher paper.

"I've been conferring with our other members of the clergy here, and we've decided upon several strategies to rouse up our community and to present our case to the school board. The first, and most obvious, is to spread the word during our sermons and to all of our other church groups."

"Secondly," he continued, grasping the sides of the podium, not for emphasis, but for support, "we will be urging selected members of our congregations to come to the school board meeting and to speak for our common cause. So we are lining up those speakers who will state the case forcefully, aggressively, with pathos, emotion, and with logic. We need to avoid repetition, confrontations, and invective during this meeting."

"Why?"

Millicent turned her head. The little man, that Guardian with the blue beret, was standing up and glaring at Brother Malcolm.

"Why what, Mr. Johnson?" asked Brother Malcolm.

"Why do you say we need to avoid confrontation with the school board? Isn't this is what this is all about?"

"Well, Jerome," said Malcolm, taking off his glasses and wiping them off. "Too many times meetings like this degenerate into our community members simply voicing their anger. It makes us seem disorganized, unprepared, and childish."

"And ghetto," said Johnson, crossing his arms. "Is that what you mean to say? Is that what you're afraid of?"

"What I'm saying," said Brother Malcolm, "is that this is our chance to convince the school board to close the door on EduNet, and on all the private charter groups trying to come into our neighborhoods. If everyone only vents their frustrations, all they come away with is the impression that we're an angry community. They might think we have nothing but our anger, that that is the definition of who we are."

"We do have a lot of anger, frustration, and aggravation," retorted Johnson, "and we need to let them know how much we're hurting."

"We will have more than enough of those types of testimonials to make them realize that."

"I think you're afraid of us being too black up there," said Johnson, stabbing his finger toward Brother Malcolm. "I think you want to cut down the number of loud stomping ghetto bitches"—a gasp went up in the room—"going up to the microphone and screaming their heads off. I think you want to turn this into a white man's game using the white man's words."

Fox had risen. "Mr. Johnson, I must ask you to sit down. This is not the time or place for you to vent your own rage. We are all here for the same reason; we are trying to stop the takeover from happening. That's our common goal. We need to think through our strategy, to plan it carefully, and to execute it flawlessly. Then we might have a chance."

Johnson stood and put on his jacket. He shook his head and laughed. "You're playing the white man's game, all of you, and the sad thing is I don't even think you know it."

"Out of curiosity, Mr. Johnson," said Brother Malcolm, still at the podium. "What should we do that would convince the school board to stop the EduNet takeover?"

"I think," said Johnson, placing his hands on the back of the chair in front of him and leaning forward, "I think we need to take to the streets. I think we need to have demonstrations, rallies, even do civil disobedience. You know, get people to lie in the road and stop traffic and shit."

"That," said Brother Malcolm, nodding, "can be effective for getting attention, but in the past, violence has proved to be far less effective than negotiating."

Johnson laughed. "You niggers are crazy," he said.

Millicent saw Malcolm stiffen, and she felt her own anger rising. Why did these young people have to use that word? Even now, decades later, whenever she heard it spoken, she still felt the pain and humiliation of having it thrown at her like a brick or whispered behind her back like the hiss of a snake, and the shadow of it clinging to her like a stranger following her home at night.

"Mr. Johnson, " said Brother Malcolm, "I must ask you not to use that word in my presence. I—"

"That," retorted Johnson, "is a prime example of how out of touch you are with today's black culture. That word does not mean what it used to mean. It's not a bad word anymore."

"Really, Jerome Johnson. Really?"

Millicent glanced over. Serena had risen from her seat and was glaring at Johnson. "If that is the case, Mr. Johnson, if this word no longer has the negative connotations as you suggest, would you like to tell us how you might react if a white man came up to you and said 'hey nigger'? What would you do? Would you say, hey dude, what's happening and exchange a high-five with him? Would you?"

"That's different—" Johnson began.

"Don't you interrupt me, young man," Serena said curtly. "I am not nearly finished with you yet."

"I'll tell you what you would do," she continued. "You'd get up all in his face and state you don't have to put up with this kind of racism and abuse and discrimination. You might very well strike this man. I could see that. I could easily see that."

She paused a beat, glaring at him.

"Now I know you and your group do a lot of good in the community. You do your tutoring groups and outreach programs and you have your food pantry, and all of that is excellent work, powerful work. You are an asset to this community. But I'll tell you this, young man, don't you ever use that word in front of me again, or I'll be up in your face. Do you understand that?"

Johnson stood with folded arms, glaring right back at her.

"You say," Serena continued, "that this word has no negative aspects when your generation uses it with each other, but then you turn around and say that if any white person would use the very same word toward you that you would retaliate. Why does your generation have this schizophrenic outlook when it comes to this word?"

She paused.

"The word is demeaning and insulting when a white person uses it toward a black. We can all agree on that, I think. Right?"

Johnson just glared.

"It is just as insulting when one young black man uses it to demean another, but they just don't see that. They don't understand that when they use that word they are exposing their own self-loathing and low self-esteem. Your generation jokingly refers to each other this way, and I guess you think it's cool, but when you use that word—in any context— you become the very same thing that the white man who calls you that is saying. It's not in your control. When you a call a friend that word, you become the white man's version of that word. Words are powerful. It's that simple."

She nodded emphatically and then sat down. Millicent reached over and squeezed her leg. "Thank you," she whispered.

Johnson stood, arms still folded, shaking his head.

"All right," he said. "I'm not going to argue with you, Ms. McDaniels; I have too much respect for you."

He turned to Brother Malcolm at the podium.

"Brother Malcolm, you, and, I'm assuming your colleagues, want to make this a civilized kind of presentation to prove that we are a reasonable community. That's the way you think we'll be heard. Fine. But I think you're wrong. Our community has always been looked at as inferior, criminal, and amoral. We can throw all the logic and coherence and courtesy we want at them, but they will never stop believing we're less than them."

He paused and glanced around the room. Millicent saw a couple other people nodding.

"The only way," Johnson continued, "that we get listened to and looked at as any kind of group that matters is when we put up a powerful presence. Now Malcolm X—yeah," he said, nodding at Brother Malcolm, "that Malcolm said 'by any means necessary', that the black man needs to defend himself, his loved ones, and his community however he needs to. That is my belief, and that," he said, picking up his backpack, "is what I will be telling my people to do. You might be the voice of reason here, Brother Malcolm, but I will be the voice of change."

Johnson turned and stalked out of the room. Brother Malcolm watched him go silently.

Reverend Lee stood up. "I also would agree with Brother Malcolm. We need to be rational and coherent, but I also do believe that Jerome also has a point. We need a strong and vocal presence; we cannot look weak. However, I do think that this strength can be shown with numbers, not with disobedience, and that, perhaps, a bit of demonstration might not be a bad thing for our cause. But, for now, for today, I agree with Brother Malcolm. Let's line up our speakers and our arguments to make the strongest impact."

A murmur of agreement rose from the crowd. Reverend Lee sat down. Brother Malcolm nodded toward him.

"I would now," said Brother Malcolm, "like to ask our representatives from the political arena to speak. First of all—"

The meeting went for some time; the alderperson spoke, saying that she would ensure that there would be a strong police presence and that security in the building would be tight. The director of the Boys and Girls' Club, Ulysses Ewell, also spoke, pledging to spread the word among his members and to bring a contingent to the meeting. He was a good speaker, his message simple but assured. Millicent could have listened to him all day.

Representative Fox then spoke at length—weary length—about his proposed bill to raise accountability standards for private charters and how community support would help get it through the Senate. Millicent wished she could take her shoes off; her bunions were starting to ache. He finished up by saying that even though Mr. Ricks and other members of the Custer staff could not be present, they would be rallying parents and students and bringing some of them to the rally as well. Serena stood up.

"I," she said, "will also be working with the Custer staff as well as the school administration in order to bring these students and their parents to this meeting. Theirs will be the most urgent and potent message."

She sat down. That, thought Millicent, has to be her world's record shortest speech. Maybe her feet hurt, too.

Finally Fox finished up and Celeste Hightower rose and went to the podium.

"I am here," she said, "as a representative from Mayor Ledanski's office. The mayor told me last night that he still had not made up his mind whether to throw his weight behind our public schools during this crisis or not."

She paused. Dead silence.

"To be frank," she continued, "he told me his faith in our public school system has been tested over the past few years. He wants to believe in public schools; like so many of you here, he went to public school. But the numbers are bad, people. You know that. That's why EduNet got its foot in the door."

She paused, looking around the room.

"And I," she continued, "was sent here today to observe and report, but I wanted to get up and tell you that I am going back to tell the mayor he needs to throw his support behind you and our public schools. The passion I have seen here tells me that this is a necessary battle, a battle that we need to win, and that with a passion like this, our public schools will get better. That's what I'm going to tell the mayor."

A few people applauded. A person would think you're running for office, honey, thought Millicent.

"All right, then," said Mr. Fox, "let's get things rolling. Brother Malcolm or I will be in touch with all of you. Thank you."

The meeting dispersed. Millicent rose slowly and turned to Serena.

"I guess the cat had your tongue, Serena. I don't know when I've heard you speak less."

"Hush up, Millicent," she said. "My sciatica hurts so bad I couldn't say anything more. I needed to move."

"Hello, Ms. McDaniels," said a voice from behind Millicent. She turned. It was Ulysses Ewell, the Boys' and Girls' Club director. She smiled.

"Hello, Ulysses," said Serena, hugging him. "It has been a long time, hasn't it?"

"A few years," he said. "I graduated back in, oh, nineteen eighty-five, I believe."

"Those years fly by, don't they?" said Serena.

"They do that," he said, glancing at Millicent.

"Excuse my manners," said Serena. "This is Millicent Maxwell, a very dear friend of mine."

He nodded and extended his hand. Millicent took it, smiling slightly. She looked sideways a bit and saw Serena giving her the eye, as if she knew what she was thinking.

"It's a pleasure," he said. "Any friend of Ms. McDaniels' is a friend of mine."

Millicent, as usual, found herself tongue-tied. She whispered a thank you and smiled again.

"So what do you think, Ulysses?" Serena asked. "What's this going to look like?"

"I don't know," he said. "It sounded good. I just don't know. I hate to be negative, but I've almost never seen none of these things pan out. People end up arguing, fighting; we decide to hold out on each other. We just never seem to be able to hold it together."

"Well," said Serena, "maybe with Brother Malcolm at the point, we'll be able to keep a solid front."

"If he can make it," said Ulysses, looking at her strangely. Millicent saw that Serena didn't catch it right away.

"What do you mean?" asked Millicent, "If he can make it?"

"Well, I thought you knew," he said. "I thought everyone knew. Brother Malcolm has pancreatic cancer."

Serena gasped and put her hand to her mouth. "Oh, my Lord, no," she said.

"Yeah," said Ulysses, "he's been sick a while, and it's bad. Terminal. He told me the other day he figures he might have six or seven Sundays left."

"We'll pray for him," said Millicent. "And we'll be in touch."

Ulysses nodded and left.

"Well," said Serena, once he was out of earshot, "there goes the coalition. Without Brother Malcolm holding it all together, we will be flying in seventeen different directions."

She leaned over to pick up her handbag and sighed.

"This is bad, honey," she said, turning to Millicent, who saw, shockingly, tears in Serena's eyes. She had never in her life known Serena to cry. She was too tough, too determined, too single-minded to cry.

"This is real bad."

Chapter 21

The bell to begin Dave's third hour World History rang. Some of the kids were still out of their seats, talking and messing around. Daquone was standing in back talking to Travion while Tiana and Laqueesha were sitting down but talking and giggling about something.

"All right, everyone, let take our seats and quiet down please," he intoned, striking the teacher tone—loud enough to carry, clipped enough to be taken seriously—automatically. Daquone and Travion both sat, continuing their conversation, while Laqueesha kept talking, even though Tiana was now trying to ignore her. Olive and Darrel had already started work on the DoNow, while Carlos was leaning back in his desk and staring out the window.

"Settle down," he said again, and the class finally quieted down. They were squirrelly today.

"Today's DoNow," he said, "is not about the Mayans or any of our other Middle-American civilizations. It is about us. It is about today. Who would like to read it out loud?"

Violet Adams raised her hand. Violet was, by leaps and bounds, Dave's finest student. She had first been his pupil as a freshman when she had come in fresh, eager, ready to learn and had been, arguably, one of the brightest kids he'd ever taught. She was a straight-A student her first year and was still on track to be class valedictorian.

"Yes, thank you, Violet," he said. "Whenever you're ready."

She peered up at the DoNow question.

"What," she said, "is it best way to change the world?" She smiled and chuckled.

"What is it, Violet?" asked Dave.

"Nothing, Mr. Bell. That's just a little big for a DoNow question, isn't it?"

"It is," he said, "but we're here to answer the big questions, aren't we?" She nodded, and then bent over her paper and started writing.

Dave glanced around the room. Most of the students were on task, although Daquone and Travion were still whispering.

"Daquone. Travion, let's get to work, please."

Carlos was still gazing out the window. Well, that wasn't terribly unusual. He was a nice kid, but not very focused. Dave walked over and gently tapped his desk. Carlos looked up, surprised. His eyes were bloodshot and he seemed tired.

"You with us today, Carlos?"

"Yeah, Mr. Bell," he said, and opened his notebook.

Dave thought about taking Carlos out to the hallway and having a one-on-one conversation with him, but that would probably embarrass him. He made a mental note to check with the school social worker about his situation—there had been some troubles at home before, and maybe he had something funky going on there again. It wasn't like Carlos to blow off assignments. He continued walking around the room. Travion was writing something down, while Daquone had scribbled down one or two sentences: just enough to get by, but nothing more. That was Daquone. Mr. Minimum.

Although things had been improving. Since Dave had started the lunchtime tutoring sessions between Darrel and Daquone, his grades had improved enough to keep him on the basketball team, and Darrel seemed more accepted by his classmates. Dave wasn't sure if Daquone was looking out for him—probably not—but the fact they were working together seemed to be helping Darrel's social status.

"Okay," he said, "that's enough time, I think. Who would like to answer today's DoNow? What can you do to change the world?"

He scanned the room. Tiana raised her hand.

"Yes, Tiana."

She looked around the room, making sure everyone was watching, and read, "The way I can improve the world is by being nice and good to everyone I meet and not be negative or say negative things. If I stop from negative actions, people will be nicer."

"Very good," said Dave. "You would set a better example. Good. Anyone else?"

Travion raised his hand. "Yes, Travion?"

"I wrote that if we can stop the violence in the streets, all the shooting and killing, then maybe we can make the world a better place."

"Good, Travion," said Dave, "although the question was what can you—you specifically—do to improve the world. What could you do as an individual to stop all the violence out there?"

Travion frowned and shook his head. "You know, Mr. Bell, there's so much people getting mad and fighting out there; it happens all the time. I don't know if I could do much of anything on my own without getting killed myself."

"What if someone you knew had a gun? Would you tell the police?"

The class muttered. Dave heard the word "snitch" repeated several times.

"Nah, Mr. Bell," said Travion, "I couldn't do that. I couldn't snitch on nobody."

"Not even to save a life?"

"Now, wait a minute, Bell," chipped in Daquone. "You just not getting it. You don't get what it's like where we're at. You can't talk to the police without getting yourself killed or worse. Snitching is unacceptable where we're at."

Several of the students were nodding.

"So," asked Dave, "what would you do, Daquone, if somebody was coming after you or someone in your family with a gun?"

Daquone shrugged. "You defend yourself."

"How?"

Daquone shrugged again. Dave looked around the room; nobody was making eye contact. Not even Darrel. He could pursue this line; in fact, he probably should, but it wouldn't go anywhere. And he had other fish to fry, anyway.

"Okay," he continued. "Who else? How can you, as an individual, change the world?"

Olive raised her hand. Dave nodded to her.

"We can work within the system," she said. "We can demonstrate, we can go to rallies, we can take to the streets like they did for Trayvon Martin and Dontre Hamilton and Eric Garner and Michael Brown, Jr. and Tamir Rice and Freddie Gray." She paused. "And all the rest."

"Who the hell are you talking about, girl?" asked Laqueesha. "Who are all those people? I know they ain't your boyfriends."

A couple students giggled. Olive turned in her chair and glared at Laqueesha.

"What, girl?" asked Laqueesha. "You got something to say to me?"

"Yeah," said Olive. "I do. I'll tell you who all those people were. Not are. Were. They were African-American citizens killed by the police for no reason. They were just black folks doing what they were doing and who got killed for nothing more than that."

Laqueesha shrugged.

"So," continued Olive, "you're telling me you don't even recognize the names Trayvon Martin or Dontre Hamilton?"

"I don't know any of those people," Laqueesha retorted. "And I don't want to."

"You couldn't, anyway," chipped in Violet. "They're dead. Murdered."

"That's their own fault," said Laqueesha. Olive shook her head.

"Girl," she said, "you better get your head off your smartphone and into the real world. We're getting picked off right and left by the police, shot for nothing, and you don't even know about it. Try watching the news"

"I got better things to do than watch the motherfucking news," said Laqueesha.

"I guess being ignorant takes up all your time," said Olive.

Laqueesha rose up out of her seat. "Don't you be calling me ignorant, bitch, or I—"

"That'll do," said Dave. "Sit down, Laqueesha." Somewhat surprisingly, she did. She usually wasn't very good at letting things go.

"I'd like to see both of you after class," said Dave. Olive looked up and nodded. Laqueesha put her head down on her folded arms, which was also very unlike her.

"All right," Dave continued. "What about Olive's point? Does going out and protesting do any good? Can that cause change?"

Darrel raised his hand. Dave nodded to him.

"Yes," he said. "Protests about Trayvon Martin and in Ferguson, Missouri caused change. Charges were brought against Zimmerman for shooting Trayvon."

"And motherfucker got off," someone muttered from the back of the room. Probably Daquone.

"Language, please," said Dave, an automatic response. "I understand this is a very controversial issue, but let's stay calm, let's keep our cool." Someone in the back of the class snickered.

"So," continued Dave, "if I'm understanding you, when a person demonstrates or protests, then that might help cause change?"

Most of the class nodded or murmured agreement.

"No."

Dave looked over. Carlos was leaning back in his seat with his arms held flat out on his desk. He glared at Dave and then shifted his gaze over the entire class.

"Nothing's going to change," he said. "Not for us. Never. It never has and it never will. We can go out there and protest and rally and lay down on the highway and shit, but that's not going to do any good at all, man. Nobody cares. Like what Olive was saying about Trayvon. He got shot by some white vigilante and the cops weren't going to do nothing. Then all the black folks and activists protested and got him arrested and put on trial and shit, but then he gets off. What's the point, man?"

"Well," said Olive, "the rallies and protests got him arrested at least. That's a start."

"So what, Olive?" said Carlos. "So what? The cops who killed Freddie Gray all got off. The cop who shot Dontre Hamilton lost his job, but he ain't going to jail. We ain't nothing, man. We don't matter. As long as we stay here in the hood and kill each other and don't fuck with the white population, then they're happy. That's where they want us to be. That's exactly where they want us to be."

The class was silent. Even Daquone. He was leaning back in his desk chair with his hand over his mouth.

"No." It was Violet, her voice rising. "We have to make it right. We can't stop fighting. Maybe you want to give up, Carlos, and say, yeah, we're nothing, but I ain't giving up."

"All right," said Dave. "Thank you, Violet. I think all of us should think about what she just said. We all have a choice; we can sit back and let things go on the way they have been and hope nothing happens to us, or we can work to make things better. We can protest, we can rally, but the one most important thing we can do is to vote."

"I can't vote yet," said Daquone. "I ain't old enough."

"Then tell your parents, your uncles and aunts, anyone who's old enough to vote. Make sure they're making their voice heard."

"Yeah, Daquone," said Travion. "Tell your mama." He leaned close to him. "Or I will."

"Shut up, Travion."

"All right," said Dave. "Travion, are you through?"

"Sorry, Mr. Bell."

"All right," said Dave. "That was a good discussion, a really good discussion, but we need to move on. Before we do," he said. "Does anyone have anything to add?" He glanced at Carlos, who had put his head down on his desk.

"Okay. Our lesson today," he began, "is going to be about the Bill of Rights, specifically the First Amendment. Today we're going to focus on freedom of assembly," he continued, going up to the Smart board, "which is one of our basic rights in this country." He brought up a copy from the First Amendment to the board. "It's guaranteed in our Bill of Rights. It guarantees that our voices can be heard." Well, he thought, here we go. "I don't know if any of you know about this," he said, sitting on the edge of his desk, "but someone is trying to take over your school."

"What?" asked Daquone. "What are you talking about?"

"There's a private company called EduNet that wants to take over Custer and turn it into a private charter school."

"They can have it," said Carlos.

"So what?" said Laqueesha with her head still down.

"What it means," said Dave, "is that most of your education would take place online and that you would no longer have regular teachers."

"Who'd be running the class?" asked Darrel.

"I'll do it," said Daquone, standing up. The class tittered in response. "Time for the next generation, Mr. Bell."

"Sit down, Daquone." He shrugged and sat.

"To answer your question, Darrel, this EduNet company would hire people who have never been trained as teachers. A lot of their applicants have never been in a classroom before."

"What if we had questions about the lessons?" asked Tiana.

Dave shrugged. "I don't know."

"What about grading?"

"What about our lunches? We still get lunch?"

"What about basketball? And football?"

"I don't know." He paused. "What we do know is that if we want to keep good teachers, fair grading, and all the other services you get here: the extra activities like team sports and drama and band, then we need to fight for our school." He glanced around the room; most of them were paying attention. Even Laqueesha had her head up now.

"Teachers here, the community, and many of the parents are upset about this. There's going to be a school board meeting to finalize whether or not this is going to happen."

"How long before they take over the school?" asked Darrel.

"This could be starting at the beginning of next semester," said Dave. "As I understand it, this company is ready to move in with their computers and new staff right now."

"Do you think it could be better?" asked Darrel. "A better situation?"

The question took Dave aback; he opened his mouth and then shut it.

"What I mean is," said Darrel, "do you think maybe some students might work better online than in a classroom? I was home schooled before I got here, and I did okay. In fact, I got a lot more done because there weren't as many distractions."

"This is not home schooling," said Dave. "This is different. Your mother was a certified teacher; she knew how to write lessons and grade you and structure your learning. The people that this company will be hiring won't have the faintest idea how to do that."

"Man," said Travion, laughing and pointing at Darrel, "you had your mother as a teacher? That be sketchy, man. That just be wrong."

Darrel slouched down in his desk. Dave could have kicked himself; he knew better than to expose a student in front of his classmates like that. He'd slipped. He'd been so goddamned desperate to get these kids on board against EduNet that he'd screwed up.

"Hey."

Dave looked up. Daquone was pointing his finger at Travion.

"Shut up, man. Leave him alone," he said.

"What?" said Travion. "Oh, do you take lessons from his mama, too?"

"Shut up, motherfucker," said Daquone.

"That's enough," said Dave. "Travion, you come see me after school for a detention." He nodded to Daquone. "Watch the language, please." He waited a moment for the tension to ease.

"So," Dave said, sitting on the edge of his desk, "what I'm hoping we might do is to see how our democratic rights work in the real world. There will be a lot of people at this upcoming school board meeting, people who don't want this to happen: parents, teachers, a lot of people from the community."

He scanned the room. Almost everyone was with him. Darrel was one of the few exceptions; he was staring down at his hands.

"So," he said, "what I'm offering is an extra grade for anyone who comes to this school board meeting as part of the protest."

"How big a grade?" asked Olive.

"Well," he said, "I was thinking of making it the equivalent of a test grade."

A murmur went up from the room.

"But as part of the grade requirement, you'd have to show up, picket—"

"What's that?" asked Laqueesha. "What's picket?"

"Holding up a protest sign and marching," said Olive without turning around.

"And perhaps speak about why it's important to keep our schools public. The more you do," he continued, "the better your grade."

The kids were excited, already talking to each other and making plans about going there together, making a party out of it. Fine. Whatever brought the bodies in.

"How do we know?" someone asked over the buzz in the classroom.

Dave looked for the voice and found Darrel staring at him.

"How do we know what, Darrel?"

"How do we know public schools are better than this new company?" he asked, a challenge in his voice: a new note for Darrel.

"Well, we don't know everything about their plans, but what we do know is that they don't provide a lot of the same services public schools do," Dave said. "They have nothing for special education, no money put aside for extra-curricular stuff, and they're not hiring qualified teachers."

"Public schools have all that, they do all that. You say we'd be better than this company, right Mr. Bell? So then why do public schools have such huge dropout rates, why are city ACT scores lowest in the state? I mean, I don't know, Mr. Bell. Maybe these guys deserve a chance."

Dave took a breath, getting ready to explain how the problems of the community could not all be solved by public schools alone, but Darrel was staring up at him, angry, hurt, as vulnerable as he'd ever been. Dave just nodded. He couldn't contradict the boy: maybe another time, but not today.

"Good question, Darrel."

And the kid had a point: a valid point. It was funny he hadn't really considered it fully before, really thought it through. The usual argument—the reflexive argument—was that there were other factors causing poor performances in the district and that you couldn't blame everything on public schools. But had they done enough for these kids? Was it possible that EduNet might be better for these kids than their public schools? No. He looked out over the class. Some of them, Olive, Darrel, Violet, and a few others were staring up at him waiting for an answer.

"Well?" asked Darrel.

"Darrel," he said, "all I can tell you is what I know from my own experience. Our schools aren't perfect. As you said, graduation rates, dropout rates, and ACT scores are really bad. Students here don't perform as well as they could, but there are other problems: homelessness, poverty, drugs, gangs, child abuse, and teen pregnancies. There's only so much we can do during the school day."

"Maybe this EduNet could do it better," asked Darrel.

The whole class was silent, listening now.

"Could they help our homeless students? Would they? And what about child abuse? Poverty? Will they provide free lunch to students living below the poverty line like we do? I think the answer to those questions is no. I think they'll be plunking you in front of computers and telling you to learn and that will be how they set up their curricula. And, most importantly, they will not be providing qualified teachers. The teachers here, the good teachers like Mr. Reynolds, Mrs. Benjamin, Ms. Finster, and me, have been teaching for years. We know how to teach, how to get through to you."

"So," he said, motioning to Darrel, "what do you think? Do you think they might be better for you?"

Darrel shrugged and said, "Probably not," but he didn't sound convinced to Dave. He looked out over the rest of the class.

"What do the rest of you think? Should we fight this?"

A couple kids shrugged. No one was going crazy defending their school.

"Anyone?"

"Well, Mr. Bell," said Olive, "even you have to admit this is not a very good school. We all know it." She smiled. "We know you work really hard and that most of the teachers here do, too, but it's too crazy here to learn a lot and the stuff we do get—with a few exceptions—is way too easy."

Heads nodded and a murmured agreement drifted through the classroom.

"Yeah, man," said Carlos. "Nobody here is going anywhere except maybe the real smart kids, and they're probably going to be behind the white kids when they get to college, too."

"So what do you think?" repeated Dave. "Is it worth it? Or should we let this EduNet come in and make a bunch of money off the services you're supposed to be getting? The money for your bus passes and free lunches and other services is going to be going straight into their pockets."

"A change might be good," said Violet. "If we could really learn like we should be learning."

"Anyone else?" asked Dave. A feeling of desperation was starting to rise in him, and his stomach began churning.

"Yeah, it's worth it." Dave looked for the voice and found Daquone looking at him and nodding.

"How do you mean?" asked Dave.

"Well," said Daquone, slouching back in his desk, "I know what Olive is saying about how crazy the schools are, but that's not just on the school. Part of that's on us. I mean, take me for an example. I don't like school. I only come here because I can play ball, so I come into my classes with an attitude and give all my teachers a hard time. The good teachers," he glanced up at Bell, "push me to get my stuff done and to do my best. They don't have to do that; a lot of teachers don't bother. But the good ones try to set me up to do all right when I get out, but most of the time I don't listen. That's on me, too."

He sat up and crossed his arms. "I guess what I'm trying to say is yeah, this school doesn't look good. Cops are here every other day, half the students don't come, and we're not doing well on the tests, but I think it would be a lot worse without our teachers. That's it, man."

"Thank you, Daquone," said Dave, nodding to him. Daquone nodded back. A voice in the wilderness, thought Dave, a voice from the oddest damned source.

"Well," he said, "I'd like you to think about this, what we spoke about today. Think about what you would want your school to look like, to be like." It was only fair. Before this, as far as he knew, no one had ever asked the kids what they wanted. "And my offer still stands. If any of you want to come to the school board meeting and speak"—God help us, he thought—"or picket and protest, you will get extra credit. Significant extra credit. Any questions?"

"A test grade, right?"

Dave nodded. He felt bad having to bribe the kids, but it was—he hoped—for their own good.

"Okay," he said, "today we will be studying about the right of assembly. Olive?"

"Yes, Mr. Bell?"

"Would you hand out these worksheets, please?"

She came up and he handed her the pack. She took them, and then leaned in close to him and whispered, "I think we need this school the way it is. I think we need the best teachers we can get." She smiled and went to start passing out the sheets.

Dave shook his head. Just when you think you knew these kids, they turn around and surprise the hell out of you. He brought the outline up on the Smart Board.

"Point number one," he said, pointing to the outline and reading, "is the right of the people peaceably to assemble. What does that mean?"

They went through the first part of the worksheet point by point. The bottom half was independent work for them to complete at the end of the class hour, work that would be graded. With fifteen minutes left in class, he got them started on the assignment.

"Okay," he said, "let's go. We only have about fifteen minutes. Remember this is for a grade."

Most of them were on task and focused. Even Carlos was doing it.

"Darrel?"

He looked up.

"Could I talk to you outside for a minute?" Dave led him out into the hallway. There were a few kids down the hall talking in front of an open locker, but Dave ignored them.

"Hey, Darrel," he said, "I just wanted to apologize in case I embarrassed you in there. I didn't mean to mention that your mother did your home schooling."

Darrel shrugged. "That's all right," he said. "Don't worry about that, Mr. Bell."

"And I also wanted to ask you," he continued, "if you really think that this is a such a bad school?"

Darrel shrugged again but remained silent.

"I mean, don't be afraid to tell me what you really think," said Dave. "I'd appreciate your point of view."

Darrel sighed.

"This school is crazy," he said. "You know that. The kids are crazy. They're wild, they don't care about their education, and they just want to play around. I see that and I think, man, this is not what school is supposed to be. If you're asking whether I think these other guys could do better?" He shrugged again. "I don't know. But I do know this isn't working."

Dave nodded. Fair enough.

"Okay," he said. "Thank you, Darrel." They returned to the classroom. Laqueesha was on the phone, Daquone was yakking it up with Travion and Olive and two other kids had their smartphones out. Dave flipped the lights on and off. The smartphones disappeared and the conversations stopped. He sat at his desk and leaned back, surveying the room, his class, his students. His life or what was left of it. As the wise man once said, everything you know is wrong. Well, he thought. So I'm wrong. What the hell do I do now?

Chapter 22

Sandra sat a corner table, her phone on the table in front of her. Eddy's was crowded. She hated these places; even though she had ordered only a simple espresso, they had taken seven minutes to get it to her. It was ridiculous. And not even that good. She ran her eyes over the room, wondering which patron might be the mysterious phone caller from the night before. Not the teenager with the tattoo of the Chinese dragon on his arm. Not the three-piece suit reading the paper.

She sipped her espresso and continued scanning the room. There was a serious bicyclist, dressed in his neon Italian racing uniform. Not him. Too conspicuous. She continued her scan. There was a guy looking out the window. He was youngish, probably late twenties, dressed in jeans and a black turtleneck. He looked complicated. Sensitive. Maybe he was the midnight caller; after all, he was trying awfully hard to look sophisticated and European. No, she decided. He was all fluff. Too much the poseur. Her phone rang suddenly. She looked quickly around the room, but that did her no good. Half the people there were on their phones anyway.

"Hello?"

"Hello, Ms. Feeley." It was the man from the night before.

"Where are you?"

"Ah, I have to apologize, my dear. I was unable to make it there in person this morning. However, I did send one of my representatives, a very pleasant man. I think you'll like him."

She leaned back in her chair.

"Who are you?" she asked.

"All good things to those who wait. I know you're a very busy person, and I'm sure you're impatient to get started. My associate is wearing a Navy pea coat and is sitting directly to your right. His name is Joe Sykes, and he'll tell you everything you need to know."

He hung up. She stared at her phone a minute and then raised her eyes. The man—Joe, apparently—was looking at her and smiling.

"Your boss couldn't make it," she said.

"I know," the man said, taking a sip of his coffee, "but this type of meeting isn't exactly his style, anyway. May I join you?" he asked, indicating the empty seat at her table. She nodded and he moved over directly opposite her.

"My name is Joe Sykes," he said, "and I work for Adrian Cole." He looked at her and she nodded in acknowledgement.

"We are usually free-lancers, working as consultants for companies who need our rather specialized services. Everyone does sooner or later."

She nodded. She knew about them. These guys were janitors; they cleaned up corporate messes quickly and quietly.

"EduNet brought us on board some time ago to help facilitate this project with Custer High School. Mr. Leach called Mr. Cole to help as a personal favor to him." Sandra nodded again, trying hard not to look surprised. Mr. Robert Price Leach was the CEO of EduNet.

"There were a lot of loose ends to coordinate with this project, as I'm sure you well know, and Mr. Leach, being acutely aware of the political pressures and the public tension surrounding it, decided to bring in Mr. Cole."

"I'm sorry," said Sandra, "but I find this all a little hard to believe. I've been working on this project for nearly three years, and I never heard of you being attached to it before."

"Well, the reason you didn't know about us is simply because Mr. Leach wanted it that way." He leaned back in his chair. "Do you remember when Senator O'Malley was on the fence about the legislation to end collective bargaining? The only Republican in the senate who was hesitating?"

Sandra nodded. That had been a tense moment. Had he not voted against the unions, the Custer takeover never would have gotten started. "He changed his vote at the last minute," she said.

"Yes, he did," said Mr. Sykes, and smiled. "He finally realized that collective bargaining for public employees was not in everyone's best interest."

"Are you trying to tell me that you were responsible for getting him to change his vote?"

He smiled again, a smile without warmth or feeling, a grin on a clown mask.

"We had a little talk with the senator the night before the vote," he said, "and he came around to the practical point of view."

Sandra thought a moment; was it possible? She remembered that O'Malley had qualms about voting with them because he represented a college town in the northwestern part of the state and half his constituency was either professors or university employees. Voting for it would have been political suicide for him. In fact, everyone had assumed the bill was dead in the water until he came out of his office the morning of the vote and announced that he had decided to toe the party line and vote to end collective bargaining, which had opened the door for EduNet.

"Yes," she said. "I remember."

"Would you like other examples of our intercessions?"

She shook her head. She felt a sudden urge for a cigarette but tamped it down.

"No," she said. "I believe you."

"Good," he said. "Would you like another coffee?"

She shook her head.

"No? All right. Let's get down to business. I'm sure you're impatient to know why we needed to see you."

"Yes," she said. "You—your associate—mentioned Mr. Paige last night. Does Mitchell know about you?"

"He knows who we are and what we do, but he was not aware that we've been involved with the project. Only Mr. Leach knew that. Until now."

"Mitchell doesn't know?" she asked. A wave of anger swept over her followed by another wave of—what? She felt anxious, quivery, like she was getting ready to start a race. Butterflies.

"No," he purred. "Only the three of us. And now you."

"What do you want?" she asked curtly.

"Mr. Leach has had some serious doubts about Mr. Paige for some time," he said. "In the nine months he's been involved with this project, Mr. Paige has shown signs of excessive emotional instability, poor judgment, and recklessness. There have been several occasions when Mr. Leach believes his behavior put the project in jeopardy."

"I don't know what you're talking about," said Sandra, racking her brain. It was true, Mitchell was brash and abrupt with his people, but she had never known him to do anything to jeopardize the project.

"Well, let's see," he said, cupping his face in his hand. Sandra noticed one of his fingers was missing. For some reason, that fact took her aback, and made her even more wary of this man; for the first time, she felt a real sense of danger.

"He has had numerous instances of loss of self-control, sometimes to the point of violence. Once, during a meeting, he overturned a chair while one of his team members was still in it."

Sandra nodded. She remembered that.

"Another time, during a rage, he flipped over his office desk."

Sandra shrugged. "Okay, he's got a temper. Everyone knows that. I don't see how any of that constitutes a risk to the project."

"There have also been other transgressions," said Sykes, looking down at his coffee cup.

"All right," she said, impatient suddenly. "Spill it."

"Most recently," Sykes said, leaning closer to her, "he attempted to coerce two of your classroom observers in order to get them to change the status of their reports. As you know, Miss Feeley, that is in direct conflict with company policy. Besides being illegal. If that fact were to get out, it would put the entire project in jeopardy."

Sandra leaned back. That idiot. That fucking idiot. She told him they had the observation problem under control, but—so like Mitchell—he had to go and take matters into his own hands.

"I see from your face that you are not surprised that Mr. Paige might have done this."

"I am surprised he didn't consult with me before doing something like this," she replied.

"We all were surprised," said Sykes, leaning back in his chair, "after all, you are the associate executive vice-president, directly underneath Mr. Paige."

He said the last part with a relish that made Sandra look up. What was this man implying? A kernel of fear started hardening in her stomach. It was against company policy for employees to sleep together, and while it wasn't usually considered an egregious offense, these guys could make it as egregious as they wanted. And who knew what they had. Pictures? Videotapes? Jesus Christ.

"So what does all this mean for us and the project?" she asked. "What are the consequences of Mr. Paige's, um—" she looked for the word—"misstep?"

"This indiscretion of his?" Once again, that smarmy quality surfaced in his voice. "I guess, as with all indiscretions, that depends upon who finds out."

"Who knows about it?" she asked quickly.

"Well," he said, smiling slightly, "you know, of course, and Mr. Cole and myself know because we were the ones he approached to fix this little matter just last night. Mr. Paige had been unsuccessful persuading one of the observers and needed us to finish the job."

"He came to you?" she asked, finally unable to conceal her surprise. It was what they'd discussed, but he'd gone ahead without her. "I don't understand something," she said.

"Yes, my dear?"

She smiled slightly, concealing her growing distaste for this man, and leaned toward him.

"If you're working with Mitchell on this," she said, her voice low, "then you're in it just as deep as he is."

He raised his hands as if in surrender.

"Miss Feeley, you have to understand that we work under the radar. No one will ever acknowledge we have worked for EduNet. We," he said, leaning back and smiling, "are invisible. Completely invisible."

He took another sip of coffee and shrugged.

"We could," he said, "go to see Mr. Leach about this matter, but we are hoping to still salvage success from what is rapidly becoming a fiasco. We believe the less he knows about this the better."

She sat a moment, staring into her empty espresso cup, trying to decipher the puzzle. If everything Sykes had said was true, Mitchell had broken company policy and maybe the law. He could be reprimanded by the company, but probably wouldn't be prosecuted. EduNet wouldn't want the publicity. If Leach decided to follow through with any reprimands or terminations concerning this, Mitchell would be left out in the cold: no bonus, no promotion, and probably no more career. And if news of their relationship got out, she'd be going down with him. If she dodged that bullet, however—she stopped a moment and glanced out the window, consciously avoiding eye contact with Sykes. If she dodged the bullet and Mitchell didn't, the Custer Project would be hers. All hers. She took a deep breath and turned back to Sykes.

"So," she said, "what do you want from me? Why are you telling me all this?"

"Mr. Leach," said Sykes, interlacing his fingers, "and Mr. Cole are very careful men. They like to prepare for all possible contingencies. If, as we fear, Mitchell Paige will continue to demonstrate questionable judgment regarding the Custer takeover, it may become necessary to remove him."

Sandra kept her face blank. She reined in everything pulsing through her.

"If it becomes necessary to relieve Mr. Paige," continued Sykes, "we'll need to have someone ready to step in and take over operations as seamlessly as possible."

She kept her silence.

"You, of course, are that logical candidate. You have been working on this project since the beginning and know it inside out. In fact," he said, leaning forward, "Mr. Leach believes you have a better grasp of it than Mitchell."

She felt herself frowning. "I've only met Mr. Leach once at a company fund-raiser. He doesn't know me."

"I'm afraid he does. He's been following your career quite closely. He scans your reports, your evaluations, everything. He's quite interested in you."

"Is he?" she said.

"Yes," replied Sykes, "and he's told me he has all the faith in the world in you. He's very confident that—if faced with an adverse sort of situation—you would do the right thing. He believes you are, and I quote him, "an infinitely moral person.""

"Really?" asked Sandra.

"Really," said Sykes. "He is sure that you, when faced with a tough choice, would always do the right thing for him, the company, and yourself." He smiled. "Even if that choice might be difficult and could involve forsaking former colleagues."

"What do you mean?" she asked.

"Anytime a higher-level employee is brought up on disciplinary charges, there must be a hearing in the Human Resources Department. Mr. Leach is confident we can count on your cooperation in such a matter."

They wanted her to testify against Mitchell. That's why they were meeting here.

"What if I would decide not to cooperate?" she said. "What if my moral sense tells me to stay on the sidelines?"

Sykes looked at her with those icy blue eyes. He was no longer smiling.

"I think you'll find we can be quite persuasive."

"Are you threatening me?" she asked.

He shrugged. "There's no need to." He reached into his pocket, pulled out an envelope, and tossed it onto the table. "A picture is worth a thousand words," he said, smiling.

He glanced at his watch again. "If you'll excuse me," he said. "I have someone waiting for me. I don't want to leave him hanging. By the way," he added, "if Mr. Paige needs to be terminated, you will be contacted. I'm sure we can count on your cooperation." He nodded his head and left.

Sandra picked up the envelope and pulled out a thick packet of photographs. She looked at the one on top and immediately recognized her apartment. Her bedroom. Her bed. Her. And Mitchell. She paged through the photographs slowly, deliberately. There she was on top of Mitchell. There was Mitchell taking her from behind, his favorite position. She riffled through them: dozens of photos taken—as far as she could tell—since the beginning of the affair. So. If she refused to play along and set up Mitchell, they would blackmail her. If she did play along, she might help Mitchell save himself, or, if he blew it all up, he would be removed and she would be the new director of the Custer Project. And that would mean a promotion. A big promotion.

She got up and shrugged into her coat. Either Mitchell staying on or her taking over would be better than the affair becoming common knowledge. That would ruin them both. She stepped outside into the lightly falling snow and reached into her purse for a cigarette. She lit up and stood there a moment, savoring the cool autumn air as the smoke swelled her lungs.

Sandra went to her car. She slid in behind the wheel and started it up. She leaned back, finished her cigarette, tossed it out the window, and grasped the wheel in both hands. Something was bothering her. Cole and Sykes seemed to have everything under control, so why bring her in? Why take all those pains? Why not just show her the pictures in the first place? It was almost as if they were playing with her—and with Mitchell—playing them like fish on the line. She put the car in gear and swung slowly into traffic, pondering.

Chapter 23

The taxi stopped in front of his building; Mitchell paid the cabbie, got out, and limped over to the elevators.

"Hello, Mr. Paige," said a voice behind him. He turned and saw Angela DiCaprio.

"Hello, Angela," he said evenly. Technically Angela was a colleague, but privately, he couldn't consider her as anything but an employee, especially after knowing she'd had cancer. "How are you today?"

"I'm all right," she said. "Are you all right? I couldn't help seeing that you were limping."

"Yeah, I'm good. I just stepped on a little glass this morning. Nothing serious." He smiled slightly.

"Well, this is going to be an exciting week," she said. "It's almost like our Super Bowl."

He turned to her and smiled but said nothing. Angela stood next to him then, silent—finally—and waited with him for the elevator. It arrived and they got in. She punched her floor and he punched his.

"Mr. Paige," she said and he turned. "I just wanted to say that it's been a pleasure working with you on this project. I think you're one of the best vice-presidents here, and I don't think anyone else could have navigated this project as well as you have." She nodded.

"Thank you, Angela," he said and actually meant it. He was used to employees—colleagues—bullshitting him and could smell it from a mile away. This was sincere; he could tell she meant it. "That means a lot to me."

"Of course," she said. "Oh, I meant to tell you sooner but it slipped my mind. Mr. Leach was trying to reach you this morning."

A bolt of anxiety shot through him. He had sort of been expecting to hear from Mr. Leach as they reached completion, but not this soon.

"What?" he asked, leaning toward her. "What did he want?"

"I don't know," she said, leaning back into the wall. "I only heard from Monica that he had called your office this morning. Early. About seven, I think."

"Thanks for letting me know," he said, unable to keep the sarcasm out of his voice.

"I'm sure it's a congratulatory message, Mr. Paige. I can't really imagine it would be anything else."

Mitchell nodded and made himself smile, but jabbed at the button to his floor again. Dumb bitch. How would you know whether the project—the ninety-five percent of it that's outside your specialized area—is going well or not? Shit. The elevator door opened and Angela got off. He nodded to her and jabbed at the close door button. He racked his brain. They had a good handle on the community angle of things; they'd gotten good intelligence from the mayor's office and were already working on a strategy to handle the meeting. They were under control politically; he'd been handling that himself. Maybe Angela was right. Maybe this was an early congratulatory meeting.

The door opened and he walked off, trying to conceal his limp, but his foot was throbbing and he could barely put any weight on it at all. He got to his office and stopped at Monica's desk.

"Hello, Mr. Paige."

"Hello, Monica," he said and waited. She was sorting through folders on the desk. When she realized he was still standing there, she stopped and looked up at him.

"Yes?" she asked. "Is there something I should be doing?"

"Do I have any messages?" he asked, trying to contain his growing irritation.

"Let me look," she said, opening her notepad, but then stopped. "I'm sorry. Mr. Leach called this morning, early, before I got in, and said he'd like for you to call him."

Idiots, he thought. I'm surrounded by fucking idiots.

"Did he say what he wanted?"

"No, sir." His irritation must be showing. Monica never called him sir unless she knew he was pissed off.

"Okay," he said, moving toward his office. "Could you get him on the phone for me, please?"

"What did you do to your leg?" she asked.

"Nothing," he said. "I'm fine." Fucking idiots.

He went behind his desk and sat down. He lifted his pants leg and examined the injured foot. His sock was wet with blood. He didn't dare take his shoe off; he knew he'd never get it back on again. It hurt like a motherfucker, too. He buzzed Monica.

"Yes, Mr. Paige."

"Hey, Monica, could you do me a favor and call Dr. Lewis? I might need to go and see him this afternoon."

"What should I tell him the problem is?"

They would need to know. "Tell him I cut my foot and it's still bleeding. I think I might need stitches. Oh," he added, "could I have some coffee?"

"Okay." She hung up.

Thanks for all the sympathy, he thought, and eased his leg out in front of him. It wasn't so bad if he didn't put any weight on it. He closed his eyes a second and tried his breathing exercises, hoping it might help with the pain. It didn't. He heard the door open and opened his eyes. Monica put his coffee on the desk and turned to leave.

"Monica, have you called Mr. Leach?"

She shook her head. "No, I haven't had a chance yet."

"As soon as possible," he said and she made a face.

Mitchell stared at the phone a second and then pulled out his cell. He dialed Sandra's number.

"Hello, Mitchell," she said.

"Where are you?"

"On my way in." She paused a beat. "I had a little trouble with the car." She sounded odd.

"Oh, nothing serious, I hope," he said, listening closely.

"No, Triple A got it going right away. What's up?"

"Well, I just got a call from Mr. Leach, the big kahuna, saying he'd like to see me."

"Did he say why?" She sounded guarded.

"No, but I think it might be to congratulate me for a job well done. Don't you?"

"Maybe," she said, "but I wouldn't count my chickens before they're hatched. We're not there yet, Mitchell."

"Everything is a go. The only serious obstacle left is that goddamned school board meeting, and you're on top of that." You'd better be, he thought. "I got a call from the mayor's office yesterday and got the low-down on how they'll be working the meeting. You need to get in touch with them today."

Another beat. "Yeah," she said. "It's still going to be tough, though. Those things can be unpredictable. All the people, the emotion; it all feeds off itself."

"Are you worried?" he asked.

"A little," she said.

His office phone buzzed. "I've got Mr. Leach on the line," he said. "I'll call you as soon as I can." He hung up with Sandra and stared at his phone. It buzzed again. He took one deep breath, two, and picked up the receiver.

"Hello," he said, trying to sound as cool and capable as he could.

"Mitchell, how are you doing?" asked the feathery high voice on the other end of the line. "This is Robert Price Leach."

"Hello, Mr. Leach, how are you?"

"Things are looking good." He sounded abstracted, as if his mind was elsewhere.

"That's great," said Mitchell, injecting as much enthusiasm into his voice as he could.

"Listen, Mitchell, I was wondering if you could come up to the office this morning at about, let's say ten-thirty. Does that work for you?"

"Sure thing, sir. I'll see you then. Should I bring anything?"

"No, we won't be getting technical this time. I'll see you then."

"Yes, sir." He was about to add something when Leach hung up. Well, not much to go on there. He redialed Sandra's number.

"Hello," she said.

"Are you still driving?"

"No, I actually just walked into the building. What did Mr. Leach say?" she asked, still with that worried note in her voice.

"Not much. Just that he wanted me up in his office by ten-thirty. That's forty-five minutes."

"Just you and him?" she asked.

"As far as I know," he said. "No one said anything different. Why?"

"Mitchell," she started.

"What?"

"Remember how you always used to tell me not to assume anything? To check and double-check before moving ahead?"

"Sure," he said. "I tell everyone that."

A sigh from the other end. "Yeah. Well, I think that might not be a bad thing for you to remember today."

Something wasn't right. Sandra knew something. He thought he heard a strange echo on the line. Where was she?

"Are you waiting for an elevator?"

"No," she said. "I'm taking the stairs."

"Are you fucking crazy? That's twenty-three floors."

"Well," she said, "I need the exercise, and, I don't know, I just wanted to walk."

"All right," he said. "I should go."

"Call me after the meeting," she said.

"Sure thing. Later."

He hung up and glanced at his watch: thirty-five more minutes. Mitchell stretched his leg out and winced; it seemed a little better, but not much. He wondered if he could scare up some painkillers around the office. Somebody had to have a prescription. A thought struck him; Sandra had mentioned that Angela had gone through surgery for cancer. Maybe she had some Vicodin or something.

Sandra would be fine; once she got rolling, she was good, very good. Tough, focused, but sympathetic. Plus she was a woman; she had that warmth, that sensitivity, that compassion for people; but she could afford to be sympathetic. He was the one who had to make the tough calls. Calls with balls. And plus she actually knew some of these community people. She would do great at the meeting. He buzzed Monica.

"Hey, Monica," he said. "Could you get me Angela on the phone?"

Chapter 24

"Hello, Mr. Leach. You asked to see me?"

"Yes, Mr. Cole. Please come in and have a seat."

Cole entered the office. It was the first time he'd been there; for all the work he'd done for this man, he'd only seen him face to face once before, and that had been in a conference room. His office was large but sparsely furnished. Windows covered the entire wall behind the small metal desk, but the curtains were drawn, leaving the room in a twilit atmosphere. Cole glanced around the office; it was furnished in a somewhat Nordic minimalist style: a lot of bare wood and shiny metal. The lone decoration was an oversized chessboard on an ornately carved wooden stand that dominated the center of the room. A recessed spotlight shone on it. Surprising. He would have guessed that Mr. Leach might be more of a mahogany and teak sort of executive—wanting to exude that aura of sophisticated richness. Most of them did.

Mr. Leach motioned him to sit. Cole settled in the chair opposite the desk and crossed his legs. Mr. Richard Price Leach sat down across from him. He was a smaller man, a little below average height. He sported a full head of rich silver hair, carefully combed, and also wore a short Van Dyke type beard. He carried some bulk on his slight frame, but Cole wouldn't have labeled him fat. He stared at Cole appraisingly, unabashedly. Leach had intense deep brown, nearly black eyes that stood in sharp contrast to his hair. Cole was unable to distinguish the man's pupils from the dark of the irises.

"Well, Mr. Cole," he said abruptly, "thank you for coming to see me." His voice was higher but with a rough and grainy quality, as if he had at one time been a smoker.

"My pleasure, sir."

"Is it?" Leach pursed his lips.

"It is."

"I hope you are being sincere with that comment, Mr. Cole. I'll tell you something right now. I don't care for pandering from my employees."

Leach lowered his head and peered at him from under his eyebrows for a moment. Interesting, thought Cole, returning the man's stare. An odd sort of opening gambit. He didn't reply.

"How are things going with the Custer takeover?" Leach finally asked.

"Everything is going well, Mr. Leach. I can tell you that we are fully prepared to implement the final stage."

"Good," said Leach, leaning back in his seat. "Very good. You've done an excellent job for us on this project, and I wanted to thank you personally. And," he added, sliding a thick envelope across the desk, "to show my heartfelt appreciation."

"You're very welcome, sir," said Cole. He did not touch the envelope. Not yet. "I appreciate the fact that we were given a free hand to implement our policies. It enabled us to be much more efficient."

"You were that," said Leach. "The way you handled the O'Malley matter was superb. I thought we were done for after that scumbag left his party."

Leach stood and strolled over to the far wall and stared out as if the curtain were not between him and the window. "How are things set up for the school board meeting?"

"Well," said Cole, "we have our agents in place. Two of them have attended some of the community meetings and will be able to apprise us of any changes in their plans. Captain Phillips of the fifth precinct will be notified by our agents as soon as the trouble begins. He'll be prepared to move in promptly. The media has also been handled. We have a man monitoring the feed. We will control every image leaving that room."

"How will you trigger things?" asked Leach, still staring at the pattern on the curtain.

"One of the community activists, Jerome Johnson, has a bit of a temper. Our man will provoke him to violence and make it seem as if he is the instigator as well."

"Is your man good?"

"Very good."

"He's done this before?"

"Yes, sir."

"All right," said Leach. "Very good. Violence at this meeting will make those people look bad, like savages, the animals that they truly are."

Cole nodded. That had been the strategy from the beginning, to discredit any community movement in order to create sympathy for the charter program. Leach put his hands behind his back and strolled over to the chessboard. He glanced at it, and then leaned over and moved one of the black knights.

He looked up suddenly.

"What," asked Leach, "about the matter we discussed earlier? That problem with Mr. Paige. Is there any progress with that?"

Cole took a breath.

"Well, yes, Mr. Leach, as a matter of fact, there has been a development."

Leach stood there, staring down at the board and frowning. Cole waited a moment before continuing.

"As I mentioned previously, I got a telephone call from Mitchell Paige. I went to visit him at his request."

Leach looked up sharply and frowned.

"What did that little asshole want?" he asked. Despite himself, Cole was taken aback by the man's sudden fierceness.

"Apparently he was having some trouble with one of the required observations at the school. It seems that one of the observers filed an inappropriate report."

"How exactly was it inappropriate?"

"It was positive," said Cole. "It seems as if the observer thought the teacher did an excellent job with his class."

Leach snorted and walked back behind his desk. He sat down suddenly.

"What a goddamned idiot," he muttered. He shook his head. After a moment, Leach leaned back in the chair and looked at Cole. "So what did Mr. Paige want from you?"

"Well, he managed to change the mind of one of the employees, Mr. Willard, by himself. Unfortunately, he did it in the presence of the second employee, Mr. Brown, whom he failed to convince. Mr. Brown actually quit the firm before reevaluating his report, so Mr. Paige wanted me to step in and persuade him to amend the evaluation."

"What did you say?"

"I told him we'd do it."

Leach nodded and grunted.

"We started the process this morning and I should be hearing from my associate any time now."

Leach nodded again.

"Good," he said. "Very good. You know," he continued, "what Paige did could be construed as grounds for dismissal. Coercing an employee to falsify a public report."

"That's what I was thinking, sir."

"But I won't do that," said Leach, standing again. He strolled slowly over to the chessboard and stood on the opposite side, behind the white players. He stared at the board a moment and then raised his eyes to Cole.

"I want Mr. Paige to never work in an executive position again. Anywhere. He must be expelled from the business world, excommunicated from the corporate culture. And," he added, "that's why you're here, Mr. Cole. To assist me in this."

Leach stared at the chessboard a moment. Cole watched as he picked up one of the white bishops, pocketed it, and then strolled over to the opposite side where he moved the black queen. He waited.

"Had you ever met Mr. Mitchell Paige before?" asked Mr. Leach, eyes still glued to the chessboard.

"No, sir," answered Cole.

"What did you think of him?"

"He was about what I expected, sir: ambitious, driven, but also arrogant, condescending, pretentious. Intelligent, but not very sensible about the choice he makes."

"They're all cut out of that mold these days," said Leach softly, almost to himself. He continued starting at the board. "Did you know he's gay?" he asked suddenly.

"I did, sir."

"Did your homework, huh?" Leach chuckled, a sound like sandpaper tearing.

"Yes, sir. We have very extensive files on all of our employees. Plus, as you know, the company performs exhaustive psychological profiling on every prospective candidate. Nothing remains hidden."

Leach nodded.

"But it must be said," continued Cole, "that even though Paige has gay tendencies, he never seems to have acted on them; if he did, he's extremely discreet."

"Not discreet enough," muttered Leach, looking over at Cole. "You see, Adrian, I know a few things about our Mr. Paige." He leaned toward Cole, emphasizing his words. "He is not to be trusted."

Was this the source of Leach's animosity toward Paige? His sexuality? Cole watched him carefully, looking for clues. Nothing. It didn't make sense. Mitchell had done an excellent job implementing the project. By most of the standard metrics, Leach should have been singing his praises. And if he wanted to fire him, he had more than enough cause. This excessive animus was puzzling.

"So," asked Leach. "What is the plan?"

"Plan, sir?"

"The plan for the removal of Paige."

"Well, I have already begun to work on some of his psychological soft spots, his self-loathing and his homophobia. To, as you know, exacerbate his stress level, to increase the chances of him acting out."

"Good," said Leach, nodding. Cole wondered if he should tell Leach he had tried to trigger his instabilities, to stir the pot by kissing him as if he were a woman. Not yet. It might antagonize Leach, and that wouldn't do; he seemed too unpredictable, too unstable, although now he seemed calm enough looking down at the chessboard. Abstracted.

"Do you play chess, sir?" asked Cole, curious about this man. He always found it interesting to investigate subtleties of human behavior and motivation, but sometimes that knowledge had to be approached from the side, as if hunting big game.

Leach looked up as if surprised by the question.

"Play? As in play with others play?" He laughed, a loud raucous bray that echoed in the bare room. "No, I don't play with others. Too boring, Adrian. Too predictable. I set up problems, chess problems. And then," he said, waving a finger in his direction, "then I solve them."

"I see," said Cole.

"I need you to do that job for me," said Leach. "And soon."

Cole nodded. "Paige," he said.

"Yes. I need you to get rid of Mitchell Paige."

Cole considered a moment; ordinarily, he would preform a task with no questions asked. But this one had raised his antennae. Something felt wrong here, and Cole was not going to put himself at risk without knowing more, even if it meant offending his client.

"These directives make the removal process much more difficult," he said. "If I may ask, sir, why do we need to get rid of Mr. Paige in this fashion? It seems unnecessarily risky to go to such lengths."

Leach took a deep breath, let it out slowly, and turned to Cole.

"All right," he said. "You're a good man. You deserve to know what you're dealing with. When Mitchell Paige first came to work here, I welcomed him with open arms. I treated him like a son. But then, Mr. Cole, he betrayed me."

Cole nodded, waiting for more. Leach continued staring at the chessboard.

"I mentored him and watched him rise through the ranks, but then I began to notice gradual changes in him: the way he would look at me during our weekly meetings when he thought I wasn't watching; the way he spoke to others about me, the lies he started spreading about me." Leach toyed with a black pawn.

Cole watched him closely, his radar up. Mr. Leach seemed to be going to a strange place. A dark place.

"And then I found him out, Mr. Cole." He looked up at him, his eyes motionless black pools.

Cole said nothing, keeping his face as expressionless as possible.

"You see, Mr. Cole, I discovered Mitchell Paige has been plotting a takeover for months. He wants my job. He's out to ruin me. I need to protect myself. I need to get rid of him. And, for this betrayal of my trust, he must be punished. He must be expelled."

"I see," said Cole. "How exactly did you come to this realization?"

"You might think I'm presumptuous for saying this, but," Leach put a finger in the air and walked back to the windows, "I have a special ability to see into people. I've been able to do it my whole life. I see their desires, their fears, and—sometimes—I even see their thoughts."

He turned to Cole and smiled broadly for the first time, exposing perfectly formed and impossibly white teeth. They had to be processed.

Treated somehow. Bleached. Nothing was that perfect; something like that wasn't possible in nature.

"I amaze you, don't I?" asked Leach. "Well, you're not alone. Many people have been surprised by the fact. Surprised and amazed."

Cole smiled and nodded. Very well, he thought. Let's see if he can read my current mind wave.

Leach moved back toward the desk. He raised his head suddenly, as if hearing something. "You probably think I'm a bit strange," he said.

"Of course not," said Cole, after a beat.

"Well," he continued, "Let me explain what I know about our Mitchell Paige." The man took a deep breath. "I've seen an ambitious mind full of hateful infection—pus—that soaks into every aspect of his being. He is poisonous because he cannot treat others with any sort of respect." He looked up at Cole. "You see, Mr. Cole, he hates himself too much to care for others. Anyone. Including me."

Cole nodded. Our Mr. Leach, he thought, seems to be slightly delusional.

Leach scowled, strode quickly around the desk, and leaned over Cole sitting in his chair. "Evil," he hissed, his face inches from Cole. "He is evil."

Cole almost turned away. The man's breath was foul, reeking of something chemical, rotten and bleach-like at the same time.

"Mitchell Paige," Leach continued, "must be removed from my presence."

The phone rang suddenly. Leach stood up and pressed the intercom button.

"Yes," he said, his voice controlled and even.

"Mr. Leach?" crackled a voice from the speaker.

"Yes, my dear."

"Sir, security called and wanted me to tell you that there are protesters in front of the building. They're picketing against the takeover."

"Thank you." Leach went to the windows and pressed a button. The curtains drew away from the windows silently. He gazed downward a moment and then gestured to Cole.

"Come here a moment, Mr. Cole. Take a look."

He walked over. Down on the street, thirty-four stories down, a group of about twenty or thirty protesters marched in circles on the sidewalk opposite the building. They held signs that were too far away for Cole to read. A few of them looked as if they were yelling and raising their fists, but for the most part, they seemed peaceful.

Leach grunted. Cole glanced over at him. The man was shaking his head. He grunted again, a low guttural sound, almost a growl.

"Fucking niggers," he said, almost spitting the words. "Fucking spics. Filth. I never could stand them. They're nothing but ballast on our society, drowning us all with their deadweight."

Leach turned to look at Cole, who said nothing, but nodded.

"All right," he said, turning away from the window. "Let's get to work. I'll make sure the police get down here and break up that jungle party. You," he said, pointing his finger at Cole, "need to work on erasing Mitchell Paige from my presence." He turned and looked out the window again. He held out his hand, spread his fingers wide, and stared at the protesters between the spread fingers.

"The hand of God," he said, his voice loud and strident, "will come crashing down on all of you."

The intercom buzzed again. Leach stood at the window, staring at the protesters through his outstretched fingers. Cole finally leaned over the desk and pressed the button.

"Mr. Leach, sir? Mitchell Paige is here to see you."

Well, thought Cole. Curiouser and curiouser.

"Very good, Louise," answered Leach, still gazing through his spread fingers. "Give me a moment." He turned and smiled. "Surprise, Mr. Cole," he said.

Leach stood up straight, dropped his arm to side, and motioned for Cole to follow him. He gestured to an alcove between the window and the wall. Cole hesitated a moment, wondering when this surreal episode would end, and then stood where Leach indicated. He said nothing, hoping his displeasure wasn't evident to the other man.

"Mr. Cole," whispered Leach. "I'd like for you to listen in on this conversation. Listen to this man. Listen to his naked ambition: it shows. Oh, it shows. And watch me play him like a chess game; he will suspect nothing. I believe this may be very enlightening for you."

"Of course," said Cole. Leach moved quickly to the wall and pressed a button. The curtain slid past Cole, leaving him fully concealed from the room. He turned slightly, allowing himself room to lean against the wall between the windows and the curtain. He glanced out the window. Police were starting to arrive at the protest. Members of the EduNet Security team were beginning to stream out of the building. They began surrounding the protesters, who continued marching in a circle.

Outside the curtain, he heard Leach tell his secretary to let Mitchell in. The door opened and he heard someone enter. Mitchell Paige. And he was dragging a foot. It would seem as if Mr. Paige had somehow hurt himself since last night.

"Thank you for coming in, Paige," said Leach. "I appreciate it."

"Anytime, sir." Mitchell's voice was level and modulated, but Cole could hear the tension in it.

"First of all," said Leach brusquely, "I'd like to thank you for all the hard work you've done on this project. We couldn't have done it without you."

"Thank you, sir."

"We are very near completion, correct?"

"Yes, sir. And it's very satisfying to bring this home to you."

"To me?"

"Yes, sir. I feel I can almost lay this project at your feet as a tribute," said Paige.

Silence. Cole could imagine Leach sitting there staring at Paige the same way he had stared at him. He almost felt sorry for Mitchell.

"Paige," said Leach, his voice low, "tell me about this problem with the observation reports."

"Sir?" asked Paige, his voice splitting with tension.

"The observation reports. First of all, I've learned that there were a number of unsatisfactory reports, reports which stated that the Custer teachers were doing exemplary work. How did that happen?"

"Well," said Mitchell, stumbling over his words. "It's hard to say, sir. We followed every protocol and took every precaution in hiring and training our representatives, but these deviations took us completely by surprise. It was the human factor, sir."

"How?" roared Leach suddenly, his voice harsh and rasping and unexpectedly loud. "How," Leach continued, "did this happen?"

No answer. Cole couldn't even hear Paige breathing anymore.

"And why," continued Leach, "did you try to coerce these observers into changing their reports?"

"Sir," stuttered Paige, "we only did that to ensure that everything would stay on schedule. We didn't want there to be any glitches in the timeline."

Cole heard Leach getting up and saw his shadow rise beyond the curtain. He came closer and stopped directly opposite, as if he were staring through the curtain, Cole imagined. As he had done with him.

"In this universe, Mr. Paige," said Leach, his voice low, almost a whisper, "we are confronted with choices. On one hand there is virtue, righteousness, morality, and justice." His voice began rising, hitting the words like a Baptist preacher. "On the other hand there is decadence, greed, and perversion."

Leach remained directly in front of him; Cole could smell his fetid breath through the fabric. He turned his head to keep from gagging.

"I know you, Mitchell," he whispered. "I know what you're up to. Did you think you could fool me?"

"Sir?" Cole could hear the naked bewilderment in the other man's voice.

"I should get rid of you for this fiasco with the reports, Mitchell. I should fire you on principle, but I've decided to give you one more chance."

No response. Smart move, thought Cole.

"Are you good, Mr. Paige, or are you evil?" boomed Leach suddenly, the voice so strident and different from Leach's usual tone it almost seemed disembodied to Cole, a voice from beyond.

Cole could almost hear Mitchell squirming.

"Well, sir," said Paige. He sounded at a loss. "I think there's good and evil in everyone. How could one person be completely good or completely evil? People are more complex than that."

"People are more complex than that?" Cole saw the shadow in front of him move back toward the desk. "No. That's not true, Mitchell." The shadow raised its hands. "I will show you the truth."

"Yes, sir."

"I, Mr. Paige, am good. I personify good." Cole could hear him sitting down.

Cole heard sirens and glanced behind him out the window. More police had arrived at the protest below. A couple of paddy wagons had pulled up, and at least five squad cars were parked opposite them. Cops in riot gear stood shoulder to shoulder with the EduNet security forces. The protesters had stopped marching and stood in a line with raised fists, shouting at the cops and security forces. A voice distracted him.

"Evil is what I am fighting," Leach was saying. "The people, the filthy animals, who are attempting to feed off the government and to bleed us hardworking citizens dry. That, Mr. Paige, is evil."

"What you did with these reports was both evil and good. I don't agree with your methods. I feel you degraded yourself." Cole heard a low grunt, and then a snort, almost a chuckle. "However," he continued, "I believe you did the wrong thing for the right reasons. You helped the company. You helped our society. And that, my son, is forgivable."

"Thank you, sir." Paige's voice was almost a whisper. Cole heard more sirens and turned back to the window. Smoke billowed over the sidewalk now and people, cops, protesters, and security were scurrying everywhere. Cole saw a security guard wrap a young man in a headlock and pummel his face with a short baton. Cops lined up in a row, holding their clear riot shields up as protesters bombarded them with bricks and rocks. A young woman ran into the street, apparently blinded by the smoke, her face covered in blood.

"What I find unforgivable," Leach continued, "is perversion and greed. Those who cannot control their own animal impulses, their natural sexuality, are weak. Evil is a lack of strength. We need to recognize that to conquer it."

Cole turned toward the room; there was something new in Leach's voice, something sticky, something clammy.

"Paige, my boy," he said. "You must find that strength. You must conquer that evil inside you."

There was a pause. Cole listened and finally heard Paige take a breath.

"Yes, sir. I'll try, sir."

Cole heard an earnestness in his tone that was—to him—somewhat surprising.

"You must do more than try," said Leach. "You think of things that are wrong. I know you do. You desire things that you should not desire. You must stop that. You must do it immediately."

"I will, sir," said Paige. Cole thought he heard a hitch, almost a sob, in Mitchell's voice.

Cole heard Leach stand and open the desk drawer. He took out something and laid it on the desk. It sounded heavy.

"Yes. You will," said Leach. "Now take off your shoes and socks."

Chapter 25

Millicent lay as still as she possibly could, even though the gravel felt sharp beneath her cheek and the acrid smell of asphalt filled her nose. She figured if they thought she was out or hurt, they wouldn't mess with her anymore. And so far, so good with that, she thought. Even though I've been stepped on a few times. Another cloud of smoke began blowing over the road toward her. She held her breath and waited for it to pass. If she was lucky, it would drift right by. That must be that tear gas; she had never experienced anything like it, not in all her days. One breath and you were crying, coughing, blind, and throwing up. Helpless. Like a sick baby. That's when she had gotten hit and went down. When she was helpless. They had to wait until an old lady was helpless before they knocked her down. What kind of people were these?

The cloud passed over her and she breathed again. She blinked as her vision slowly began to clear. By some miracle, her glasses had stayed on during her ordeal. The first thing she saw was a young girl, no more than eighteen or nineteen, lying next to her on the ground, unconscious, blood all over face. The poor thing had her skirt all hiked up showing her underthings. Beyond her, she could see a young man, one of Jerome Johnson's people—they all wore those hats—doubled over as a policeman kept beating on him with his baton. He was joined by one of those security guards in blue, the EduNet people, on the beating. The boy went down, and the two of them continued kicking him and laughing. There was a row of people on the sidewalk lying on their stomachs with their hands cuffed behind them. Some of the people were groaning. A couple of them were bleeding. The smell of vomit was everywhere. She didn't see anyone she knew. She sure didn't see Serena.

Cautiously, slowly, she lifted her head and peered around. There was still some scuffling going on beyond the bank of smoke that still hung over the sidewalk, but there were no police near her. She rolled on her side and tried to kneel up, but there was something wrong with her leg. It didn't want to move. A sharp pain shot all the way up her side. She stopped moving to catch her breath, then felt someone coming near her and lay still and shut her eyes.

"Oh, baby," a voice said.

Millicent opened her eyes and there was Serena kneeling next to her, big as life.

"You're late again," said Millicent. She tried to smile, but had no idea what it might look like, no idea what condition her face was in.

"I didn't get your message until half an hour ago. By then, it was already all over the radio and the television. What possessed you to come down here with these radicals?"

Another pain flew up her side, forcing all the breath out of her lungs. She might have said something but wasn't sure. Things went dark.

Millicent opened her eyes. Serena was standing over her, talking to someone in a white jacket. She tried to speak but something had been placed over her mouth. When she tried to take it off, she realized she couldn't move. They'd strapped her in. She started talking, telling them to let her go, that she hadn't done anything. She saw Serena kneeling down next to her.

"Hush, now, Millicent," she said. "These nice people are going to take you over to St. Rita's. They think you might have broken something and want to get you to the emergency room as soon as they can."

Millicent started shaking her head and telling her no, no hospital, she wasn't going to any hospital, she hated them.

Serena put her hand on Millicent's.

"Don't worry, now, baby," she said. "I'm going to ride in the ambulance right alongside of you. I'll be right there."

Millicent took a breath, a shallow breath, it hurt to breathe now, and nodded. She felt them lifting her up and then wheeling her. Then something clanked and suddenly she was lying inside the ambulance. Serena was sitting right next to her, holding her hand. The young man sat on the other side of her, fiddling with some sort of equipment. The ambulance started moving.

"Why don't you use the siren?" asked Serena.

"This isn't really an emergency," said the medic. "Your friend is in no immediate danger. We don't want to tie up traffic if there's another life-threatening situation out there."

Serena nodded.

"I don't think we need this anymore," said the EMT, lifting the mask from Millicent's face.

"Thank you," said Millicent. "I do not like that thing over my mouth."

"I could tell," he said, "but you have to promise to tell me if you start feeling dizzy or lightheaded. All right?"

Millicent nodded.

"Okay," he said, "could you tell me where it hurts?"

She did, describing how it hurt, when it hurt, and how bad. He nodded.

"Okay," he said. "I'm going to have them send you right up to x-ray when we get there."

"Did she break something?" asked Serena. The medic shrugged.

"It's possible," he said, "but we won't know more until we get the x-rays."

Millicent shut her eyes. Please God, she thought, do not let it be my hip. I could not stand to be laid up that long. And she knew some people broke their hips and never got over it. They just curled up, dried up, and drifted out. Please God, she thought. Not me.

"Millicent?"

She opened her eyes. Serena was looking down at her, frowning.

"What happened out there, Millicent?"

Millicent thought a moment, sifting through the images of the smoke, the tears, the sounds of wood hitting flesh and bone, sirens, the screaming, the swearing.

"First," she said. "It was quiet. Jerome Johnson, that young man from the meeting, was there handing out signs. They told us to march in a circle on the sidewalk across the street from the building."

"Why were you out there?"

Millicent tried to remember. Then it came to her.

"Reverend Lee called," she said, "and he said there was going to be a small and peaceful demonstration in front of the EduNet building. He was there, and I saw him helping people after the fights started. Jerome John-son and his crew were there, and I was a little worried they were ready for something, but they were good. They were peaceful."

She stopped, remembering a moment.

"Ulysses was there," she said. "You remember him from the meeting. I didn't see anyone else I knew." She took another breath. It didn't hurt so bad this time. "Jerome did a good job. He had things organized. He told us to stay calm, not to yell, not to be confrontational or to throw anything. And we were good. We were just marching, chanting some things, you know, like 'free our schools', 'keep public schools public', you know."

"Uh-huh," said Serena, grasping her hand more tightly.

"Then all of a sudden we see all these men in blue jackets coming out of the building. You know, they were wearing the jackets like sport coats. It turned out they were security. That's what Jerome said. At first, we thought they were just going to stand there, you know, make a line be-tween us and the building. And they did. At first. But then the police cars starting rolling up with sirens and lights going. Everything. Then one of the big police trucks, you know, like the UPS truck, comes rolling up, and all these cops in riot gear come out. Well they formed a line right in front of the security line."

She took another breath. The pain was almost gone. A wave of warmth passed through her and she closed her eyes. She looked up just a moment later. Serena was still looking closely at her. I better keep going, thought Millicent. Serena does get impatient.

"So," she continued, "we were watching all this happening and some of the young men were getting a little angry. A couple of them began yelling at the police and shaking their fists, but that Jerome came right over and settled them down. 'Don't give them what they want' he said. 'Don't play into their hands.' Well, Serena, things happened quick after that. Somebody threw something. A rock, I think, and it bounced off one of the policeman's shields. Then something popped and there was smoke everywhere." She felt the tears welling in her eyes as the images started replaying themselves to her.

"And then, Serena, then, they were just on us. The police weren't bad, they was just pushing us back. It was those guards, that security. They had these sticks they were beating us with. I saw one of Jerome's people go down with a big gash on the side of his head. And Jerome, too, but these guards were not letting up when we went down. Nope. They were kicking and beating us all. I saw Ulysses go down and I was going over to him when something hit me and everything went dark."

She stared up at Serena. "Sorry, Serena," she whispered. "That's all I remember."

"That's fine, baby," said Serena, grasping her hand with both of hers. "That's just fine."

Millicent looked up at her face and wanted to tell her not to cry, that she was going to be fine, that she was feeling better by the minute, that she was sure all those fine strong men—especially Ulysses—were going to be fine, too.

"Hey, Serena," she said. "Don't cry, baby. As soon as I get home, I'll make you some of my Apple Crumble. Because," she whispered, pulling Serena closer, "the good Lord himself, if ever he would come down to earth again, could not resist the taste of my Apple Crumble."

She heard Serena chuckle as she closed her eyes and let the warm darkness, like the river on a summer night, flow over her.

Chapter 26

Dave looked across the table. Beverly looked nice tonight, very nice. She was wearing a black satiny type of dress that showed off her curves quite well and she had done something to her hair, though he couldn't say exactly what. She looked up suddenly from the wine list and smiled.

"What do you think?" he asked.

"I don't know," she said. "You're the wine expert. What do you like?"

"Well," he said, leaning over and taking the wine list from her, "the Chianti is really nice here, but the Burgundy, the 2009 Drouhin, is drinking really nicely now."

"Really? How do you know?"

"I had some just the other night." He raised his eyebrows. "I do my homework."

"I see. Well, I guess I'll have to trust your judgment. Let's go for the Burgundy."

"You won't be disappointed."

She leaned forward and whispered, "I'm sure I won't." He felt a tingling go through him that he hadn't felt since high school; this woman knew how to flirt. The waiter came and he ordered the wine, asking it to be decanted at the table. While they waited, she chatted about Celia, her daughter, and all the tribulations she had been going through on the JV volleyball team.

Dave listened, nodding and clucking when appropriate, and concentrated on keeping his eyes on Beverly's; they kept pulling downward toward her breasts, which lay nestled in the black satiny valley of her dress. He was genuinely sympathetic to what she was saying; he had raised three daughters himself and had ridden through the rough patches of mean girls, queen bees, all the middle school cliquey shit, and boys, boys, boys, but he was fighting a rising tide of hormones he hadn't felt for years. And, oddly, unpredictably, an erection that wouldn't quit. It was embarrassing.

The wine came and the waiter opened it. Dave crossed his legs as he decanted it, hoping to regain some control of his libido. He poured them both a glass, took their orders and left. Dave raised his glass.

"To us," he said. She smiled and raised her glass in return.

"Yes," she said, "to a new beginning. And it's a good thing we got started. 'Lovers ever run before the clock'".

"Shakespeare?" he asked.

"Yes," she giggled. "How did you know?"

"Oh, just a guess."

They ate, talking about work, colleagues, and the upcoming key school board meeting as they finished off the Burgundy before they left. It so happened that Celia was doing a sleepover with a friend, even though it was a school night, so Beverly had told him they'd have the house to themselves. Dave followed her in his car as they drove through the old East Side neighborhood where she lived.

It occurred to him on the ride over that he had made no provisions for birth control. He wasn't sure if Beverly used any—from what she said, it didn't seem as if she had much use for it these days—or if she had gone through her change in life and didn't need it anymore. And he was not about to ask about that. He could have kicked himself for not stopping and picking up some rubbers before meeting her at the restaurant. Well, perhaps he was being too optimistic anyway, although if he was still any good at reading the signs, there seemed to be a pretty good chance he wouldn't be sleeping alone tonight.

She pulled into the driveway next to a bungalow nestled behind a big oak tree, now naked of its leaves. Its black branches reached high, blanking out large parts of the house and sky. He pulled up in front of the house. Beverly stood on the porch, waiting for him.

"Nice house," he said.

"Well," she said, finding her key, "don't look at it in the daytime. It needs a lot of work."

She opened the door and went in. Dave followed. Like so many of the old East Side bungalows, this one had finished oak floors, white plaster walls with molding, and the little stained glass windows on either side of the china cabinet. The furniture was very nice, though it looked a little worn. But who am I to talk, thought Dave. This place is a mansion compared to my house.

"Give me a minute," said Beverly. "I need to freshen up. Make yourself at home. There's a few bottles of wine in the rack next to the china cabinet. Why don't you open one up?"

"Okay," he said. He bent down over the mini-rack. There was a moderately good Chianti, a Pinot he had never heard of, an Australian Sauvignon Blanc, and—surprisingly—a very nice, and expensive, Bordeaux. It was tempting, but, well, maybe he should open the Chianti.

Dave grabbed it, went to the kitchen and rummaged through a kitchen drawer until he found the corkscrew. He opened it, and looked for some wine glasses, found only the stemless kind—oh, well—and poured out two glasses, put his nose in one and inhaled deeply. Yep. Just as nice as he remembered. Very nice Chianti. He returned to the living room with glasses and wine in hand and settled himself onto the couch.

"I see you're making yourself at home."

He turned and saw Beverly standing in the arch between the living and dining room, wearing black satin—again—pajamas. They were styled like men's pajamas, but were cut differently. For a woman. They hung very nicely. He smiled.

"I think we both are," he said.

She came and sat beside him. He handed her a glass of wine and they sipped it, glancing at each other shyly, almost coyly. My God, thought Dave, you'd think we were a couple of teenagers, but, he reflected, they weren't young and fresh like kids, but worn and wounded, rejected—badly—by those closest to them and still not past licking their wounds.

Without thinking about it, he leaned over and kissed Beverly softly on the lips. She gasped a little, surprised, and then returned it. His hands cupped her face, then reached over to the back of her neck, holding her head to his as he kissed her lips, her cheeks, and her neck. His hands began roaming over her body, finding her thighs, her breasts, her belly. He felt her hands reaching toward his hips, undoing his belt, and reaching for his zipper. She stopped suddenly.

"What?" he said.

"We should probably go to the bedroom," she said, smoothing her hair back with both hands. Her pajama top had come undone and he could spy one breast hanging loose in the folds of the flimsy fabric, the nipple peeking out at him as she moved.

"Okay," he said, grabbing his glass and the bottle of wine. "Lead on, MacDuff."

"Oh," she said, grabbing him by the front of the pants and leading him upstairs, "now you think you can seduce me with a little Shakespeare?"

"Well," he said, shrugging, "maybe."

She giggled as she led him through the door and into the bedroom.

* * * * *

They lay together, not speaking. He felt a delicious chill as a breath of air tickled the sheen of sweat on his naked body. Beverly lay next to him, still breathing a little heavily, her hand clamped onto his like a vise. He closed his eyes; this had been really nice. He had almost forgotten—his body had almost forgotten—the sensations, the smells, the slap of flesh on flesh. Sex. Finally. Thank God.

"That was really nice," said Bev.

"Well," said Dave. "It was okay, I guess."

"Shut up," she said, elbowing him. "You were barking like a dog."

"Yeah," he said. "You're right. It was very nice."

He lay back a moment, relaxing, truly relaxing, for the first time in months. He let his mind drift a moment, roaming from point to point, until suddenly the image of Darrel slumped at his desk popped into his mind.

"What?" asked Beverly, who, he supposed, had been drifting, too. He must have jumped or made some sort of noise.

"Nothing," he said. "I just remembered something that happened in my third hour this morning."

"What, anything bad?" Beverly asked, her voice suddenly pointed in the darkness.

"No. I was talking to my kids about going to the school board meeting, you know, and me giving extra credit for it, and I was talking to them about how much better public schools were than the charters."

Beverly sat up and flipped on the bedside lamp.

"Okay," she said, laying back down and snuggling in close. "So?"

"So one of my kids, one of my best students, said that maybe EduNet running the school or even going to a different school might not be such a bad idea."

Beverly cupped her hand under her chin and leaned over him.

"Which kid?"

"I don't know if you know him. Darrel Ridgeman. He's a little guy."

"Sure I know him. He's the home-schooled kid who knows almost everything. A real braniac."

"He's a nice kid," said Dave, feeling defensive of Darrel all of a sudden. The other kids called him a braniac sometimes; it wasn't meant as a compliment.

"Of course he is," said Beverly, "but he doesn't really fit into the school. He's not really a public school kid."

He turned his head and looked at her.

"What I mean," she continued, "is that he's not part of the social climate there. He doesn't have a lot of friends, he doesn't do any extra-curriculars, and he doesn't get the culture; you know, the music, the clothes. He didn't grow up with it."

He nodded. She was right.

"So," she continued, "it's no wonder that he doesn't think Custer is a great school. It's not what he's used to."

"A couple of other kids agreed with him," said Dave, squirming a little. He felt warm; he wasn't used to another body so close to his.

"I bet they were pretty good students. Not great, but pretty good."

"Yeah," said Dave, turning his head to look at her. "How did you know?"

Beverly sat up and reached for the glasses of wine. She carefully handed one to Dave and sipped her own.

"One thing you know about kids—teenagers—is that they're going to find fault with authority, right? Their parents, the establishment—"

"Right on," he said.

They both smiled at the expression. Dave knew it had been years since he'd heard it. "—the government," continued Beverly, "and, of course, their school. It's what they do at this age."

"So you think our kids are happy where they are? That they like it there?"

"Yeah," said Beverly, drawing her legs up under her chin. "I think most of them are happy there."

"I don't know," said Dave. "I wonder if some of them might think they're getting shortchanged. They see kids from other schools—white kids, mostly—getting better grades, better test scores, better opportunities, and going to better colleges. Or going to college, period, and they wonder why it's not happening to them."

"That's a big question," said Beverly, draining her glass. "Big enough for another glass of wine." She sat up and refilled her glass.

"It's not the teaching," she said, after taking a sip. "God knows we work our asses off, and for the most part, the faculty here is pretty good. I think there are a lot of things: poverty, apathy, mistrust of the system, and a general decline in the valuation of education." She turned and smiled at him. "How's that for a mouthful?"

"Pretty good," he said. She was right, but these were the same old arguments he'd been hearing for the past thirty years.

"So what's bothering you, Dave?" she asked.

"It got me thinking," said Dave, "about whether we're right." He turned and looked at her. "I'm wondering if public schools are really the best thing for our kids."

"You think EduNet would be better?"

"EduNet? Hell, no." They both chuckled. "But," he continued, growing serious again, "I have to wonder if we're defunct and we don't know it."

"Well, let's see," said Beverly. "We teach our students, we motivate them, we provide supplies for most of them." Dave nodded. "We feed them," she continued. "Two meals a day. We counsel them, we—for all intents and purposes—parent them, we advise them, we accommodate them, and we discipline them. We show them love. For some of them, the only time they see it at all during their day. Do you think they would be getting that much from a private charter? No." She shook her head. "No way. I think until we finally start taking poverty seriously, we're not going anywhere with all these problems."

Dave nodded. She was probably right. But how was he supposed to tell Darrel that without alienating him? Yeah, Darrel, we're doing everything we can, but your community and your culture are too fucked up for us to help you out. Sorry, buddy, but you're screwed. The same as your daddy was and the same as your granddaddy was. It's just the way things are.

"Penny for your thoughts," said Beverly, cuddling in again.

"I was just wondering," said Dave, staring at the ceiling, "for all the years we've been teaching, things have never really improved that significantly, right?" He didn't look at her, but felt, rather than heard, her affirmation. "So that begs the question, why are the parents and the community so attached to public schools? Why don't they want something better?"

"They know," said Bev. He looked over at her, sitting up, the light framing her naked body in dark heavy lines.

"They know what?"

"C'mon, Dave," she said. "Use your head. They know the obstacles that these kids are facing. They see it every day, a hell of a lot more often than we do."

"Yeah," he said, still not convinced. "So?"

"So," she said, "they know we're doing the best we can because they're doing the best they can."

"But it's not enough," said Dave.

"No," she said, taking another sip of wine. She drew her legs up tighter against her torso. "It's not enough, and it's frustrating, but it's all they have. They want their kids to be successful, to be doctors, lawyers, CEOs, like all of us, but we're all they've got."

"What about private schools? I don't mean the private charters, but what about the Catholic schools, the Lutherans?"

"Remember Lionel Little?"

He thought a moment. Yeah. Three or four years ago. A pretty bright kid who was acting out in school because he was bored; his mom had pulled him out and put him in a predominantly white Catholic school.

"Yeah," he said. "I remember him. His mom sent him over to St. John's. Whatever happened to him?"

"I happened to see her at Walmart the other day. He was miserable over there. He had nothing in common with the kids there and he felt ostracized. His mom transferred him over to Central the following year." She shrugged. "Academics and grades and opportunities were important to her, but so was his happiness. He graduated—from a public school—and got a scholarship to Ohio State. Success is possible."

He shut his eyes. That was a risky argument; she was opening herself up to being called an elitist—or a racist.

"I don't know," said Beverly. "I know that what I've been saying sounds elitist, but it's not. You know that. I just know in Lionel's case he didn't want to be pulled out of his school, his neighborhood, his whole life. How would you feel if your parents had sent you away to school? I know it happens, but these kids feel marginalized anyway, even in their own neighborhoods."

Dave felt himself drifting as Beverly continued talking. He was slipping into a sleep state, aware but not, slowly moving images forming on the edge of his subconscious. A face started forming, one he didn't know. Yet. Yet. He did know it. As it slowly came into focus, he felt his chest tighten and his breath catch in his throat. He jolted suddenly and completely awake.

"What?" asked Beverly.

"Oh, man," said Dave, breathing hard. His heart was racing.

"What?" she asked, putting her hand on his chest. "Were you having a bad dream?"

"Yeah, I guess so," he said, sitting up and putting his head in his hands. Who was it? Who had he seen in the dream?

"Here," she said, handing him his glass and looking warily at him. She's probably wondering if I sleepwalk or something, thought Dave. He closed his eyes, trying to resurrect what he had seen. No dice.

"I think this whole thing is getting to you, Mr. Bell." She pushed him back down. "You need to lie down and relax."

He lay there a moment, breathing, Beverly's hand on his chest. He felt himself drifting again, drifting into sleep, oblivion, and the dread of his dreams.

"David?" she asked.

He opened his eyes and looked at her sitting next to him, naked as a baby. He had to smile.

"Would you mind if I turned on the television? I like to catch the news before I go to sleep."

"Sure," he said, and fluffed up his pillow.

She got the remote control and flipped on the TV. Dave reached for his wine glass.

"Jesus."

He looked up at her. She was staring at a shot of a riot. Tear gas flooded the street as police and security goons beat on protestors. The caption underneath read, 'Rioters attempt to storm EduNet Building.'

Dave looked closely at the crowd but didn't recognize anyone. Beverly turned up the sound. The newscaster's voice boomed out suddenly.

"The protest began peacefully but violence soon escalated after members of the crowd began throwing objects at the policemen. Police, as well as members of the EduNet Security Team, moved in quickly to secure the riot scene."

More footage flashed of people running. An older woman lay still on the street, her leg skewed off at an odd angle. A row of people lay facedown on the sidewalk, handcuffed. Beverly turned and looked at him, aghast.

"What's happening, Dave? What does this mean?"

"Shit," he said. "Just shit."

Chapter 27

"You went ahead and decided without me?" whispered Serena into the phone.

Millicent smiled. Even Serena's whispers sounded loud. She glanced over at the television mounted on the wall. Her leg was throbbing again; she pressed the button and raised the bed slightly. Millicent took a breath. They told her she had two broken ribs for sure, and that she had some internal bruising, but they weren't sure about her leg. Maybe it was broken. Well. God would provide. She glanced up at the television.

The news was playing footage of the protest again — for the seventh or eighth time by her count, and she'd only been watching for half an hour. She recognized the shot, the one where the boy got smacked from behind, right in the head, and went down like a sack of potatoes. He looked as if he should have been in school.

"I don't care if this is an imperative," said Serena, glancing back toward Millicent. "I should have been there." She listened a moment. "I would have been at the rally, Reverend Lee, had I been informed in a timely fashion. I didn't hear until one hour before."

Millicent could hear the reverend's deep baritone rolling out of the phone — too light to make out the words, but big enough to recognize. He'd been brave tonight, not fool brave enough to take on the police: that was always a losing proposition, but brave enough to carry out Mrs. Forrester, who'd gone down almost immediately. Millicent wasn't sure if she'd been hit by something or had fainted from the shock of it all because it was — well — shocking. There weren't too many other words for it. No one had expected the police to come after them like that. It had been crazy.

"All right," Serena was saying. She seemed calmer now. "If you say so." Her voice flared up again, still a whisper, but penetrating. "I was not there, so how can I possibly provide an opinion?" She listened a moment. "Well, Reverend, maybe he did do well at the rally, but he is young and

227

he is a hothead. He might light this whole thing up. I would personally go with that Ulysses. He is more mature, more level-headed, more experienced." She glanced over at Millicent and shook her head. "You want me to speak at the school board meeting? You all just decided that? Well, thank you, Reverend, for letting me know in your timely manner. I really do appreciate that." She listened a moment, then grinned and chuckled. "All right, Reverend, all right."

Millicent watched the footage of the riot loop through again. Part of her kept hoping she might see herself up there.

"All right," Serena was saying, "I'll come down there a little later."

The door opened and her doctor walked in. He was a young man, lean, an Indian, not an American Indian, but an Eastern Indian. Dr. Singh. His velvety dark hair was neatly combed to the side. He was dark. He's almost as black as I am, thought Millicent, almost smiling. He came to the foot of her bed and glanced at her chart, then moved to the side of the bed.

"Hello, Mrs. Maxwell," he said. "How are you feeling tonight?"

"I'm not too bad, doctor," she said, "except my leg is still hurting a little bit."

"I'm not surprised," he said, glancing at her chart. "That was a nasty injury you had."

Millicent looked over toward Serena, who had hung up on the Reverend when the doctor came in. Now she was hanging back by the other side of the room, arms crossed. Millicent motioned for her to come over. She had told Serena she wanted her there when the doctors talked; she wanted to be sure she was able to understand what they were saying. Between their jibber jabber and the drugs, she wasn't sure she would get things right. Serena came to the other side of the bed and took Millicent's hand. She looked at Dr. Singh expectantly. She looked anxious, almost cowed.

"This is my friend Serena, doctor. She's here to translate."

The doctor smiled. Serena smiled back hesitantly but gripped Millicent's hand more tightly.

"Well, I have good news and bad news," said the doctor. "The good news is that your hip is fine. There is some bruising around the soft tissue there, but the bone is sound."

Serena sighed and nodded. Millicent saw her mouth, "Thank you, God."

"Now the bad news is that you do have a hairline fracture of your femur, which is the long bone of your leg."

"That doesn't sound too bad, doctor," said Serena, her tone rising.

She's getting herself back, thought Millicent. Whatever scared her had gone back down.

"Usually not," said Dr. Singh, "but whenever an elderly person breaks a bone, especially a long bone, there is a much greater risk of complications and infection. It is worrisome."

"What do we do?" asked Serena, her tone big and steady.

"The leg is immobilized for now and it is late, so we will put the cast on tomorrow. It will be a big one, extending from here," he said, indicating Millicent's hip, "to here," pointing down toward the ankle. "It will be difficult for you to move around."

"Well," said Millicent, "I suppose I could use a cane."

"Or a walker," said the doctor. "That's what we usually recommend."

Millicent actually snorted and put her hand over her mouth. She could barely believe that sound had come out of her mouth. Serena giggled.

"I," said Millicent, trying to regain her dignity, "am not using a walker. Walkers will guide you right into the nursing home."

"Well," said Dr. Singh, "they will give you everything you need tomorrow." He put his hand on sidebar of the bed. "I must also say that we are also a little concerned about your internal injuries, Mrs. Maxwell. We are still seeing some slight, very slight bleeding, and we would like to monitor your condition for a little longer."

"Is that really necessary, doctor?" asked Serena.

He glanced up at her and leaned on the bar. "Yes," he said, quietly, surely, definitively. "It is." Serena nodded.

Millicent looked up at her and shrugged.

"I will order you something to help with the pain in your leg," said the doctor, "and if you need anything during the night, just ring for the nurse."

"Thank you, doctor," said Serena. Dr. Singh nodded to both of them and left.

"Well," said Serena, "you've got a long road ahead of you, baby, but I'll be there with you every step of the way."

"Hmph," said Millicent, "I want you right next to me on your own walker rolling on into Riverwest Providence."

Serena laughed. "You got it, baby," she said. "You got it." Millicent started giggling too, and then yawned.

"All right," said Serena, "I'm going to go and let you get some rest, but I'll be back tomorrow morning."

"Okay," said Millicent. Her eyelids were suddenly heavy. Serena's voice seemed to be coming from a distance now, from across the room. She felt something—a hand—touch her forehead and stroke it gently. She stopped on the edge of sleep and teetered there, like a child balancing with one foot on the curb, and smiled.

"Good night, Mama," she said. "Good night."

Chapter 28

Joe leaned over the backgammon board, his head in his hand, thinking.

"So Mr. Leach told me he needs evidence," said Cole, "proving Paige is—as he terms it—a sexual deviant. The gay angle. That's how he wants us to play it."

"Really?" asked Joe. He took another sip of bourbon. "What sort of evidence? Videotape? Eyewitness?" He didn't ask why. Why didn't matter.

"Yes," said Cole. "Something like that." He had turned and was staring at Joe, the darks of his eyes like open graves.

Joe looked back at him a moment and then nodded. "Sure. We can do that."

"All right," said Cole, sitting down again. "Personally, I would prefer taking care of this without the sexual angle, but, as you know, the client is always right."

Joe felt himself frown. It seemed to him that Cole's voice had gone a little noble. He'd heard that tone before, when cops said they would only go so far, that they had limits. He leaned over and moved a marker.

"So, Joe," asked Mr. Cole, looking at the board. "Any ideas?"

Joe nodded. "Yeah. Let's do it at the school board meeting. We can set him up real easy there. There's going to be fireworks anyway, right?" He smiled at Mr. Cole, who smiled back.

"So," continued Joe, "we know Paige will be pissed off, anyway. It won't take much to set him off. We make it look like he's the instigator."

"That would certainly help other aspects of the case. Can you do it?"

"Don't worry," said Sykes.

Cole nodded as he considered the board.

"Then," continued Sykes, sipping his bourbon, "then we take him out of the room and make Mr. Leach happy. After we're done, there won't be any doubt he engages in deviant behavior."

He held out his glass and Joe touched it with his own. A few drops sloshed out as the tumblers made contact and splashed on the table. Joe leaned forward quickly and swabbed them up with his shirtsleeve.

"Thank you," said Cole, smiling. "You are, in every way my dear Joseph, a master cleaner."

Chapter 29

Sandra pulled into the school parking lot. It was already getting hard to find a space. She glanced at her watch. Six forty-five. The meeting was due to begin at seven-thirty. It looked as if it was going to be a full house tonight. She parked the car, turned it off, and sat a moment. It was time. Showtime. Time to put on her game face. The event had finally arrived, and she should have been elated, overjoyed, pumped. But the truth was that she couldn't have felt worse about it.

She was about to help eradicate a public school, probably the first of many, to dismantle part of the community, part of her own past, part of herself. She wouldn't be who she was if it wasn't for her school. Not this particular one, but one just like it. And she was about to begin the process of wiping all that out. She fumbled in her purse, found her pack of cigarettes and lit one up. She'd smell like smoke, but she didn't give a damn anymore; she didn't care who knew.

Sandra opened the door, dropped the cigarette, and stepped on it. She stood and surveyed the full parking lot, took a deep breath, and squared her shoulders. They were in for a fight. She was here to do a job, and she planned on doing it. There was no other choice. She had made a commitment to EduNet, to Mitchell, and to herself, and—like it or not—she was going to follow through with it. Sandra locked the car and started toward the brightly lit school door. Had she known then what she knew now, no, she would not have signed up with EduNet. But she hadn't known. She had signed up with them, signed up to make her name in the corporate world and to make her big bucket of money. And she was probably going to end up with both. Lucky her. Lucky fucking her. Sandra walked into the door, nodding to the school security guard standing there. He smiled at her and she smiled back. Well, she thought, that's probably the last friendly exchange I'll have all night.

* * * * *

Dave sat in his classroom. It had always seemed odd to him, whether it was during parent teacher conferences or open house or working late, how different his classroom felt at night. He knew it was absurd, but it always seemed to him as if time stood still then, as if the world were caught in amber, trapped in the dark, as if in a dream state. Without the students, without the energy, without the light or the noise, the room was not a classroom anymore, a holy place of learning; it was only a room, and an ugly room at that: walls painted that pukish institutional green, desks set in straight rows facing the much bigger teacher desk, and beige blinds covering the windows that stretched down to the air vents on the counter.

His room was waiting. It was holding its breath, anticipating the day, the children, the light coming from outside those windows and from within those young and fragile eyes. It was waiting for him and his craftiness, for the magic that only happened during the school day, magic that was coy, hiding between the pages of battered textbooks and crinkled worksheets, behind furrowed brows and dull pencils, but magic that—when it struck—pounced suddenly, or deliberately, into the hearts of children. Sometimes it came with laughter, joy, affirmation, sometimes it traveled with pain, sorrow, or compassion. It was everywhere.

Dave stood and stretched, stood a moment gazing out the window into the darkness, and opened his desk drawer. He fumbled around, looking for his Tylenol bottle. Of course it wasn't there. Shit. Well, even if he had found it, it probably would have been empty. He glanced at his watch. Seven. He'd better get down there. He walked to the door, took one more look at the empty room, as still as a crypt, flipped off the lights, and shut the door.

* * * * *

Sandra walked into the George Armstrong Custer Auditorium. It looked a lot like the way she remembered Central's Auditorium back when they weren't afraid to spend money on building their schools: there was a tall proscenium arch over the stage, and behind it—if it was like Central—a state-of-the-art backstage area with a light board, a fly rail, the whole nine yards.

The Channel Seven news crew was setting up its camera in one corner while Channel Five was already running tests on the opposite side. Wall to wall coverage, thought Sandra. Wonderful. Just what she needed—more pressure. Three long tables stood on the stage with microphones set in a row like crows perched on a telephone wire. She surveyed the stage. Nobody was sitting down yet, although a few people were milling around behind the seats. Sandra recognized a couple of the school board members, Mark Maris and Milton Gorski, who were engaged in friendly conversation. That wasn't surprising. They both owned their own businesses and were conservatives and deeply pro-privatization advocates: big allies of EduNet, a part of her team.

She had never met them before but knew their histories and politics intimately. In fact, she knew a lot about all the board members. That had been part of her job. She glanced around, looking for Mitchell. Not here yet.

"Excuse me," said a voice at her elbow. Sandra turned and saw a youngish African-American woman, dressed in a black sleeveless gown.

"I'm sorry," the woman continued, "but I wanted to introduce myself. I'm Celeste Hightower from the mayor's office. I'm here tonight as a community liaison."

Sandra nodded, recognizing the name. The mayor had wanted someone to act as his eyes and ears at the community meetings concerning the takeover, someone discreet, Mitchell had said. Well, thought Sandra, this sweet young thing is about as inconspicuous as a butterfly on a corpse.

"I'm Sandra Feeley from EduNet," she said quietly, not wanting to attract attention. Not yet.

"I know who you are," whispered Celeste, extending her hand. "This is so exciting. It's going to be a new chapter in the history of this city. Of this state. Of education in general."

"Yes, it's going to be quite the show," said Sandra. Hopefully not a shit show. "So," she continued, "should we be expecting the mayor tonight?"

She knew full well he would never show at anything as controversial as tonight's meeting, but they still—after all this time—didn't know where the mayor stood on the takeover. Somehow he'd successfully straddled the issue for over three months. Maybe, she thought, maybe Ms. Hightower might give us a little insight as to where our good mayor might land.

"Unfortunately, no," said the girl. "He had a previous engagement, and won't be able to attend tonight, but he sends his full support and approval to everyone here." She leaned forward and whispered, "It was really nice meeting you, Sandra. Good luck."

Sandra glanced around the auditorium. From where she stood below and to the side of the stage, she could see the seats were filling up. Pairs of school security guards were already stationed at every exit. From what she could see, it mostly looked like families and just plain folks. Citizens. Most of them were chatting and getting settled, as if they were getting ready for a night at the theatre. There was a group of youngish looking guys wearing blue berets sitting about halfway up near the aisle and another one sitting near the front. The Guardians. She'd heard about them from Mitchell: some sort of militant community activist group. They looked pretty grim.

She glanced at her watch. Quarter after seven. Okay, she thought. I have time to freshen up a little. After all, there are TV cameras out there. She looked around a saw a bathroom sign a little farther down the hall. She went in. After fixing her make-up, she glanced at herself in the mirror. Good. She looked good. She squared her shoulders, straightened her jacket, and strode out into the hallway. The first thing she saw was Mitchell standing by the stage door. He looked irritated.

"Jesus," he said. "It's about time. You're late."

It just fucking figures, she thought, walking up to him. Somehow, some way, he always gets the upper hand. Sandra took a good look at him; as usual, he looked good, really good. Too good. He was wearing his charcoal Armani suit, a blue silk shirt with a pale lemon tie, and his black Florsheims. The outfit screamed success, money, and privilege. He looked like a million bucks. Exactly the wrong message they wanted to send tonight. Money was not supposed to be part of the equation, and yet here he was standing here dressed like fucking royalty. Plus, his hair had been freshly cut, and he looked as if he'd been to the spa. His whole appearance reeked of money.

"What?" he asked. "Don't you like my outfit?"

"You look good," she said, trying to squeeze the irony from her voice. He had no clue how inappropriate this was. Well, she thought, it wouldn't do any good to let him know now; it was too late to do anything about it, and all it would do would be to set him off. And the last thing she needed was a surly Mitchell next to her up on that stage.

"You, too," he said. "You look great."

"Thanks," she said. She looked closely at him. He looked all right, together. Prepared. Except he still seemed to be favoring his leg.

"How's your leg?"

"Good. My foot, actually, but it's fine."

They looked at each other a moment.

"Are we ready?" she said.

"Yeah," he said. "Sure. But we have a few minutes."

"I know, but I thought we could go over a few things. I was going to review some of the details and maybe point out some of the school board members to you. You should probably know who's in our corner."

"Well," said Mitchell, raising his arm and fixing his cuff, "I know we have Maris and Gorski in our pocket for sure, and probably Wallace. Jackson, Rosicky, and Dupree are on the fence, although Dupree can be swayed. Robinson, Sanfelippo, and Montoya are probably unreachable."

"I'm impressed," said Sandra. "You did your homework."

"Hey," said Mitchell, shrugging. "I do the politics, remember? That's my area. This part of it I know better than you know your spreadsheets and data. In fact, despite what you think, I do know all this stuff. Inside and fucking out. So. I think we were able to reach Rosicky and Dupree. Jackson was more of a tough nut, but we'll see."

"This is not going on behind closed doors anymore, Mitchell. These guys can't just go off the tracks because of some backroom deal they made with you. They're going to have to answer to their people out there, their constituents."

"Well," said Mitchell, "never underestimate the power of the almighty buck." He smiled at her, winked, and held out his arm. Sandra looked at him, grinning at her like a monkey, took his arm, and nodded. They walked through the door and onto the stage.

* * * * *

Serena had submitted her speaking slip to the secretary an hour before. Two minutes to say her piece. That was absolutely ridiculous. No one was going to pull a stopwatch on Serena McDaniels; she would say what she had to say and that would be that. She took her seat in the section of the auditorium reserved for speakers. Two or three other people she didn't recognize were there: one older white man in a three-piece suit and an elderly woman with her arm in a sling. One of the survivors of the riot, or I should say the massacre, thought Serena. Well, good for you.

She craned her neck, scanning the crowd for Lilly Robinson, the president of the board. She and Lilly went way back; she had taught Serena's children at Carver Elementary, had gone into administration, then had retired and run for the school board back in 1996. And she had towered over it ever since then, piloting policy that aided families, schools, and neighborhoods. She was—is—thought Serena, a monument to her community and her people.

Our community, thought Serena, glancing around her. Our nation. Look at us. A people strong and united: educators, pastors, lawyers, doctors, and plain old working people: all of us, all of the diaspora, the scattered. Their allies were in attendance, too, the other people who cared about right and wrong: Hispanic people, Hmongs, white people, especially the Custer faculty, and others: decent people, God-fearing people, just people. She waved at some of the acquaintances and families she knew from church and everywhere else: the Williams, the Tribletts, the Robinsons, and there were the Ruffins. She hadn't seen them in forever.

"Why, hello there."

Serena turned. Lilly Robinson. That was the way of it—the person you are looking for is always the last one you find.

"Hello, Lilly," she said, standing up and wrapping her in a hug. Lilly was tiny, no more than five foot in tall shoes, and her age had made her look even tinier. She probably had never weighed more than one hundred pounds in her life. She stepped away and gave Serena a good look.

"Look at you," said Lilly. "You haven't changed a bit. How long has it been, Serena?"

"It's been so long that I don't want to know."

The two of them laughed loud and long like nothing had changed. And, thought Serena, it really hasn't changed. Our education system has been under fire, and our neighborhood children are at war with each other, but there wasn't anything too much new about that.

"Let's have a seat," said Lilly. "My feet hurt." They sat and Lilly leaned in close. "I think it's a toss-up right now. We have four to stay public, myself included, three to go private that will not be swayed, and two that might land on either side of the fence. All we need is one."

Serena nodded. That was pretty much the way she had figured it, too, except she only had counted on three to stay public.

"Did we get DuPree?" she asked.

Lilly shook her head. "Not yet. He's holding out. Uh-uh. Billy Rosicki came over to us this morning. He was saying he'd been getting some pretty strong pressure from lobbyists over in Madison and that he'd be damned if he was going to let any crooked politician tell him what to do."

That is a bonus, thought Serena, because no one ever knew what that crazy old man was going to do.

"So without DuPree," she said, "that leaves Willie Jackson."

"Yes, it does," said Lilly, frowning. "I don't know what's in his mind anymore. He's been worried about his business. He's been saying he can't find help from the neighborhood, that the kids who apply to work at his stores can't do any math or write worth a damn and that they quit after their first paycheck. I don't think he believes in public schools anymore."

Lilly frowned and glanced up at Serena, who said nothing. They both knew there was a grain of truth in what Willie was saying. It seemed that no matter what they did or how hard they tried, that the quality of education was slowly spiraling downward. Some people blamed teachers, some the curriculum, and some the culture: the constant distractions of computers and video games and social networking and twittering and God knew what else. And some people blamed the disintegration of family. That argument hit Serena directly in the heart every time and she knew Lilly felt the same way.

"Serena," said Lilly. She was looking at Serena, concerned.

"I'm sorry, honey," said Serena. "I was just thinking."

"I know." She patted Serena's knee. "Say, how is Millicent Maxwell? I heard that she was beaten up in yesterday's demonstration."

Serena nodded. "Thank you for asking. She has a broken leg, but seems to be doing all right. The doctors are worried about infection; they're keeping her in the hospital a few days."

"Thank God for that."

Serena nodded. She glanced over her shoulder, hoping to see Reverend Lee in the crowd. Not yet. And there, near the back, was someone she recognized but couldn't place. A white man in one of those Navy pea coats, and... well, that was the only thing she could remember about him for the moment.

"Serena."

She turned. Lilly was standing up. "You're drifting again. You better get ready for that speech of yours." She gestured up toward the stage. "I've got to get up there, honey. It's time."

Serena stood and they hugged.

"God bless you, Lilly, and let's stop this thing in its tracks."

"I know we will, baby. I know we will." Lilly turned and walked to the stage door. Serena watched her and then sat, waiting her turn, waiting her turn.

Chapter 30

I t was packed. Dave had never remembered the auditorium being so full, not even in the days when the school had been at its capacity of about a thousand students. He looked around, wondering where he could sit and then saw Knox, sitting in a side section close to the front with Zoe Ralph and Mr. Reynolds, waving at him. He weaved his way through the crowd over to them. They had reserved a row for the faculty.

"Dave," said Knox, breathlessly. "We saved you a seat."

"Thanks," said Dave, exchanging greetings with the others. There was a largish group of Custer faculty, maybe fifteen or twenty of them. He edged into the row and sat. Knox was next to him, clutching his ticket tightly as he leaned over and whispered into Zoe's ear.

The crowd—a lot of families and community members—had signs and placards friendly to the cause, but that was a given, that was what they had counted on. Corporate powers never surfaced at events like this; they did their dirty work behind closed doors. Dow had never shown up during the rallies in Madison during the sixties, and Boeing had never appeared at any sit-ins to explain their side of the story. They only spoke to the lowly serfs when they were forced to, and they were being forced to do so today. By the people: these people.

He scrutinized the stage. Lilly Robinson was slowly making her way toward her seat. It wouldn't be long now. The two EduNet representatives were already seated and shuffling papers. Dave was surprised to see that one of them was the woman who had interviewed him—or had tried to—the other day. She was speaking to the suit next to her, pointing out something on her laptop. He looked like the archetypal corporate clown with his thousand-dollar Armani three-piece and designer haircut. You could look at him and honest-to-god see what a royal dick he was; she, on the other hand, hadn't seemed quite so bad when they'd met. What was her name? Something Irish with an "F". Finney? Fenton? No, Feeley. That was it.

Directly in front of the stage, taking up the first three rows, was the reserved section for speakers. Dave recognized some of the popular voices of the black community. There was Serena McDaniels, Alvin Fox, and Reverend Lee. Funny that Brother Malcolm wasn't there; he was always a strong presence at these functions. There were also some parents he knew, Mrs. Blanque, for one, and there was Darrel's mom sitting next to her. And there was Ethel sitting ramrod straight in her chair as she listened to Mrs. Ruffin. Good. He hadn't been sure whether Ethel was going to make it or not.

A blare of feedback flooded through the auditorium. Lilly Robinson was leaning into her microphone.

"Ladies and gentlemen, will you please take your seats? We'll be beginning in just a few minutes."

The few people still standing in the aisles found their seats. The wired podium stood at the foot of the stage. Dave craned his head around, scanning the crowd for Beverly one last time.

"Will the meeting please come to order?" Lilly Robinson started banging her gavel on the table. A couple board members hurried to their seats.

"Let's take roll call. Is the reporter ready?" The recorder nodded, hands poised over his machine.

"Let's start with the roll call."

The crowd settled back, waiting expectantly.

"William Jackson?"

"Here."

"William Rosicki?"

"Yo."

"Loretta Sanfelippo?"

"Present."

"Buford Wallace."

"Present."

"Mark Maris."

"Yeah."

A slight mutter rippled through the crowd; Maris had a history of backing up the voucher programs.

"Iris Montoya?"

"Present."

"Milton Gorski?"

"Here."

"And I, Lilly Robinson, president, am also present. Let the record show there is full attendance of the school board."

Lilly settled back into her seat, looking out over the auditorium. Dave couldn't see her very well from where he was, but he could see her starting to hunch her shoulders, the intensity starting to build in her.

"Ladies and gentlemen," she said. "We all know why we're here. This is a public hearing on the subject of whether George Armstrong Custer High School should be shut down and reopened as a private voucher school to be run by the EduNet Corporation."

A chorus of boos billowed down the auditorium floor. Lilly waited a moment for it to diminish and then leaned forwad to continue.

Maris stood up. "I move that we hear testimony concerning the EduNet proposal to place Custer High School under new administrative reorganization."

"I second that," said Gorski.

"So carried," said Lilly, and banged her gavel.

"First, we will be seeing a presentation from representatives of the EduNet Corporation." She paused and peered down at the notecard in her hand. "Mr. Mitchell Paige, Executive Vice-President in charge of Operations, and Ms. Sandra Feeley, Associate Vice-President, will be presenting an overview of the takeover project."

She turned to the side table and nodded. The Feeley woman turned to Paige, who nodded to her. She leaned forward into the microphone in front of her.

"Good evening," she said. "My associate, Mitchell Paige, and I are here tonight to help make this school a better place for your children to learn, a better place for your them to grow, and a safe place for the entire community."

The crowd started muttering as soon as she opened her mouth. A few boos cascaded over the seats. This is going to be a rough night, honey, thought Dave, unless you grab this crowd and don't let go.

"We're here to tell you about EduNet and how it can improve your lives and the lives of your children." At this point, the corporate logo flashed onto the screen behind her.

"Last year," she continued, leaning forward into the microphone and raising her voice above the murmur of the crowd, "only sixty point nine percent of seniors in this school district graduated. In this school, only fifty-two percent of students who entered as freshmen graduated." She paused. No one was booing now. "That's only a little more than half. Of the students who did graduate, the median grade point average was a one point five: a 'D'. At this school, the student average for the ACT test was a median score of thirteen out of thirty-six."

She paused a moment, folding her hands on the table in front of her.

"That stinks," she said. She waited for the murmuring to die down.

"That's right," she repeated. "It stinks. Every parent, teacher, and administrator in this room should find all of these numbers completely unacceptable. You should find this school and this school system unacceptable. The numbers don't lie, and they're all telling us the same story. Your children are failing, and this school is failing. Public schools are failing. And frankly, you, as parents, are failing." Another murmur went through the crowd. Feeley rode it out, waiting until it died down. "We think," she said firmly, "that EduNet can do better."

Dave sneaked a look to his left. A few people were still grumbling, talking to their neighbors and disagreeing, but quite a few of the families, parents of kids he had taught and was currently teaching, were nodding slightly.

"EduNet has a track record of success comparable to the best private and public school systems in the country. We've demonstrated that with our combined programs of live classrooms and online programming."

Sandra pressed a button on the remote in front of her and scrolled through until she reached a bar graph labeled achievement.

"As you can see," she said, "this graph shows the increase in performance in the Gundry school in Baltimore that was closed and then reopened under EduNet supervision. Achievement in reading went up eight percent the first year and then twelve percent more the second year. Achievement in math went up nine percent the first year and then twelve the second year. ACT scores went from an average of fifteen to twenty-one in two years. All these are significant increases. We saw them in Baltimore and there's no reason we can't see them here."

Dave looked around. He saw the Williams, Olive's parents, sitting stonily with arms folded. The man next to them was leaning forward with his elbows on his knees, listening intently. They were all listening. And starting to wonder if this woman could be right. Keeping Custer public could be a harder sell than he thought.

Sandra Feeley was going on and on about achievement rates and student satisfaction and all the other skewed statistics they'd boiled up. She began explaining a chart about ACT scores, using a laser pointer to indicate some of the details about her model school. The red dot jumped and bounced atop and around the green and purple bars like a drunken Tinkerbell.

Dave suddenly thought he smelled something burning, a sharp odor, electrical, like a short circuit, coming somewhere behind him, and he turned to see what it was. Everyone behind him was focused on the stage; no one else seemed to notice it. His face felt hot suddenly and he turned back toward the stage, but could not make out Sandra Feeley at all anymore. He blinked. Her dress was a streak of blue smeared across a white and red background that was bleeding together into a blend of glowing color that grew brighter and brighter until it became a searing brand reaching past his eyes and stabbing into his brain.

He shut his eyes, waiting for the pain to ebb, and then opened them again. The light, the pain, was gone now, but the stage, the room, everything was still a blur. He could still hear Sandra, but she sounded as if she were inside a cave, her voice echoing more and more rapidly until it became nothing but a high-pitched trill. He put his hands over his ears and shut his eyes again. Breathe, he told himself. Breathe. It'll go away. It'll stop. It always had before, but it had never been this intense, this painful. It had never lasted this long before.

Dave leaned back in his chair and opened his eyes; everything was still blurry, but getting better. He could actually see the outline of the table and Sandra Feeley, even though he couldn't make out too many details. But his vision was getting better. The people in front of him, next to him, were in perfect focus. He glanced to his right. Knox was leaning back in his seat with his arms crossed, scowling. Zoe was texting something. Good. No one had noticed. Good.

He brought his attention back to the Feeley woman. She was talking about their model, the Gundry school, and what a success it had been. A film about it was beginning; Knox leaned over and said something to Zoe who nodded and held up her smartphone. She was filming the meeting, probably to post on Facebook. Good idea. Let the whole world see. Let the kids see it.

The video played, showing black kids sitting in their classrooms, listening closely, raising their hands obediently, being model students in every way. The teachers were young, attractive, and black. Everyone in the film was black. Everyone in the film was well-dressed and pretty. Everyone in the film was perfect.

Dave heard some chuckling to his left; a man was watching and shaking his head. A few other people in the audience seemed amused, but quite a few others were absorbed in it. One woman was shushing her husband. A mixed bag, thought Dave. It looked as if the presentation was hitting more than missing. Their response was going to have to be good. Very good.

"So," Sandra said, "in conclusion," and a few people applauded — more ironically this time — "what we at EduNet would like you to come away with is this. We know how to run efficient, effective, and excellent schools. You just saw one in the Gundry school. Two other high schools have started up this year, and we have three more K-12 institutions planned for next year. What we want," she said, pausing and looking out over the audience. "What we want is to bring that level of excellence, efficiency, and effectiveness to you and your community. We want to bring greater opportunities to your children. We want to give them a fair shot; we want to level the playing field."

"Thank you," said Feeley, leaning forward. She took a long drink of water and then placed her hands on the table.

"All right," said Lilly, leaning too close to her microphone again. It began squealing and she leaned back suddenly. "Sorry about that," she said. A wave of laughter rolled down. "Well," she said. "Mr. Paige, would you like to say anything to the people gathered here tonight?"

He started to lean into the microphone in front of him, but Ms. Feeley leaned over from her chair and caught his sleeve and whispered something to him. Dave's vision was still a little blurry, but he thought he caught a little urgency in her body language. Maybe. He blinked again. Paige said something to her and she leaned back in her chair, a vision of surrender.

"Thank you, Ms. Robinson," he said, "my name is Mitchell Paige." To Dave, his voice, high and a little nasal, sounded confident to the point of arrogance, almost snide. "We can make this school work again, and work better than it ever has before. EduNet is an outstanding program with an incredible track record. Ms. Feeley has told you how it's worked in Baltimore and elsewhere and how other urban communities all over the country are jumping on the bandwagon. You can't afford to pass up this opportunity. This is your chance to make something out of yourselves, something out of your community, and something out of your children."

That was a stupid goddamned thing to say. A rustling, as if everyone in the crowd had begun fidgeting simultaneously, rolled through the room like waves breaking on a shore. Dave could feel it, and then the muttering began, louder than before. Feeley seemed to feel the restlessness, too. She leaned over to Paige, put her hand over his mike, and whispered to him. He waved her off impatiently.

"So, in conclusion," he said, "we're here to answer any questions you may have about us or our program. Thank you." He leaned back with his hands folded over his stomach. He has absolutely no clue, thought Dave. Paige stared out over the crowd who stared right back at him. The applause was conspicuous in its absence.

"All right, then, Mr. Paige," said Ms. Robinson, her voice stony. "Thank you. Now, we have a list of people who have expressed a wish to speak tonight. We have limited that number to thirty and will be asking that everyone keep their remarks under a two-minute time limit so we can get out of here before midnight." She smiled and cocked her head. "I know it may be difficult for some of you to do that, so I will be gently reminding you when and if you go over that limit."

Some laughter peppered the crowd.

"I also know," she continued, "that this a volatile issue. Some people in the community have been up in arms about this matter and, as a result, there have been some incidents of violence. Some people have been hurt, seriously hurt. We do not want any repeats of this violence. We are here to

247

help decide what's best for our children and our community. Therefore, if there are any outbursts or inappropriate displays, those people responsible for them will be immediately removed and prosecuted. We've gone to the extremes of bringing in extra security," and she nodded to them, stationed near the exits, "and the mayor has ordered a police presence be on standby near the school."

A few people stood up, and one, a youngish black man near the back, sitting near the Guardians, stood up and started shouting something about freedom of speech.

"Please," said Lilly, "let's get settled down. Now I don't like this any better than you do. I don't believe the police have any business around this meeting, but it's out of our hands. This is something the mayor has decided. Now, we can go ahead and ignore the police outside and have this meeting and decide this issue, or we can decide to vent our anger and frustration and disrupt this entire proceeding and go home. So let's keep our cool and get through it."

Everyone except the young man reluctantly sat back down. He continued standing defiantly for a moment, and then finally took his seat.

"All right," said Lilly. "The first person on our list is Dorothea Blanque."

An older black woman near the front stood and made her way to the podium set up in the aisle. Her arm was in a sling and a large bandage covered the cheekbone directly underneath her left eye. She was dressed in blue warm-up suit and tennis shoes. The woman walked slowly up to the podium and leaned into the mike.

"My name is Dorothea Blanque," she said, "and I am here to support our public schools. I went to school here some years ago, I won't tell you how many, and I was taught well. Public schools work in our best interest, in the best public interest. I learned about unions in Mr. Packard's U.S. History class. I don't think EduNet will be teaching us about no unions. I read *The Jungle*, that book about the meat-packing industry in Chicago. I don't think EduNet will be teaching our children about greedy corporations. And you know why?" she asked, turning to the people beside her. "Because they are a greedy corporation."

The crowd roared its approval. Dozens rose and started shouting. Lilly Robinson started banging the gavel and shouting into her mike for everyone to quiet down. The woman at the mike raised her hands and the crowd quieted down.

"EduNet is trying to steal public money for their private endeavors. They are in it completely for the money. I don't believe they care about us or our community or our children. Don't believe what that nice white lady tells you. I know who they are. They will do anything for the money." She raised her arm in the sling. "I can testify to that. I was there the other day when their people came and beat us with sticks and gas because we was getting in their way. Some of my fellow protesters are still in the hospital. That," she said, pointing at Sandra, "is exactly who you people are. You are thugs and you are bullies, and you are criminals. Thank you."

She turned and walked slowly back to her seat. The crowd rose up and applauded, a few of them shouting and gesturing angrily at the stage.

"Please," Ms. Robinson was saying as she pounded her gavel. "Please." The noise finally subsided as Dorothea reached her seat. Lilly sighed.

"I know," she said, "that this is an emotional issue, but I must ask you again to please conduct yourselves in a mature and respectful manner. If demonstrations like this continue, we'll be forced to postpone the meeting and hold it as a closed session. Is this understood?"

The crowd muttered. Someone yelled, "We need to speak."

"Then speak," said Lilly, her voice firm, "but speak in turn and speak with respect. Ask your questions, air your opinions, but please don't turn my meeting into a circus." She took the list and smiled as she read the next name.

"Mrs. Ethel Benjamin."

Ethel stood up and made her down the row, people standing to let her through. A couple reached over the backs of seats to say hello or shake her hand. How many of the people here were taught by Ethel Benjamin, thought Dave. Or Reynolds? Or me? He felt a surge of pride as Ethel walked down the aisle and up to the mike. She was the best of them. Definitely. Ethel reached up and pulled the mike down to her level, then squared her shoulders and stood straight.

"Hello, Ms. Robinson," she said, "and members of the school board. It's my pleasure to stand here tonight to address you. I've taught here at George Custer High School for forty-four years. I see many of my old students here in the room tonight." There was scattered applause, and, as

Dave scanned the crowd, he saw smiles and nods throughout the rows of people. The guy in the red t-shirt sitting to his left chuckled and said to his companion, "Man, that old Mrs. Ben was tough as nails. She was the one nobody messed with."

"I wanted to repeat a lot of what's been said here," Ethel continued. "Public schools are the fabric of our communities. We need them to maintain our way of life, our culture, and our awareness of the outside world. Ms. Blanque was correct when she said that public schools teach everything to everyone. We have no other agenda here except to show our students the light of truth. Corporations like EduNet have their own agenda. In fact," she said, unfolding a sheet of paper she'd been carrying in her hand, "EduNet is part of a corporate family that has huge interests in the energy business. How do you think they would feel about me teaching *Silent Spring* or Mr. Reynolds teaching his Aquaponics unit? Probably not very well."

Dave found himself nodding. He was not alone in the room.

"I am also concerned," she continued, "about our special needs children. The famous Gundry school of Philadelphia has no special education facilities or staff in their building. What do we do with them, Ms. Feeley? Can you tell me that? What do we do with our Down syndrome children, our autistic children, and our cerebral palsy students? Where do we put them?"

She paused a moment and stared up at the EduNet people. The Feeley woman actually squirmed a bit while Paige merely slouched back in his chair, crossed his arms, and smiled. Dave nodded; he had seen a thousand of his students do that over the years; the body English was clear enough: "you can't tell me what to do." He nodded. Good stuff, Ethel. Good stuff. She took a breath and straightened her shoulders.

"What about our students who are homeless, who come from dysfunctional or abusive homes?" asked Ethel, still staring straight at Sandra. "You see private voucher schools are not required to service every student. By law, public schools must serve every student who walks through those front doors. So Ms. Feeley and Mr. Paige may decide that your son or your daughter is too much trouble or costs too much to teach here at their exclusive EduNet Academy. They can recruit whom they want, teach whom they want, and kick out whom they want."

Ethel put her hand over her mouth and coughed slightly. You could hear a pin drop, thought Dave. Just like one of her classrooms. She cleared her throat and continued.

"Public schools are also accountable to the cities and the communities that they serve. At Custer, and all across the district, we have to report test scores, GPAs, graduation rates, suspension rates, and a budget report. Private vouchers like EduNet do not have to maintain any sort of minimum performance rates. They are not accountable to anyone."

Lilly Robinson leaned forward in her seat.

"I'm sorry, Mrs. Benjamin, I'm going to have to ask you to finish up. Your time is up."

"Thank you, Lilly," she said. "I only have one more brief point, and that has to do with our teachers. Since collective bargaining for public employees was outlawed in this state, we've been losing our best and our brightest. As I said earlier, I've been a teacher for forty-four years. Many of my most experienced colleagues have retired, and others have left for positions in other states, even other countries. The profession is no longer attracting young people willing to commit their lives to teaching. The private vouchers have a reputation of hiring non-qualified teachers without experience and without the proper background to lesson plan, instruct, or manage their classrooms. They are hiring unqualified people to teach your children. And that is a shame."

She took a step back from the podium and pointed a finger at the EduNet side of the table.

"You may not know it, my friends," she said, "but you are ruining public education, and with that, you are ruining this country: without a strong public education system, all of our most basic freedoms will be at risk."

She turned back to Lilly and the rest of the board.

"I hope that these representatives from EduNet will answer my questions, and I hope that you members of the school board will make the right decision. Not everything in this country should be privatized, especially not our schools. Thank you."

Ethel turned to leave the podium. A few people started applauding, then a few more, and then some stood. The applause grew and cascaded as Ethel went back to her seat. A few called out approval. Dave heard a few shouts of "Yeah, Mrs. Benjamin" and the like. She'd made a strong case, as least as strong as Feeley's.

"To address Mrs. Benjamin's questions," Sandra was saying as the applause died down, "I'd like to say first of all that our online course software system addresses every type of student need possible. It covers every grade level and every type of learning style."

"But," a voice from the crowd shouted, "do you take care of the special education students? A lot of them need more than some computer program."

"No," said Paige brusquely, his tone assertive and final. Dave saw Sandra open her mouth and then close it, and then set it in a firm straight line. Dave thought she seemed just a little unhappy with her colleague.

"No, we don't," he continued. "We can't do that and remain cost-effective. This is why public schools are failing. They over-extend themselves. We've discovered programs like special education, music, and the arts are simply not necessary for young people coming into today's economy."

A woman wearing a Chicago Bears sweatshirt sitting two rows in front of Dave stood up.

"What about my Tiffany?" she asked angrily. "She has autism. Where is she supposed to go if your school is not able to take her? She deserves an education, too."

"Public schools," interjected Sandra, shooting a look over to Paige, "in this district will continue to provide special education services. That has been one of their specialties over the years and is one of the few areas where they still excel."

"Well then," said the woman, "let me get this straight. First of all, you've been saying that public schools are not doing their job and are as bad as they can be, and next you're telling me that my Tiffany is not good enough for your school and that I need to send her back to the public school. Is my daughter not good enough for your school?"

"Well," said Sandra, "that's not quite right. If your child has special education needs, then our school is not good enough for her. We admit that. We tell you because we want the best for your child, for every child, and we believe the public schools do a better job at special education than we do. We don't want students coming to us unless we can do the best possible job for them. So if we are not the best school for them, we will refer them to the best school for their needs. If that's not us, fine. We don't matter. Your children matter."

The woman sat down, still grumbling, not looking very happy, but apparently stalled by Feeley's argument.

"In terms of accountability," Feeley continued. "We have very high standards that we adhere to at EduNet. We don't need special government boards and agencies looking over our shoulders ensuring that we're doing our jobs. You just saw our annual report. That is how we do things."

"How can we trust you?" said a voice next to Dave. He glanced sideways. Knox had shouted out the question and was now ducking behind the seat in front of him.

"Trust our record," said Feeley. "Trust our graduation rate and our ACT scores. Trust our high attendance rates and our low suspension rates. That speaks to our effectiveness."

"All right," said Lilly. "Next on our list of speakers is Nathan Durham."

An older white man dressed in a three-piece suit stood and inched his way down the row, and then slowly made his way to the podium. He suit was wrinkled, and his tie seemed a little askew. It looked as if he hadn't worn it in a long time. In general, he had a generally unkempt appearance; his white hair stuck out from the side of his head and it looked to Dave—even from that distance—as if he hadn't shaved recently. The man shuffled down the slightly sloped floor to the podium, grasping the backs of chairs to balance himself as he made his way down.

"Hello, Mr. Durham," said Lilly gently, as the man grasped the podium and balanced himself, looking around through his thick-rimmed glasses.

"Hello," he said, in a surprisingly robust and deep voice. "I'm Nathan Durham and I've lived in this neighborhood since nineteen fifty-nine. I live over on Dorchester and Grant. I've been here a long time, longer than this school has been here. I remember when they were building it back in the sixties. It used to be a good school. This used to be a good neighborhood. You could leave your door unlocked at night, you knew everybody in the neighborhood and everybody knew you. Everybody took care of everybody else. Now it's all gone to hell. Nobody cares. People let their kids run wild up and down the streets, you hear that damned loud rap music and you hear guns going off all the time."

He paused and ran a hand through his wild hair. The crowd, which had been murmuring and grumbling as the old man had been rambling on and on, now quieted, waiting. Dave glanced at Lilly Robinson, to see if she might stop the old man, but she sat impassively, staring at the stopwatch in front of her. Durham glared at her a moment.

"It's not the school that's bad," he blurted suddenly, his voice blaring like a foghorn. "It's these kids. It's not the teachers or the principals or you damned politicians up there," he continued, pointing a shaky finger at the board. People in the crowd were talking loud, some angry voices rising above the general tumult. "It's those kids," Durham continued. "They're nothing but hooligans. Criminals."

The woman in the Bears sweatshirt stood again and pointed at Durham. "You're talking about my daughter, my Tiffany. You're calling her a criminal."

"Well, she is," retorted Durham, turning to face her. "I'm sure she's out there with the rest of them walking the streets all hours of the night, stealing stuff."

"Tiffany never stole anything in her life," the woman retorted, her voice now louder than Durham's, "and she never walked the streets in her life. You don't call my little girl a prostitute."

A woman in blonde braids stood and started shouting with Tiffany's mother, something about disrespecting her daughter because she was impaired. More and more people were standing, some edging out into the aisle. Just like a fight in the hallway, thought Dave. Everybody has to see it. He noticed a few people taping the confrontation with their smartphones.

Lilly banged her gavel on the table; Dave realized she'd been doing it for some time. Durham stopped first, and then the woman in the braids stopped. Tiffany's mom was determined to get the last word in.

"Oh, forget it," said Durham, throwing up his hands and turning his back to her. "I can't talk to you people, anyway."

Tiffany's mom cocked her hip and put her hand on it.

"What do you mean," she said, her voice as low and powerful as a panther, "you people?"

There was a dead silence; Durham scowled out at the crowd as he scanned them.

"I mean you people," he said. "All you people out there. All you people in my neighborhood."

"You mean," said Tiffany's mom, taking a slow step toward him, "us black folks? Is that 'you people?'"

Durham looked at her, his scowl fading, and then turned back to the mike.

"You mean," said Tiffany's mom softly as she took another step toward him, "us niggers?"

Durham turned suddenly. "If that's what you want to call yourself, then yeah," he said, "you niggers."

The room exploded. Tiffany's mom came flying down the aisle, moving incredibly fast for a woman that size. A big man with a goatee grabbed Durham by the shoulder and pushed him into the podium as a woman in flowered print dress tried to hold him back. A security guard rushed in and pushed the larger man back as Tiffany's mom finally got to Durham. She came on him swinging both fists and screaming her head off. Another security guard pulled her off the old man. She looks familiar, thought Dave. I think I know her. Or her kid. Dave realized there weren't actually that many people up; it looked worse than it actually was. Two of the guards were escorting Tiffany's mom and her friend out while another was herding Durham up the aisle past the jeers of the crowd. Lilly was still hammering on the table until the noise started to subside.

"That," she yelled suddenly, standing up, "is enough." It was loud enough that the crowd quieted enough for her to assume a normal tone. "That," she repeated, "is enough. By all rights, I should cancel this meeting immediately. If we can't act like civilized human beings and have to behave like a mob, then we won't be having this meeting." She stopped and surveyed the room. Most of the people had already sat back down. A few people were still milling around in the aisles, but crept back to their seats under the fierceness of her glare.

"That was your free pass," she said. "One more and we're done. Everyone has a right to an opinion. That's the law. We have a responsibility to behave like adults even if we get upset. You are all adults. You know that."

The crowd sat quietly. Dave looked around again and thought he saw Beverly in the far corner, but he couldn't focus on her. Tiny lines shimmering like cut glass bisected his field of vision, hovering in the upper regions of his sight; when he tried to focus on them, they disappeared. He squinted, trying to see into through the shimmering island to the dimness on the other side, when a roaring, like a heavy sea, buffeted him from the side. No, he thought, not again, not this soon, and shut his eyes tight, but not soon enough to stop the dazzling hammer of light that came crashing down on the crown of his head, knocking him back into his seat and driving him back into darkness, into complete and utter oblivion.

Chapter 31

Mitchell watched the old white guy, Durham, acting up with the two black women, and almost laughed out loud. He couldn't help himself. The guy was fucking nuts; he just didn't give a shit. Durham reminded Mitchell of his Uncle Steve, a retired pipefitter who, after he got into his mid-seventies or so, seemed to lose all his filters, all of his natural restraints. He just said whatever he was thinking out loud. He didn't give a shit about what people thought anymore. It got him into trouble—just like it had almost gotten Durham killed—but part of Mitchell admired the freedom to behave like that, to say fuck it to propriety and political correctness.

He glanced over at Sandra, who was watching the Robinson woman talk to the assembly in the auditorium as if they were children. She was nervous, but she had been doing pretty well keeping a lid on things.

"Next," said Robinson, "is Ms. Serena McDaniels."

A tall black woman arose and edged her way out of the aisle. There was something about her that caught the eye. Not so much in the way she dressed; that was pretty run of the mill, but more in her bearing, the way she held her head. Proud and dignified. She looked almost, well—Mitchell searched for the word: regal, that was it. Regal.

The woman reached the podium and nodded to Robinson, the board and then turned her eye to Sandra and Mitchell.

"Good evening," she said, her voice carrying through the public-address system and into every corner of the auditorium. It wasn't necessarily a penetrating voice, but it was one that demanded attention. She could be executive material, thought Mitchell, watching her closely. Definitely. She's got the confidence, the bearing, the attitude. All we'd have to do would be to get her a proper education, an MBA.

"My name is Serena McDaniels. I've worked with many of you in this room, and I wanted to let you know that I am in complete and non-negotiable opposition to this takeover. I am here to tell the people at EduNet that this school is not for sale." Mitchell nodded; she had a nice cadence going, a real revival type feel to her speech. The crowd responded, making sounds of agreement.

"Let me repeat that," she continued. "This school is not for sale. This community is not for sale. Our children are not for sale. Slavery is over, and this would most definitely be a form of slavery." Shouts of yes, it is, uh-huhs, and even a hallelujah came floating down from the auditorium.

Slavery? thought Mitchell. Are you kidding me? He glanced over at Sandra with raised eyebrows; she glanced back at him with narrowed eyes. She even shook her head slightly. He smiled at her, looked back toward the woman, making a show of nodding seriously as she spoke.

"Yes, slavery," continued the McDaniels woman, as if reading his thoughts. "Selling our children's futures is just another more modern, more subtle, and more powerful form of enslavement." She paused a moment.

"Selling this school would cleave us from our past," she continued. "And historically, this type of activity was yet another tool of the slave trade, the deliberate act of separating a person from their past, making them dependent on the master. Selling this building to an outside mercenary corporation would be ripping us away from our past, tearing our memories away from us, and destroying our heritage."

Heritage, thought Mitchell. What heritage? What the hell is she talking about: the gang and drug culture? The single parent culture? The heritage of entitlements?

"Many of us in this room went to Custer High School five, ten, fifteen, twenty, or more years ago; some of us were many more years ago," she continued. A few people laughed. "We were taught here, we made life-long friends here, and we grew up here. This school was where we first voted, where we went to dances and performed in concerts, where we attended homecomings, and it was the place where some of us met our future wives and husbands. It was a place we attended when we were young, and it's the place we gather now. It is indeed a powerful part of the common tradition of our community."

"So," said the woman, "While we know that our school has fallen on hard times and that we will all need to work together in the future to ensure our children's success, it is just as important that this building continue to remain a public non-for-profit school and community center. It should not be owned by outside forces. It belongs to us. It belongs to all the people here and all the people who have been here."

More yeahs and right ons and smatters of applause rolled down from the crowd, mounting in volume as the woman went on.

"We have seen mounting attacks on our public education system over the past decade," she continued. "Our teachers have doing more with less. They are doing simply phenomenal work, and now they need our support more than ever. We cannot let these people come into our city, take away our children's school, their teachers, and the center of our community. I say this to the school board; we have to stand strong and vote no to this proposal. Thank you."

She turned and started back to her seat, proud in bearing and regal as a lioness. The crowd started applauding and then stood as she made her way back to her seat and sat down. Lilly turned to Sandra.

"Would you care to respond?" she asked. Sandra took a breath and leaned into the mike.

"Yes, I would," said Mitchell quickly, into the mike. Sandra started to say something, but Mitchell held up a hand.

"First of all," he said, "I'd like to thank Ms. McDaniels for her heartfelt and eloquent remarks. We know that any change of this magnitude is never easy, and that EduNet will do everything in its power to ensure a smooth transition." He paused. The McDaniels woman was sitting with her arms folded, glaring at him, smirking.

"Secondly," he continued, staring straight at the McDaniels woman, "I'd like to say that far from enslaving anyone, as Ms. McDaniels seemed to be implying this renewal would do, I think this EduNet project will, on the contrary, be liberating you."

The room seemed to take a collective breath. Mitchell paused to take a drink of water. He glanced at Sandra, who was covering her mouth with her hand.

"As my colleague was saying earlier," Mitchell continued, gesturing toward Sandra, "almost all levels of achievement in this school—in most of the public schools in this district for that matter—have been substandard, below average, and, in a word, atrocious. Is that," he said, "really what you want for your children? If it is, hey, fine, stay with the status quo. Stay with this school. Tell your representatives on the school board that you're perfectly happy watching your kids fail year after year and fall deeper and deeper into the cycle of poverty."

Mitchell paused. He thought he heard a sort of humming or buzzing coming from the crowd, a deep sound, a rumbling, almost a growl. He looked out over the vast room. A sea of faces stared back at him. Sullen. Angry. Well, too bad. Maybe it was time they heard the truth and recognized their responsibilities.

"Crime and drugs and lack of parental responsibility are only a part of the problem. The culture is part of it, too. You know this. I know it. Everyone knows this. In short, unless something changes, this school will continue to fail. Your community will continue to fail. Your neighborhoods will continue to fail, and your children will continue to fail unless you do something positive and assertive to improve your own situation."

"Our children are not failures." The voice resounded throughout the entire room, like a bell on Sunday morning. It stopped everything. The same woman, McDaniels, was now standing and pointing at him, her finger like a pistol aimed at his head.

"You don't know, Mr. Paige," she said. "You don't know what it is to be black in this city." A wave of applause greeted this. "You don't know how many obstacles and barriers our families have to go through in order to provide for our families, to keep them safe, and to educate them. We do everything humanly possible to make our children everything they can possibly be. For you to insinuate otherwise is just wrong."

Mitchell opened his mouth to speak but felt a hand on his arm. Sandra. He turned to see her leaning into the mike.

"I'm sure Mr. Paige meant to say that all we want is to give your children more opportunity, more hope."

Mitchell pulled his arm from her grasp and glared at her.

"That's not what I heard," called out a voice from the audience.

"Me, neither."

"Nor I," said the McDaniels woman. "I heard him say he was going to stop poverty, change our neighborhoods, change our culture, to—what was it you said, Mr. Paige—oh, that's right. Liberate us. You said you were going to liberate us. You hear that?" she said, turning to the crowd behind her. "He's going to liberate us. He's going to free the slaves. Let's hand it to our own young Mr. Lincoln." She turned and gave him an exaggerated bow.

Boos cascaded down from the crowd. A few people were up out of their seats yelling. Lilly Robinson was pounding on the table in front of her.

"No," Mitchell was yelling into the mike, trying to get over the noise of the crowd, "that's not what I was saying." It was no use. They couldn't hear him.

He turned to Sandra as a crimson streak careened past the corner of his vision. In almost that same instant, something popped behind him. Red white chunks, drops of water flew over him, on him, wet junk was all over him. As soon as the smell struck him, he knew: something had thrown an apple that had hit the wall behind them. It had come damned close to hitting him. He was covered with bits of it. Sandra, too. She was standing now and brushing it off her. The crowd was standing, laughing, jeering, trading knuckle bumps or high fives. Some looked angry. Others looked scared. McDaniels and some others were screaming at him. Screaming at Sandra. Fuckers, he thought. Rotten motherfuckers.

Robinson was banging her gavel loudly. Slowly, the people resumed their seats and quieted down. Sandra moved to his side of the table, picking up bits of apple. He noticed her hand was shaking.

"I think we've heard enough," said Robinson, laying down her gavel and glaring out over the crowd. A protest rose from the crowd; Robinson beat it down with her gavel. Sandra stood up and tried to speak, but was shouted down.

Lilly turned to the crowd and said, "This meeting is over. I think it's about time for the board to retire and this meeting—" and then dodged as another apple, and then another, and then more, flew past them. Something hit him directly in the chest. He looked down to see rotten shards of tomato coating his suit.

He stared at them: these people, he thought. How dare they? He could feel the rage growing, blossoming in his chest, the crimson flower opening behind his eyes, staining his vision red. There they are, he thought, standing out there with their fucking hands out every day of the year. Fucking niggers. He felt his fists clench, taking on a life of their own, and leapt up.

"Shut the fuck up," he screamed. "Just shut the fuck up, you god-damned stupid fucking niggers."

Sandra and Lilly both gaped at him. The crowd roared and then surged toward the stage as one single mass.

"The police," screamed a voice from the back, "the police are coming. The doors in the back of the theater slammed open and officers clad in riot gear burst into the room. Something flashed and exploded near the middle of the far aisle as police swept through the crowd. Smoke started billowing from the back of the room. People were screaming, leaping over seats and running everywhere.

Mitchell saw a couple of the security guards come down toward the front where the crowd was still trying to climb the stage. The nearest guard was knocked off his feet as soon as he got near the growing knot of people next to the podium. He went down and Mitchell lost sight of him. They were swarming down the aisle, screaming and coughing from the smoke. Tear gas. Police were on the stage now, escorting the board members off the stage. One had Sandra by the elbow and was pulling her away.

Mitchell tried to follow but felt something pulling him by the leg. He turned and white light flashed, impact—thunder—and then momentary blackness. His legs buckled. Mitchell regained balance momentarily and turned to see a fist cocked over him, and then felt another crash of thunder on the side of his head. He felt himself going down to his knees, then his hands. Someone had him by the collar then, and he was up on his feet again and being pushed and supported at the same time. He felt another hand holding him by his pants, pushing.

They were moving, off the stage into light, through the door and into a room. The hands pushed one last time, hard, and Mitchell smashed into a metal door and collapsed onto the cold tiled floor. He lay there a moment, his head pounding. He slowly raised himself on his hands and opened his eyes. A vast white structure loomed in front of him like a statue of Buddha—the toilet; he was inside a stall in the bathroom.

"Hey, man," the voice hissed.

It came from behind him somewhere. Mitchell waited, bracing himself for another blow. The pain slowly ebbed and his vision cleared; he could now make out the beige and yellow tiles on the floor spattered with red droplets. Blood. His blood. His hand went instinctively to his face and then something had him by the collar again, yanking him back onto his knees.

"You ain't calling nobody nigger now, are you, boy?"

Mitchell heard a metallic clink, felt something cold on his wrist, and then his arm was yanked forward. He heard another clink and looked up to see both of his hands cuffed around the pipe behind the toilet. He pulled back instinctively, but it was too late.

"What do you want?" he asked. His tongue seemed thick and gummy. Blood in his mouth. He tried to spit but couldn't.

"I don't want anything," said the voice. "I'm just holding you for someone."

Mitchell craned his head around slowly, careful not to jostle anything loose. A man stood in the doorway of the stall. He was a big man, dressed in a black warm-up suit and wearing a mask, a red ski mask. Mitchell closed his eyes. He heard the door open and footsteps come in. Then he heard the click of a lock.

"Hello, Mitchell."

The voice seemed familiar. He turned his head. A second man stood there in the doorway of the stall. He was average height, wearing a black turtleneck and one of those Mexican wrestling masks: an ornate crimson skull, the eyes rimmed in brilliant orange and blue. Los Muertos. Death. Beautiful death.

"What do you want?" asked Mitchell. A strange sort of buzzing started in his head. Everything seemed to be in slow motion, misty, like a dream.

"I want you, Mitchell," said the man in the mask. "You know I've always wanted you."

The man's hands went to his belt. He was wearing black leather gloves—nice ones—and Mitchell watched, fascinated, as the man started undoing the belt. Strange. One of the fingers of the gloves didn't quite move with the others, staying straight as the others bent and unfastened and unzipped.

The big man stepped past him into the stall and Mitchell felt him pulling him up on his feet. He pushed him up against the cold metal wall and leaned against him, holding him there with his weight. Mitchell pulled his head up, wanting to say he needed to get out, he couldn't breathe, when he felt something go around his mouth. A gag.

It hit him then, like an icicle through his brain. He threw himself furiously back at the man leaning on him, causing him to step back and then he turned slightly, raising his knee, before the weight crushed him against the wall again, pinning him. Mitchell felt hands going to his own belt, undoing, unfastening, and he flailed his body as much as possible, but he couldn't move. He felt his pants slide down to his knees and someone else move up behind him and place hands on him.

"I've always wanted you, Mitchell," the voice hissed in his ear. "Always."

* * * * *

Dave opened his eyes. The light was gone, but his head felt like a broken light bulb. He smelled smoke and saw people running down the aisle. Someone was shaking his shoulder and he turned to look, but his head, his eyes, his body would not obey. He tried to speak and heard gurgling as he tried to more clearly articulate his words. What the fuck is happening, he thought. What is it? A face loomed before him; he blinked and focused. Will. He looked closely at him and said, "Dave. Can you hear me, Dave? Dave?" He tried but nothing worked. Nothing.

"Call 911," said Will to someone to his side. Knox? Zoe? Zoe. She had the phone. She always had the phone.

"What is it?" Knox.

"I think he's had a stroke." He knew that voice. That was Will again. Stroke was significant, he knew, but he couldn't quite place exactly what it meant. A spell, maybe? He remembered his mother talking about those. He felt hands.

"No. It's better not to move him. Wait for the EMTs."

Shit. They were taking him to the hospital. He would have to get a sub for tomorrow.

The smoke—where was it from?—drifted over them. More people running. Screaming. What was happening? Someone grabbing his shoulder. A voice.

"Mr. Bell. Mr. Bell, what's the matter?" He recognized it but couldn't quite place the name. Oliver? Maybe. No. It was a girl's voice. He felt tired. His eyes closed and he drifted.

"David," another voice said, close, clipped, stern.

He opened his eyes.

Ethel. She stood in front of him, peering down, looking into his eyes.

She nodded and said, "David, you need to stay awake until we get you to the hospital. We believe you've had a stroke. Stay still and try to relax. We'll get you there as soon as we can."

His vision started clearing. Faces floated in front of him. Youngsters. Students. His students. There was Darrel and Daquone and Olive. Then a stranger wearing some kind of uniform bending over him, asking him his name, street. He tried to speak but couldn't; his mouth wouldn't work. He felt himself being lifted—deadweight—and placed on a bed, or a stretcher, probably one of those collapsible ones. Sure. He felt movement and looked up as they started pulling him out of there. There was Will, up there and walking next to him. Ethel was right behind him. Then they were out one of the exits and into the parking lot filled with red and blue flashing lights. Cold. He felt himself rising and then being pushed and he was in a car, the ambulance, and they were already putting stuff into him, an IV and whatnot. He was in bad shape, he knew, he must be, but he barely felt anything. All his worries and tensions had evaporated and he was in a bubble of contentment: no worries, no anxiety, no responsibilities, no knowledge.

* * * * *

Sandra looked back as she was being pulled across the stage; the cop had just grabbed her without saying a word and was brutally dragging her away. She'd lost Mitchell during the first part of the melee and was trying to locate him. He was right next to her when that big guy had leapt on the stage; she scanned the side and saw someone being half-pushed half-carried out. She caught a glimpse of the man's coat: it was Mitchell. She planted her feet and pulled back hard from the cop.

"Let me go," she yelled. "My friend is back there."

The cop glanced back and shook his head. She couldn't see his face under the plastic visor.

"We're not going back in there," he said. "Not on your life. I'll get you to a safe zone and you can come back for your friend later."

"No," she screamed and started to struggle. The cop simply pulled her to him, put his arm around her waist and carried her through the exit behind the stage and into the parking lot where some of the other board members were standing. At least a dozen police cars and a few paddy wagons were parked there, lights blazing. A couple ambulances were stationed there, too.

Lilly Robinson looked as if she were in shock. Gorski and Rosicki were already in a brightly lit corner of the lot, talking to one of the TV news team.

Shit, she thought. That's right. The TV stations were here. They caught everything. When the city turned on their televisions tonight and saw what Mitchell had done, the deal would be screwed.

Sandra leaned against the wall and crossed her arms. She felt ready to cry but had to keep it inside her—at least for a while. She had to be ready to make a statement. The news guys would surely want one. She glanced around her; maybe it was a good thing Mitchell wasn't there.

More paddy wagons rolled in. What a mess, she thought. What a fucking mess.

She glanced as a young man, a skinny thing with big black glasses and no more than twenty, came trotting up to her.

"Excuse me," he said. "Are you Sandra Feeley from EduNet?"

She nodded.

"I'm from Channel Seven. I'm Matt. I'm just an intern, but I know that Miss Knowles would like to interview you. I'm supposed to ask if you'd like to do one."

Sandra just nodded. She would be expected to make a statement. The boy nodded back and trotted to the TV truck.

God, she could use a cigarette, but her purse was back in that riot somewhere. She glanced back at the exit. No dice. A cop was standing there. She looked around the lot, hoping to see if someone had lit up; maybe she could bum one. There was the intern trotting toward her again.

"Hey," he said, "could you do the interview now? Would that be okay?"

"Sure," she said. The boy motioned for her to follow him. They crossed the lot, heading toward the bright lights.

"Hey," she said suddenly, on impulse. "I don't suppose you have a cigarette, do you?"

He stopped immediately and started digging into his shirt pocket. He pulled out a crumpled pack of Marlboros, dug one out, and handed it to her. It was flattened and bent, but it looked like heaven to her.

"Thanks," she said, taking it. The boy—Matt—took out a lighter and fired it up for her. She leaned in, lit it, and took a deep hit. God. That tasted good.

"That looked pretty intense in there," he said. "I saw the footage. It was nuts."

"Yes, it was," she said, taking another hit.

"So what started it?"

She looked at him. "What?" she asked.

"What started the riot? We saw that somebody threw something up on stage and then there was a lot of yelling, and then all hell broke loose, but we lost the signal for a second. The mikes went out. Did you see anything specific?"

She shook her head and he nodded and then pulled out another maimed cigarette and lit up himself. They missed it, she thought. How in God's name had they missed what Mitchell had said?

"We're ready," said Matt. Sandra nodded, took one last puff, and followed him under the TV lights. A young woman with bobbed blonde hair stood staring at a notecard as another woman touched up her make-up.

"Hello," she said, spying Sandra. "Miss Feeley, I'm so glad to meet you. I'm Irma Knowles. I'm a reporter from Channel Seven and I wanted to interview you about the disturbance tonight. Now, you're the representative from EduNet, correct?"

"Yes."

"And you were here to address the crowd about EduNet?"

"Yes, we wanted to inform the public about our program and to help them understand why having EduNet come in would work to their advantage."

"Okay," she said, scribbling on her notecard. "What happened?"

Sandra told her exactly as she remembered it, leaving out only one detail—the fact that Mitchell had incited the riot.

"Okay," said Ms. Knowles. "Do you know what started this disturbance, what the flash point was?"

Sandra pretended to consider a moment, then shook her head.

"I don't know," she said. "I can't say. There was a lot of yelling and then they just started rushing the stage."

"Okay," said Knowles, making a final note. "I think we're set. We'll go on in about ten minutes. Are you good? Do you want water or coffee or anything?"

"I'd love some coffee, and I don't suppose you'd have a cigarette, would you?"

"Sure," said Knowles. She grabbed her purse and started digging around in it.

Man, thought Sandra, I've got to start hanging out with reporters more.

The interview went very smoothly. Knowles was good; she asked almost exactly the same questions as she had during the prep. There had been no surprises, and—as far as she could tell—it looked as if EduNet would come out looking as pure as the driven snow. Man, thought Sandra, puffing on another borrowed cigarette. How fucking lucky can you get? She stood near the exit, waiting impatiently for the all clear to get back in. Mitchell had still not shown up.

She was worried and wanted to get hold of him before any of the other TV crews did; he needed to know that he'd gotten away with screaming the word "nigger" at a crowd of black people. Her anger began to once again supersede her concern for him. What was wrong with him? Why would anyone do that? She took another furious puff.

"Miss," the cop was saying. "You can go in now."

Sandra thanked him and went back into the school auditorium. There was still a pall of smoke in the air and the odor nearly made her gag. The place was empty except for a few cops checking behind some seats and some of the security guys talking together in a knot near the back. She found her purse and coat where she had hung them up, and went up to a cop in the aisle.

"Excuse me," she said. "A friend of mine and I got separated during the, um, disturbance. Do you know where I could find him?"

"You need to check with the people outside," said the cop. "They'll know if he was arrested or—"

"Miss?" asked a voice behind her. Sandra turned. A man in a rumpled brown suit was standing slouched with his hands in his pockets. He was tall with graying hair and had the beginnings of a belly poking out behind his tie.

"Yes?" she said.

"I'm Detective Fields. Are you one of the corporate people who was here at the meeting?" She nodded. "Okay. I think we have your associate in back here." He produced a notebook and flipped through it. "Mitchell Paige. We're interviewing him at the moment."

"Why?" asked Sandra, a sudden feeling of weightlessness flowing through her gut. "Is he in trouble?"

"No," said Fields. "Not at all. Not at all. He was actually the victim of a crime. We're interviewing him for some details while he receives medical attention."

"What happened?" asked Sandra.

"He was assaulted," he said. "The injuries aren't serious, but we need to do some testing to continue the investigation."

"Testing?" What was he talking about? What kinds of tests would they need to take to determine an assault?

"What happened?"

"Well, apparently someone blindsided him on the stage, knocked him silly, and then took him into the bathroom where he and another assailant continued assaulting him."

"How is he?"

"Not bad, considering. Some cuts and bruises and a possible concussion and some, um, well, some tearing of tissues and bleeding."

"What? What does that mean? Tearing of tissues?"

The term was trying to click with something in her brain, but it couldn't quite connect. Fields looked at her a moment and then looked away, but not before she caught the beginnings of a grimace on his face.

"What?" she said.

Fields shrugged and said, "Well, Miss, to be honest, we believe it was some sort of sexual assault."

Sandra swallowed as she felt the taste of vomit rising in her throat. She turned away and ducked her head. Raped. They'd raped him. And she knew. She knew it wasn't anyone here from the meeting. It had been Cole. Or Sykes. Or the two of them together. This knowledge had been rooted so deeply inside her she had no doubt it was true. Sykes—in so many words—had said they were going to get him, and she had never doubted they would do something: but not this. She turned back to the cop.

"Who did it?" she asked, hoping they'd caught them somehow.

"We don't know at this point. They were wearing masks. We figure it was someone from the crowd. I understand he did a pretty good job of riling them up."

"Can I see him?"

"Let me ask him. What's your name?"

She told him and he disappeared behind the stage. Sandra stared behind him a moment and then sat in one of the folding chairs still standing on the stage. She sat still a moment, staring at the smoke drifting slowly over the seats. It was quiet. A few voices, speaking low.

"Miss?"

She turned. That detective, Fields, stood behind her, his hands still in his pockets.

"No," he said gently. "He said no, he doesn't want to see anyone right now. I'm sorry."

Sandra nodded and got up. She thanked the officer and strode out the back. The school board members were gone, the TV crews were packing up, and most of the squad cars were gone. The wind was picking up; the cold bit on her face and it felt good. She walked through the lot, the horror and sorrow, the pettiness of it all, following her as closely as a hungry dog.

Why? She understood that they had to get rid of Mitchell, that they had their job to do, but not like this, not like this, not yoking him to this bare shame, this utter humiliation. This wasn't just duty. It was spite, venom, hate. And now the cold felt even better as it found her eyes, her tears, and her guilt, that deep guilt. She felt the iciness worming its way inside her, chilling her as surely as death: it was her fault. Yes. As sure as if she had been there and cheered them on, it was her fault. She gazed up at the clear winter sky, lit with the jagged sliver of pale moon, and knew that she would never see Mitchell again. She stopped and stared at the stars. It had been a long time since she'd done that, and they were bright, brighter than she remembered. She used to know some of the constellations, but not anymore. No. She ducked her head and continued on to the car. No. He would not be seen again.

Chapter 32

Ethel pulled into the school parking lot; it was still dark out, but the eastern sky was beginning to blush with color. A couple inches of snow had fallen during the night. Not enough for them to call off school, but just enough to be an annoyance. She pulled into her space and parked. It wasn't really her place, but since she was always the first one there she got first choice, and this one was always her first choice.

Ethel gathered her briefcase and purse and went inside; the halls were empty. The cleaning crews were gone and the secretaries had not yet arrived. Her footsteps echoed off the bare linoleum as she made her way to her room. She flipped on the lights, settled in, and started writing the day's assignments on the chalkboard. Ethel preferred the chalk over those electronic Smart Boards and even those fancy whiteboards. It was nothing rational, she knew; she just preferred them.

Ethel glanced at her watch; she still had forty-five minutes before school started. She sat down at her desk and took out the papers she had corrected the night before, placing them in the correct wire basket: biographical essays about Emily Dickinson. Funny. They never used to make her so tired. Now she could barely stand to read them; of course, most of them were simply awful. And, of course, it had been a late night. She and Eric had gone up to St. Mary's to visit David again and not gotten home until after nine.

It was hard, seeing him strapped in the wheelchair and still unable to speak. He had lost a lot of weight. His left hand was all right, perfectly functional, but his right had been paralyzed and was permanently curled into a sort of hook. She could barely stand to look at it. Dr. Verlani told them Dave had suffered a massive stroke after probably suffering a series of small ones, and that while therapy might help some, chances were slim that David would ever be able to speak again. Or walk without assistance. She had brought him some magazines and some non-fiction books, historical fiction, the ones he liked, and she had talked to him at length, giving him the latest school gossip, but there had been not a glimmer of recognition or reaction. She had to wonder: was it dead inside there, like being asleep, or was poor David trapped inside his own body? How horrible that would be.

Ethel took out her thermos and poured herself a cup of coffee. No. Nothing seemed to be registering with David. Not his daughters when they arrived or left. Not his ex-wife when she arrived and stood simpering in the doorway. Not Beverly when she came and sat with him for hours. Not Will when he came in with a six-pack to watch college football bowl games with him. Not even the news that Custer had been taken over by EduNet. She told David every last detail of the—very—hostile takeover. How the local news had smeared the black community and the entire public school system, blaming the riot on them and not on that idiot from EduNet who had stood up on stage screaming racial epithets loud enough for the whole world to hear. Which begged the question, she had said to David; she had heard it, dozens of people in the audience had heard it, and some members of the school board had heard it. So why hadn't the television cameras picked it up? Why had it been buried? There had been several postings of the riot on social media, but they had all disappeared within hours. It was if it had never happened.

They had fought it as hard as they could, Lilly and Serena and the rest, but the board had voted with EduNet. The riot had turned the tide against them. Mr. Ricks was out; he'd been fired and replaced by an EduNet representative. They were hanging onto the faculty for now, but they would probably turn the entire staff over at the end of the year, herself included. Well, that was all right. She'd had a good run, and it was nice in a way to know that this would be the last year; she would appreciate it more. Ethel startled as a knock came on her door. A youngish woman stood there. Ethel took a moment to place her. She was the one who'd been up on stage during the riot.

"Hello, Mrs. Benjamin," she said. Ethel nodded.

"I'm Sandra Feeley," she said hesitantly. "I'm one of the vice-presidents at EduNet."

"I recognize you," said Ethel. "You were at the school board meeting."

"Yes," Sandra said. "I was the liaison. I spoke to the crowd on behalf of EduNet."

"Yes."

Ethel took a moment to appraise this one. The girl seemed nervous, a little apprehensive, but that had to be because of the situation. She sensed a toughness about her; Ethel had seen that at the meeting and she thought she could see a bit of it now. She'd also shown she could think on her feet.

"Have a seat," she said. The girl settled herself. "How can I help you?"

"Well, I'm assigned here to direct the transition," she said, brushing a strand of hair from her face. "We're putting in the new computer rooms and getting all the WiFi and programs set up." She stopped and smiled, obviously waiting for a response.

Ethel waited. There was nothing in that little speech for her, and she had no reason to give the girl any of her approval. She'd eventually get around to telling her why she'd come to see her. The girl smiled slightly and then continued.

"I wanted to talk with you about a couple of things," she said. "First of all, that teacher who had a stroke at the meeting. Mr. Bell. I met him on a visit here last fall and I was just wondering if you've seen him? Do you happen to know how he's doing?"

Ethel paused a moment. "We saw him last night at the St. Mary's Rehabilitation Center, and for all intents and purposes, he's now a vegetable. He cannot speak or walk. No one is exactly sure what he knows or understands."

The girl looked shocked and then upset, which was exactly what Ethel had intended: to shake her up a little bit, to make her uncomfortable. If she wanted the truth, fine, she'd get it.

"I'm sorry," said Sandra. "Did you know him well?"

Ethel shrugged. "We worked together a very long time. Over thirty years."

"I'm sorry," she repeated. She stared down at her hands as she spread them wide in her lap, obviously uncertain how to continue.

"How else can I help you?" asked Ethel. The girl looked up suddenly, and Ethel saw that the toughness, the determination, was back in her eyes.

"I wanted to ask you a favor," she said. "We're looking for someone here to head the faculty. It's a new position. You see, a lot of the people we'll be hiring won't have much classroom experience and we would like to have someone on the staff who will help mentor the new teachers coming in."

"Will you be keeping some of the current staff?"

Sandra nodded.

"Yes," she said. "I have a fair amount of latitude implementing our program, and I've decided to keep a fair amount of the present faculty."

This was new. Ethel had been under the impression the entire staff would be turned over in order to hire younger—and cheaper—teachers.

"Why?" asked Ethel. "Why would you want to keep us?"

"You know the students, you know the parents and some of the other people in the community. We're hoping you can help us make a smoother transition. There's still a lot of hostility out there towards us."

"What about compensation?"

"You, as the head of faculty, will be receiving your present salary and benefits. The other teachers will be starting at our normal pay rate with compensation for experience."

"What kind of numbers are we talking about for them?" asked Ethel.

Sandra shrugged. "Anywhere from thirty-five to fifty-five thousand. Our regular health plan will be made available to them."

Ethel nodded. She had seen the health plan: fifteen hundred a month for family coverage with a three thousand deductible in a closed network. It was probably the cheapest plan possible. And there would no longer be a pension plan.

"You won't be keeping too many teachers on those salaries," she said.

Sandra shrugged. "It is what it is," she said.

Ethel leaned back. She had seen the EduNet curriculum. It was very heavily internet-based; most of the time kids would simply be plugged into computers. Classroom instruction would be reduced to three hours a day, spent mostly on reinforcing the online material, and it looked as if the people they would be hiring would only be required to have a bachelor's degree. No teaching experience. The new teachers would have no experience lesson planning, managing classrooms, or implementing curriculum. That spelled failure. The students would suffer. Her students would suffer. That would not do.

"I'll do it with a few conditions," she said.

Sandra nodded. "All right. What are they?" She produced one of those electronic tablets and turned it on.

"First of all," said Ethel, "I want comprehensive training sessions for all the new teachers. Lesson planning, management, and all the other skills they will not be coming in with. Secondly, if I am head of faculty, I want a team of my own to help implement these sessions. And I want them compensated at their present rate of pay."

Sandra finished writing it all down. "Who exactly are we talking about?"

Ethel thought a moment. "Mr. Reynolds, Mr. Baker, Ms. Ralph, Mr. Ellison, and Mr. Knox."

"I think we can maybe swing three teachers on those terms, but not all five."

"All or nothing," said Ethel. Why the hell not? She had nothing to lose.

"I'll see what we can do."

"Secondly," said Ethel, "I want to see something done for our children with special needs. We need to address that."

Sandra shook her head. "No, we've already determined that's impossible. The expenses are prohibitive."

Ethel looked at her and did a little quick calculus. Could she get away with pushing for this one? She pondered. No. Probably not. This young woman was tough and she had boundaries she was not going to stretch. And Ethel could see she was not one to bend. So, she thought, I won't go for what I want; I'll go for what I need.

"All right," said Ethel. "Here's the bottom line. I have one student, Jeremy Davis, who has Down Syndrome. He's been here three years and considers this his second home. I want him to be able to stay and finish out his education here."

"How do you know him?" asked Sandra. "You're not a special ed teacher."

"Let's just say I'm looking out for him as a friend of the family," said Ethel. "I promised his mother I'd watch out for him."

Sandra had stopped writing and was staring at her tablet. She swallowed. Ethel wasn't sure, but she thought she could see the girl's eyes getting shiny. She had seen enough teen-aged girls on the verge of tears over the years to know when someone was on the edge. Typically, Ethel would have wanted to console the person, but not today. This wasn't about support or teaching or even common human decency. This was business. This was about her kids.

Sandra looked up and smiled. Ethel saw she'd been right, and that the girl had fought it back.

"Yes," she said, her voice firm. "Yes, I can do that for you. In fact, I can guarantee it." She stood up. "I'll communicate to the board and get back to you about your other conditions." She turned to leave.

"I have a question," said Ethel. Sandra turned to her.

"Whatever happened to the young man working with you during that meeting? I heard he got beat up. There was even a rumor going around that he'd been killed."

"No," said Sandra. "Nothing quite so dramatic. He did get assaulted and is taking some time off to recover. We expect he'll be back with us in about three months or so."

"He's lucky to be alive," said Ethel. "That was one stupid goddamned thing to say."

Sandra nodded.

"You're lucky it wasn't picked up by the TV cameras, otherwise, EduNet never would have gotten the contract."

Sandra nodded again and took a breath. Ethel waited. Nothing. No clue.

"All right, then," said Sandra. "If there's nothing else, I need to get back to the office. I'll be in touch."

"Good," said Ethel. "I'll speak to you then."

She left and Ethel stood up slowly and walked to the window overlooking the school courtyard. The sun was above the horizon now and the sky was as clear as clear could be. It was going to be one of those beautiful winter days where the sunlight cut as sharply as ice and the cold honed both the mind and the senses. Winter was by far her favorite season. She loved the sense of stimulation but also the isolation, the silence of it, how the snow damped sound and gilded everything so beautifully.

She crossed her arms and gazed out at the courtyard. Well, it wasn't much, but it was certainly better than what they had been expecting. If Sandra followed through, and she was able to keep her core of staff and be able to teach these youngsters how to teach, well, maybe, just maybe, her students would actually have a fighting chance. It still was not a public school. It never would be. Nothing would take the place of the school she had taught in before those damned politicians had taken their hatchets to it. Teachers had been able to make teaching a career, instead of a stepping stone or an afterthought, which was what most young people considered it now. Now, thought Ethel, gazing out at the pristine beauty of the new snowfall, we're becoming extinct. This is our ice age, our last gasp. She smiled slightly and turned back to her classroom. The day was about to begin.

Chapter 33

The sun had not yet climbed over the mountains. It still amazed him how the hills could hold the sun hostage until at least eight in the morning, how the jagged range could steal the dawn. It would remain pre-dawn, gray for hours, and then the sun would suddenly emerge full-grown and as bright as mid-morning: no colors, no blushing sky, just day, as if a light switch had been turned on. He missed the slow sunrise over the lake as he missed little else from before. He had no other misgivings about leaving everything else behind him: his career, his condo, or his life.

After the tests had come back and the doctors had given him a clean bill of health, a company lawyer had contacted him. He was duly informed that EduNet would no longer require his services, but partly as a settlement for his injuries and partly as a severance, he was to be given a three million dollar bonus. All he had to do was keep his mouth shut.

It was over and done. His career was finished as soon as he had opened his mouth at that meeting. He knew that; he wasn't stupid. He also knew no one would ever employ him as an executive or in any kind of management capacity again. He was now the invisible man. He was an untouchable. He had no name. And he had nothing more to lose, so he took the money and left for nowhere in particular, looking for nothing in particular.

Now, three months later, he was still an invisible man. He wasn't the only one; he could see that now, see the others who floated through this life, ghosts, touching no one. Others were here, too, but he knew no one, and no one knew him. He was solitary now and learning to enjoy it as his mother had enjoyed it on the vast barren prairie. He had time to think but he didn't want to think. He wanted oblivion, but silence and solitude were the closest he could get.

His climb to the top had taken up all his time, all the hours of his adult life, and a good part of his boyhood. He felt diminished, as if he'd lost a limb. Empty. Even after three months. But he was rediscovering himself, redefining himself, coming to terms with who he was; he was starting to understand why his mother shunned people and avoided relationships. He walked out to the balcony and gazed at the emerald mountains jutting out of the beautiful blue-green sea. He was starting to notice things like that; he was starting to appreciate some of the little things.

He dressed and went out into the balmy tropical air; it was warm even at this time of the morning. The village was already bustling. He stopped for a coffee at his usual café and then continued on to the beach. He sat down at his usual spot, on a bench that faced the ocean. He sipped his coffee and leaned back on the bench, closing his eyes and letting the sun warm his skin.

Adrian Cole had entered his dreams the night before. Again. He had come to see him in his old office. They had talked a long time, telling the deepest and darkest secrets, and then held each other and kissed long and slow, and then done more and more. Much more. He opened his eyes abruptly, shutting out the shadowy images with the bright light of day. He had been thinking of Adrian Cole a lot, ever since the night in his condo. The man was with him constantly, beside him, in his ear, inside him. He filled the tranquility, the black peace inside him, with another—slightly lighter—shadow.

He finished his coffee and left his bench, his beach, returning to his apartment. He went over to his desk, opened the drawer and removed the pistol. It was a nice one, a Glock nine millimeter, a Desert Eagle. He walked over, sat on the bed, and held it as he did every morning, watching his own reflection in the chrome finish, tilting it forward and back to capture the gleaming sun. It fit perfectly in his hand. The weight of it and the coldness of the metal were always somehow refreshing. He traced his fingers along the shaft, down the handle, and back around the trigger. It was a beautiful piece of workmanship. Exquisite. He put the gun in his mouth, gazed at himself in the mirror, curled his index finger around the trigger, and, after a moment, he removed the gun. It wasn't time. He put it on the table, took out the clip, and cleaned it as he did every morning, as he would every morning until the day when he would finally—inevitably—have to use it.

Acknowledgements

I would like to thank Ms. Kira Henschel for her steadfast support, enthusiasm, and advice as my publisher. I would also like to thank Tom Biel and David Thome for their help and advice as authors, Michael DiMilo for his outstanding artwork, Dennis Curley for his editing advice, Bob Carter for his photographic skills, and also Matt Linn and Jim Koeper for their legal expertise. I would like to express my gratitude to Mark Bradley, Paul Carter, Maryann Carter, Frankie Carter, Kent Mueller, Janie Hatton, Judy Gundry, Rich Curley, and Mark Mamerow for their input as early readers of my manuscript. I would also like to thank the rest of my family, particularly Sue Kletzke Carter, Susanne Carter, my wife Kris, and my daughter Frankie for their unwavering support and refusals to let me get too cocky.

About the Author

Geoff Carter grew up attending public schools in the Milwaukee area, eventually graduating from the University of Wisconsin at Madison with a degree in Communication Arts. He has been teaching English in Milwaukee Public Schools for twenty-eight years in both traditional and non-traditional settings, working almost exclusively with at-risk students. Carter is a proud and active member of the MTEA, the local teachers' union.

He holds a PhD in English and has also taught at the University of Wisconsin-Milwaukee.

Carter lives in Milwaukee. He is married to an extraordinary woman and is the proud father of a remarkable daughter. In his spare time, he enjoys fine wine, sailing, fly-fishing, organic gardening, and reading.